A DISTANT HARBOUR

Jessica Blair lives in Ampleforth College on the edge of the North York Moors. Married, with three grown-up daughters and a son, she now devotes her time to writing. She is the author of *The Red Shawl*, the story of the Whitby whalers and the women they left behind.

JESSICA BLAIR

A Distant Harbour

HARPER

HarperCollins*Publishers*
77–85 Fulham Palace Road,
Hammersmith, London W6 8JB

First published in Great Britain by
Judy Piatkus (Publishers) Ltd 1993

1

ISBN 978-0-00-785031-0

Printed and bound in Great Britain by
Clays Ltd, St Ives plc

For Joan

with thanks for the faith and encouragement
which never faltered

ACKNOWLEDGEMENTS

My grateful thanks for help in a variety of ways go to: Geoff and Dominic Hudson for solving navigational problems; Ken Forster for information on Pictou; John Quigley for information on New Bedford; Raymond May for medical information; Paul Hudson for publicity material; Lynn Curtis for advice and for being such a kind and brilliant editor; my publishers for all their help; Joan and my family for constructive criticism and guidance coupled with an unending patience.

Chapter One

Ruth Fernley tossed and twisted in her sleep. The nightmare darkened her mind just as it had done every night for the past three months.

Towering waves crashed down, pounding and bruising her body. They dragged her to the depths of the ocean and then thrust her upwards, surrendering her to the heaving sea. Struggle as she might, fight as she could with what strength she had left, her plight was hopeless. Her cry for help was lost in the howling wind and the splintering of timber on the rocks which claimed the London Packet a few miles south of Whitby. The sea swirled around her, hungry for a final victim. Water filled her mouth. She gasped for air. She reached out, seeking some support against the clutching sea.

Her cry split the still night in the turret bedroom of Rigg House, lonely on the precipitous cliffs south of Whitby.

She sprang up in bed, gulping air deep into her lungs. She was soaked in sweat, as if drenched by the sea. Her eyes, wide with the nightmare horror of near drowning, stared unseeingly at the wall opposite her four-poster bed.

She shuddered violently as her surroundings became a reality. The sea had not won. She was here, safe in Rigg House.

Tension drained from her. She sighed, folded the bedclothes back and slid slowly out of bed. She picked up a robe from the back of a chair and slipped it round her. She ran her long fingers through her copper-tinted hair and, with a slight shake, sent it cascading to her shoulders.

As she had done every night for the past three months,

she walked slowly to the window and gazed out across the cliffs and beyond to the sea. Tonight earth and water were bathed in a sheen of pale light which filtered through the glass to highlight her delicate skin and proud, high cheekboned features. The world was silent and only the minute undulations of an almost calm sea broke the stillness.

If only it had been that way when the London Packet had sailed out of Whitby. She would have been safe in London now, with Matthew, the man she had come to need when her marriage to David Fernley was slowly destroyed by ambition, jealousy and hatred. Instead Matthew was dead, drowned in that nightmare storm of which, unknown to the rest of the world but for two people, she was the sole survivor.

Waves crashed across the stricken ship eager to break Ruth's grip on the rail. The wind, howling in its fury, sought to fling her into the boiling cauldron that swirled around the doomed vessel.

When the London Packet struck the rocks it had been everyone for themselves, but Matthew had stayed beside her, helping her reach the rail.

'Hold on, love!' She caught his warning before it was whisked away on the wind. She glanced round, overawed by nature's viciousness. A gigantic wave towered over them, seeming to hang in mid-air while gathering more strength. She cowered in wide-eyed terror. Then it was falling, falling, crashing down with unrelenting force.

Matthew flung himself towards her in an attempt to give her more security but in that moment, when his grip had slackened, the wave struck.

Ruth felt the brute force of it. She was flung to her knees but somehow, in desperation, managed to hang on to the rail. Gasping for breath, she struggled for survival, looking to Matthew for help. Instead she saw him lifted and tossed, like some piece of flotsam, over the side.

'Matthew!' her scream pierced the wind.

There was no answer, no cry for help. One moment he was there, alive beside her, the next he was gone.

She sank to the sea-swilled deck, overwhelmed by desolation, oblivious to the howling wind and raging sea, but still her outstretched arms clung to the rail, an automatic grasp at life.

The crack of breaking wood pierced her bemused mind and she felt herself falling. Fear gripped as the sea closed over her head. She was numb to the surging water, helpless in its power. It thrust her upwards. She broke the surface and found herself still clinging to a piece of timber that had once been the rail. Some distant, inbred instinct told her to hang on, that there was a chance. A wave carried her away from the rocks. Some of its power seemed to have gone from it. Was it her imagination or was the storm subsiding?

She shook the water from her face and looked around, desperate for help. There was no one. The ship had gone, only a few floating timbers remained.

She propelled herself to a large piece of wood and transferred her grip. The sea still ran strongly but it had lost some of that cruel force. It closed around her, washed over her and she felt its power tug at her, dragging her under. She came up, gasping and coughing water. How many times it threatened to deny her life she never knew but forever in her mind was the instinct to hold on to the floating spar.

Her brain and body were numbed by the callous beating of the sea until hope began to drift away.

Water broke over her head. Her grip slackened. She fought to hold on, fought against the pull which threatened to take her from her saviour. Something tightened under her arms. She felt herself drawn upwards. The water no longer swirled around her body; instead she felt something hard against her back. It hurt and that sensation drove some comprehension back to her mind. Hands were grasping her, hauling and dragging, fighting the sea for her life.

The boat dipped then rode high on a wave. Whoever held her used that motion to help him make the final pull. She was dragged over the gunwale and tumbled into the bottom of the boat. There, face down, she retched and retched, spewing water until she lay spent with the exertion but filled with joy and relief.

Though still tossed by the waves, Ruth sensed that the boat was under control and that the fury had gone out of the storm. She turned over slowly, curious to see who had braved the raging sea to rescue her. She looked up at the figure at the tiller, skilfully manoeuvring the boat so that it was not swamped.

Francis Chambers!

The shock of seeing the man whom she had engaged as chief clerk to her husband David's whaling firm drove the last remnants of confusion from her mind. She lay there amazed, staring up at him, drawing assurance from his strength and the bold way in which he challenged the storm. His legs were braced against the bottom of the boat; his strong hands held the tiller, commanding it to do his will. The muscles under the saturated shirt which clung to his body were iron hard. Water streamed from his hair. He brushed it impatiently away and set his face to the wind.

Ruth read determination to survive in the set of his whole body and in the defiance in his eyes.

He glanced down at her. A reassuring smile touched his lips as he yelled above the howling wind, 'You're safe, Mrs Fernley. The worst is over.'

Ruth nodded acknowledgement and struggled into a more comfortable position. She moved closer to him as if she needed his closeness to give her strength.

Braced against the tossing boat, she struggled to speak.

'I didn't know you could handle a boat. And to risk your life . . . why?'

He looked down at her and as their eyes locked Ruth sensed a tingle suffuse her body for even here on storm-wrenched waters she saw adoration and desire in his dark eyes.

'You, Ruth.' His voice was charged with emotion. 'I was on the quay when word came that the London Packet had foundered. I lost no time. You were on board. It was you I had to save.' His lips tightened. 'I was determined the sea should not have you. Thank God I found you!'

'Thank God you cared,' she breathed. Her mind was a whirl. She had never thought of Francis as any more than an employee. Oh, she had been aware of him as a man, confident, strong and athletic-looking, but it had never gone beyond that.

Now she realised that she must have meant much more to him or he would never have taken to a wild sea in the hope of saving her. Had he nursed a secret desire, a thwarted passion for her? Maybe she could use it to her advantage, and besides he was far from unattractive . . . This was the first time he had used her Christian name and she liked the way he said it.

And she did owe him her life.

The boat dipped into the waves, sending spray over them, but Ruth did not care. She was safe. The wind was easing and with it came a lessening of the sea's ferocity.

When the storm had passed and the sea settled, Ruth had had time to think. What was left to her? Where could her life go? Her marriage was in ruins. She had finally broken the bond with David when she had stepped on board the London Packet with Matthew. Now he was gone. Yet here was Francis who had risked his life for her, who on his own admission had come only for her. Her mind began to seize on the opportunity.

'Were you the only one to come?' she asked.

He shook his head. 'No, but the others were driven back. The rescue boat nearly made it but was struck by a freak wave and turned turtle. Reckon all hands would be lost.'

'Then I could be the only survivor?'

'Most likely. Unless anyone managed to get ashore, which I doubt.' Francis surveyed the clearing sky. 'I think we can head for Whitby.'

'No, Francis, not Whitby.' Her voice was soft and pleading. 'Take me to Rigg House.'

'Rigg House?' he queried, puzzled.

'Take me there and then I'll tell you why.'

Francis altered course and manoeuvred the boat to a safe anchorage at the foot of the cliffs below Rigg House, which stood in isolation three miles along the coast from Whitby.

He secured the boat and showed Ruth every attention and care as he helped her scramble to the top of the cliffs. They hurried quickly across the rough grassland to the high wall surrounding the bleak-looking home. In a few moments Francis was tugging at the bellchain.

They heard bolts being drawn back. The door inched open just far enough for the occupant to peer out.

'Mrs Judson, Emily, it's me.' Ruth's tone was low and supplicating.

In that same instant Emily recognised her and threw the door wide open.

'Oh, Mrs Fernley, what's happened?' she cried at the sight of the two shivering and sodden figures standing before her. 'Come in, come in.' She stepped aside, and as Ruth and Francis entered the house, closed the door behind them.

'I was on the London Packet – it went down. Francis saved me. We need your help.' For the moment Ruth made the explanation brief for she was beginning to tremble with cold. A further explanation could come later.

'Thank God he was there.' Emily nodded her approval of Francis. 'Now come, the pair of you.' She led the way quickly up the stairs. She opened the second door along the landing and turned to Francis. 'You'll find towels in the top drawer of the chest and some clothes of the late master's in the wardrobe.'

'Thank you, Mrs Judson.' He made a slight bow and went into the bedroom.

'I put the clothes you left behind when the master was killed in the turret bedroom. I knew it was your favourite. I hoped you'd come back one day, but not like this.'

'Thank you, Emily.' Ruth hugged her, glad that she still held a special place in Emily's affections, a place she had won the first time she had come to Rigg House with Jonathan.

'I'll get some warm drinks and something to eat. Come down as soon as you're ready.' She turned on her heel and hurried down the stairs.

Ruth smiled to herself as she walked to the turret bedroom. She wondered how Emily would view her if she knew the truth; if she knew that Jonathan had been Ruth's half-brother, but that she had allowed them to be lovers before revealing her true identity to him and then, when out riding, deliberately forced him off the cliff to his death. And after all her efforts her plot misfired when Jonathan's will, the one she had forced him to make in her son's favour, was invalid.

She changed quickly and hurried downstairs. She wanted a word with Emily before Francis appeared.

'Ah, you look better. More like my Ruth,' beamed the housekeeper when Ruth entered the kitchen.

It was a large room with a huge open fireplace along one wall. A kettle, puffing steam, hung from a reckon and some bread cakes were warming in front of the fire. Bacon sizzled in a pan and two eggs, ready for cracking, rested on the table, set for two.

'I feel better,' Ruth smiled. 'And that smells good.'

'I've set for you to eat in here. I thought it would be warmer for you.' Emily sounded apologetic for not arranging a more elegant setting.

'It will,' Ruth reassured her. 'Now, tell me, I knew you were still here but what is to happen to the house?'

'It's mine.' Emily gave a delighted smile – a rare sight for it broke down the armour of reserve in which Emily cloaked herself. It was a trait which was off-putting to strangers, especially as her tall, gaunt figure seemed to give the impression she was looking down on the person confronting her.

'Yours?' Ruth showed surprise.

'Yes, ma'am. You remember the master left all his possessions and lands to some cousins? Well, they didn't want Rigg House, being content with the estates round Cropton and everything else he left. So because of my loyalty to him, they made me a gift of Rigg House, either to spend the rest of my days here or sell as I saw fit.'

Excitement gripped Ruth. This couldn't be better. The door opened and Francis came in.

'Good gracious,' gasped Emily. 'I thought you and my late master were roughly the same build but I didn't expect such a perfect fit.'

Ruth eyed him critically. Francis was tall, well-built, and had a figure which carried these clothes well. He was lean, muscular, hard of jaw, and his bearing spoke of pride – but pride held carefully on a rein. His eyebrows were smooth and beneath them brown eyes sparkled with a zest for life, softening the harshness which could creep into his features at odd moments.

He was her saviour, someone who had risked his very life for her. He was no longer a mere employee but a man who, she realised, was conscious of his own attraction and knew how to manipulate it for his own ends. She sensed they were two of a kind. He would have to be watched but she knew she would enjoy the challenge. And she had one advantage: she knew she had what he desired and could exploit it for her own ends. She would enjoy playing him as a fisherman plays a fish and would land him to do her will.

Warmed by their food and drink, fussed over by Mrs Judson, the horrors of the sea receded and were banished from Ruth's mind as she busily laid plans for the future.

'Sit down, Emily. I have something I want to say to you both.' Ruth indicated a chair at the table. As the housekeeper sat down Ruth glanced from one to the other. 'I want your help. I have much I want to do, and to achieve it, it is essential no one should know that I'm alive. Everyone must think that I'm dead, lost in the shipwreck. I need you to keep my secret and I need your loyalty. You will not go unrewarded.'

Emily and Francis, surprised by the request, exchanged glances.

'Ma'am, you know you can count on me for anything,' murmured Emily Judson, who had always idolised her.

'Thank you,' replied Ruth with a smile of gratitude. 'Francis?'

For a brief moment he hesitated then said, 'Of course, but what's this all about?'

'You will have to know more, of course, but that later. Emily need know no more for what she doesn't know won't harm her.' Ruth looked at her, seeking her agreement on that point. Seeing her nod, Ruth went on, 'Emily, I have one more thing to ask you. I need somewhere to live, somewhere where I will not be seen.'

'Ma'am, Rigg House is yours for as long as you want to use it. It will be a pleasure for me to have you living here, someone to look after.'

'Thank you.' Ruth sank back in her chair with satisfaction. Things could not have gone more satisfactorily. Now there was only one more thing to achieve this night if she was to hold Francis in her power and she anticipated no trouble with that.

'Come with me and I'll show you the rest of the house, Francis,' she said, rising from her chair.

'Will you want anything else, ma'am?' asked Emily.

'Nothing, thank you.'

Ruth led the way from the kitchen and took Francis through the house. He made the usual comments of admiration for the way in which the house had been furnished and tastefully decorated, but paid more attention to Ruth herself who subtly led him on.

'This is my favourite,' she said, opening the door of the turret bedroom. Francis stepped inside and she closed the door. The room was big and semi-circular, projecting over the north-east corner of the house. One wall was draped with tapestries of hunting and sea scenes. A large four-poster bed, its head against the wall, occupied a central position with a small table to either side. An escritoire and a dressing table, each with its own chair, were placed against the wall and a long curved window seat was cushioned and trimmed with matching material.

'You can see the sea from here.' Ruth crossed to the window.

Francis came to stand beside her. Far beyond the bottom of the cliff, gentle now after its fury, the sea stretched to the horizon.

Ruth shuddered as memories of those nightmare moments tumbled back on her. Francis put his arm around her and turned her to him. She looked up into his penetrating gaze. 'There's no need to be frightened any more. You're safe. I'll always be here when you need me.' His words were soft, caressing, reassuring.

'Francis,' her voice was husky. 'I'll never be out of your

18

debt for saving my life, but what made you risk yours?'

'I told you in the boat – you.' His grip tightened round her waist and he pulled her closer. She did not resist. 'I've always loved you, ever since you interviewed me for the job, but I could not make it known to you. You had . . .'

She raised her finger to his lips and stopped his words. 'I have no one now,' she whispered, her eyes beckoning.

He met that look for a brief moment then his lips found hers with a demanding passion which was returned, kiss for kiss.

'Oh, Ruth, Ruth! How I've longed to do that,' he gasped.

'There can be more,' she whispered.

She felt the tension in his body, sensed the excitement coursing through his veins, matching her own heightened desires. She felt his fingers on the buttons at the back of her dress and started to undo his shirt. Then she brushed him aside, shed her clothes quickly and was waiting for him on the bed, arms outstretched by the time he had finished undressing.

With passion spent they lay silent in each other's arms until Francis turned on to his stomach so he could look into her eyes. He kissed her lightly on the lips. 'Now, Ruth, what else have you to tell me? What is it that Mrs Judson need not know? Why do you want people to think you dead? But first . . . Jonathan Hardy who lived here. Were you and he lovers?'

'I'll not fence with you, Francis. I'll not hold back. Yes, Jonathan and I were lovers until his untimely death in a fall from the cliffs.' There was no need to tell him who had caused that fall.

'And Matthew? You were going with him to London?'

'Yes. I needed him in a different way, different even to my husband. He was there when my marriage was break-ing up, more than a friend, and I think we'd have stayed

19

together in London. But that was not to be. Now I see I was weak in running away. Why should I, and leave those damned Thoresbys to get away with everything?'

Francis noted the hatred that had come into Ruth's voice. 'But I thought the Fernleys and the Thoresbys were the best of friends?'

Her lips tightened. 'You thought wrong then. Oh, David was always besotted with them – in fact I wouldn't be surprised if he'd been under Jenny's skirts but I can't prove it.

'But what happened? We were expanding, taking on a second whaleship as you know. I'd gone into debt with it, expecting a good return when David came back from the Arctic. Instead the whaling season was bad and *The Lonely Wind* was badly damaged, needing costly repairs. And how was she holed? Through David saving that damned Adam Thoresby and his ship! Thoresby got off scot-free and now Fernley's faces ruin. That was the last straw. I decided to leave with Matthew.'

'And now?' prompted Francis as she paused for breath.

She gazed deep into his eyes. 'Revenge,' she hissed. 'Revenge on the Thoresbys. And that's why I want to be believed dead and why I need you. You can be my eyes and ears, letting me know what is happening in Whitby while I work out how to get my own back on David and his precious friends. Tomorrow you return by boat in your own clothes. Say you were blown ashore up the coast. And then I depend on you for news.'

'You'll not keep me away.' Francis kissed her, long and hard. Her arms twined around his neck and it was a long time before she let him go.

Two days later Francis let himself into the garden of Rigg House through the small door in the wall. He was bursting with news.

'Where is she, Mrs Judson?' he asked when she let him in.

'In her room.'

Emily watched him take the stairs two at a time. She pursed her lips and raised her eyebrows. There was something in the wind, but it was no concern of hers, she supposed.

Francis burst into the turret room where Ruth was sitting on the window seat. She saw the excitement in his face as he crossed to her.

'News!' he cried as he sat down beside her. 'First, Adam Thoresby was lost with the rescue boat.'

'What?'

'Second, and this is something you can build on,' he went on quickly, ignoring her shocked expression, 'I now work for Fernley and Thoresby.'

'Don't talk in riddles,' she snapped irritably.

'The Thoresbys wanted to finance David to save his ships. He would only agree if they took a share in his firm. Then it was decided that they should amalgamate, pool ships and crews, so the new firm of Fernley and Thoresby has been created.'

Ruth was astounded. The husband she had come to despise for his weakness and credulity had been saved. Those damned Thoresbys again! They had been thorns in her side ever since she had come to Whitby.

'Damn, damn, damn!' she hissed through tight lips.

'But isn't this all the better? Won't your revenge be all the sweeter? Now you can lay plans to ruin the Thoresbys, really ruin them, because I'll be right at the heart of everything,' pressed Francis.

Even as he was speaking Ruth's mind had been racing ahead. 'You're right!' Her eyes were wide with excitement as she grasped his hands. 'This is better than ever. We can ruin them and enrich ourselves.'

'By the way, the new ship is going to be called the *Ruth*.'

'The *Ruth*? How touching. I didn't know David cared,' she remarked sarcastically.

Over the succeeding weeks they laid their plans carefully as Francis reported daily on the progress of the repairs and kitting out for the first voyage of *The Lonely Wind*, the *Ruth* and the *Mary Jane*, sailing under the colours of the new firm, Fernley and Thoresby.

'Fernley and Thoresby.' Standing by the window in the moonlight, remembering the events of the past weeks, Ruth spat the words with venom. Her firm, the first she and David had created, was now linked with the Thoresbys. No doubt prim and proper Jenny was helping to run the firm she, Ruth, had created. But Jenny had suffered a loss too, lost her Adam, taken in the storm while searching for survivors from the London Packet. Ruth felt no sorrow for her. Hadn't she spelt trouble ever since David came to Whitby and met her thirteen years ago? He had denied feeling any affection for her but Ruth had known otherwise; the embers between them had never died. Well, with Adam dead and Ruth too so far as anyone but Emily and Francis knew, they'd think themselves free to marry. David a bigamist! What a shock he would get when she finally chose to let the truth be known. Ruth gave a little chuckle of satisfaction at the thought. All in good time for there was more to her plans than that . . .

Nightmare over and her resolution strengthened, Ruth went back to bed.

Chapter Two

'Ship ahoy!' The cry from the lookout on the main top gallant rang clear on the piercing Arctic air.

David Fernley started. He had placed the sharpest eyes in Whitby in that position to get the earliest sighting possible.

'How many?' he yelled.

'Two,' came the reply.

Tension drained from David. *The Lonely Wind* and the *Mary Jane* were safe.

'Whither away?' he called.

'Larboard bow.'

He crossed the deck, swung on to the bulwark, grasped the ratlines and climbed the rigging to get an early view of the two whaleships. As soon as they were in sight he shouted instructions to the helmsman and within the hour the *Ruth* was sailing slowly past the other two ships, with welcoming yells being exchanged between the crews.

Before the *Ruth* was level with the *Mary Jane*, David saw Ruben peering intently over the rail, eager for the news David was carrying.

'It's a girl!' he yelled, a broad grin breaking out across his weather-worn features. 'Both all right.'

Ruben punched the air with delight.

David laughed at his brother-in-law's joy. He was pleased that his own delayed sailing, awaiting the completion of the *Ruth*, had enabled him to bring such good news to Ruben.

David turned his attention to manoeuvring the *Ruth* to a safe anchorage against the pack-ice in line with the other two whaleships belonging to the firm of Fernley and Thoresby. A rope ladder was thrown over the side and by the time David was on to the ice, Ruben Thoresby was waiting to give him an enthusiastic greeting.

He and David slapped each other on the back. 'What's Katie like?' he asked eagerly, savouring the name he and Jessica had picked before he sailed.

'Beautiful,' grinned David. 'Much like her mother.'

'Then she will be.' Ruben pictured his wife's dark eyes, deep mysterious pools sparkling with life, heightened by her pale oval face and cloud of dark hair, tumbling to her shoulders. At this moment, with this news, the desire to hug her and tell her how much he loved her, even though the child was not his, was almost overpowering.

'James Humphries? Did he try to contact her?' Anxiety dimmed Ruben's enthusiasm.

'No,' replied David firmly. 'He married Catherine Howard, or rather her fortune. Spends a lot of time in London. Thee need have no worries about him. He'll never risk losing Catherine's money by acknowledging Katie as his.'

Relief showed in Ruben's eyes. 'I'd fight him every bit of the way if he tried! Katie belongs to Jessica and me.'

David gave him a friendly tap on the shoulder and turned to greet the man hurrying across the ice towards them. Jim Talbot had served him faithfully as mate on *The Lonely Wind*, and David had promoted him to captain when he had taken command of the new ship, the *Ruth*.

'How did she sail?' asked David, inclining his head in the direction of *The Lonely Wind*.

'As good as ever. Wouldn't know she'd been damaged,' replied Jim.

'Good. And the whaling?'

'Both half full. And you?'

'Nearly the same,' said David. 'But I broke off to keep this rendezvous.'

'We should have full ships by the end of the season.' Ruben glanced at Jim for confirmation.

'Aye,' he agreed. 'Reckon we want to be further west.'

David nodded. 'We'll give the crews a break for twenty-four hours and then head west.'

'I see you named the new ship *Ruth*?' commented Ruben, a note of curiosity touching his voice.

'Aye,' replied David slowly. 'Ruth once meant the world to me. We loved each other, then I came to Whitby . . .' His voice faltered. 'We were ambitious, maybe too much, so maybe it was the cause of all our troubles.'

'Thee weren't to blame, Davey,' Ruben tried to comfort him. 'Ruth betrayed your trust.'

He shook his head slowly. A wry smile touched his lips. 'We were both to blame, I more than her perhaps.' He shrugged his shoulders. 'We had some good times.' His mind pictured the poor downtrodden lass he had loved in Cropton, the waif ill-used by her step-father and un-acknowledged by her real father, the squire. Then he saw the girl he had rescued and married whose aristocratic blood gave her a confidence which took them into Whitby society and nurtured his ambitions. 'Ruth became a fine woman. She still has some place in my heart. She didn't deserve to go down with the London Packet.'

'Was she found?' asked Jim.

'No.' He shuddered. 'I hate the thought of her lying somewhere at the bottom of the sea.'

'Try not to, Davey.' Ruben placed a comforting hand on his arm. 'It's right we remember the dead, but life is for the living.'

David shrugged. 'Thee's right, Ruben. And we've got young 'uns to think about. My Kit, your Katie, and Jenny's Anne. Our firm will be theirs one day.'

'Hurry, Anne, I don't want to be late!' Jenny called from the bottom of the stairs as she pulled on her black gloves.

She glanced in the mirror, adjusted her black bonnet and smoothed her black woollen dress before taking a matching cloak from the peg beside the front door.

'Coming, Mother.' Anne's voice, clear and precise, was accompanied by the sound of her hurrying footsteps. She tripped lightly down the stairs, a twelve-year-old whose natural vitality had been sadly shadowed by the loss of her father three months ago.

Jenny turned to greet her daughter whose outfit was almost a miniature replica of hers. The resemblance did not end there for Anne's looks and disposition came from her mother while her eyes were those of her father, deep, dark pools flooded with life. Whenever Jenny looked into them she saw Adam, the man she had loved with all her devotion and passion. The man she still loved. How often she had cried in the stillness of the night and bemoaned the fact that he had given his life trying to save others. 'Lost at Sea' was etched on his gravestone in the windswept churchyard high on the cliff near the ruined abbey. He had been a man of the sea, born to it, lived for it, and was taken by it.

'Mama, when can I wear pretty clothes again? I'm tired of always wearing black,' asked Anne, as she watched her mother pull the cloak around her shoulders and pin it with a large jet brooch shaped like a whale, a present from Adam carved by his own hand.

'Soon, love, soon.' Jenny's voice was soft, gentle, flowing with a Yorkshire lilt without any of its harshness. Convention decreed a period of six months' mourning but she knew it was hard on children and had decided that after today she would release Anne from the bond. In fact, she too felt the need to escape from the drabness of everyday black which hung on her like the pall on Adam's coffin. It was custom to mourn the dead but her reasoning told her she was really mourning for herself and the great sorrow Adam's death had brought her. But he would want her to go on living, for herself and for Anne and those dear to her. She would miss him no less if she wore one of the pretty dresses she had in the wardrobe upstairs.

Her eyes brightening with excitement, she cried, 'Hang convention! Let's put on something really nice.' She grabbed Anne's hands. 'We love your father no less.' She started up the stairs, sweeping Anne along with her.

Eagerly Anne matched her mother's pace. Enthusiasm danced in her eyes. 'I'll put on my yellow taffeta dress, the one Daddy liked.' Laughter rang in her voice.

'And isn't that a better way to remember him?'

They reached the top of the stairs. 'We'll have to be quick,' called Jenny as they went to their respective rooms.

A few minutes later they both reappeared, Anne in the dress she'd said she would wear and Jenny in a green skirt and white bodice with a grey mantle around her shoulders. She carried a deep blue woollen cloak and both of them laughed when Anne said 'Snap!' for she too had chosen a cloak of exactly the same colour.

They hurried downstairs and paused only for Jenny to remove the jet brooch from her black cloak and pin it to her blue one.

They stepped outside into Henrietta Street, cut along the face of the East Cliff overlooking the harbour. Jenny locked the door, then, taking Anne's hand, set off for Church Street. Neighbours, chatting on their doorsteps, nodded or said 'Good day', but she knew that after they had passed whispered comments would be made that Jenny Thoresby had thrown off her widow's weeds and her husband dead only these three months! But she didn't care. Life had taken a new turn and she sensed that Adam would have approved.

Henrietta Street joined Church Street, the main thoroughfare on the east side of the River Esk, close to the foot of the Church Stairs, the one hundred and ninety-nine steps which climbed the cliff to the parish church.

Church Street, flanked by houses and shops, bustled with activity. Housewives, out shopping, seeking to stretch their meagre money as far as possible, jostled with sailors aiming to spend some time in an inn or heading for a ship. Artisans hurried to their work, chandlers hastened to complete a deal, and barefooted urchins played chase through the throng of people.

Narrow yards climbed the cliff face giving access to the red-roofed houses which seemed to stand one on top of the other. On the opposite side of Church Street similar ways led to the staithes beside the river. Across the Esk lay a smaller area of houses under the shelter of the West Cliff, whilst higher fine new terraces were expanding as the better off sought a change.

It was an area which Jenny loathed after her experience there as a child.

Her mother, a girl from a well-to-do family, had married a self-made whaling captain who could not change his rough ways even after moving to the better-class area on the West Cliff. He was ostracised by her friends and eventually, devastated when his wife was killed eloping with a lover, hanged himself. Jenny found him at their fine house and had loathed the West Cliff ever since, regarding it as an ill-omened place. Unwanted by her mother's family, she was taken in by her father's life-long friend, the ex-whaler Tom Holtby who ran the Black Bull public house on the east side of the river. Growing up amongst the whaling fraternity, she met and fell in love with Adam Thoresby, only faltering in her choice when David Fernley came to Whitby and she nursed him after an injury sustained while saving Adam's life on his first whaling voyage.

But her mind was far from those days now as she hurried to her mother-in-law's.

Reaching a two-storeyed cottage close to the far end of Church Street, the name 'Harpoon House' carved on a piece of wood over the front door, she rapped the brass knocker and turned the handle.

'Just us,' she called, stepping inside, and closed the door behind her. Anne ran ahead along the passage and opened the door to the kitchen. She liked coming to her granny's.

'Hello,' she cried as she burst into the room. She ran to her granny who was sitting in a chair beside the fire mending some socks.

'Hello, sweet.' Emma Thoresby's pale face lit with a welcoming smile. She dropped her mending into her lap and hugged her granddaughter with a joy which never diminished no matter how often Anne visited her. She saw Anne as a replacement for her own Lucy who had never been strong and had died young.

'Hello, Ma.' Jenny spoke from the doorway then crossed the kitchen to give her mother-in-law a kiss.

'Hello, luv.' Emma smiled at her daughter-in-law and held her hand that moment longer, expressing a deep unspoken affection.

As she had entered the kitchen Jenny had caught a momentary glance of surprise cast at her apparel. There might be a touch of disapproval in it but Emma Thoresby would not criticise. People should follow their own feelings on the matter of mourning and she would bear Jenny no ill will for wanting to be done with the outward symbols.

She herself would continue to dress as she was now. Her full dress was of black poplin with long sleeves tight at the wrist. Around her shoulders was a black fichu and a head-fitting cap, of matching material and colour, was tied under her chin.

Care-worn lines etched features which had met calamity with calm serenity. The fear which had always stalked her mind, but which had never been allowed to show, had been realised with the loss of her husband, Seth, and her eldest son to the sea. It was still there for now her Ruben sailed the Arctic in search of whales.

Released from her granny's arms, Anne peeped into the cradle set to one side of the polished, black-leaded fireplace.

'Shhh, don't wake Katie, she's just gone off,' said Emma.

'Hello, Jenny. Anne.' Jessica greeted them quietly as she came through the back door from the yard.

Though Jessica made no comment, Jenny saw approval in her sister-in-law's eyes as she realised the mourning black was gone.

She was glad for she valued Jessica's opinion. She had taken to David's sister the very first time she had come to Whitby and had been delighted when she had gone to live with him and Ruth after they had established themselves. She had approved of Jessica's friendship with Adam's brother Ruben, but frowned on her association with the aristocratic James Humphries, a tempestuous affair which left her pregnant and suicidal. Ruben saved her from death and then married her so that he would be thought the father of her child.

Jessica's smile was warm and there was laughter in her dark eyes now though they could cloud over with concern for anyone in trouble. She went to the mirror and tightened her hair into a bun at the nape of her neck. Anne watched. She liked her aunt's hair when it cascaded to her shoulders, reflecting and shining in the light.

Jessica turned from the mirror and peered into the cradle. 'She's well away, Ma.'

'Aye. And don't ask me if I'll be all right. I've got my little helper.' She put her arm round Anne standing beside her chair. 'Off with thee. See that Fernley and Thoresby is thriving. Thee owes it to Ruben and David – and to Adam. You know he would have approved.'

Jessica took her brown cloak from the peg, swathed it over her blue poplin frock trimmed with white lace, and put a blue bonnet over her hair.

'Thee both look proper ladies.' Emma gave a nod of

approval. They kissed her and Anne, and left the house.

They hurried along the east bank of the river past the tall-masted ships tied up at the quays. These vessels, rising and falling with the gentle movement of the water as the tide challenged the river, were a scene of constant activity.

Dockers stripped to shirt and breeches to find some relief from the warm sun were busy unloading timber from the Baltic countries, spices from Africa and wines from Portugal. Others were loading sailcloth, butter, bacon and ham, while a continuous chain of men carrying sacks of alum kept up a regular rhythm, going up one gangplank and back by another.

Whitby's position as a leading English port had always made Jenny proud and today she found her pleasure in the familiar scene renewed. It was as if it was a signal to throw off her mourning, as if Adam was saying: 'Get on with your life. Miss me but don't be sad. There's still a life to be lived.'

The quays throbbed with life. Some sailors hurried to their ship. Others, already aboard, leaned on the rail and called and joked with girls making their way to market. A group of women, bonnets firmly tied beneath their chins to keep their hair in place, stood at a long table. They handled sharp knives with the dexterity of experts, cleaning and gutting a haul of fish as it was brought from a nearby smack.

Jenny and Jessica nodded at acquaintances and bade others, 'Good morning.' They turned into the flow of people crossing the drawbridge, along the quay on the west side of the river to a blue door in a block let off as offices to all manner of firms connected with the shipping life of Whitby.

Opening the door they stepped into a passage from which a flight of stairs gave access to an upper floor. The passage led to a door at the back while on the right were two more doors. Jenny opened the first of these. Two men, one in his fifties, the other still in his teens, glanced up from the ledgers in which they were writing.

Seeing Jenny, they immediately jumped down off the tall stools which enabled them to work at the high sloping desks in comfort.

'Good day, Ma'am,' they both said in unison.

'Good day, Mr Swan. Good day, Danny.' Jenny smiled and nodded to each in turn. 'Is Mr Chambers in?'

'In his office, Ma'am,' replied Mr Swan.

'Your mother well, Danny?' asked Jenny lightly.

He swallowed hard. His eyes widened. Here was Mrs Thoresby, shareholder in the firm he worked for, speaking to *him*. 'Er, er. . .' Mr Swan's elbow in his ribs seemed to propel the next words from him. 'She's very well, Ma'am. Very well.'

'What else?' hissed Mr Swan, embarrassed that his charge should forget something.

'Er, thank you, Ma'am,' spluttered Danny.

Jenny smiled, amused at the apparent upheaval she had caused in the quiet office. 'Remember me to her.' She recalled his mother from school, it seemed like a lifetime ago, and knowing how it would help the family, had been only too glad to take Danny on as an office boy and trainee clerk.

'Yes, Ma'am,' he replied. He glanced down at his shoes then shuffled them as if trying to hide the fact that they were dusty.

Jenny nodded and rejoined Jessica in the corridor. 'He's in,' she said, and started to mount the stairs.

At the first landing she turned to a door painted the same blue as the outside one. The stairs continued up two more storeys where some merchants had offices.

She tapped on the door and, followed by Jessica, entered a spacious office from which two tall windows gave a fine view across the harbour to the East Cliff. Paper, sticks and coal were laid in the fireplace in readiness for the weather's turning colder. Above the mantelpiece hung an oil painting of the *Mary Jane*. On either side shelves held models of the *Mary Jane* and *The Lonely Wind*, soon to be joined by one of the *Ruth*, as well as some scrimshaw, log books and ledgers. Two easy chairs stood one on either side of the fireplace, while two high-backed chairs stood in front of a large table behind which Francis Chambers glanced up from the letter he was reading.

As soon as he saw his visitors he jumped to his feet and with a broad smile came round the table to meet them.

'Good day, ladies. It is a pleasure to see you.' His glance moved over them swiftly and admiration glinted in his eyes. He knew how to make women feel special.

He also knew he looked good in his fawn trousers with a slightly darker stripe and matching tail coat cut away at the waist. The tapered lapels were the continuation of a turned-up collar, inside which a white cravat was neatly tied at his throat. His black leather boots were as bright as a mirror.

He bowed as he took Jenny's hand and then Jessica's. 'Please, sit down.' He stood beside the chairs, attentive to his visitors' comfort, and then moved back to his chair behind the table. 'As I said, it is a pleasure to see you.' The statement had now become something of a question. He was seeking the reason for their visit. He sensed it was official and was curious. Neither of the Mrs Thoresbys had ever visited him before.

'Mr Chambers,' Jenny began.

'Francis, please, Mrs Thoresby,' he interrupted, holding up his hands.

'Very well, Francis.' She inclined her head in acknowledgement, knowing full well that he would never expect to be as familiar with either her or Jessica. Charming as he might be, she knew that he realised the relationship between them would never be more than employer and employee. 'We are very appreciative of the way you have run the business through all our troubles and hope that you will continue to do so. The late Mrs Fernley was certainly a good judge when she employed you.'

Francis inclined his head, humbly acknowledging her praise.

'We appreciate the way you handled the creation of the new firm of Fernley and Thoresby, and decided to stay with us and run things while our menfolk are away in the Arctic.'

'It is my pleasure and my duty, Ma'am,' he replied smoothly. 'They can't hunt the whale and be here to attend to the business. Captain Fernley, with Captain Thoresby's approval, briefed me thoroughly in what they see as a path towards gradual expansion.'

'I'm sure he did, and we are delighted for you to continue that way, but we feel that as shareholders we should know more about the business and develop an interest so that we can take an active part in it.'

Though he was thrown momentarily by this unexpected request, Francis suppressed his reaction. 'Well, I'm sure there's no need to trouble yourselves.' He embraced them both with his comment. 'Ladies and business . . . well, you know how it is?'

'Ah, that may be so in most cases,' cut in Jenny, 'but Mrs Fernley – God rest her soul – showed the way, and with our husbands dealing with the practical side of the business we feel we would like to be doing something to help. Don't we, Jessica?'

'We do,' she agreed. 'And we have the children to think about. Some day this firm will be theirs.'

Francis pursed his lips and nodded. 'Well, I must say, you are to be commended for your ambitions. But don't you think the business is better left to someone who, though I say it myself, knows more about it? It will take an awful lot of your time to learn it.' His mind was feverishly seeking every possible way to put them off. He didn't want them nosing around; wanted them kept at a distance. Come too close, become too enquiring, and they just might upset Ruth's plans for which he was already laying the foundation.

'Mrs Fernley did it and she had no one to teach her,' pointed out Jessica.

'Yes, Ma'am, but she must have had a gift, an aptitude for business,' said Francis, leaning forward in his chair.

'And so might we.' Jessica's voice was crisp with determination. She wanted to be as much a part of Ruben's life as she could be, and his life was whaling.

'Business and pleasure can be mixed, Francis. Many a deal is sealed at social occasions,' Jenny put in.

He stiffened. This was a side of life which he had found barred to him and it annoyed him. Oh, he could deal with the bosses but only in the office; he was never invited to their houses, to their get-togethers. Though they respected his shrewd dealings and his apparent loyalty to his employers, he remained an employee, one with whom it did not pay to mix socially. Now the two Mrs Thoresbys were sticking their noses in. It was as if they didn't trust him and it implied he was a mere employee – he who had been running the firm alone without any trouble.

He hid his annoyance and said, 'As you say, Ma'am, those social occasions can be important.' He paused a moment then added: 'I wouldn't know just how important, never having experienced them myself.'

The note of sarcasm in his voice was not lost on Jenny but she chose to ignore it, saying instead, 'They *are* important. That is why we would like to know more about the business. You never know what may crop up, and it would be a pity to miss something which could be advantageous to us through plain ignorance. I know the late Mrs Fernley turned such occasions to her advantage. There's no reason why we can't, provided we know what we are talking about.'

'Very well, if that is what you wish. When would you like to start?'

'At your convenience.' Jenny glanced at Jessica for her approval, which showed in a slight inclination of the head.

'Well, shall we say Thursday, the day after tomorrow?'

'Right.'

'Two o'clock?' suggested Jessica.

'Admirable,' replied Francis, his easy manner hiding the chagrin he was feeling.

'Thank you for your time,' said Jenny, rising from her chair. 'We'll get along and leave you to your work. Sorry we caused an interruption.'

'Not at all,' he said, pushing himself to his feet. 'It has been a pleasure, and I look forward to Thursday.' He ushered the ladies to the door and bade them goodbye. As it closed behind them, he turned with his back to it, raised his eyes heavenwards and cursed to himself.

He would have to be extra careful. He could direct their attention as he willed, but he must not give them one small cause for misgiving nor withhold information which might make their husbands suspicious on their return. He crossed the room and sank on to his chair behind the table. He opened a ledger, flicking through the pages, examining figures and making adjustments.

Francis Chambers rode out of Whitby on the east bank of the river. Although he had ridden only occasionally since coming to Whitby, as a youth he had learned to ride on his uncle's farm near Guisborough.

Rigg House had become a second home for him since that first night with Ruth. Although Emily Judson did not fully approve of their closeness and held her judgement of Francis Chambers to herself, she was slowly coming round to accepting him. After all, he had saved Ruth's life, and she always seemed happier when he was around.

Francis had soon realised that the daily journey to and

from Whitby necessitated that he should take up riding again and so he bought a horse and arranged stabling for it during the day, along with the coaching horses at the White Horse in Church Street.

Now he turned his mount up the cart track which led to open grassland stretching to the cliff edge. To his left the gaunt, crumbling ruins of a once thriving monastery rose in silhouette in the evening light. Beyond, the tower of St Mary's Church, beaten by the winds of many decades, watched over the final resting places of Whitby sailors, like some unmovable guardian.

But he saw nothing of these for his mind was too preoccupied with the problems which had arisen since he had received his visitors, and he was too intent on reaching Rigg House as quickly as possible. Though eager to reach Ruth with his news, Francis nevertheless exercised caution for no one must know of his final destination. As far as anyone in Whitby was aware, he was now living in Robin Hood's Bay.

Satisfied that there was no one about, he cut across the grassland for the last half mile to the house. He dismounted at a wooden door close to the northwest corner of the sheer wall which surrounded the house. He drew a key from his pocket and unlocked the door. He led the horses into the grounds and locked the door behind him. Then he took the horse to the stable and quickly went through the daily routine of unsaddling and rubbing down.

The grounds were tidy. Four men kept them so, hired once a month by Mrs Judson who let them in, paid them and saw them go.

On those days Ruth did not walk in the grounds. To the outside world she was dead, and that same world ignored Mrs Judson — 'the recluse of Rigg House' as she was known, living her lonely life behind locked gates and locked doors. Of such places and such people superstitious folk created tales which they came to believe were true.

Local people kept away from the vicinity of Rigg House, especially at night.

This reputation suited Ruth, once it became known to her through Francis, and she encouraged him to spread stories. They gained with repeated telling among Whitby folk, steeped in sea superstition, and country folk, brought up on tales of witches, elves and hobs.

Francis crossed the open ground to the house. It was square-shaped with a turret rising at the north-west corner like some warning finger, its windows in the upper rooms like eyes observing events in the land beyond the house. He reached the stone path which surrounded the building and walked briskly to the front. A short flight of steps, lined by matching stone balustrades, led to a double-door. He jerked hard on the iron door pull and heard a bell jangle in the depths of the house. He counted to five and repeated his action, then a third time: a signal insisted on by Ruth, though he deemed it over-cautious when he was the only one with a key and all entrances, even the imposing front gates, were kept locked. He could not see anyone bothering to scale a seven-foot wall. But Ruth wanted it that way, so that way it had to be.

A few minutes after the last sound had died away, he heard the huge bolts being drawn back. A key turned in the lock and the door inched open. Francis knew the exact position to stand so that he could be identified.

'It's me, Mrs Judson,' he said to the eye which peered out at him.

The door swung wider. Emily Judson stepped to one side without a word and closed the door after he had entered the house. She turned the key and pushed the bolts back home.

'Mr Chambers,' Emily greeted him, and drew herself up straight.

She started to move ahead of him but he stopped her. 'It's been Mrs Judson and Mr Chambers for the past three months. Can't it be Emily and Francis now?' He noted her reaction at the thought of such familiarity, taking it almost as an affront that he should want to address an older woman by her first name. 'Look,' he hastened to add, 'I know we respect each other and, more importantly, we're both devoted to Mrs Fernley. I know you would do anything for her, indeed are doing, and so would I. We are allies.' He lowered his voice conspiratorially. 'We share a secret, and so I think it would be friendlier if we used our Christian names. We need mean no more by it than that, I assure you.'

While he had been speaking, Emily had observed him with a steady gaze. She liked him; he had saved her mistress from the sea and he was good for her. Ruth was always happier, lighter in mood, when he was here.

'Come, what do you say?' he pressed her, a twinkle in his eyes.

She met his smile and relaxed. 'Very well. Emily and Francis it shall be.'

His smile broadened. 'Good, Emily.' Impulsively, he gave her a hug.

She stepped back quickly as he released his hold. 'Tut, tut, Francis! It doesn't give you licence for more familiar gestures.' There was a snap to her voice but he could tell she hadn't really been offended.

'Where is she, Emily?'

'The withdrawing room.' She started across the hall towards the rear of the house. 'Tell her I'll bring some supper in directly.'

'Thanks.' Francis called after her. He laid his hat on a table at the foot of the curving stairs, then crossed the hall to the withdrawing room, knocked lightly on the door and opened it. He stepped inside the room, thinking not for the first time how grand it was with its high ornate stucco ceiling. The walls were papered in green with a flowered motif. Above the elaborately carved oak mantelpiece hung a large mirror. The fire was laid but not alight and the fire-irons, resting on a brass fender, brightly polished. The alcoves on either side of the fireplace housed two matching inlaid tables. A large settee faced the fireplace and two easy chairs were set to each side.

Ruth was sitting in a window seat to catch a little more light for the embroidery she was doing.

'Francis,' she greeted him, and he noted there was pleasure in her voice. She laid down the embroidery and took his hand as he sat down beside her. 'What news?' she asked, searching his face. She detected unease. 'Something's troubling you. What is it?'

He frowned. 'I had a visit from the two Mrs Thoresbys today.'

Ruth scowled. Her insides still churned at the mention of the Thoresby name. 'What the devil did they want?'

'They told me they want to take more interest in the business,' he explained.

'What?' She was half astonished and half amused. 'They should be at home looking after babies, cooking, sewing, knitting. I hope you put them off?'

'I tried but it was no use. They insisted. I didn't want to press too hard in case they wondered why I didn't want them around.'

Ruth looked thoughtful. 'Mmm, you're right. It just means you'll have to be careful what you explain to them.'

'I've been giving that some thought,' he said. 'Enough to make them think I'm showing them everything and sufficient to allay the menfolk's suspicions when they get back from the Arctic. But it'll need more care and vigilance.'

'You'll do it, Francis, I know you will.' A sparkling gleam had come to Ruth's eyes.

'After they had gone, I decided it was time to work on the plans we've made over these last three months. I negotiated the first transfer of funds.'

'You did!' An excited timbre came into her voice. At last things were underway. Now there was more meaning to her seclusion, more desire to fulfil their plans, more of an urge to pursue revenge to its ultimate conclusion.

'I went to see M . . .'

'No names, Francis. Better that only you know who you are dealing with,' she put in quickly.

'He invoiced me for services to some equipment. I paid him and he made a deposit in an account in the name of R. C. Shipping.'

'Who are they?'

He smiled. 'R for Ruth. C for Chambers.'

She laughed. 'Stupid of me.' Then she eyed him more seriously. 'But you can't sign for cash. The bank might be suspicious as to where you are getting the money, and I certainly can't – I'm dead.'

'True,' he agreed. 'We don't draw on the money. My friend, let's call him that, is R. C. Shipping. To all outward appearances, it's his firm.'

'But can we trust him?' she asked with suspicion. 'Couldn't he take the money for himself?'

'In theory, yes, but he won't. I have a hold over him which you need not bother about. He knows I could ruin him and prefers to take the ten per cent of whatever he deposits for us in R. C. Shipping, rather than face ruin.'

Ruth smiled. 'You're a cunning bastard, aren't you, Francis Chambers?'

He grinned. He sensed her mood lighten, that she was pleased their schemes had been put in motion, and squeezed her hand. 'We'll succeed, Ruth. Nothing more certain.'

'I know we will, and it will be all the more satisfying to do it right under their noses.' She flung her arms around his neck and hugged him tight. Then she would have moved back but he held her. She felt the strength of his arms, the firmness of his body, and the warmth of his breath upon her neck as his lips pressed against her smooth skin.

She relaxed, let her body take on an enticing softness. His mouth sought hers. She surrendered for a few moments and then matched his ardour with equal ferocity.

Chapter Three

'Whaleships! Whaleships!' The cry rang through Whitby's narrow streets. It spun off into the yards and along the alleys. It stormed through open windows and brought doors crashing wide. People poured into the streets, left their drinks unfinished, shelved their work and hurried to the cliff tops or made for the piers and the staithes. Whitby ships were in sight. Their menfolk were home.

These were special men. Whalers. Men who risked their lives in the cold and ice of the Arctic to hunt sixty-foot whales from tiny open boats with hand-held harpoons, in order to add to the prosperity of this thriving Yorkshire port. They were men apart, men with an aura. They were not only sailors, they were explorers sailing unknown waters, and hunters who stalked big game. These Greenland men, as they were known, were special, and in recognition of it Whitby always turned out to give them a heroes' welcome.

'Whaleships! Whaleships!'

The cry reached the house in Church Street. Emma Thoresby turned from the sink to see her two daughters-in-law springing to their feet. Excitement shone in their faces, but she also noted the touch of sadness in Jenny's eyes, as she felt the pang in her own heart.

This was the first time she would not be greeting the return of her eldest son. This was the first time Jenny would not be welcoming her husband home. Emma's heart went out to her daughter-in-law. She knew what it was like to lose a husband to the sea, and knew that all the pain would be dragged up again with the return of the whaleships. But Emma knew too that Jenny would go to the cliff top as she had always done.

She would seek, knowing all along that it was useless. She would recall all the times she had watched Adam, first as a mere crewman, then as a lineman, a boatsteerer, a harpooner, and finally as captain of the *Mary Jane*, returning from the Arctic. Now the *Mary Jane* would sail into Whitby without him, commanded by his brother Ruben.

'Ruben!' The word escaped from Jessica's lips charged with expectation.

'Away wi' thee, lasses,' cried Emma. 'Leave the bairns wi' me.'

Jenny paused. Her eyes met Emma's. Each knew Adam was deep in the other's thoughts. Emma gave a brief nod in which Jenny read understanding and approval of her wanting to be on the cliff top. She turned, grabbed her red shawl and ran from the house after Jessica.

'Come on, slow coach,' called Jessica, laughing. She had never once considered the possibility that the *Mary Jane* might not be one of the ships approaching Whitby. Jenny hoped and prayed that Jessica would not be disappointed for with that would come anxiety. Was Ruben all right? Was he going to return at all?

They twisted quickly through the crowds moving along Church Street and climbed the Church Stairs, impatiently tolerating the throng of people who barred quicker progress.

Clearing the Church Stairs they ran to join the crowd gathering along the cliffs. Jenny found a gap and wormed her way to the cliff edge.

'Is it them?' panted Jessica, eager for her to make an identification. She knew that Jenny, from years of observation, could recognise a vessel long before most folk.

Her gaze cut through the distance and flicked across the three vessels moving steadily far out on the North Sea.

'The *Mary Jane!*' she whispered.

'Ruben!' Jessica's voice was filled with relief amidst the excitement. He was safe. He was home. Dancing with joy, her eyes turned to her sister-in-law. Her words froze on her lips. In Jenny's transfixed gaze she saw sadness and a cry to heaven to let her be strong enough to bear this homecoming. She realised how deep the hurt must be still. Jenny should be greeting Adam, thrilling at his safe return, eager to feel his arms about her, anxious for his kisses. Instead she would return to a lonely bed and her memories. She put a hand lightly on Jenny's arm. 'I'm so sorry,' she whispered.

Jenny started. Forcing back the dampness in her eyes, she turned to Jessica and smiled. ''Tis I who should be sorry. I mustn't spoil your joy.' She hugged her sister-in-law. 'That's the *Mary Jane* out there! That's Ruben!'

'The others?'

Jenny turned her attention back to the sea. '*The Lonely Wind*, and though this is the first time I've seen her coming home, I feel sure it's the *Ruth*.'

The names of the ships rippled through the crowd, like wind through corn. Three of Whitby's ships were safe.

Jenny glanced down at the red shawl she held in her hand. Tears came back to her eyes. She had waved it at the start of every voyage which Adam had made, a sign of her continuing love while he was away. And she had always used it as a welcoming signal on his return. Now it would wave for him no more. Instead it would wave for David Fernley, but without the deeper meaning reserved for Adam.

She turned her attention back to the three ships, directing her gaze to the mastheads. A few moments later she grasped Jessica's arm. 'There's bone!' she cried. 'Bone at the masthead on all three! Full ships!'

The two friends hugged each other joyously in the exciting knowledge that all three ships had had a successful voyage. Their firm, the new firm of Fernley and Thoresby, risen from the ashes of Ruth's and David's enterprise, could not have had a better start.

David Fernley watched the familiar Yorkshire coast approach as the *Ruth* beat her way home, nearing the end of her maiden voyage to the Arctic. The towering cliffs of Boulby and Kettleness relented a little between Sandsend and Whitby, to rise swiftly and allow only a narrow passage to the sea for the River Esk. It was to that river, around which Whitby clung to the steep cliffs, that he directed his vessel. He glanced across at *The Lonely Wind* and the *Mary Jane*. They were already allowing him to take the lead, to be the first of them to pass into the river, a privilege granted to a whaler returning from her first voyage.

In spite of his elation at returning with a full ship, and the knowledge that the firm of Fernley and Thoresby had had a magnificent start, David felt a pang of regret. How he wished his dear friend, Adam Thoresby, had been bringing the *Mary Jane* home. With no husband to welcome today, Jenny would not be on the cliff to raise a red shawl. Even though she had once promised to be on the cliffs whenever he returned, he could not expect her to tear her heart open by watching the *Mary Jane* return without Adam.

With the ship moving into quieter waters, thunderous cheers broke out from the crowds on the cliff tops, along the staithes and the quays. Whitby folk gave their whaleships the homecoming they deserved after contesting the rigours of the Arctic, and these three were coming home full, bringing more prosperity to the port.

There was something special about the pride which filled David as the cheers reached his ears. Here was success. Three ships in which he had a share, full ships, bringing a substantial profit for his newly formed firm. This was something he and Ruth had dreamed about, had aimed for, until she became over-ambitious and it all ended in tragedy. Now she would not raise a welcoming white shawl for she lay beneath the waters somewhere off this rockbound coast.

He raised his arms in acknowledgement of the welcome and his eyes turned to the cliff top. He started. A red shawl! It waved. Jenny was there!

'Take her in, Luke!'

'Aye, aye, sir!' The mate, Luke Dobson, took command.

David swung on to the gunwale, grabbed the shrouds and climbed the ratlines to gain a more prominent position. Holding on by one hand, he swept his cap from his head and waved it vigorously. He saw the red shawl move faster and knew he had been seen. All thoughts of the past, of Ruth and of Adam, were swept from his mind. Jenny was there! She had come to welcome him just as she'd said she always would.

Someone beside her was waving and jumping up and down with excitement. It could only be his sister. She would be thrilled to be greeting Ruben after his first voyage as captain. This was a great time for them.

The three ships moved steadily upstream, passed beyond the bridge which linked the east and west banks, and sailed into the section of the river which was used as the inner harbour. They were carefully manoeuvred to the quays along the east bank. Ropes were thrown out and eagerly taken to make the ships secure to the quayside. Already people thronged the quays: wives thankful that their husbands had survived another whaling season, and eager to feel their strong arms around them; mothers grateful to have their sons home again to fuss over; and fathers, ex-whalemen perhaps, eager for talk which would transport them back to the Arctic and relive in some small measure that mysterious call of the north which still haunted their minds. Merchants, knowing by the bone at the masthead that the whaling had been good, were wanting to learn more about the catch, while prostitutes were eager to offer their services to men back from Arctic isolation.

The gangways were run out and sailors swarmed on to the quay to be hugged and kissed in a joyous reception reserved only for the Greenlandmen who battled with the dangers of the Arctic.

David watched from the ship, delighted with the happiness generated by this homecoming. His dark, deep-set eyes roamed casually over the milling crowd then stopped and focused on one figure, a red shawl around her shoulders. Jenny! He held her in his gaze. The girl of nineteen to whom he had offered his heart was now a fine woman of thirty-two. His eyes never left her as she wove her way through the crowd towards the gangplank. She saw him, smiled and waved, and he raised his arm in reply. He moved quickly to the gangplank and met her on the quay.

'Jenny!' The one word was full of feeling. He took her outstretched hands, gripped them with a gentle firmness and bent to kiss the cheek she offered him. 'I didn't expect . . .' he said as he straightened up and stepped back, still holding her hands.

'I once said I would always be here to welcome you home,' she replied.

'I know, but this time . . .' he said gently.

Jenny gave a wan smile. 'But the arrival of our whaleships is something special and Adam would have wanted me to be here.'

David nodded. 'Thank thee for coming, from him and from me.' The trials of the tragedy and its aftermath had left their marks on her once flawless ivory skin, but the beauty was still there and her voice was still smooth, gentle and caressing.

'How did the *Ruth* handle?' she asked, casting an eye over the ship.

'Splendidly,' he replied with enthusiasm. 'She's a good ship.'

'I'm so pleased.' The love of ships, gained from her seafaring father, was in her eyes as she let them range over the three vessels before settling on the *Mary Jane*. For a moment tears dimmed her eyes as all the times she had been at the *Mary Jane*'s gangplank to welcome Adam filled her mind. She started. 'No need to tell you where Jessica is.'

David laughed. 'This will be a happy time for them. How are Katie and Anne?'

'Both well,' said Jenny.

Any further conversation was halted by the arrival of Francis Chambers. 'Good day, Captain Fernley. Welcome home.'

'Thanks,' replied David with a smile as he took Francis's proffered hand.

'No need to ask you if you've had a good voyage,' he said enthusiastically. 'With bone at the masthead on all three ships, this is certainly a great start for Fernley and Thoresby.'

'Thee's dead right,' laughed David. 'Have thee got someone lined up for the blubber and the whalebone?'

'Not only lined up,' replied Francis, a touch of pleasure in his voice at being able to bring David Fernley good news, 'contracts are signed already.'

'So quickly!'

'Aye. As soon as I knew there was bone at the masthead, I concluded the preliminary negotiations which I had made a week ago and made a firm deal.'

'Who with?'

'Albert Fisher.'

'And he squeezed an extra shilling a ton out of him,' put in Jenny.

Surprised, David glanced at her. 'Oh, so thee knows about the deal?'

'Yes. Jessica and I decided we would take more interest in the firm and be a help, especially when you and Ruben are away. Ruth did it so why not us?' Jenny paused then added quickly when she saw the momentary flicker of pain cross David's face. 'I'm sorry.'

'No. Don't apologise,' he said. 'I shouldn't feel anything.'

'Oh, I got the contract signed by Frank Watson, Mrs Thoresby,' said Francis quickly, diverting their attention back to business.

'Good,' she said enthusiastically. 'He'll take all three shiploads.'

'He couldn't refuse after dealing with you, Ma'am.'

'What's all this?' asked David.

'Well, I thought you'd be taking all three ships to the Baltic for timber so I approached Frank. He was interested in taking two as he usually does. I tried hard to persuade him to take all three but he was a bit stubborn so I invited him and Hester round for tea — I know his weakness for cream cakes. Result — you've just heard what Francis said.'

'Well, I'll be darned!' laughed David. 'Good for thee. I see we'll have to watch these ladies, Francis, they'll be taking over.'

He laughed, only to him it was not amusing.

From the window in Rigg House, Ruth watched Francis hurry across the lawn from the door in the wall. He was tall and well-built, wearing his clothes well.

His purposeful walk took him beyond her sight. She remained deep in thought, looking out of the window, until she heard the doorbell clang and Emily's footsteps cross the hall.

Francis hurried in, allowing the door to slam behind him. He crossed the room quickly, took her hands in his and kissed her on the cheek.

She sensed he was bursting with news and responded

eagerly. 'Come on, tell me! I know three ships are back, I saw them from the turret.'

'All three were ours,' he replied, his eyes sparkling. 'And all were full.'

'Wonderful.' Ruth's face broke into a huge smile. 'Plenty of profit for us to take.'

'And not only that, Jenny has persuaded Frank Watson to take all the timber the three vessels will bring from the Baltic. I took the contract for him to sign today.'

'Even better,' she cried. Her enthusiasm swept them both into laughter and it seemed to finalise the bond between them, drawing them irrevocably together in a secret which neither of them would dare reveal to anyone else.

With a decision made to sail to the Baltic in ten days' time, David left the preparations in the capable hands of Ruben, Jim Talbot and Luke Dobson, and took the opportunity to visit his son.

He took the carrier's cart, bound for the market town of Pickering, as far as the lonely inn at Saltersgate. The sign, with its painting of a wagon and horses, creaked on its hooks, charging the silence with foreboding. David wanted no reminder of the night, thirteen years ago, when as a youth of eighteen on his way to Whitby to join the whalers, he nearly ran foul of the 'Gentlemen', leaders of the notorious smugglers on the Yorkshire coast. He shouldered his bag and set off across the moors for Cropton.

The sun shone from an almost clear sky, drawing the deep hues of the heather into a mass of purple. This was a season that David had always loved and, in spite of the years away from country life, he found there was still a kind of magic in these wild, isolated places.

He eased the pack on his shoulder and lengthened his stride. He breathed deep of the warm air, so different from the icy sharpness of the Arctic. A red-brown flash rose from the purple as a grouse, disturbed by the human intruder, took flight with a deep whir from its strong wings. Its plaintive cry faded into the lonely distance.

Two hours later, David paused where the heather and bracken gave way to a wooded hillside. Beyond the trees, protected from the north winds by a slope, stood a cottage from which smoke curled lazily to settle in a dark streak, willed into movement by the gentle breeze. Even from this distance David could sense the calm peace around the cottage. It was just as he had always known it during the first eighteen years of his life. For a moment he wondered if he had been wise to leave that life thirteen years ago to achieve a desire to sail with the whaleships. Couldn't he have had peace and tranquillity here with Ruth instead of the turbulent life which had come with his ambitions?

David threw off the thoughts as quickly as they had come. If he had stayed here he would never have fulfilled himself. The past was the past, not to be dwelt on, while the future was filled with enticing prospects. Whaling was his life, the country a haven which offered a pleasant escape for a short while.

David started down the slope and followed a path through the wood from which he emerged into a field which ran all the way to the cottage. He was halfway there when he saw his mother step outside. She shielded her eyes against the brightness for a brief moment, seeking to make out what stranger was approaching. 'Davey!' Her excited shout split the air.

Martha Fernley, her heart racing with joy, hurried towards her son.

'Ma!' he called and started to run. He saw his father dash through the doorway of the cottage, closely followed by David's younger sister, Betsy, and his brother John.

A few moments later David was hugging his mother tightly. There were tears of delight in her eyes as she buried her head against his chest, clinging to him, fearing that he would be gone in a minute if she did not hold on to him.

'Hello, Pa.' David held out his hand while still holding his mother.

Kit Fernley took his son's hand in a firm grip. His eyes shone with pride. 'Good t'see thee, lad. Welcome home.'

'Thanks, Pa.' David released his grip and turned his mother so that he could link arms with her and at the same time receive Betsy's greeting. His eyes were full of admiration as his sister ran towards him. She had grown into a fine young woman. Of medium height, she was well-proportioned, not plump but solidly made, and her rosy cheeks marked her out as a lover of the open air.

'Davey!' The joy she put into that one word showed the deep affection she had held her eldest brother in ever since childhood. She hugged him and kissed him on the cheek.

'Thee looks as well as ever, Betsy,' smiled David, then added with a twinkle in his eye, 'Not married yet?' It was a question which passed between them whenever they met.

'Get on with thee,' she laughed, giving him a playful tap on the arm. 'I'm content with Ma and Pa, and now with your Kit to look after . . .'

'How is he?' broke in David eagerly.

'Just fine,' she replied. 'Isn't he, Ma?'

'Grandest bairn I've seen,' smiled Martha.

'John.' David took his hand in a grip which signalled brotherly affection.

'Davey.' John's voice was soft and warm. A year younger than David, he was stronger, and broadened by farm work on the land which he loved. He never ceased to appreciate the changing seasons, the challenge of wresting a living from their temperamental attempts to upset routine. Now his square face glowed with the pleasure of welcoming his brother home.

'How long is thee home for, lad?' asked Kit as they walked back to the cottage.

'A week, Pa. We sail for Memel in ten days, for timber,' explained David.

'Only a week?' sighed Martha, disappointed that she would not have her son for longer.

'Sorry, Ma,' he said. 'Now where's that son of mine?' he added eagerly, to take his mother's mind off their parting even though it was a week away.

'He's upstairs in Betsy's room.'

'Have a look at him,' put in Betsy. 'But don't go waking him,' she added on a note of warning. 'I've just got him off to sleep.'

Martha and Betsy accompanied David upstairs. There he found his son fast asleep, looking so contented with not a care in the world. His right hand was knuckled at his mouth and he gave a little sigh as Betsy pulled the eiderdown straight though really it needed no adjustment. The wooden cot, made by John, was lined with white linen and was as spotless as the white sheet and pillow.

'Kit,' David whispered, his eyes fixed lovingly on his son. Martha and Betsy withdrew quietly to leave them alone.

He continued to stare in wonderment at the tiny figure sleeping peacefully. 'Oh, Ruth, if thee could only see him, thee'd love him.' The words formed soundlessly on his lips and in his heart he cried out: 'Where did we go wrong, Ruth? Where? So much happiness could have been ours.'

When he went downstairs to the large kitchen the first thing he did was to thank the family for looking after his son.

'It's nothing,' said Martha. 'We're delighted to have him.'

'He's no trouble,' added Betsy. 'Biggest problem is stopping Pa and John spoiling him.'

'Don't blame us, eh, John?' grinned Kit. 'No telling what womenfolk get up to when we're in t'fields.'

'Well, no matter, I'm grateful to you all.'

Martha and Betsy were busy setting the table for the evening meal and John was mending the fire. His father was sitting in one of the two wooden chairs beside the fireplace, charging his pipe. It was a familiar scene to David. It had gone on like this day after day, week in and week out, month following month, throughout the years. Routine, regular, hardly varying. It was warmth and security built on understanding and love.

'Thee's in John's room. Thy bed's always made up,' said Martha as she started cutting a loaf of bread.

'Thanks, Ma. I'll take my things up.' David grabbed his pack and started for the kitchen door. He paused and looked back. 'That's a good smell,' he said glancing towards the big pan hanging on the reckon over the fire.

'Stew,' said Betsy.

'Thee'll be ready for it,' said Kit, 'after that moorland air.'

'I am that, Pa!'

A few minutes later, washed and with a clean shirt on, he sat down at the table with the rest of the family.

His father sat at the head of the table, and David thought that he was stooping just a little more than he had been when David had brought young Kit here prior to sailing for the Arctic. Years of farming toil, of lifting heavy sacks, of handling sheep and cattle, of scything and stooking, of being out in all weathers, were taking their toll. But his father still had a sparkle in his dark eyes and made light of any aches and pains.

David glanced at his brother. He knew John would ease their father's labour as much as he could. There was power in his arms for two men and he was not one to shirk his duties.

Betsy ladled stew on to plates and Martha brought them to the table.

'Looks good,' said David, eyeing the meat, potatoes and vegetables. He reached for some bread and took some of the pickled red cabbage offered by John.

'Now I have time to ask, how's Jessica?' asked Martha as she sat down.

'Very well, Ma. Taking an interest in the business now. She was a great help while I was in the Arctic. She saw that my house was ready for me when I got back. I've got one in Henrietta Street now.'

'Near where you used to live?'

'That's right, before I moved across the river.'

'And Katie?'

'She's a grand little thing,' replied David. 'Thee'll have to come to see her, Ma.'

'Maybe Jessica will come home sometime.'

'Of course she will,' said David. 'Now what about your news? How's the new landlord?'

'Considerate. Very different to old Squire Hardy. We hardly knew t'young un, Jonathan.'

The name pierced David's mind. He could hear Ruth flinging the facts of her association with her half-brother at him; how she had used him and sent him to his death, only to find her schemes to gain his wealth thwarted by his cunning. David started. His father was going on.

'After he fell from the cliffs at Whitby, the estates passed to a distant cousin, Cornelius Hardy. Be about your age. Married to a nice lass. They've reviewed the whole estate and all the tenancies.'

David sensed an undercurrent of excitement around the table. He glanced round his family. His mother was sitting contentedly in her chair as if a burden had been lifted from her. John was trying to keep a smile of pleasure from showing. Betsy gave the appearance of hugging herself, while his father's weatherbeaten face seemed to be released of its careworn expression.

'What is it?' asked David. 'What have thee to tell me?'

'New squire's given us the cottage!' announced Kit.

'What!' he gasped, staring incredulously at them all.

'It's true, Davey,' beamed his mother. 'Gave it to your Pa for long and faithful service to the family. He also said he wanted to relieve any worry about what would happen to Betsy when we passed on.'

'This is wonderful news,' cried David. 'Now I know why thee thinks he's a good landlord.'

'And that isn't all,' put in John enthusiastically. 'He's given me a permanent job on the estate and he's renovating several of the old cottages and giving me the chance of the first one ready.'

'So thee and Phoebe . . .'

'That's right. Now I have a permanent job, we'll marry as soon as the cottage is ready.'

'I'm happy for all of you, and it's a worry off my mind.'

The week passed quickly. David relaxed in the carefree atmosphere. He loved playing with his son, helped with some refurbishments to the cottage, walked with Betsy and enjoyed the company of them all in the evenings around the fire. The talk flowed from country matters to the sea, whaling and David's business. Ruth was never mentioned for the family feared that it would reopen old wounds, something they did not want to do while revelling in their own good fortune.

Goodbyes were hard and David left with a promise to come again soon and to bring Jessica with him.

The break had given him the opportunity to review his own future so that, after taking his pack to his house on Henrietta Street, he make his way quickly to Jenny's.

'David.' She greeted him with a smile when she opened the door. 'Come in, it's good to see you.'

She closed the door behind him and he stepped to one side to allow her to lead the way into the kitchen. 'Don't mind it in here. I was just folding these clothes.' A basket, with a pile of neatly folded clothes next to it, was set on a table against one wall. A kettle hanging on a reckon over the fire began to spout steam. 'Just right for a cup of tea.' She went to the tea pot which was warming on a hob beside the fire and poured boiling water into it.

'It's good to see thee, Jenny,' said David, sitting down in a Windsor chair beside the fire. 'How has thee been?'

'Fine, thanks.' Jenny crossed the room to a cupboard and produced two cups and saucers. She placed them, along with two plates, on the table. 'I'm getting settled down. Taking an interest in the firm helps.'

David nodded. He did not remark on it but he knew she must be missing Adam till it hurt, because he, at this moment, was missing the presence of his friend. Adam had always seemed to fill this house with life; now that old atmosphere was missing.

'When did you get back?' she asked, going to the pantry.

'Just now,' he replied. 'Took my things home and came straight here to see how thee is.'

She came from the pantry carrying a tin and a plate pie. 'I must have known it.' She smiled. 'Got your favourites here.'

'Good.' He grinned in anticipation of enjoying the pie which he knew must be apple. There could only be one thing in the tin: that mouth-watering fruit cake which was Jenny's speciality.

'How was everyone at home?' she asked as she returned to the pantry.

'All well,' he called. 'Little Kit's a fine baby.' He went on to tell her about the cottage and John's good fortune while she brought out some cheese and poured the tea.

'How's Anne?' he asked as they settled down at the table.

'Very well,' replied Jenny. 'Growing so fast, at twelve she's quite the young lady. She's at her gran's.'

They exchanged news while they ate and when she had cleared away, David made his request. 'I want to see the sea, Jenny. Walk with me on the cliffs.'

She hesitated. Memories of shared moments came tumbling back; times shortly after David had come to Whitby when they had been close.

'Please, Jenny,' he pressed.

She met the appeal in his eyes and knew she could not refuse an old and dear friend. 'Very well.'

He helped her into a brown coat and picked up the red shawl from the back of a chair. 'Want this?' he asked.

Jenny nodded, took the shawl and draped it round her head.

'Will it wave when I leave for the Baltic?' he asked.

'It will, Davey. You should know better than to ask,' she answered quietly.

He stepped towards her but she turned and opened the door into the passage which led to the front door. 'We'd best be going.'

They walked from the house in Henrietta Street to the Church Stairs, nodding to acquaintances, exchanging greetings with friends and aware of glances cast in their direction by gossiping groups. They climbed the hundred and ninety-nine steps steadily, pausing to gaze across the red roofs to the new town growing on West Cliff on the opposite side of the river.

They walked beyond the church and took the path to the edge of the cliffs. The day was fine with a warm sun only occasionally cooled by a passing cloud. The air was clear, sharpened by a fresh wind, and left a knife-edged horizon beckoning to distant waters. The cry of soaring seagulls and the low boom of breaking waves sealed the moment in David's mind as he stopped and gazed across a gently running sea.

Jenny stood beside him silently. She did not want to mar these precious minutes for him. From his expression she could see that David felt himself at home, that this was where he belonged.

David started. 'Sorry, Jenny, I was miles away.'

'That's all right.' She smiled. 'I know you, David Fernley. I've walked these cliffs with you before.'

'Walk with me now,' he said, a catch in his throat.

They turned and strolled along the cliff edge in silence, each lost in thought.

'Davey.' Guessing where his recollections were taking him, Jenny broke the silence. 'We've started well with the business. Are you happy with the organisation?'

He stopped and looked deep into her eyes. 'Forget the firm. It's thee and me I'm concerned about.'

'David, please,' she started, a perturbed look clouding her eyes, but he silenced her with a gentle touch on her lips.

'Let me say what I want to say. Thirteen years ago I walked these cliffs and proposed to a girl I had fallen in love with. She turned me down and married my best friend. Would she turn me down again?'

'Oh, Davey, don't ask me.' There was anguish in her voice. 'I don't want to hurt you again.'

'Then don't,' he cried. 'Marry me.' He grabbed her hand so that she could not turn away from him.

A vulnerable look had come over her face and for one moment he wondered if he had broken a friendship but in his heart he knew it would take more than that to turn Jenny away from him.

'Davey, I can't!' she repeated.

'Why not?' he pressed. 'It makes sense. Thee's lost Adam, I've lost Ruth. We're both free. I've always loved thee. I know I nearly won thee all those years ago. Thee felt something for me then, it can be rekindled now.'

'Stop, Davey. Stop!' Jenny's face creased with anguish, her eyes filled with tears. She knew she was on the point of tearing David's heart in two. She would give anything to avoid that but could see no way of doing so. She had loved him when he first came to Whitby but not in the way he had wanted. It was Adam whom she loved differently, Adam whom she had married. Though she still loved David in a way it remained the same as it had been all those years ago. Jenny stared into his eyes with a look which pleaded for him to understand. 'I can't marry you.'

'Thee can,' he cried. 'We've no ties.'

'I have,' she returned. 'I still love Adam.'

'Jenny, he's dead.' He saw her wince and hated himself for being so blunt. 'I'm sorry,' he added gently. 'But it's a fact of life. Thee's alive and life is for the living. Adam wouldn't want thee to mourn forever.'

'I know that, and I won't,' said Jenny. 'I'll live my life as I see it. Hopefully I'll enjoy most of it but Adam will always be close to me, and it will be him I'll always love.'

'I'm prepared to take that on,' he said.

'I wouldn't allow it. It wouldn't be fair to you. I couldn't let you live in the shadow of my love for Adam. You deserve better than that. David, please.' She laid a gentle hand on his arm. 'I do love you, always have, but in a special way that doesn't run as deep as my love for Adam. If I married you there would always be that barrier between us. Please, for your own sake and for mine, don't ask me again. Don't spoil the deep friendship and understanding that we have. Let us remain as we always have, two people who share the love that goes with a deep friendship.'

David swallowed hard and bit his lip. There was so much he could say but he knew it would be useless. Behind her words he recognised a finality and he thought too much of her to try to overwhelm her feelings. 'If that's the way thee wants it,' he said quietly, unable to disguise the disappointment in his voice.

Jenny smiled, a comforting, understanding smile, as she reached up and kissed him on the cheek. 'Dear David, you will always be special to me.'

He took both her hands in his. His words matched the

depth of her feeling. 'And thee is to me. Thee always have been and always will be.' He kissed her on the lips and she did not resist. 'If ever thee needs me, whatever for, just call and I'll be there.'

He held her hand until they reached the top of the Church Stairs and walked back down to the town.

There was a sense of urgency about David's request that Ruben, Jessica and Jenny should meet him at his house on Henrietta Street. He gave no hint as to why he had called this meeting and all three, talking among themselves, could find no possible reason for it.

The voyage to the Baltic had gone well, with all three ships bringing cargoes of first-class timber to Whitby. The red shawl had waved from the cliff top and David knew that his relationship with Jenny remained as it had always been.

Now she made her way to David's, in the company of Ruben and Jessica, wondering what it was that David needed to talk to them about the day after his return to port.

He welcomed them warmly, and when they were all comfortably seated handed them each a glass of Madeira. He stood in front of them, raised his glass and said, 'Our firm of Fernley and Thoresby has got off to a fine start. Three full ships from the Arctic, a good price for the blubber and whalebone, followed by a successful voyage to Memel. And thanks to Jenny, all the timber sold at a good price. Here's to continued success.'

All three acknowledged his toast then sipped at the Madeira, waiting for him to go on. He hesitated, trying to choose his words carefully.

'Go on, Davey,' prompted Jessica. 'I'm sure that isn't why thee brought us here.'

'Thee's right, Jess,' he said. His glance took in all three and he read the curiosity and anticipation on their faces.

'While we sailed to the Baltic I had time to do a lot of thinking. I came to a decision. I'm going to make Luke Dobson captain of the *Ruth* and I'm going to London.'

'What!' all three gasped at this sudden and unexpected announcement. They knew from the fact that he was relinquishing the captaincy of the *Ruth* that his going to London would be for a considerable time.

Their exchange of glances spoke of bewilderment and confusion.

'What on earth for?' cried Jessica.

'Thee's just said the firm's going well, why this change?' Ruben demanded.

'Why are you going to London?' asked Jenny, though in her heart she knew the real answer.

'Hold on,' smiled David, raising his hands as if to parry the questions. 'I've thought this over carefully and it makes a lot of sense. The firm is on a sound footing. Ruben is a capable captain, so is Jim Talbot, and I'm sure Luke Dobson will be. Jenny and Jessica are learning the business rapidly from Francis Chambers. The business is in good hands. In London I'll look for ways to expand, possibly branch out into more distant voyages. After all, firms there are sending whaleships to the Pacific. Maybe that's where we should turn our eyes. We'd escape the hazards of the Arctic.'

'I think we need thee here,' put in Jessica. 'Thee has more experience of running the firm than any of us. After all, thee and Ruth did so.'

'That's true, Davey.' Ruben lent weight to Jessica's point. 'I'm no businessman. I'm a sailor, a whaleman. I wouldn't be happy behind a desk.'

'I know exactly how thee feels,' replied David. 'I'm the same, but I'm not suggesting thee give up the sea, only keep an eye on things when thee's ashore. I'm sure even that won't entail a great deal with Jenny and Jessica involved all the time.'

Ruben nodded but did not look at all convinced that it was a good idea for David to leave.

'Davey, don't forget young Kit. What about him?' Jessica sought another way to hold her brother back.

'He'll be all right with Ma and Betsy.' He gave a little laugh. 'It isn't as if I'll be away for good. I'll come back to Whitby as often as I can, depending on developments in London. I'll go to see Kit then. He'll not be forgotten. None of thee will.' He glanced at all three. 'Don't look so glum. As I said, I can see ways to help develop the firm.'

'It seems your mind is made up,' said Jenny quietly.

'It is.'

'Sleep on it, Davey,' suggested Ruben.

'No need.' He shook his head. 'I had plenty of time to think about it on our voyage to Memel. Nothing will make me change my mind.'

'When will thee go?' asked Jessica.

'I've booked a passage for a week tomorrow. I'll see Chambers later today, make sure everything is shipshape. Tomorrow I'll go to Cropton, then I'll be back here with a couple of days to get ready for London.'

Silence filled the room, as if this moment was seeing the end of an era, then Ruben spoke. 'Jess, why don't thee go with Davey? It's an opportunity for thee to visit your parents and have a chaperon both ways.'

Her eyes brightened but she made a protest. 'I can't leave thee, Ruben.'

'Of course thee can,' he replied reassuringly. 'Thee may not get an opportunity later on. This is a good chance. It's only going to be for three or four days and then we'll have the rest of the winter together.'

'Ma would love to see thee,' said David.

Jessica looked at her husband with love in her eyes. She was so glad she had found her true love with Ruben and that her affair with James Humphries had come to nothing. 'Well, if thee's sure . . .'

'Of course I am, love.' Ruben stood up and held out his hands to his wife.

She rose from her chair and came to him. 'Thanks, Ruben. Call for me, Davey.'

'Six o'clock,' he replied. 'Carrier leaves at half-past.'

'I'll be ready. See thee when I get back, Jenny.'

Jenny nodded and came to her. She gave her friend a hug and said, 'Have a good journey.'

David saw his sister and brother-in-law from the house and when he returned to the room found Jenny deep in thought. She looked up when he closed the door.

'I'm the real reason you're going to London, aren't I?' she said quietly, holding his eyes with hers.

Denials sprang to his lips but he could not utter them. He could not be dishonest with her. 'Well, I suppose so, but nevertheless it can be turned to the firm's advantage.'

'But I feel as if I'm driving you away!' Tears were gathering in Jenny's eyes. 'Whitby's been your life. The whalers, the Arctic . . . Oh, David, you'll miss them all so much. London's not for you.'

'Maybe, maybe not,' he said wistfully. 'There comes a time in every life when we must look to new beginnings. This is probably mine.'

'What will you do?' she queried with concern.

'I'll contact one of the whaling firms, maybe get the captaincy of one of their ships. I'll see how things work out.'

Jenny dabbed her moist eyes. 'Forgive me, Davey.'

He came to her and took her hands in his. 'There's nothing to forgive. I'm going of my own free will.'

'Don't forget me, Davey, though I don't deserve remembering.' She felt as if something of the past, which she held very dear, was being taken from her.

'I could never forget thee, Jenny.' He bent and kissed her on the cheek.

As he drew back she saw a love in his eyes which she could never return.

'David, be happy. Look to the future. You'll find some-one else.' Her kiss was gentle and she left the house without looking back.

The westering sun flamed the red roofs of Whitby as Francis Chambers hurried to the East Cliff. He climbed the Church Stairs without a pause and, on reaching the cliff top, lengthened his stride towards Rigg House. He had the key to the door in the wall in his hand and opened it with the minimum of delay. He did not pause to admire the flowers, so eager was he to impart his news to Ruth.

He rang the bell at the front door and waited impatiently for Emily to come. When she did so he burst past her with a haste which startled the housekeeper.

'Withdrawing room?' he called over his shoulder.

'Madam's not down yet,' she replied.

Francis changed the direction of his stride without stopping. He threw his hat on a chair and bounded up the stairs two at a time.

Emily gave a little grimace as she closed the front door and turned to see Francis hurrying along the landing at the top of the stairs.

He flung open the bedroom door without knocking and gave it a push to close it behind him as he strode into the room.

Surprised by the sudden intrusion, Ruth, sitting in front of a dressing table brushing her copper hair, swung round on her stool. Her pink silk dressing gown hung open, exposing a brocade corset, stiff with whalebone, which raised and revealed firm, rounded breasts. Her white drawers gave way to black net stockings while her under-skirt lay still unattached over the back of a chair.

She flicked the gown across her and obscured Francis's devouring gaze as he crossed the room.

'Don't you knock . . . ?' Ruth's indignant tone was

swamped as he grabbed her round the waist, pulled her to her feet and smothered her with kisses.

She pushed against him until she was able to gasp, 'What's all this about? Why all the excitement?'

He released her and stepped back. His eyes danced with exuberance. 'Captain Fernley's leaving Whitby, and going to London,' he announced excitedly.

The full impact of his words not making themselves felt, Ruth stared at him. 'You mean for good?'

'Well, practically,' replied Francis.

'But why?' she asked, still incredulous. David was so steeped in Whitby and its whaling, had been ever since he had seen the whaleships on his first visit at nine years old, that she would never have believed anything would drag him away. She sat down on her stool.

'Said he wanted to see how London firms were seizing new whaling opportunities, especially in the Pacific. He thinks it might be advantageous for Fernley and Thoresby to look into such possibilities.'

Ruth's thoughts were racing. She only half heard Francis as he went on: 'He's briefed me on the development of the firm and allowed me more authority.' He stopped his pacing and swung round to face Ruth. 'This gives us even better opportunities to ruin him, just as you wanted.' His jaw muscles twitched as a feverish excitement gripped him. He saw riches tumbling into his lap and, as this brought disaster to David Fernley, Ruth would be ever more grateful and ready to ply him with favours which would fulfil his cravings and desires.

She nodded slowly as if agreeing with what he said but her thoughts were elsewhere, trying to probe the real reason for David's unlikely decision to leave Whitby.

About to go on, Francis stopped. He saw the faraway look in Ruth's eyes and knew better than to break her concentration.

She stared unseeingly past him, her mind probing,

searching and then discovering. She knew! Her woman's intuition had given her the reason. Jenny had turned him down! David was trying to escape. A chuckle started deep in Ruth's throat. As delight took hold of her she hugged herself and started to rock backwards and forwards as the thought of Jenny turning David down became more of a certainty.

Unable to understand, Francis stared at her.

'She refused him! She refused him!' The words, though quiet, were suffused with joy. Her laughter grew and the rocking became swifter until she flung her arms wide with ecstasy and her piercing cry, filled with elation, penetrated every corner of the room. 'Jenny refused to marry him!'

'All aboard! All aboard!' The shout came loud and clear from the decks of the *Capella*.

'Best of luck, Davey.' Ruben's hand gripped his. 'Take care.'

'I will. Thanks, Ruben.'

''Bye, David. Remember us.' There were tears in Jessica's eyes as she turned to her brother.

'Of course I will.' He kissed his sister on the cheek and then took her in his arms. They hugged with all the deep affection they felt for one another.

'A present for thee,' whispered Jessica as they parted, and slipped it into his hand.

He looked down to see a cross, delicately carved from Whitby jet, lying in his palm. 'It's beautiful, Jess. Thanks.' He hugged her once again.

'All aboard!'

The final cry drew them apart. David took off his cap and passed the chain and cross over his head.

He turned and hurried aboard the *Capella* and stood by the rail as the gap between ship and quay widened. His hand, raised in a parting gesture, received an acknowledgement from Ruben while Jessica wiped her eyes before replying.

The *Capella* moved out into the river and headed for the sea.

A solitary figure on the cliff top waved a red shawl.

'Goodbye, Jenny love,' David whispered. He fingered the jet cross hanging close to his chest. 'And I'll never forget thee, Jessica lass.'

Chapter Four

The *Capella* moved steadily up the Thames under a clear blue sky. The air was sharp but ahead the smoke from the coal fires of the city hung like a pall. The voyage had been uneventful with the ship making good time in a smooth sea.

With the branch pilot in charge of navigating the busy river, the *Capella*'s captain, Simeon Midgley, relaxed a little, though responsibility for the vessel's safety still rested on his shoulders. Alert, his eyes darting everywhere, he kept watch on situations developing on the river.

'First time to London, David?' he asked as he crossed the deck.

'Aye, Simeon, it is,' he replied, straightening up from the rail. 'How many times for thee?'

Simeon laughed. 'Lost count.' The Whitby man, after sailing with Cook, had returned to his home port where he gained promotion on ships plying regularly to the capital until he became master of the *Capella*. He and David were acquaintances and respected each other's seamanship in their different callings. 'Yon's the docks of the East India Company,' Simeon pointed out.

David had been admiring the fine vessels, East Indiamen as they were called. He had heard of them but had never seen one and now realised why they were known as the lords of the ocean. Not only were they big, bigger than he had imagined, they were magnificent and seemed to know it for they appeared to be floating proudly in their own special dock, scorning all other shipping.

Simeon saw David staring wide-eyed at the forest of masts filling the Pool of London. There were ships everywhere, moored to the quays along the banks or moving along the fairway, and all around them activity, the whole scene swarming as if it could never be still.

'Ever seen so many ships, David?' laughed Simeon.

'Never,' he replied, with a slight shake of his head to emphasise his disbelief at the scene.

'Yon's three of thy lot.' Simeon pointed to three vessels lying still at the quayside as if trying to recuperate after battling with the sea.

David gazed in the direction indicated by Simeon and felt a thrill of pride as his eyes settled on the ships. Whalers, unmistakably. Purposeful, tough. They were his life and his reason for being here. On the way south he had wondered if he had done the right thing in leaving Whitby, and on the way up the river, seeing the teeming activity, his doubts had been strengthened. But now, seeing the type of ship with which he was familiar, his mood lightened.

'Come for the whalers?' asked Simeon.

'Aye,' replied David. 'Should have told thee before.'

'No reason to. Thee's thy own master.'

'Going to see what the whaling trade holds here. See if Fernley and Thoresby can find something to its advantage,' explained David.

'Main firm is Samuel Enderby and Sons.'

'Heard they'd been into the Pacific?'

'Aye, they did. The *Emilia* rounded the Horn in eighty-nine, got back here the following year with nearly one hundred and fifty tons of sperm oil, and a report of whales off the coast of Peru. Sent a flurry through London's whaling fraternity, I can tell thee.'

'Might look at these Enderbys,' said David thoughtfully.

'Do, but better still go to Hartley Shipping in Copper Street,' Simeon advised. 'A good, solid firm. Dominic

Hartley's a grand old man, been in shipping all his life and in whaling the past twenty years. Mention my name, tell him I sent thee.'

'Thanks, Simeon. I'll do that right away.'

All further conversation was cut short as Simeon supervised the docking of the ship and the disembarkation of passengers. David said goodbye to him and was grateful for Simeon's directions to Copper Street.

Before he had gone very far he felt himself lost in the swirl of life around him. He felt as if he was walking on the brink of two different worlds as well-dressed merchants and shopkeepers hurried about their business which brought them into contact with the dockers and unskilled labourers essential to their trades. Barefooted urchins in filthy rags chased by, almost knocking over a young girl who had just sold some oranges to a finely dressed lady in a sedan chair. David pitied the two men having to carry her in the heat of the afternoon, but they plodded on through the dust and squalor of the narrow London streets. Clerks hurried about their business, carrying notes and messages, contracts and bills relating to the many goods which poured in and out of the leading port in the world. Many held handkerchiefs to their noses, trying to ease their breathing in the smoky atmosphere which added to the filth and dirt of the city. David found himself longing for the clear air of the sea and the Arctic.

Following Simeon's directions, he wended his way through the bustling crowds, alert for pickpockets and keeping a tight hold on his pack. Turning into Copper Street he found some relief from the hustle. The street was quieter, more concerned with business than the general flow of life. Small groups of men could be seen, well-dressed in coats short to the waist but cut away to tails at the back, knee-length breeches worn with calf-clinging hose and black shoes with silver buckles. Some carried canes and most wore a low-crowned, small-brimmed hat.

David heard figures quoted and goods mentioned and guessed that trade was being discussed or deals being made. Less ostentatiously dressed clerks plied their way between business premises, and youths stirred the dust as they ran by with messages.

David glanced at the plaques beside the doors until he found the one he was looking for. It announced Hartley Shipping in bold lettering on highly polished brass.

The building was double fronted, with the stonework well pointed and the windowframes in good condition. The brown door was freshly painted and the windows on either side were polished. David's favourable impression was strengthened when his knock was answered by a smiling youth with an accent foreign to his ears. 'Good day, sir. What can I do for you?'

'I'd like to see Mr Hartley,' replied David.

'I'm sorry, sir. Mr Hartley's not in today,' the youth answered breezily as he flicked his lank blond hair back off his face. He pursed his lips into a serious expression. 'As a matter of fact, sir, he's rarely in these days. Don't know when he'll be in again.' David's heart sank, but before he could make any comment the youth went on, wiping the solemn expression from his face with an open, all is not lost, smile. 'But, sir, you can see Miss Hartley.'

David was about to say he would come back another day when the youth stepped to one side with a flourish, allowing him entrance which he could not refuse.

He moved past the youth who, though his clothes were of good quality, seemed to be unable to wear them with any degree of tidiness. The youngster closed the door with an exaggerated gesture, bringing it just short of crashing shut.

'This way, sir,' he beamed, round face sparkling as if it had been newly scrubbed.

He led the way along the passage which was lit from a skylight above the front door. He paused at a door on the left, opposite another which David surmised had been deliberately left open to assuage the curiosity of the three faces turned in his direction while pretending to be occupied with other things.

The youth gave a distinctive rap on the door, paused a moment then opened it with the same sort of flourish as he had used to admit David to the building.

'Ma'am, a visitor for you,' he announced.

'And who might it be?' The voice was soft but authoritative.

'I don't know, Ma'am.' The youth sounded embarrassed.

'Oh, Billy, haven't I told you always to ask the name?' The admonishment, though gentle, was no less telling.

Billy dropped his gaze to the floor and shuffled uneasily. 'I'm sorry, Ma'am. I forgot.'

'Well, come along. Do it now.'

Billy straightened and turned his head to David. 'Who shall I say is calling, sir?'

'Captain David Fernley.'

Billy pushed back his shoulders. Gone was his embarrassment. 'Ma'am, a visitor. Captain David Fernley,' he announced firmly.

'Very well, show him in.'

Billy glanced at David and gestured with a slight bow. 'This way, sir.'

David thanked him as he stepped into the room. Billy closed the door quickly and a moment later David heard the door across the passage close.

A young lady rose from the desk close to the window. 'Captain Fernley, I'm sorry about that. Billy is bursting with life but he forgets so easily.' There was a gaiety about her which David found appealing. She seemed amused by Billy's ways but the laughter was not unkind. David was drawn to the eyes which had an unusual depth to their blue. They were friendly and warm yet at the same time alert and he knew he was coming under a quick but thorough scrutiny and assessment. It was a first appraisal, which would be amended for better or worse later, but he guessed it was more often than not accurate from the first.

'Lydia Hartley,' she introduced herself, extending her hand.

He took it and felt a gentle response to his grip. 'Pleased to meet thee, Ma'am.'

'Ah, from Yorkshire, I think.'

'My accent's so obvious?' he grinned.

'Not as marked as some,' she replied. 'And what brings you to London, Captain Fernley? Please do sit down.' She indicated a leather-upholstered armchair as she went back to her chair behind the desk.

She smoothed her high-waisted linen dress before sitting down. Its deep yellow looked cool on this hot day and complemented her flaxen hair which was drawn up on her crown and neatly pinned in place. David imagined it loosened, tumbling to her shoulders, shimmering in the light like a sundrenched waterfall. He felt there was a calmness to her, as if she would never grow flustered, and this was reflected in her complexion which was smooth, clear and unlined.

'I'm a whaling captain, done all my sailing out of Whitby,' he explained. 'The firm of Fernley and Thoresby, of which I have a third share, is doing well, so I thought I would come to London to see what possibilities it had to offer us.'

'Does your firm want to expand here?' asked Lydia.

'I would think not, but maybe the South Seas could offer us an alternative to the Arctic.'

'Ah, but whaling in the Pacific is different to whaling in the Arctic.' In her warning David sensed a deep knowledge of the trade.

'I would expect that.'

'So you would like to experience it before deciding

whether to direct your firm there?' queried Lydia with a quizzical raising of her eyebrows. She was curious. This man, whom she judged to be about her own age, was good-looking in a rugged sort of way. He was marked by the wind and sun but she also detected lines of strain, as if life's offerings to him had not all been easy. There was about him an air of regret and his dark eyes held sadness as if he had suffered losses from which he was trying to escape.

'Possibly. Maybe I could do a voyage from here?'

'You seem uncertain?' There was irrefutably probing behind her soft tones.

David shrugged his shoulders. 'Who knows what life may bring? But I know I'll miss the Arctic.'

'They tell me it's a magical place.'

'Aye, it is. There's something about it which, in spite of the dangers, draws thee back again and again.' A faraway look had come to his eyes and she knew that for a moment he was no longer in a shipping office in London.

'Then why are you here?'

'I told you why.'

'But there are other reasons, I suspect?' Lydia put the question, then, regretting it, went on quickly, 'Forgive me, I shouldn't ask. It is no business of mine. The reasons you gave are good enough.' She changed the tack of the conversation. 'How did you come to find Hartley Shipping?'

'I came down on the *Capella*, Simeon Midgley, captain. He and I are acquainted. He told me to come here and make myself known to Dominic Hartley.'

'Ah, Simeon, an old friend of my father.' She nodded her understanding. 'He doesn't come to the office very often. Leaves me to run the firm.'

'Thee?'

She laughed merrily. 'You seem surprised. Why shouldn't a woman be capable of running a shipping firm?'

David smiled. 'No reason at all. I'm not entirely surprised. My wife ran our firm until she was drowned. Now my sister, her husband and the wife of my friend who was lost in the same tragic accident run the firm, so thee sees I'm used to ladies having a finger in shipping affairs. But although I've seen it work in Whitby, I didn't expect to find it happening here in London.'

'Well, you're seeing it now,' grinned Lydia.

'And I'm sure thee's as capable as we men.'

She inclined her head graciously. 'Spoken like a true gentleman.'

He smiled and their eyes held for a moment.

'Look, David. May I call you David?'

He acknowledged her request. 'Of course.'

'Well, David. I have something in mind which might help you, but I would rather discuss it with Father first. Now, you must meet him. Besides, he'll want to hear news of Simeon. My carriage will be here in an hour, you must come home with me.'

'That is very kind,' he said, and started to rise. 'I must find somewhere to stay.'

'No need. I'm sure my father will insist on your staying with us, at least for the time being.'

'But I couldn't impose . . .' he protested.

'It will be no imposition, I can tell you. My father will be delighted. He'll love to yarn about the sea. You'll be doing him a favour. I know he gets sick and tired of female company. I'm an only child and there's only the housekeeper, Mrs Dove, at home. So you see, I would deem it a favour if you'd stay.'

He smiled. 'How can I refuse?'

As they left the building Lydia took David into the room across the passage. Immediately she entered the four clerks jumped off their high stools and stood with pen still in hand. Billy beamed while the other two clerks, whom David judged to be in their late twenties, were more solemn-faced. An older man rose from behind a desk situated close to the window which overlooked the street.

'This is Captain Fernley.' Lydia made the introduction. 'Silas Farnham, our chief clerk.' She indicated the man by the window.

'I am pleased to meet you, Captain.' The small thin man with hair greying at the temples made a slight bow.

David returned the greeting and then Lydia introduced the other two clerks as Dick Castle and Stanley Harris. 'And you already know Billy,' she concluded.

He beamed even more exuberantly.

'Pleased to meet all of thee,' said David with a glance which embraced them all but which each felt was meant for him individually.

They were making their own judgements of the stranger whom Billy had already enthused about from his first brief meeting. Their assessment agreed with his. They all liked the open, friendly face and pleasant greeting of the new arrival.

'I'm leaving now, Silas, you'll see that everything is locked up as usual?' Lydia addressed her chief clerk.

'Certainly, Ma'am.'

'Silas and his family live above the offices in the rooms which Father and I had until we moved to our present house,' she explained once she and David had settled in the coach. 'Billy is an orphan. His father was killed on a whaling voyage, so Father gave him a home, a room right at the top of the building. Now Silas's wife keeps an eye on him. Dick Castle and Stanley Harris are both married, Dick last year, Stanley three years ago. They live a couple of streets away. Do you have any family, David?'

'Aye, Kit, just a year old. He's with his grandparents.'

'Your mother and father?'

'Aye, at Cropton, a small village on the edge of the North Yorkshire moors. Pa's a farm worker.'

Lydia raised an eyebrow in surprise. 'So what took you

to the sea? I'd have thought farming would be in your blood.'

He smiled and shook his head. 'Hated it ever since Pa took me to Whitby when I was nine. I remembered the ships, especially the whalers, and from that day I was determined to become a whaleman.'

'Then you did well,' she commented.

'Aye, maybe.'

She saw the wistful look come back to his dark eyes, as if memories of the past brought into doubt his achievements as a sailor, for achievements there must have been for him to have become a captain with shares in his firm. She felt her pulse quicken and sensed her curiosity about this man intensify. She wanted to know more but would not pry.

The coach rumbled on through the rough, dry, rutted streets, many of them strewn with refuse. People streamed about their business or aimlessly idled life away. Well-to-do rubbed shoulders with the poor, beggars pleaded for alms, traders with laden baskets cried their wares. David had never seen so many people, such activity, or heard such a noise.

'Thee used to live above the offices? That would be convenient. Why did thee move?' David surprised himself with the question. At one time he would have held his curiosity back. After all, he had only just met Lydia Hartley, but now here he was asking what might be a personal question. Somehow he felt at ease with her, as if their acquaintance was old established. He sensed that she must feel the same otherwise why should she ask him, a complete stranger, to come home with her, and what's more hint that she might be able to offer him accommodation? It only needed her father's approval, and he felt that Lydia, if she wanted it, would have no trouble in getting that.

'Yes, it was convenient as you say, and many merchants and shopkeepers still live above their places of work,' she explained. 'But a drift has begun. The City is so crowded. You've seen something of that. So Father and I decided to move, get away from the smoke, get into fresher air, see a bit of green instead of nothing but buildings and roofs. Father had a house built in Russell Square, which has been developed around the open space kept by the Russells in front of their great house in order to preserve their view. It's nice there, quiet after the bustle of the City.'

David agreed with her when the carriage turned into Russell Square. The big house isolated in its own grounds overlooked a treelined square of carefully tended grass. It seemed to tolerate the houses it had allowed to share its surroundings. These houses were detached, each affording solitude to owners escaping from the turmoil of the overpopulated City.

The carriage turned into a short drive and stopped at the main entrance. Alighting with the coachman in attendance, Lydia thanked him then turned to David who had climbed out and stood beside her.

'Welcome to my home,' she said quietly.

He inclined his head. He noted she had said 'my home' as if extending a privilege to a dear friend. 'Thank thee,' he returned. 'I'm already thinking how lucky I am that thy father and Simeon were friends. But for that friendship, I wouldn't be standing here.'

'I'm glad too,' she said, quickly turning to the house as the coach rumbled away to the stables standing separate to the house on the north side. 'Come and meet Father.'

David followed her up the four steps to the front door. She unlocked it and he found himself in a spacious hall from which a curving staircase led to the upper floor. A small oak table stood against one wall and supported a swivel mirror. Beside it stood a small stand on which Lydia placed her cloak and hat. She glanced in the mirror and patted her hair.

He watched her every move, admiring the unhurried grace.

Satisfied with her appearance, she turned and smiled at him. 'Oh, I'm sorry. Force of habit. A ritual every day before I go in to see Papa. Do put your things here.' She indicated the stand.

He laid down the jacket he had been carrying, along with his cap and bag.

'Ma'am.'

David turned to see a teenage girl in a black, full-skirted dress and white apron come from a door at the side of the stairs. She was pleasant-faced but bore a shy, almost serious expression, as if she held everything and everyone in awe.

'Ah, Millie, this is Captain Fernley,' said Lydia.

She glanced at David, dropped her gaze and made a small curtsey.

'He will be staying with us,' Lydia went on. 'Please see that everything is ready in the guest bedroom, and tell Mrs Dove that there will be one more for dinner.'

'Yes, Ma'am. Will you need another cup and saucer for tea?'

'Of course,' replied Lydia without displaying any irritation that the girl would not think for herself.

Millie turned to retrace her steps.

Lydia led the way to a door on the right. She entered the room, leaving David to follow.

Even on this hot day a fire burned cheerfully in the grate, a comfort for the man who had to spend most of his time sitting in this room. It was square, a good size and high-ceilinged. Two tall windows gave a pleasant view across the square, while in the opposite wall two more looked out on to a well-kept garden, not too big but large enough to walk in. A desk occupied one corner of the room positioned to give a view of the square. A settee was set at an angle to the fireplace. Lydia greeted an elderly man sitting in a wing-chair opposite it.

'Hello, Papa.' Lydia's voice was light and gay. She kissed him on the cheek.

'Hello, my dear.' The broad smile held a deep affection while his brown eyes not only expressed the admiration he felt for his daughter but also revealed his undeniable love. He patted her arm as she kissed him.

'Father, I've a visitor for you,' she said, straightening and turning towards David.

'Oh, delightful, delightful,' cried her father with genuine enthusiasm. He half turned in his chair to see who the visitor might be.

'Papa, this is David Fernley – Captain Fernley from Whitby. David, this is my father.'

He extended his hand as he reached the chair. 'I'm honoured to meet thee, sir.'

Mr Hartley's grip was still firm though not as strong as it once had been. 'I'm pleased to meet you, Captain Fernley. A man of the sea, you're welcome here.'

'Thank thee. But, please, not Captain – David.'

The older man leaned back in his chair with a chuckle. He had noted that his daughter had used this stranger's Christian name when she first made the introduction, and he inferred that she had taken a liking to him in the short time she had known him, which he knew could only have been since she'd left home that morning. 'Very well, David it shall be. So, Lydia,' he turned to his daughter with a twinkle in his eyes, 'do you think it should be Dominic?'

She laughed. 'Well, Papa, why not? Two seamen together.'

Mr Hartley turned to David. 'There you are, David, she approves, so I'm Dominic.' He extended his hand again as a second introduction.

David took it and with a grin said, 'Very well, sir.'

'No,' came the sharp reply, 'Dominic.'

'Dominic.' David broke into laughter at the mischievous twinkle in Dominic's eyes.

'Do sit down, David.' He indicated the chair which Lydia had drawn up close to her father's.

David waited for her to be seated and then sat down.

'Does Millie know we have a guest?' asked Dominic, glancing at his daughter.

'Yes,' she replied. 'She'll be bringing tea in a moment.'

'Good, good. Now, David, what brings you to London?'

As he explained, he was able to study the older man. He judged him to be in his seventies. Though his full cheeks and ruddy complexion tended to hide the fact, his neck had begun to show signs of ageing and his broad hands had started to wrinkle. His hair had thinned from the front, leaving a bald patch. There was an air of joviality about the man and an impression that he was thankful for the way life had treated him. He had little to complain of, had lived life as he'd wanted, and bore only one or two regrets: the loss of his wife after a long happy marriage, and the death of his son before the boy was two. Now he adored the daughter in whom he could see no wrong.

When David had finished telling Dominic his reasons for being in London, omitting the tragic events which had dogged his recent life, Lydia put her suggestion.

'Father . . .'

'You always say, "Father" when you've something serious to say,' cut in Dominic.

'Don't tease,' she said. 'Father, David is interested in our South Seas whaling, but let's make use of his knowledge first.'

Both men looked askance at her, each wondering about her idea.

'Well,' she went on, 'we're fitting the *Hind* out for a whaling voyage to the Arctic and haven't a captain. Let's appoint David, use his experience in exchange for ours in the Pacific.'

For a moment there was silence. Then both men started to speak at once, stopped, looked at each other and David bowed graciously to the older man.

'Splendid idea, Lydia, splendid!' He slapped his thigh with delighted approval and turned to David. 'What do you say? You won't be able to sail until March, but you can come into Hartley Shipping employment right away so that you can supervise the fitting out of the *Hind*. I couldn't possibly send you to the Pacific as master right away. The whaling is basically the same but there are things which are different – trying out, for instance, and the fact that you'd be hunting the sperm whale which you will never have encountered. You can learn a lot about such things from the crew while preparing the *Hind* for the Arctic and you'll bring valuable knowledge to us – this is our first venture north for three years.'

David's mind was trying to keep pace. Only a few hours ago he was sailing up the Thames on his first visit to the capital, knowing no one, uncertain what he was going to do. And now, through a few words from Simeon, he had met friendly people and was being offered the captaincy of a vessel sailing for the waters he knew, sailing north to the land and sea which had always beckoned him with their mysterious call.

'What can I say?' His voice was filled with gratitude. 'Thee knows nothing about me, yet thee befriend me and offer me command of the *Hind*. I'm overwhelmed, at a loss for words, except to say thank thee – both of thee. I'll accept.'

'Capital, capital,' cried Dominic. He had noted the relief and pleasure in his daughter's eyes. 'Lydia's a good judge of character and I'm sure she'll not be mistaken about you.'

There was a knock on the door and in answer to Lydia's call Millie entered carrying a tray.

'Thank you,' said Lydia as she sat forward on the settee to reach the teapot.

'Ma'am, the guest room is all ready,' said Millie shyly.

'Thank you.'

The maid hurried from the room, shutting the door quietly behind her.

Lydia glanced at her father and saw a twitch of amusement at the corners of his mouth. 'Guest room?' he said teasingly.

'Well, I thought you'd like David to stay with us. You'd like to chat about the sea. Make a change for you to have a man in the house,' she explained.

'Very thoughtful of you, m'dear,' he returned with a knowing look.

'If it's not convenient . . .' David started hastily.

'Of course it's convenient, my boy,' chortled Dominic. 'Delighted to have you. Lydia's always right, I'd love to talk about the sea and it will be a change to females everywhere.'

'Thank thee. Thee and Lydia are too kind.' David glanced at her and they exchanged a smile.

Throughout the succeeding weeks and months, David enjoyed life with the Hartleys. He loved chatting with his host, hearing of his adventures at sea and of how he came to found Hartley Shipping. He learned about the opening of the Pacific by a British whaler and of the lucrative possibilities if the whaling trade was developed properly there. Dominic in his turn revelled in David's talk of the Arctic and of Whitby.

David's immediate feeling of being at ease when he first met Lydia was not ill-founded. As time passed he found her likeable, understanding, sympathetic and fun to be with. As the days moved into weeks he looked forward more and more to being with her. He enjoyed her company and was glad to escort her on visits to friends and to plays in the City, but although he sensed that she had a special feeling for him, he was still too pained by memories of Ruth and Jenny to become more deeply involved, though he had no doubt that his respect and admiration might one day turn to feelings of a stronger nature.

Lydia for her part experienced stirrings in her heart that she had never before felt for a man. Maybe she had been closeted with her father for too long but David had come like a breath of fresh air with his gentle understanding, sympathy and pleasant manners. She knew she was falling in love but kept her feelings to herself for she sensed that there were shadows over David's past. Some day, she hoped, they would be dispelled.

Christmas came and went. David sent messages and presents to Whitby via Simeon and received some in return. Lydia was pleased that he showed no inclination to return north for the festive season and in her own home made it a special occasion, reaping in return a sense of well-being and joy at David's appreciation of what she had done to make him feel part of the family.

Throughout this time he flung himself whole-heartedly into preparing the *Hind* for her maiden whaling voyage to the Arctic. The ship was ready by the second week in February and he decided to sail on the first of March.

As sailing day approached, Lydia found she could not concentrate on business in her usual way. Her thoughts became more and more preoccupied with David and how much she was going to miss him. She was pleased that he was more relaxed and that some of the shadows about him were being dispelled. She hoped that it was not only the change of environment which had brought this about but an interest in her as a woman.

When David returned to the Hartley house the evening before he was due to sail he was surprised to find that Dominic had retired early.

'He's insisting that he comes to see you sail tomorrow,' explained Lydia, 'and is getting over-excited about it. His interest in the firm has never waned but he's not been to see one of his ships sail for over two years. I persuaded him to go to bed and gave him some laudanum so that he gets a good night's sleep.'

'A wise precaution,' agreed David. 'And we must see that he wraps up well tomorrow. There could be a chill wind blowing off the river.'

Lydia smiled. 'You're so thoughtful, David. Thank you for all you've done for Papa.'

'I've done nothing.' He tried to dismiss her gratitude.

'Oh, but you have. Another man to talk to about ships, the sea and whaling has revived his interest and enthusiasm. I'll always be grateful to you for that. But I'm chatting away and you'll want to get changed. A glass of wine when you're ready.'

After David had freshened up and changed he joined Lydia in the withdrawing room. She poured two glasses of Madeira and handed one to him. She raised hers. 'To a successful voyage and may God go with you.' The words caught in her throat and her eyes were damp.

He raised his glass in acknowledgement. Their eyes met and Lydia felt her pulse race for she detected in David's dark, haunted gaze a glimmer of affection. But what sort of affection? As a friend for a friend or did it run deeper?

'I'll miss you, David. I have a special regard for you,' she said quietly.

'And I'll miss thee,' he returned, holding her gaze. 'Thank thee for all thee's done for me.' She started to deny that she had done anything but he stopped her. 'Thee'll never know how much. Thee befriended a stranger in a strange city. Thee opened thy home to me and became a very dear friend who helped to ease a lot of the hurt I was feeling. Thee gave me a ship at a time when I needed something to occupy my mind. Thee took me into thy circle of friends and thee's been a wonderful companion.' He reached out and took her hand in his. 'I will ever be grateful to thee.'

His touch set Lydia's heart pounding. She wanted him to go on, to take that one step which would match his feelings to hers. He bent forward and kissed her on the cheek, a friendly kiss of gratitude, while her heart cried out for him to take her in his arms and kiss her as a lover.

He would have drawn his hand away but she held on to it. 'David, do take care. You are very important to me, I want to see you back safely.'

He could not mistake her true feelings. They were written in her eyes, in the way she looked at him, and in her touch. It would be easy for him to sweep her into his arms; he liked her, but was not sure he was ready for a deep commitment. Ruth and Jenny still seared his mind and until his love for them was finally exorcised he could not take the step he sensed Lydia would like him to take. Ruth was dead and though he sometimes thought of their good times together those memories were fading fast. Jenny was another matter. Though she had said she could love no one but Adam would time bring her to change her mind?

'Lydia . . .' David's voice was serious. He looked at her with troubled eyes. 'I too have a special affection for thee, but I can't say it goes any further than that.' He saw tears come to her eyes but she held them back. 'I don't want to hurt thee, I think too much of thee for that, and I *would* hurt thee if I gave thee false hopes. Who knows? When Whitby is out of my system maybe . . .'

'Say no more, David,' she broke in quietly. 'I understand. I've asked cook to prepare a special meal. Let's not spoil our last night together.' Her voice was choked with tears. She raised herself on her toes and kissed him gently. 'My thoughts will be with you every moment, and I'll be here when you get back.'

She turned and walked towards the door. David reached out as if to stop her then let his arm fall to his side.

The day was bright. A fresh breeze blew along the river and sent the small cotton-wool clouds moving in steady lines across the sky. Dominic insisted on seeing the *Hind* sail and, suitably attired against the cold air, rode with Lydia in the coach to the quayside. He chatted excitedly, recalling the days when he prepared to sail.

The coach rumbled on to the cobbles. The coachman hauled on the reins, steadying the two horses with gentle calls which were interrupted with explosive expletives thrown at the people who showed reluctance to get out of the way of the coach.

Fathers and mothers were there to see their sons leave. Wives with baby in arms and children clinging to their skirts wept their goodbyes to husbands and were jostled by others who, once the ship sailed, would leave the quay with a light step, thankful to know where their husbands would be for the next five months. Old sailors hung around, mesmerised by all the activity but remembering it was much the same in their day as they yearned to be young again. Barefooted urchins had no interest in the sailing but used the people in the crowd as obstacles in their games of chase. Sailors took last-minute supplies on board, urged on by the shouts of their superiors.

David, on the deck of the *Hind*, turned his eyes everywhere, noting that all was going as he wanted it. He missed nothing, even the most cursory glance formed an indelible impression on his mind. His eyes swept to the quay and saw the coach making slow progress to the gangway.

'Mr Kemp!' His voice cut sharply across the deck to the mate who was making a last-minute check on the security of the whaleboats slung on their davits. 'I'm going ashore.'

'Aye, aye, sir,' the six-foot mate replied and immediately

took on the mantle of extra responsibility the captain's absence entailed.

David hurried to the gangplank and was on the quay as the coach drew to a halt.

'Hello there, Dominic. Pleased thee came,' he cried as he opened the door of the coach. 'And thee too,' he added, turning to Lydia.

'Nothing would have kept me away,' she replied. She loved the excitement of sailing days and had readily accompanied her father when he had cultivated the habit of being there to see his ships sail. When he broke this habit she had clung to the tradition. She envied the sailors and the ships that took them to new horizons and distant worlds. But today her enthusiasm was tinged with regret. Sadness clouded the excitement for the *Hind* would be taking David Fernley away, a man she had come to respect, admire, and – dare she admit it to herself? – love.

But she hid her regret, subdued her sadness and outwardly enjoyed all the flurry that surrounded a ship's sailing.

'All ready, my boy?' asked Dominic, his eyes roving over the rigging and across the deck, taking in all the activity of which he had once been so much a part.

'Yes. I've only a few minutes. The boats and ropes are in position, ready to take us to mid-stream.'

'Have a good voyage, lad.'

David grinned. 'A full ship for thee, Dominic.' He took the proffered hand and felt affection in the firm grip. 'Thanks for all thee's done for me.'

'Nothing! We've done nothing! Only too pleased to have you.'

'Thee's done more than thee'll ever know. And thee.' He turned to Lydia and took her hands gently in his. 'I can never, ever, thank thee enough.'

'David, we were pleased to help.' Her words came quietly, almost sticking in her throat. 'Come back safely.'

She held on to his hand a moment longer.

'I will.'

Their eyes locked, held by different feelings but not so very far apart.

'All aboard! All aboard!' The cry from Jeremy Kemp split the air, bringing the moment of departure upon the crowd.

Extra bustle and movement swept across the quay like the breaking of a wave.

David made one last goodbye to his friends, felt the extra pressure on his hands from Lydia as she wished him well. He turned and hurried to the gangplank.

Lydia held the tears back. How she wished she could leap from the coach and give him one final hug and kiss, just as wives and sweethearts were doing along the quay, but it wouldn't be proper. David reached the deck, turned and waved. She raised her hand in reply and wished it was raised in welcome.

Chapter Five

David thanked the pilot and watched him swing over the bulwark to move agilely down the rope ladder to the boat which would take him back to land. The pilot steadied himself, turned and saluted, a compliment which David returned.

Once the boat was clear of the *Hind*, he turned his attention to taking her north. He knew his real trial with the crew had begun. Over the previous weeks he had got to know them and they him. He felt sure he held their respect for his no-nonsense, firm approach and the efficient way he had handled the preparations for this voyage, but he also knew the ultimate test was his seamanship, his handling of the vessel and themselves under both favourable and trying conditions. He was determined to show them that a Whitby sailor was every bit as good as a seaman from the capital.

His orders came crisp and clear and the *Hind* burst into activity as men climbed the rigging and moved on to the yards to release the sails. Eager to take advantage of a southerly wind, he piled on the canvas. Great sails unfurled and burst their brilliant white against the blue sky. Caught by the wind, they billowed. The *Hind* answered their call and sped eagerly away from the mingling waters of river and sea. Her bow cleaved through the waves sending them hissing along her sides to foam behind her as they sought their own tranquillity from the intruder which headed north.

David breathed deeply. The sharp air driving into his lungs brought a feeling of well-being. This was where he belonged. The sea. A ship beneath his feet. Strong wind in the sails. He was home.

He kept the coast in sight until he had passed beyond Yarmouth Roads when he altered course for the Yorkshire coast. The weather still ran fair with the chalk cliffs of Flamborough Head in sight, then on to the more familiar landmarks of Filey Brigg, laid down by the Devil, and the Norman castle high on the cliffs above the old fishing town of Scarborough. Precipitous heights at Ravenscar gave way to Robin Hood's Bay but rose again as the graveyard of many ships driven on to hull-tearing rocks. David shuddered at the sight which darkened his mind with recollections of that fateful day when Ruth and Adam had been taken from him.

'Mr Kemp!' David tore his mind from the tragedy.

'Aye, aye, sir.'

'We'll take her into Whitby.'

'Aye, aye, sir.' Jeremy did not question but let the orders fly. The captain had a right to take the ship where he saw fit and no doubt Captain Fernley was taking the opportunity to visit his home town.

Men scaled the rigging and furled the sails under Jeremy's watchful eye. He cajoled and urged, offered advice and appreciation, bringing the best out of the crew. Under David's skilful guidance the *Hind* came in graciously to Whitby, attracting the attention of those in the close proximity of the river and the quays. David automatically glanced to the cliff top. There were no crowds, no welcoming red shawl. How could there be? But a new excitement gripped him at the thought of giving Jenny, Jessica and Ruben a surprise. He looked in the direction of the familiar quays. The *Mary Jane*, *The Lonely Wind* and the *Ruth* were there. They had not left for the Arctic.

'Mr Kemp!'

'Aye, aye, sir!' The mate crossed the deck quickly.

'We'll be here a week. Give the crew shore leave as thee

93

sees fit. Thee's in charge. I'm gannin' over the moors t'see my son. Have the *Hind* and the crew ready to sail a week today.'

'Aye, aye, sir.'

'And, Jeremy, see the crew conduct themselves right proper in Whitby,' he added with a knowing nod.

'I will that, sir,' grinned Jeremy.

Once ashore, David made his way quickly to the *Mary Jane*. He eyed the ship on which he had made his first voyage with admiration. She had none of the grace of the merchantmen across the river but there was something special about her. She was small, workmanlike, tough, with a certain purposeful beauty that any seaman would admire. She hugged the quay, tranquil, taking a respite before she sailed to meet the rigours of the Arctic.

A burly figure watching the activity on the quay from his one eye leaned on the rail near the gangplank: Jamaica. No one had ever heard his real name; he had gained this sobriquet from the place where he had lost his left eye, now covered by a black patch. He was tall, broad-shouldered and with a well-proportioned body which spoke of power. He was the best harpooner sailing out of Whitby. David had learned much from the mate of the *Mary Jane* who had served the Thoresbys, Seth, his eldest son Adam, and now young Ruben, for nearly twenty years and never been tempted by another vessel.

'Jamaica!' David's voice was filled with delight at seeing his old friend.

The mate straightened and turned his head to see who called. Seeing David break into a run, a grin broadened across his face, tempering the severity of the scars which ran across his cheek from the mutilated eye.

'Captain Fernley!' Jamaica was down the gangplank and on to the quay in a matter of seconds. He grasped David's outstretched hand in a grip which expressed pleasure at seeing him, the man he had watched progress from a raw country boy to a talented whaling captain.

They hugged each other with back-slapping exuberance. 'Thought thee were in London, Cap'n.'

'Davey to thee, Jamaica,' laughed David with a playful punch. 'So I was. Firm of Hartley Shipping was fitting the *Hind* out for the Arctic. Hadn't a captain so here I am.'

'So thee came in on that?' He nodded towards the *Hind*, a note of contempt in his voice.

David chuckled. To Jamaica no ship was a good ship unless it had been built in Whitby. 'She is not so bad. Made good time.'

'Ugh! Wait 'til the Arctic tests her.'

'Ruben aboard?' asked David.

'No. He's gan to see Chambers. We sail tomorrow. Thee'd better be with us so's we can keep an eye on that old tub.'

'Then thee'll have to wait for me,' laughed David. 'The *Hind*'s here for a week. I'm over the hills to Cropton after I've seen to a few things here. Must be off. I'll see thee where the whales spout.'

'Aye. If that gets thee there!'

David gave Jamaica a friendly slap on the shoulder and hurried along the quay to find Jim Talbot and Luke Dobson, captains of *The Lonely Wind* and the *Ruth*, arranging their final sailing details. With greetings and good wishes exchanged, he hurried to the office of Fernley and Thoresby.

Ruben greeted his brother-in-law with enthusiastic delight. 'We've missed thee, Davey. Whitby isn't the same without thee.'

'Thanks,' he replied. 'I've missed Whitby. London's too big, too crowded.'

'Then thee's back for good?'

'No. Just brought a whaler in. I'm captain of the *Hind*.'

'Thee'll sail with us! It'll be as if thee'd never been away.'

David shook his head. 'Given the crew shore leave for a week while I go to Cropton, but we'll arrange a rendezvous.' He turned to Francis Chambers who had hidden his surprise at seeing him. 'How's business, Francis?'

'Good, Captain Fernley. Everything's in order. Captain Thoresby was just setting some final details which need seeing to while he's away. The concern . . .'

'No, I don't want to know,' cut in David with a dismissive shake of his head. 'If Ruben's satisfied then I am. Have the ladies been troubling thee?' he added with an amused twinkle in his eyes.

'Oh, no,' Francis was quick to reassure him.

'We have implicit faith in thee. Don't let them bother thee. I'm sure they don't mean to.'

'We get on well, Captain Fernley.'

'Glad to hear it.' He turned to Ruben. 'If thee's through here I'll walk with thee to see Jessica.'

The two whaling captains strode through Whitby's streets exchanging news, with Ruben eager to hear all about the Port of London and David's connection with Hartley Shipping.

Jessica's surprise changed to excitement when her brother walked into the house on Church Street. Questions poured from her lips as he told her and Ruben about London and about the Hartleys while they enjoyed a meal of stew followed by bread pudding.

'Thee'll stay the night with us?' she suggested.

'No. I'll sleep aboard the *Hind*. Save upsetting thee here,' he replied.

'It's no trouble. Thee knows that.'

'I do, but with the bairn thee's plenty to do. Besides I'm to be up early to catch the carrier's cart. I'm gannin' to see Ma and Pa.'

Jessica knew it was no use pressing her brother once his mind was made up and it obviously was from the determined note to his words.

David did not return directly to his ship when he left Jessica and Ruben but made his way along Church Street, lit by the occasional whale oil lamp, to Jenny's.

In answer to his knock the door was opened by Anne who gaped in amazement as she held her oil lamp high to cast light across the features of the man she'd thought was in London. 'Mam,' she yelled excitedly, 'it's Uncle Davey!' She turned and ran back into the house, leaving David to close the door and follow her.

Jenny, thinking that Anne had taken leave of her senses, had not fully comprehended the meaning of her words when David walked into the kitchen.

Jenny's gasp of surprise was drawn out as she stared wide-eyed at the man who had stepped out of her life seven months ago, a man she had missed as a dear and special friend.

'Jenny.' He held out his hands as he crossed the kitchen.

She responded and in their touch each knew they still held a deep affection for one another. Nothing had been marred by David's hasty retreat from Whitby. He kissed her lightly on the cheek and, after an admiring glance, turned to Anne. 'How's my favourite girl?' he asked.

'Better for seeing thee,' she replied quickly.

'Ah,' smiled David, 'thee's sharp. A little flatterer.' He winked at her. 'And a pretty picture. Almost as pretty as thy ma.'

'Now who's the flatterer?' laughed Jenny.

Two hours flew by with Jenny and Anne wanting to hear all about London.

'The *Hind*'s here for a week,' he explained as he took his leave. 'I'm over the hills to Cropton in the morning but I'll see thee when I get back.'

As he walked to his ship, his mind dwelt on Jenny. There was still a place in his heart for her. It had not lessened in his absence. Though he knew she still felt the same towards him, he was certain that her love for Adam was still dominant in her heart. Was he foolish to hold out a hope that one day she would accept him as her husband? Hadn't she indicated that she wanted no more of their relationship than as it had been when she married Adam? Shouldn't he accept that and get on with his own life, look to the future? But with whom? Lydia?

Lydia – the young woman who had befriended him when he reached London, just as Jenny had done when he first arrived in Whitby, a raw young man from the country seeking a ship. That friendship in the capital had been so important to him. Now as he walked through the dark streets of Whitby to the cold loneliness of his cabin aboard the *Hind*, he realised how much he would miss the warmth and homeliness of the house in Russell Square and Lydia's companionship. Or was it more than that? He felt a stirring in his heart as he conjured up a picture of her. Her smile, warm and reflecting her enjoyment of life, accompanied by a gaiety in her laugh; her flaxen hair, neatly pinned in place when she drew it to the crown of her head, and her deep blue eyes which had expressed a love for him which he could not mistake. Should he have responded more positively instead of keeping his feelings under rein? Had he been blind to much of her charm which now began to dwell in his mind? It drove away the thoughts of Ruth which had begun to wriggle their way in with a tempting: 'Compare her with me. Remember the way I loved thee. We were good for each other. We conquered Whitby together – me the country waif, thee the farm lad. We should never have let it go wrong. Could Lydia do the same for thee as I did?'

'Aye, she could,' muttered David viciously to drive Ruth from his thoughts. 'She has poise and charm, she's pretty. She has a business head but is not over-ambitious, and she'd be a steadying influence if ever my ambitions tried to run away with me. Though that is unlikely after my experiences with thee, Ruth.' He faltered. 'Aye, but we did have it good once, didn't we, Ruth? Thee loved with a passion that made the nights more than exciting. How I missed thee in the Arctic. Why did we have to go wrong?'

He shuddered and tore his mind back to the present and to tomorrow when he would see his son.

Ruth could not sleep. She tossed in her bed, annoyed for allowing the news which Francis had brought her – that David was in Whitby – to affect her in this way. He was near. The boy she had loved through her poverty and ill-treatment at the hands of her step-father in Cropton. The young man who had stood up to him and saved her, who had married her and taken her off to Whitby. The seaman whose ambitions she had shared and helped. Life had been good then. Davey! Suddenly she longed for the feel of his strong arms around her, to experience once again the power of his love as it had been after his absence in the Arctic. Then there had been passion which her body cried out for. Francis's love making never matched the passion she had felt in David and that was what she wanted now.

She cursed. Why the hell had he come back? She had thought with his going to London she would be purged of him forever.

Oh, Davey, why do you disturb me so after what we went through? It would have been all right if you hadn't loved that bitch Jenny. Though she chose Adam, you still loved her though I was the one who took you to owning your own ship. Maybe I did stray too, but I wouldn't have if it hadn't been for your feelings for Jenny. All right, I was ambitious but so were you. Maybe we both got carried away, went too far so that our love soured? Oh, Davey, why did we go wrong? Where did we go wrong? We were good for each other, needed each other. But that bitch had to come between.

Ruth's mind darkened with hatred.

Her and the Thoresbys. I'll bring them down! I'll make

them pay — and you for loving her. If my ambitions lie in ruins so will yours, but mine will rise again, built on the firm that started as our creation but which you have almost given over to them. And the sooner I do it, the better. I'm fed up with being cooped up in here!

She swung out of bed and walked slowly to the window. Her gaze flitted across the moonlit landscape, the ruined abbey, gaunt and mysterious, the cliffs towering above a sea gentle in motion pricked by the shimmering light from the clear night sky.

Soon she would be free. She smiled at the pleasure there would be in revenge. The Thoresbys would be crippled and she would be far away, carving out a new life in another land. Plans had been formulating in her mind, secret, only to be told to Francis near the culmination of his efforts. She needed him for that and would salve her need with his devotion until she needed him no longer.

A week later, back from Cropton and from saying goodbye to Jenny, David climbed the gangplank, determined to keep a rendezvous in the lonely wastes of the Arctic.

The crew were pleased to see their captain back in good form and good humour. They were tired of their break in Whitby. They had enjoyed themselves within the bounds set by Jeremy Kemp but were now ready to get on with the job they had left London to do.

David felt their mood and after a brief word with Jeremy to check that all was well, his orders rang clear.

'Get singled up!'

'Loosen fore top'l!'

'Hoist it!'

The ship was a hive of activity as the crew sprang to obey with a keenness which was not lost on him and which augured well for the voyage.

'Let go fore and aft!'

Ropes were eased from the capstans on the quay and as

they slipped free were quickly hauled on board, coiled and stowed.

Only those about their business saw the *Hind* ease away from the quay on the ebb-tide, a different departure from that afforded her in London and different to those sailings from Whitby which lingered in David's memory. Here she was a stranger and though those who saw her manoeuvre through the narrow open drawbridge and gain speed as the wind filled the topsail wished her a safe voyage, there were no crowds giving her a rousing send-off as they would one of their own.

To David, standing close to the helmsman, it was a strange feeling, almost eerie. But the day was fine, the blue sky dotted with fleecy clouds, evenly placed, moving steadily under the influence of the gentle breeze.

The *Hind* headed for the sea. David glanced to the cliff top. No crowds. No well-wishers. Only a solitary figure. A red shawl swirled. Jenny! She had kept a promise made all those years ago. David's heart went out to her. He gave a wave of farewell. A sign of deep friendship. He sighed, wishing it had been more, then his mind strayed to another departure little over a week ago and he felt his pulse quicken as he thought of Lydia with her hand raised in farewell.

'Get aloft!' Jeremy's voice boomed across the deck, breaking into David's confused thoughts. He raised his hand one final time to wave to Jenny then turned his attention to the activity on the ship.

Men swung on to the bulwarks, gripped the rigging and climbed quickly upwards with the dexterity of long experience to loosen the main topsail.

The *Hind* left the river and felt the lift of the sea. Her bow cut through the waves, curling the water back to hiss along the side before being left to regain the tranquillity disturbed by the ship's passing.

David was pleased that the wind was a favourable

southwesterly of a strength which would make for good speed.

'Hoist y'r main tops'l!'

'Set the courses!'

'Hoist the topgallants!'

As the wind sent the large expanses of sailcloth into a billowing white tautness, the *Hind* responded and adjusted her motion to the demands of wind and sea.

These were moments which never failed to thrill David: the deck gently heaving under his feet, the creak of the ropes, the crack of the sails, the swish of the sea and the wind beating against his face. Why think of the South Seas? Wasn't this where he belonged, sailing north to answer its call?

With Shetland in sight, he altered course for Bressay Sound. The men, knowing that they would have time ashore in Lerwick, the last for five months, eagerly obeyed commands which sent them aloft to the yards to furl the sails. With the skill of experience David brought the *Hind* to berth among twenty whalers riding quietly at anchor in the Sound. He scanned them quickly but did not identify the three Whitby ships. They must have left already for the Arctic.

'The men know about being back by first light?' David eyed the mate.

'Aye, sir.'

'Good. Let 'em go.'

At Jeremy's signal boats were lowered, and with raucous shouts and laughter men swarmed into them and pulled for the shore, eagerly anticipating the whisky houses and brothels.

'Thee gannin' ashore, Jeremy?'

'No, sir. I'm shipkeeper,' he replied, taking a well-smoked pipe from his pocket and starting to fill the bowl carefully.

'I think thee should have a break,' remarked David.

'And what about thee, sir?'

He did not reply but strode to the rail. From the dozen small boats which had come out to the *Hind* while their occupants shouted their wares, hoping to find a buyer, he singled out a red-headed youngster of about seventeen.

'Hi! Thee there,' he called.

All eyes turned in his direction and boats bumped as youngsters vied for David's attention.

'Thee with the red top.'

The youngster stood up. 'Me, sir?'

'Aye. Come aboard.'

'Aboard?' The red head swallowed hard. He had never heard such a request before.

'Aye. And jump to it!'

The youngster propelled his boat to the side of the *Hind* and tied it to the rope ladder. He scrambled up the rungs quickly and swung his legs over the rail.

'Name, lad?' David asked, almost before his feet had touched the deck.

'Andy, sir.' His voice was firm, precise, and marked by a soft Shetland lilt.

David eyed him. He was well-built, not tall but tough-looking, as if he'd had, and maybe was still having, a contest with life. His face was open, alive, and his light brown eyes bright with enthusiasm even though they held a doubt as to why he had been summoned on board. His thick knitted jersey and dark blue trousers were marked and worn and his feet were bare.

'Andy who?'

'Roberts, sir.'

'Live in Lerwick?'

'Aye.'

'With thy family?'

'Nay. There's only me.'

'No one else?'

'Ma died two years ago. Never knew my father.'

David nodded. He did not pry further. No doubt Andy's birth was like others in Lerwick and David wondered how many bastards there were in the town who could lay claim to a passing whaleman as their father.

'Right, Andy, the crew's gone ashore as thee'll have seen. I'm Captain Fernley and I'm gannin' ashore too. Mr Kemp here, the mate, was gannin' to be shipkeeper but I think *he* should go ashore. Reckon thee can do the job?'

Andy gulped. 'Shipkeeper! Me? In charge o' this whaler!'

'Well, can thee?'

'Yes – aye, sir,' Andy spluttered, still taken aback by the request.

'Know what thee hast to do?'

'Aye, sir. See everything's all reet and stop anyone coming aboard who has no reet.'

'And how will thee do that?'

'Give 'em me fist if I have to.'

David laughed and exchanged a wink with Jeremy who was also amused by the answer.

'Aye, but how will thee know who has a right to come aboard if any of the crew return early, though I don't expect they will?'

'Ask 'em the name of the captain.'

'Good,' replied David, taking to his sharp-witted youngster.

'Ah, but Captain Fernley's known in Lerwick, though some will wonder why he's sailing a London ship . . .'

'Oh, so thee's heard of me?'

'Aye, sir. One o' Whitby's most experienced captains. So thee sees I'd need further identification from anyone trying to come aboard the *Hind*. I'd ask for thy name and also the mate's. Reckon no one will know that unless they have a right to be aboard.'

Amusement flicked David's lips and he saw the mate had not been offended by the unintentional put-down.

'Right. Thee's got the job,' he said. 'We'll tak' thy boat.'
The two men stepped to the rail.

'A moment, Captain Fernley.'

David stopped at the note in Andy's voice. He turned. 'Well?' His eyes drilled into Andy, trying to measure the request he sensed was coming.

Andy was almost put off but plucked up the courage to go on. He liked the look of Captain Fernley and his mate, so unlike many of the skippers who put into Lerwick. They could be harsh, abusive, cruel, and could exploit the youngsters who tried to sell them fresh vegetables, eggs, chickens and butter. He had lost goods to them and had felt the hard blows of their fists when he had protested. But he knew there would be nothing of that about these two men; they would be fair.

He drew himself up and suddenly the words were out. 'Do I get paid, sir?'

'Oh.' David looked down from his full height and put on a stern face. 'That depends on what sort of a job thee does.' For one fleeting moment he saw suspicion and doubt touch Andy's eyes. 'But thee'll get something, thee won't lose.' He glanced at Jeremy. 'Let's get ashore before he drives a harder bargain.'

David swung over the side but before his face had disappeared Andy, with an impish grin on his face, called: 'And something for the hire o' the boat!'

David met the smile, said nothing and set off down the ladder. Jeremy followed, chuckling to himself.

Andy came to the rail and watched the two men settle themselves in his boat with Jeremy at the oars. Captain Fernley untied the rope and, as the boat moved away from the *Hind*, Andy hauled the rope ladder in. David, approving of the youngster's action, glanced up and waved. Andy grinned and raised his hand in salute. He allowed the ladder to snake on to the deck and then glanced around the ship. He straightened, expanding his chest with pride.

He, Andy Roberts, was in charge of a whaleship! Maybe one day he would be taken on as a crew member. Maybe even this voyage. Would Captain Fernley sign him on? Impossible. Andy had counted the men as they went ashore and he knew the *Hind* had a full complement. But he was master of the ship until Captain Fernley returned.

Jeremy rowed the boat with strong steady strokes to the quay where they tied it close to some stone steps, greened by the wash of the sea. They carefully avoided the fishermen's nets and baskets as they strode along the quay towards the grey stone buildings set against a strip of low bleak hills.

David eyed a man mending some nets and was surprised when he recognised him. 'Alex! Alex Fraser!' he called.

The man looked up, startled. His face broke into a broad grin when he saw David. He jumped to his feet and rushed forward with outstretched hand. 'Captain Fernley! It's good to see thee.' His delight was expressed in his firm grip and David's matching pleasure was there in the friendly slap on Fraser's shoulder.

'And thee,' returned David. 'But what's this? Mending nets? Ain't thee sailing with the whalers?' He turned to Jeremy. 'Alex was one of the best mates to sail with me. Got the Shetlander's affinity to the sea. And here he is mending nets!'

Jeremy held out his hand. 'Jeremy Kemp. Pleased to meet thee.'

Alex shook hands with the mate of the *Hind*. 'Thee's sailing with a grand captain, an expert in the Arctic.' There was a touch of envy in his voice.

'Well, come on, an explanation. Why is thee mending nets?' David pressed.

'Ain't sailing with the whalers this season. Wife hasn't been too well so I thought I'd stay ashore. I'll earn some brass from fishing.'

'Thee'd get more from a whaler.'

'Aye, more than likely. But we'll survive until next year. Last season was a good one and I've a bit put by from that. With what I'll get from fishing, we'll manage.'

David knew that Alex was luckier than most due to his diligence and thrift but his fate could still rest on the whims of an unsympathetic landlord.

'Sorry about Maggie,' he said. 'Nothing serious, I hope?'

'No. She's a lot better than she was. Look, are ye goin' anywhere special?'

David shook his head. 'No.'

'I've just about finished this net, then I'm away to see some relations over yon hill.' He indicated the rising ground to the northwest of the town. 'They have a croft on the side o' Dales Voe. Why not walk with me?'

'Aye, why not?' David had little time for drinking though he would not deny any man the pleasures he sought. He turned to Jeremy but before he could raise a query the mate anticipated him.

'Thee go ahead, Cap'n. We had nothing planned.' He glanced at the Shetlander. 'See thee again, Alex. Hope all goes well for thee.' He raised his hand in salute and hurried away along the quay.

As soon as Alex had tidied up his nets and needles, the two men fell in step and started away from the town.

'I wondered what had happened when thee wasn't with the Whitby ships,' said Alex. 'Ruben told me thee had gone to London.'

As they climbed the hillside David told Alex as much as he deemed it necessary for him to know about his reasons for going to the capital.

The clouds were breaking quickly under the strengthening wind, allowing shafts of strong sunlight to scud across the hillside.

They paused and looked back. The harbour and Sound looked thick with sailing vesels, fishing boats and whalers, the odd merchantman and a few coasters, so close that it looked possible to walk from the town to the island of Bressay which gave its name to the Sound. The uninspiring greyness of the buildings which made up the town seemed to weigh heavily, as if daring the people to try to burst out from their subjugation to the landlord. Even the occasional flash of sunlight failed to raise any sparkle from the scene. It had never been a place to draw any enthusiasm from David, and he regarded it only as a place to replenish supplies, take on more crew if needed, and give the men some last contact with civilisation — if that was what it could be called — before the loneliness of the Arctic.

But he did enjoy the beauty of Shetland away from Lerwick. Now, as he stood on the hillside with Alex, he drank it in. The voes and wicks, piercing the land to the south of the town, shimmered in the sunlight. To the northeast the sea burned a deep blue beneath the clearing sky. Gulls screeched and wheeled above the water then dived to find some titbit which attracted their ever searching eye. David breathed deep of the wine-like air; the poverty and squalor but a little over a mile away drowned by the Shetland beauty.

'Would thee miss it if ever thee left?' he asked, his mind on his own situation.

'Aye. Wherever I was some part of me would yearn for the homeland. I'd miss it. But the poverty . . .' Alex paused, his deep-set eyes misting with a recollection which evoked hatred. 'And I've known it, Captain Fernley, I've known it.' There was bitterness in his voice. 'I come fra Shetland crofting stock, a life which is no more than an existence. I escaped to the whalers and I'm thankful. They lifted me out o' the harsh poverty which is the lot o' most folk on these islands.' He looked around. 'Poverty blinds thee to the beauty which surrounds thee. Scenes like this mean nothing to an empty belly. They don't fill it. Beauty can't rid thee o' a tyrant landlord who thinks more o' his sheep than human lives. If ever I left Shetland, I'd not want to return to that sort o' life.'

'That bad?' said David as they started to climb again. To him Shetland meant Lerwick, a place to hire men and buy fresh supplies. He knew little more of the land or its people.

'Aye, it can be hell. Thee'll see some o' it if thee comes all the way with me. Thee'll see poverty. It's not a pretty sight but my uncle and aunt and cousin Beth make the best o' it. They'll give thee a warm welcome.'

The two men topped the hill and paused to scan the land which tumbled before them to the long, narrow Dales Voe which widened towards the northeast and the open sea.

'Yonder.' Alex pointed to a distant croft, close to the shore, sheltered from the penetrating blasts of the northerly winds by a small projection of land.

Across the voe the land rose gently, keeping low to reveal tantalising glimpses of firths, headlands, voes and islands beyond, highlighted by sunshine and shadow.

David made no comment on the beauty of the scene; it would have made no sense to a man who knew the conditions which prevailed in the croft and the hardships faced by its occupants.

Their strides lengthened down the hillside and David, feeling warm, unbuttoned his woollen jacket. The front of his shirt was open and Alex noticed the chain around his neck.

'That's a fine-looking cross,' he commented. 'Whitby jet?'

'Aye. My sister Jessica gave it me when I left for London.'

Alex suddenly waved and identified the two figures who had emerged from the croft. 'Aunt Bab and Uncle Will.' He saw them raise their hands to shield their eyes from the sun and so have more chance of identifying the two men who strode purposefully towards the croft. Knowing they would be looking with apprehension, fearing a visit from the laird's men who could descend with their demands at any time, he raised his arms and shouted at the top of his voice: 'Aunt Bab! Uncle Will! It's me, Alex!'

The couple lowered their hands, glanced at each other, then turned their attention back to the two men and waved a welcome.

In a few minutes David was witnessing a laughing, joyous reunion.

'Aunt, this is Captain Fernley. Remember I sailed with him?'

'Aye, I do.' She looked at David. 'And he had naught but good t'say about thee.'

'I'm pleased to meet thee.' David took the thin hand which felt as if it would break if he exerted his usual greeting.

The woman smiled, revealing uneven teeth. She could only be about fifty yet her face was lined beyond its years. A sparkle had been raised in her eyes for this meeting but David judged that a deep sadness usually clouded them. Her shoulders were stooped under the trials of a hard life. In the few minutes since their arrival he had noticed her try to straighten, to hold herself more erect in an attempt to hide the toll that circumstances took of her. A fierce pride burned deep within her but it needed more than a nephew's visit to bring it back to the surface before it was too late.

'My Uncle Will,' said Alex.

The man had tried to hide his gauntness beneath a short beard and drooping moustache, but they could not conceal the hollows under the high cheekbones. His sunken eyes were touched by a haunting misery and filled with frustration and bitterness which could not be hidden by the cheerful greeting he gave David.

'Come away in w' 'ee,' Bab invited. 'It isn't much but 'ee's welcome.'

'It will be perfect, Mrs Robinson.'

'Damn landlord keeps us like this.' Bitterness was vented in Will's words. 'He squeezes us for every penny, and it's just the same if we have a bad year.' His mouth set in a hard, grim line as he cast his eyes despairingly over the harsh land. 'What sort of a living can ye eke out o' land like this?'

'Come away, Will. Captain Fernley doesn't want to hear all that.' Bab Robinson started for the croft and the men followed.

'Where's Beth?' asked Alex.

'She's away out somewhere,' replied his aunt. 'Day dreaming as usual, I expect.'

'She's well?'

'Aye, but this is nay life for a lass going on twenty-five.'

David ducked his head as he followed Alex through a low doorway into the croft. After the sunlight the gloom was intense. The only light came from a tiny window, for the broken glass of the skylight had been replaced by a scraped sheepskin and now served more as an outlet for smoke than a source of light.

The smoke stung David's eyes and sent its pungent smell into his nostrils. He gasped but stifled his cough. As his eyes adjusted to the light, he saw that the smoke curled from an open fire at one end of the room. Grey ash surrounded the few red embers in the smouldering peat above which a kettle and cauldron were suspended from the crook and links above the hearth.

'Sit down, Captain Fernley, I'll get thee a drink,' said Bab.

'No thanks, Aunt,' put in Alex quickly. 'There's nay need. Thee can ill spare the tea.'

'Hush ye, Alex. I want to. If I can't gi' a friend o' thine a cup of tea, I might as well gi' up.' Bab put a stop to any more protestations by removing the wooden peg placed in the kettle spout to prevent the water being contaminated by the peat smoke, and poured the boiling water into a teapot.

David and Alex sat on a long, crudely made wooden sofa which was set along the wall opposite the tiny blackened pane of glass beside the door. Will sat with them while his wife busied herself pouring out the tea. When she had done so she sat on a rough contraption which posed as a chair. She stooped forward and tried to stir more life into the peat with a stick. Smoked billowed upwards, to escape through the hole in the roof, and sent whorls to sting the eyes. Wiping his watering eyes David saw that the only other piece of furniture set on the earth floor was a wooden table which had been well scrubbed with Shetland soda. Set in the wall were two box beds. Their doors, which would have allowed some privacy, had long since been removed to be fashioned into more necessary items for the croft.

The Robinsons had tried to make the best of a heart-breaking situation, but if it had not been for their genuine warmth towards him he would have been repelled by the squalor. There was not one item of comfort and when he saw what passed for beds he felt he would never again see anything so uninviting. On the farm in Yorkshire he had been used to feather beds and pillows covered with snow-white sheets and pillowcases, washed and cared for by his mother who, with the help of Jessica and Betsy, had also carefully embroidered them. But here the beds were loose straw with only worn coats strewn over them for warmth.

This was worse than he had expected on approaching the croft. He had imagined some degree of comfort even though the straw roof, green from the grass and moss which had rooted, would soon need replacing. Some of the loop stones which held the fishing net stretched across the roof to stop the constant Shetland winds from blowing the roof away had been removed to block up holes in the wall.

'Thee need some repairs to the croft, Uncle,' observed Alex.

'Ach, how can I?' rasped Will bitterly. 'What wi' rent and taxes imposed by the damned landlord, it taks all my time to grub a living fra' the land and the boat.'

'Can nothing be done?' asked David.

Will gave a harsh laugh. 'Done? The only thing that's done is me! Broken on the back o' Shetland poverty. Landlord taks the fish I catch, an' butter that Bab maks from the drop o' milk fra one cow I'm allowed to keep — that's on top o' the rent and taxes. *And* he demands three days' labour fra me.'

David was taken aback by the oppression. He had heard rumours about it but had paid little attention, thinking them exaggerated. This was the first time he had witnessed it. 'Ever thought of leaving?' he asked, wiping his eyes free of the smoke-induced tears.

'I'm a Shetlander. This is home.' Will paused, then shook his head sadly. 'But who knows? It's been a bad time. Things have got worse. Maybe I would.'

'Aye, they have,' confirmed Bab wearily. 'I dinna ken what'll become o' us.'

David saw concern come over Alex's face and he knew his friend wanted to talk to his aunt and uncle. He did not want to intrude on their privacy and bring embarrassment to the older people in front of a stranger. He drained his cup and stood up. 'If thee'll excuse me, I'll take a walk while thee talks.' He stepped to the door. 'I'll be back later.'

Pleased to escape the smoke, he breathed deeply on the wine-like air, driving the acrid fumes of pungent peat from his lungs. The fresh air drove the irritation from his eyes. He wiped the moisture from them with his large red handkerchief, crammed his cap on his head and climbed the small hill behind the croft.

He paused at the top and gazed along the voe where the wind-rippled water sent the sunbeams dancing like a myriad of sparkling mirrors. His gaze moved beyond to the open sea, to the far horizon where a man could be free, where his soul could take flight and the world could be left behind. His eyes swung down to take in the shoreline of the voe more closely. The hill dropped steeply to the water but as it moved round towards the sea it eased and slipped gently to the strands of gleaming sand caressed by the lapping water.

David started forward, enjoying the peace, forgetting all the problems which beset a whaling captain – especially one captaining a crew from a strange port for the first time. He swung nearer the shore then climbed along a narrow path crossing a steep slope which plunged into the voe. At the far side the slope eased and the land tumbled in gentle folds to a tiny bay. He stopped in his tracks. The sheer beauty took his breath away. The silence was so overpowering that it would have been sacrilege to break it. The otherworldly quality of the scene seeped into him and the sensation was one which he would never forget.

The voe rippled its waters on to the glistening sand which reached towards the grassy slopes fringing the bay with a halo of green. The sun warmed the breeze-caressed bay and cast its light on the restless water, filling the scene with a shimmering life which drew David deeper into its magic. He moved slowly towards the bay.

Then he saw her.

She emerged from the backcloth of green at the far side and glided across the sward with the white-flecked fingers of water reaching out to catch at her feet. She tossed her head back, sending her long, dark hair cascading down her back, and turned her gaze to the waters at her feet.

David's pace quickened. His eyes were fixed on the young woman. They never left her even as his feet crushed the last blades of grass and reached the sand. Still she moved along the water's edge. He reached the sea oblivious to the wetness which swirled around his boots, caught in the spell which filled the bay and lifted it out of this world.

He stopped and, as if in unison with him, the girl sensed his presence and ceased to move. She looked up. Their eyes met and they gazed across a strand of time, as if this was the only moment of their existence, when the past had never been and the future would not come.

David devoured her with his eyes. Her sylph-like body was clad only in a thin, ankle-length skirt and blouse which clung to her small firm breasts enticingly. Her arms, bare from the elbow, had fallen to her sides, allowing the woollen shawl to dangle unnoticed in the water. She carried no shoes.

There was an open frankness about her face which was gently moulded around her high cheekbones and a firm, square jaw. Her lips curved through their fullness to gentle corners which seemed continually to hold an enchanting smile. Her deep blue eyes, perfectly set, brought a symmetry to her face and drew David's gaze when it might have roved elsewhere. They captured him with their vitality. They danced with light, wild and bold, when they might have been dimmed by the poverty of the islands. He could sense in them restless urges which brought her to seek unison with the sea, enticing with its promise of freedom.

He moved forward. 'Beth?' he whispered as he stopped close to her.

She inclined her head quizzically. 'How dost thee know my name?' Her voice lilted with the question.

'I came to the croft with thy cousin, Alex. I left them talking,' he explained.

She nodded. 'Fra the whalers?'

'Aye. David Fernley.'

She put no further question to him. In the silence there was no barrier. It was shared in the deep understanding of two people immediately one, as if for them time did not exist, never had and never would. They were of all time, two souls unified in an eternity of love.

The sea splashed against Beth's feet and sprayed upwards to wet the bottom of her dress, already damp from her walk in the waves. She did not notice. The man from the whaleship held her attention. The power in his body could not be hidden by his jacket. He towered over her but made no effort to dominate. She sensed a gentleness behind his rugged appearance and weatherbeaten face. There was pride in the way he held himself. In the eyes which held her she saw stirrings of laughter and joy above a deep-rooted sadness.

This man was no intruder. It was as if he had a right to be there, as if he had always been part of this place and part of her life also.

The wind blew strands of her hair across her face and she stroked them away with a graceful movement of her long fingers. The action seemed to bring them both to their senses.

'Come here often?' David asked.

'Aye.' She turned as he moved towards her and they matched their steps, walking slowly along the tiny bay, their feet washed by the curling fingers of sweeping water. 'Here I feel free o' the poverty and misery of the islands.'

'Ever thought of leaving?'

'I couldn'a leave Mother and Father.' She tossed back her hair and looked at him wistfully. 'But I do leave every time I come here. Here Shetland life canna touch me. Here I am all the things I want to be.'

'And what are they?' he quizzed as Beth, wondering why she was revealing all to a stranger, halted her flow of words.

'Those are my secrets.' She laughed gaily, eyes twinkling with a teasing delight at denying this man access to her innermost thoughts.

David smiled. Their eyes met, held, and an understanding sparked between them. His hand reached out and found hers. It was a natural coming together and Beth did not reject it. They walked slowly in silence, hand in hand.

Then as one they stopped and turned to each other. Their lips came together in a gentle caressing kiss. A tremor of passion flowed between them and David swept his arms around her, crushing her to him. She returned his kiss with equal ferocity as her arms came up round his neck and held him tightly. Their lips parted then found each other again.

At last Beth leaned back in his powerful arms and tilted her head so that she could look into his eyes. Her sadness had gone and in its place lay love and hope.

'When do thee sail?' she whispered.

'Tomorrow,' he answered regretfully.

'I'll be here in our bay every day until thee returns. Think o' me.'

'I'll never forget thee. Thee'll be with me in the far reaches of the ocean, along the edge of the ice and beyond until I'm here again with thee, my love.'

They kissed, parted and walked slowly along the beach until they could go no further. Regretfully they turned on to the grass and started back towards the croft.

'I'll be out there in the morn' when thee sails,' said Beth quietly, pointing along the spur running towards the open sea. 'At the end on Kebister Ness.'

So deeply were his thoughts engrossed with this girl that it was not until they stood on the hill behind the croft that David recalled to what she was returning: the harsh, poverty-stricken life of a Shetlander. His stomach churned. He could not visualise this carefree creature in the peat haze of the dim room he had visited. He yearned to take her away, to show her . . . He started to voice his thoughts but the words stuck in his throat. This was her home. She had not complained. He could not tear her away. He was not settled in London, didn't know if he would be. Besides, there she would be a lost soul in a teeming city. That was not a life for her. Whitby? He had broken his bonds. Would he want to return? And now he was sailing to the Arctic.

They started down the slope and were nearing the croft when Beth's mother and father appeared, followed by Alex.

Beth yelled, delighted to see her cousin. Her bare feet flew across the last few yards and she flung herself into his open arms.

'I see thee's met Captain Fernley?' he said, hugging her tightly.

'Aye,' she replied.

'Time I was getting back,' Alex said as he released his cousin.

The two seamen said goodbye and a special glance passed between David and Beth as their hands touched gently in parting.

The two men strode on quickly, pausing at the top of the rise to signal a final goodbye. David's eyes rested on the figure waving wildly in return and plucked her back to the beach where time had stood still for them both.

Chapter Six

When David turned on to the quay his attention was drawn to a group of men close to the steps to his boat. As he neared them he saw they were from the *Hind* and that they were surrounding someone lying on the ground.

At the sound of his approach one of them looked up. 'Cap'n Fernley, sir! Trouble!' The man had moved to meet him.

'What is it, Morgan?'

'The mate, sir. Fell down the steps. Broken his arm badly.'

Concerned, David rushed forward and dropped to one knee beside the mate. 'Bad, Jeremy?' he asked, perturbed by the sight of the mate's face screwed up in pain.

'Hell, Cap'n.' Jeremy winced as he held his right arm. His face was bathed in perspiration. 'Shoulder's bad too.'

David glanced up. 'One of thee, quick! Find a doctor, such as he'll be in this place.'

One of the men ran off. David took off his jacket, laid it over the mate and then gently wiped the sweat from his face.

Ten minutes later the sailor returned with a small fat man, breathing heavily with exertion and complaining at having been rushed.

'The best I could do, sir,' the sailor reported. 'He professes to be some sort of doctor.'

David cast disapproving eyes over the man whose clothes were dishevelled and none too clean. His face bore a look of distaste and his small chubby hands were grubby. David noted the black bag and wondered if it really signified anything.

'Know what thee's doing?' he demanded.

The man threw him a glance of contempt. 'Thee stick t' thy trade, I'll stick t' mine.'

David had received no answer to his question but had no choice but to let this man see to the mate. He smelt the heavy tang of whisky on him and could only hope his judgement and treatment would be sound.

The man lurched down on to one knee and bent forward to examine the mate's arm. Jeremy gasped with pain as the doctor touched it.

He grunted and continued his examination, carefully removing Jeremy's jacket, with the help of his shipmates, before slitting open his shirt sleeve. The break looked ugly with the skin gashed in three places. The doctor grunted several times as he examined the arm more closely. He paused and looked at Jeremy whose attempt to disguise the pain was not really successful.

'I'll fix thee, son, but it'll hurt,' said the doctor, quietly sympathetic.

Jeremy nodded. 'Go ahead.'

He fished in his black bag and brought out a bottle of whisky. He pulled out the cork and thrust the bottle at Jeremy. 'Drink that. It'll help a bit.'

Jeremy took the bottle in his left hand and raised it to his lips. He gasped as the whisky stabbed at his throat and fired his stomach.

The doctor chuckled. 'Strong stuff, eh? Away wi' 'ee, get some more. Plenty of it.'

Jeremy drank again and again until his mind began to feel befuddled. His attention became so concentrated on the bottle that he did not take in the words when the doctor, glancing round the watching men, said: 'Hold him still – and I mean, still!'

The authoritative tone did something to reassure David. When he was satisfied that the men had the grip he wanted, he looked at David. 'His right shoulder's out. I'll put that back first. Two breaks on his forearm, I'll do them next.' He glanced at Jeremy then suddenly gave his shoulder a sharp movement which brought a yell from the mate as pain seared through his befuddled brain. The doctor grunted with satisfaction. 'Keep holding him, but gently now.' He went about the business of setting Jeremy's arm with a quick efficiency, drawing the necessary short splints and bandages from his black bag which seemed to be bottomless.

When he was finished he took the bottle from Jeremy, grunted and raised his eyebrows when he saw it was empty. The mate was oblivious to what was going on around him. The doctor stood up and looked at David. 'Thee's the captain, I tak' it?'

'Aye.'

'Where's thee bound, Arctic?'

'Aye.'

'Then thee'll have t' sail wi'out this man.'

David nodded. 'I reckoned so. I'll have to get him a passage back to London.'

The doctor let his gaze cross the ships lying at anchor in the Sound. 'None of them will be sailin' t' London.'

'Thee knows ships?' commented David, surprised at his assessment.

A ghost of a smile crossed the doctor's face. 'A body doesn't live in Lerwick as lang as I have wi'out gettin' t' know ships. Yon's the best chance.' He nodded at a small vessel across the harbour. 'It'll be sailing for Aberdeen day after tomorrow. Maybe get a ship there for London. I'll tak thee t'see the cap'n.'

'Thanks,' replied David.

'And he canna lie there 'til the ship sails,' went on the doctor, nodding at Jeremy.

'I can find him a place for two nights,' replied David. 'With the Frasers.'

With the passage fixed, he returned to the men waiting with Jeremy still sleeping soundly in the wake of the whisky. The men had found a ladder and were ready to transport the mate.

'Morgan, thee'd better stay with Mr Kemp and see him safely back to London. Thee won't lose any money; thee'll still get thy share from the catch.'

With that reassurance, Morgan made no protest and the party, led by David, set off for the cottage on the edge of Lerwick.

Angus and Maggie, with their seven-year-old twins, Fiona and Alan, came from their dwelling to meet them.

'My mate fell, broke his arm and put his shoulder out,' explained David. 'He's been fixed up but can't sail with us. I've arranged for him and Morgan, whom I'm leaving to look after him, to sail on the *Gull* for Aberdeen, day after tomorrow. They need somewhere to stay until then. Can thee do it, Maggie?'

'Aye, Cap'n Fernley. Nay trouble. Bring him inside, lads.' Maggie, who looked pale and wan, as if just getting over an illness, had no hesitation in offering shelter. She was a tall woman of thirty or so, her fine features unfortunately marked by the harsh Shetland life, but there was pride and determination in her grey eyes. Slim and with a trim figure, she was aware of admiring glances cast in her direction, and was flattered rather than offended.

David lingered after Jeremy had been settled and the men had headed back to the quay.

'Angus, I'm without a mate and that means a harpooner as well. Any chance of thee . . .?' he asked tentatively.

'He'll come,' put in Maggie firmly.

'But, lass, I said I'd stay. Thee's not been well.'

'I know, love. But I'm almost better. I'll take care, and the twins'll see I do. Thee go. I always wanted thee to.

Maybe it's fate that thee had t'wait for Captain Fernley.'

'I need a man like thee, Angus,' pressed David.

Angus hesitated and glanced again at his wife.

She smiled. 'Away wi' thee, Angus Fraser. Thee knows thee'll be miserable if thee doesn't, an' I don't want misery about the hoose.'

Angus shrugged his shoulders. 'What can I do? I canna win.'

Ten minutes later, a pack on his back, Angus said goodbye to Maggie and his children and strode out with David, happy in his heart and thankful to have an understanding wife.

As they climbed aboard the *Hind*, Andy reported everything was in order and that he had had no trouble.

'Good. Ever been to the Arctic, Andy?' asked David.

'No, sir.'

'Then would thee like to?'

'Like to?' Andy was not sure what was meant by the question.

'Aye. Does thee want to sail with me now?'

'Thee's got a full crew, sir.'

'Wouldn't be asking if I had,' rapped David. 'Mr Kemp broke his arm so he won't be sailing. Mr Fraser, here, is coming as mate. I've had to leave Morgan with Mr Kemp. Do thee want his place?'

'Aye, sir. Aye.' Andy's eyes brightened at the prospect. He could hardly believe he was being offered a place on the *Hind* under the famous Captain Fernley. 'But I knows nowt about whaling, sir.'

'Thee'll soon learn, lad. Thee's bright enough.'

'Aye, thee will that,' put in Angus. 'Now move to it, lad. If there's anything thee wants from ashore, then off wi' thee now.'

'Nothing, sir.'

'There is,' snapped David. 'Thee can't gan to the Arctic in bare feet. Here!' David fished in his pocket and passed some coins to Andy. 'Off with thee. Get some thick socks, boots, and extra trousers and a jersey.'

'Thanks, sir.'

Andy was at the rail and halfway over when David stopped him. 'Andy!'

'Sir!'

'That's thy shipkeeping pay.'

There was a slight hesitation then Andy called, 'What about the hire of my boat?' He grinned and was gone before a laughing David could reply.

By first light all the crew were on board. All hands were mustered and David introduced their new mate. A quick check revealed that no one was absent, and, though some members of the crew still showed signs of the previous night's carousing, headaches and pains would soon disappear in the sharp air and activity of getting the *Hind* underway.

The new mate's orders were clear and delivered in a no-nonsense voice which went a long way towards gaining the crew's respect quickly. Men hastened to do his bidding, swarming up the rigging to unfurl the sails and standing by to haul the anchor.

As the cold, chill dawn rose slowly from the horizon, flowed across Bressay, slid over the whaleships, crept over the roofs of Lerwick and climbed the hills behind the town, the *Hind* slipped quietly away from Shetland.

A solitary figure stood on Kebister Ness and waved goodbye to the man who had entered her life but a few hours before. David, longing to hold her, watched Beth until he could see her no longer.

Ruth strode restlessly in the turret bedroom of Rigg House. She was tired of being confined. She longed for open spaces and for freedom. The restrictions she had placed on herself were beginning to chafe. Oh, she must keep out of sight;

let everyone think that she was dead. But was there any harm in a walk beyond that high garden wall? Few people walked these cliffs, and if she remained alert she could easily slip away before she was recognised. But should she risk it? Recognition could jeopardise her whole plan. Although Francis was carefully bleeding the firm of cash, it would take another year before they could bring it to the edge of ruin. A year! Ruth shuddered. She couldn't stand being cooped up here for another year.

She stopped by the window, gazing out beyond the wall to the open space of the cliff top. It drew her. Her spirit wanted to be free. Her fingers plucked at the skirts of her dress in irritation. She frowned, swung round suddenly and grabbed her cloak. She found a key to the door in the wall and hurried down the stairs, swinging her cloak around her shoulders as she did so.

Once outside she paused, her back to the door, and looked around. The late-afternoon sun suffused the grass with a soothing glow. Beyond the cliffs the sea stretched tranquil to the sharp horizon. Above, the sky shimmered blue, marked with wisps of high white clouds, flimsily whisked by the capricious breeze. The ruined abbey stood silent with towering walls and soaring arches a reminder of glories gone, as if to remind her of her own past, of ambitions achieved and ruined.

Ruth started and put the comparison from her mind. There was no future for the abbey. It could never rekindle past splendours. But she could. She had a future and it was already underway. Her plans would carry her to a fortune and then to achievements even greater than those she had once gained in Whitby. They would be even more delectable for they would be realised on the ruination of the despised Thoresbys, and if David fell with them then so be it.

The air was sharp, and combined with the feeling of freedom it made Ruth aware that life had much to offer if only she moulded it to her desires. Elated, she walked briskly to the edge of the cliffs, remaining alert for a sign of another human being.

She stood close to the edge, drawing in life and energy which she now felt had been stifled by the confines of Rigg House. The self-imposed incarceration must stop. She must escape more often now that she had broken away. There would be no harm even if she came only this far, provided she was careful. The resolve made, she returned briskly to the house.

'Ma! Ma!' Anne shouted at the top of her voice as soon as she entered the house in Henrietta Street when she came home from school. 'Can we go for a walk on the cliffs?' The enthusiasm and eagerness in her voice as she burst into the kitchen could not be denied.

Jenny laughed at her daughter's excitement. 'Why? What's so special about walking on the cliffs?'

'Johnny Hardcastle said he saw a mysterious lady there,' replied Anne, her words pouring out quickly.

'Mysterious? What do you mean?' Her mother gave a little snort of disbelief to calm her daughter's excitement.

'Well, he saw her and then she disappeared.'

'She couldn't disappear.'

'He looked for her and couldn't find her.'

'Maybe she went when he wasn't looking.'

'No, Ma, he said she couldn't have.'

Jenny laughed to herself at such childish exaggerations but kept a serious face when she replied: 'But she must have. People don't just disappear. Maybe Johnny was a long way off and she passed out of sight in a dip in the land.'

'He says not.'

'So you want to go to see if you can see her?'

'Can we, Ma? Can we?'

Jenny knew Anne's liking for tales of hobs and witches

and stories connected with sailors' superstitions. She realised she would be pestered until she gave way. Far better to agree and go with her than have the girl scurry off on her own without telling her.

'All right, but after you've had some tea.'

Half an hour later mother and daughter put on their cloaks and were soon climbing the hundred and ninety-nine steps, known as the Church Stairs. Anne, convinced that she was going to see the mysterious lady, was charged with excitement. She could hardly contain herself to walk beside her mother. Jenny tried to curb Anne's over-active mind. They reached the top beside the parish church and moved on through the churchyard, pausing to offer up a prayer at Adam's grave, one among so many others, witnessing the power of the sea over life. Impatiently, Anne respected her mother's wish in silence, then skipped ahead as they left the graves behind them.

The evening was pleasant, warm without being oppressive. Only the faintest of breezes rippled through the grass and silence seemed to hang in the air. The hazy sun barely managed to cast a shadow from the ruined abbey which stood gaunt, sombre and silent. Even Anne's ebullience was stilled and she walked quietly beside her mother as they moved along the edge of the cliff.

Jenny shivered without knowing why. There was no reason for it, yet she felt cold. Was there something in Anne's story? Had Johnny Hardcastle seen . . .? The word 'ghost' came into her mind. She shook herself. What on earth had put that into her mind? She did not believe in such things. A mysterious lady? That was just children's way of expressing things. Jenny smiled to herself. There was nothing so vivid as a child's imagination. But was she only reassuring herself? Jenny's spine stiffened. She was in danger of letting her imagination run away with her if she did not take hold of her uneasiness. She found herself holding Anne's hand, though she had not been aware of reaching for it. Another automatic action to bolster her confidence?

Her lips tightened in annoyance. Why had she thought that? What could there be here on the cliffs? The light was good. If they saw anyone it was sure to be a neighbour out for a walk. And that's what Johnny Hardcastle must have seen, a local woman walking on the cliffs. Though not many people did so, not now there had been rumours about ghostly movements seen around Rigg House ... Jenny almost stopped and stamped her foot in irritation at herself for letting her mind rove to such matters. What was she doing allowing such thoughts to enter her head? When she had heard such stories before she had dismissed them as just that – stories.

She glanced apprehensively to sea. A short distance offshore a bank of fog hovered like a damp, clinging shroud. It was like a curtain, reluctant to reveal what lay behind it, and in that reluctance created an atmosphere of menace.

'We mustn't be caught by that fog if it begins to come inland,' she warned.

Anne did not answer, unusual for one who was always full of chatter. Jenny glanced at her and was startled to see her face had lost its colour and that her eyes were staring from a tight, drawn face.

'You all right, Anne?' She asked tentatively.

'Yes, Mother.'

'Maybe we'd better go home.'

'Not yet, Mother. We haven't got to the place where Johnny said he saw her.'

'But we'll see nothing.' Jenny felt compelled to put certainty into her voice though in her own mind she was not so convinced.

They kept walking.

The abbey to their right seemed to rise higher, almost as if it was adopting a menacing attitude to those it regarded as intruders. In the distance Rigg House stood: black, silent, forbidding.

Jenny found her mind wandering again. Why did Rigg House have that strange atmosphere? Was there any truth in the rumours that beset the superstitious Whitby folk? To tear her mind away from such thoughts she focused it on the times she had walked these cliffs with David. How he had almost convinced her that it was him she loved and not Adam.

They had walked about another hundred yards when the sun lost some of its strength, as if a veil had been pulled over it. Jenny turned and saw that the fog had insidiously crept round behind them and was moving over Whitby. Alarmed, she swung round again and saw that ahead it had crept up the cliffs and was moving between them and Rigg House. It had all happened so quickly, so silently, catching her unawares even after she had warned against it. Now it billowed up over the cliff face, swirling around their legs. It thickened but as yet was no more than waist high. It felt damp and clammy. Jenny shivered. With the repulsive feel of the fog or at the eerie atmosphere which had come with it, to intensify the thoughts which had been dominating her mind?

'Ma!' Anne's long drawn out whisper was an amalgam of shock, disbelief, terror and excitement.

Jenny glanced at her daughter, who had stopped in her tracks. She was rigid, staring ahead with eyes wide with fright.

With the instinct of a mother wanting to protect her child, she swung round to follow Anne's gaze and saw her: a hooded figure half hidden by the fog barely a hundred yards away. The woman had her back to them. But where had she come from? Jenny could have sworn she hadn't been there a moment ago. How had she come to be there? Jenny's pulse was racing.

The fog rose and curled as if dancing around the woman.

She held her arms wide as if to embrace it, then hugged herself. She pushed her hood back and let her hair stream free. The fog flowed on from the cliffs, rising, obliterating. The figure seemed exhilarated by it and suddenly whirled round with the movement of its tentacle-like fronds.

For the briefest of moments, through a curtain of fog, Jenny saw a face.

'Ruth!' The word formed on her lips but was frozen there in terror and disbelief.

The fog rose, mocking them as it threw a curtain over the figure.

'Anne, stay here! Don't move!' Jenny's words were scarcely above a whisper but were uttered with such authority that Anne knew they must be obeyed.

She hurried forward, automatically counting her steps as she did so. A hundred paces. A few more. She should see the woman by now — if there had been one. She stopped, then turned completely round, her eyes trying to peer through the fog. She must make sure that the woman had only been a figment of her imagination. That or someone from Whitby.

No one. Damn the fog! If only it would clear. Jenny went a few more yards and stopped again. She listened, hoping to hear the rustle of a skirt, a footstep, some sound which would prove that there was nothing mysterious about the woman.

And yet she could have sworn it was Ruth. Irritated, she admonished herself for allowing her mind to play tricks on her. This damned fog created an illusion. It had masked the real person, leaving her only with an impression. Ruth was dead. How could it be her?

The breeze freshened. The fog swirled in it and in a few moments the landscape was clear. There was no one. Jenny could not believe her eyes. The woman could not have disappeared. A cold chill gripped her heart as she realised she was opposite the section of the coast where Ruth had drowned!

The sight of Anne still standing forlornly in the spot where she had left her registered on Jenny's bemused mind. She raised her hand in a half wave and Anne ran forward to her.

'Did you see her, Ma?'

'I did when you did, but there was no one here when I tried to get closer.'

'But where did she go?'

'I don't know, Anne. I don't know.'

'But you saw her.'

'Oh, yes. Johnny was right.' Jenny was getting a grip on her feelings. She must say nothing to alarm her daughter. 'So there you are.' She shrugged her shoulders. 'You've seen her. Now will you be satisfied? It could only have been someone from Whitby.'

'But we can't see her now.'

'Well, she could have gone off in the fog and been down one of those dips over there by the time the fog cleared.' Jenny waved her arm vaguely. 'Now that you know there was nothing mysterious about Johnny's lady, we can go home.'

She turned and headed back for Whitby. After a thoughtful silence Anne skipped ahead, as if all her cares had disappeared. Jenny was pleased though her own thoughts still troubled her.

She did not believe in ghosts; at least she hadn't until a few moments ago. She was aware that there were people who did and others who loved to listen to ghost stories but she had tended to ignore and disbelieve them because she had no direct experience. But now . . .

A ghost? Could she believe that? Was that Ruth's ghost? Did the restless dead come back, perhaps to make reparation? Was that the case with Ruth? Did her deeds torment her so much, even in her watery grave, that now she walked the earth seeking some way to make amends? Jenny would have liked to think so, but from her knowledge of the living Ruth could hardly believe her ghost would be so benign.

Chapter Seven

Jenny had had a poor night. She had slept little and then only fitfully. The face of the woman on the cliffs, Ruth's face, had haunted her. Sometimes mocking, sometimes menacing, it had persisted in tormenting her. She would wake from a shallow sleep, bathed in sweat, expecting to find Ruth standing over her, threatening her with the unknown. But there had been no one. She had been left trying to free herself of the belief that she had seen Ruth's ghost on the cliffs.

She needed to tell someone, needed to purge herself of this insidious infiltration of her mind. So it was that, pale and agitated, she awaited the arrival of Jessica at the offices of Fernley and Thoresby.

'Morning, Jenny.' Jessica sailed into the office with her usual liveliness, as if a fresh breeze had blown her in from the sea.

She usually caught Jenny up into her own high spirits but today had no such effect. Jenny's greeting was quiet as she looked up from the figures which Francis had presented to her yesterday and on which she had been unable to concentrate.

'Something the matter?' asked Jessica, looking curiously at her friend with a questioning frown.

Jenny hesitated. She glanced at her hands, held in front of her on the table which served as a desk.

'You'll think I'm silly,' she said quietly, raising her head to meet Jessica's probing gaze.

'Why should I? If something's bothering thee, I'm ready to listen. Maybe I can help, maybe not, but thee'll feel better for having got it off thy mind.'

Jenny wet her lips, then suddenly she was speaking, the words coming fast as if she wanted to get rid of them as quickly as possible. 'Yesterday evening Anne and I were on the cliffs. She said Johnny Hardcastle had seen a mysterious lady there, between the abbey and Rigg House. Well, Anne wanted to see, wouldn't be put off, you know how children are, so we went. I knew if we didn't she'd go up there alone without my knowledge, and I didn't want that.' Jenny paused as if she was reluctant to reveal the rest of her story.

'Well?' prompted Jessica.

She gazed hard at her friend. 'I saw Ruth!'

For a moment Jessica did not take it in, then the three words made their impact. 'Thee what?' she gasped, her eyes widening with disbelief.

'I saw Ruth.'

'Thee couldn't. Ruth's dead!'

'I know.'

'Then who did thee see?'

Jenny went on to relate in detail exactly what had happened. Jessica listened intently without interrupting until Jenny sank back in her chair almost exhausted with the intensity of her experience.

The momentary silence which followed was charged, as if her story had brought another presence into the room.

'But thee didn't see the face clearly, only caught a glimpse? Under the circumstances it would have been so easy to have imagined it was Ruth. In fact, even imagined thee saw someone. Because of Johnny Hardcastle's story thee could have half expected to see a lady, and with that in thy mind . . .'

'But Anne saw her too!'

'Couldn't she have been influenced by Johnny's story too? Even more so than thee. Where exactly was it?'

'Between the abbey and Rigg House, as I said, near the

cliff edge.' Jenny paused as if summoning strength to say what she had to say. 'It was just opposite the place where the London Packet went down and Ruth was drowned.' The words were delivered slowly to emphasise the point she was making.

Jessica stared incredulously at her. 'Thee believes thee saw a ghost, Ruth's ghost?'

Jenny bit her lip. 'Oh, Jess, I don't know what to believe.' She swallowed hard, on the verge of tears.

'Come on, Jenny, there's no such thing as ghosts.' Jessica's voice was firm, filled with conviction to drive the doubt and nonsense from Jenny's mind.

'I wish I could believe you. I didn't believe in them, but now . . .'

'Rubbish!' snorted Jessica. 'Thee's said there was swirling fog. Well, it's easy to imagine things under those circumstances. Even if thee did see someone, there must be a simple explanation.'

'I hope you're right,' sighed Jenny.

A knock on the door interrupted their thoughts. The door opened and Francis popped his head round and with a bright, friendly smile wished the two ladies a good day.

'Francis, come in,' called Jessica as he was about to close the door again. 'Since thee took up riding,' she went on as he crossed the room, 'have thee been up on the cliffs beyond the abbey?'

His mind was immediately alert. This was a strange and quite unexpected question. 'Yes,' he answered cautiously, as if trying to anticipate the next query.

'Have you ever seen a woman walking on the cliffs?'

'Alone?'

'Yes.'

Francis was aware of the two women watching him intensely, as if they were hanging on his reply, needing confirmation of something niggling at their minds.

He hesitated as if trying to recollect while his mind

raced. He could deny seeing anyone. Was that what they wanted to hear? Why the query? Had they seen someone? If so, would a denial look strange?

'No. Why? You surely aren't paying any attention to those stories circulating about Rigg House?' He gave a half laugh of contempt.

'No.' Jessica shook her head. 'But Jenny was on the cliffs yesterday and thought she saw someone she knew. A woman.'

'It was nothing.' She suddenly decided she had better try and dismiss the matter. She did not want to be derided by their manager.

'Weren't you able to speak to her?' he asked.

'It was foggy,' Jessica explained. 'When Jenny searched she found no one. And when the fog lifted, in only a matter of minutes, there was no one to be seen.'

'Who did you think you saw? Someone from Whitby?' he asked.

'Leave it, Jessica,' Jenny put in, but she would not be put off.

'No one from Whitby. Jenny thought it was Ruth Fernley.'

'Captain Fernley's wife?' gasped Francis. 'Impossible. She was drowned.' He put on a mask of incredulity while his mind battled with the obvious inference of Jenny's sighting – Ruth had ventured beyond the walls of Rigg House. Rage stirred within him. He cursed her for being so stupid, for throwing their plans into jeopardy.

'Exactly,' said Jessica firmly.

'Then Mrs Thoresby thinks she saw a ghost?' He assumed a mantle of disbelief.

'That's why we wondered if thee'd ever seen . . .'

'No,' cut in Francis unwaveringly. 'I've seen no one.' He glanced sympathetically at Jenny. 'Maybe it was a trick of the fog.'

'That's what I've been telling her,' said Jessica. 'Thee

must try to forget the whole thing, Jenny.'

'I really don't know what to believe.' She shook her head slowly. 'I'm sure I saw Ruth, but how can that be?' Dismay filled her eyes.

With work over for the day, Francis lost no time in making his way to the White Horse.

He must put a stop to Ruth's foolhardiness at once. Any indiscretion due to impatience could lead to their downfall. And just when riches were within his grasp.

He rode steadily out of Whitby, curbing his eagerness to reach Rigg House. He resisted the urge to ride there directly and used his usual circuitous way so that no one would know his destination. The longer route did nothing to calm the seething fury which had boiled inside him all day at the thought that Ruth had taken such a needless risk.

He took the horse through the side door to the stables and then hastened to the house. His lips tightened in impatience as he awaited admission. When Emily Judson opened the door he almost bowled her over in his rush to confront Ruth.

'Where is she?' he barked over his shoulder as he strode across the hall.

'Upstairs,' Emily called after him, eyebrows raised in surprise at the anger in his voice.

Francis threw his hat on to a chair at the bottom of the stairs and climbed them two at a time. He flung open the bedroom door without knocking.

Startled by the suddenness of his intrusion, Ruth turned from her seat by the turret window.

Annoyance clouded her face. 'Don't you ever knock?' She stiffened, glaring at him as he crossed the room with the door slamming shut behind him.

He ignored her remark. 'What the hell made you do it?' he demanded through clenched teeth.

'What are you talking about?' she asked haughtily.

'Walking on the cliffs! Leaving this house!' He glowered at her.

'I do what I want.' She rose from her seat, defiance in the set of her head.

'Not when it might ruin all our plans,' he snapped irritably.

'Our plans!' She tossed her head with a half laugh of derision. 'They were *my* plans. You are just needed to carry them out.'

'Right. But when you recruited me they became *our* plans and I'll not have them ruined by your foolishness.'

Ruth brushed past him. 'You don't know what it's like to be cooped up here day after day, not able to stir beyond that high wall. Hell, Francis! I just had to get out and feel some space, be on the cliffs and have nothing there before me but the sea and the sky.'

'You were seen,' he spat.

'Yes, I know. Little Johnny Hardcastle.' She gave a chuckle. 'Poor lad was scared stiff. Looked as if he'd seen a ghost!'

'Not by him. Jenny Thoresby.'

'Oh, she saw me even though it was foggy? I couldn't be certain that she had but I slipped away in the fog.' She gave a harsh laugh. 'Does she think she's seen the ghost of Ruth Fernley?'

'She doesn't know what to believe.' Francis took two paces towards her and grabbed her by the arms. 'But I do! I believe you nearly ruined everything for us.' His grip tightened as his eyes flashed angrily. 'Don't do it again or else I'm finished. Don't forget, you need me. You can't fulfil your desire for revenge without me. So think hard on it, Ruth.'

She arched away from him but his grip held tight. Her eyes flashed rebelliously. No one was going to tell Ruth Fernley what to do! 'And don't *you* forget you need me in more ways than one. Certain favours can be withheld, Francis, and I don't think you would like that.'

She met the fire in his eyes. They held each other's gaze in a moment of antagonism and defiance. 'Nor would you!' he hissed and pulled her hard against him, his mouth finding hers in a kiss which threw down all barriers and sent them both soaring.

With passion and lust sated, Ruth and Francis lay in each other's arms.

'How long before we can leave here?' she asked casually.

'October of next year.'

'Not before then?' she cried, sitting up and twisting round to face him. 'I can't stay trapped here until then.'

'Be patient, my love.' He ran his finger lightly over her breast. 'You want revenge, and you'll have it in full then.'

'But why so long?' Ruth pouted.

'We have to make it worth our while. We must want for nothing when this is over. And that means sufficient cash to do what we like. According to my estimates a good voyage by the three ships this year, a good winter voyage for timber and then another successful season in the Arctic, and we'll have what we want.'

'But suppose the whaling is not so good?'

'Then we wait longer. But don't think like that. We must prepare for success.' Francis eyed her with curiosity. 'Come, Ruth, this isn't like you. Doubts? I thought you had none. I thought revenge burned so deep nothing else mattered?'

Ruth started. What had got into her? Francis was right. Revenge first and foremost. Nothing must stand in the way. As she freed her mind from all doubts she seized on the one flaw in their schemes.

'They'll still have their ships and that means they can survive.' Her eyes narrowed as she looked at Francis. 'I want them ruined!' She said the words deliberately, to make their meaning abundantly clear. 'Sell the ships from under their noses.'

'What?' Francis gasped at the audacious demand. 'That will take some doing.'

'Maybe, but do it.' She gazed into his eyes with the intensity which marked her hatred of the Thoresbys and which told him she would brook no refusal. Then she lowered herself slowly towards him with all the seductive grace of her body, and as their bodies united she knew that Francis would do her bidding even if it meant adjusting the plans he had already made.

'It may take a little longer,' he said as he dressed.

'That doesn't matter,' she answered from the bed where she lay watching the lithe, muscular body which only moments ago had been hers. 'How much longer?'

'I said October of next year, but it might have to be the following spring, after the ships have sailed for the Arctic. I want Ruben out of the way. And I've got to get authority to sell . . .'

'I'm sure you'll manage that,' chuckled Ruth, revelling in the thought of the ships returning only for Ruben, Jenny and Jessica to find that they no longer owned them.

'Just two things,' said Francis, pulling on his breeches. 'You must not be seen by anyone. Don't forget that. If you must venture beyond these walls, be extra careful. But better you stay inside.'

'And the second?' she prompted as he hesitated.

'We must get right away after we've got what we want. Somewhere no one will find us. So give it some thought.'

'I already have. America!'

'What!' Francis was taken aback.

'Won't that be far enough? Neither of us has anything to keep us here.'

Francis chuckled. His eyes danced with amusement.

'You never cease to amaze me, Ruth Fernley. America it is!'

Maggie Fraser sat on a stool by the door of her croft two miles out of Lerwick. Hidden from the town by the rising land, it lay close to the shore, peaceful in its isolation. She leaned back against the stones, gathered from a nearby broch when she and Alex first came here newly married a year before the twins were born. Though it was late in the day the stones still held some of the heat of the sun and were a warm comfort to Maggie's backache. With the help of the twins she had been toiling to remove the grass and weeds growing among the thatch of the one-roomed croft, partitioned into house and byre to enable Alex to look after their one cow, two sheep and few hens even in the severe depths of a Shetland winter.

The twins were fast asleep in their box beds, fitted with two doors which were closed and opened by means of a finger pushed into the hole carved for this purpose.

Maggie smiled wistfully as she recalled Alex carving those holes, clover-shaped for luck for Fiona and Alan, and heart-shaped on theirs, expressing the love they shared so deeply.

The air was still and, if one forgot for a few minutes the harshness of life under the domination of the unsympathetic laird, the scene seemed to hold contentment. The sea was calm, too lazy to lap the beach. Maggie enjoyed these moments of the long summer days, the Simmer Dim, just before the onset of the brief twilight. She felt near to Alex then for he had often spoken of the northern days without night, when the silence and calm took on a magic which was pure Arctic.

She was happy – at least as happy as she could be in the struggle to make a living. But Maggie was not one to be beaten. She would make the best of what she had and what she could muster. She made what comfort she could from the two wooden chairs, three stools and a table, all made from odd bits of wood by Alex. But in pride of place was the canopied chair which she had fashioned from straw fastened to a wooden frame made by Alex. The weave was such that it was draft-proof – a boon in winter when the Shetland winds roared in anger. Maggie had said that she would make another but somehow or other there always seemed to be something else to do.

Apart from the daily chores around the croft and her unceasing efforts to keep it as snug and as comfortable as possible, she milked the cow, made the butter, gathered the eggs, did the baking, cleaned the wool, then carded, spun and knitted it.

She sighed as she recalled the daily round into which she slotted the extra tasks such as that which she had been doing today. She would have the roof ready for Alex to add a new layer of thatch to the old when he returned from the Arctic. And she would see that his boat – his clinker-built Ness yoal – was ready so that he could get in some fishing before the winter storms. His yoal was his pride and joy. A man of the sea, he was a true Shetlander – a fisherman with a croft. His crofting came second but he realised that all had to combine for him to eke out a living which sometimes barely rose above an existence, with the laird forcibly buying in their produce at low prices yet charging exorbitant rents. Alex and Maggie counted themselves lucky that he could earn something on the whaleships to supplement their meagre income. She hoped that whaling was good this time for it would mean something extra, and Captain Fernley had always been more than generous.

Though times were hard Maggie knew she had a lot to be thankful for and only regretted that they could not help Alex's only relatives, his uncle and aunt and Beth. Bowed down by their poor land, heavy taxes and ageing before their time, they seemed to be succumbing to poverty with little prospect of bettering their lives.

Maggie knew she was lucky. She had a good man who had his family at heart and worked hard for them. How she wished he was here! She missed him so much. She closed her eyes and dreamed.

How long she sat there, transported to Alex on his ship, she never knew. Only the harsh crash which split the silence jerked her back to reality.

Startled, she opened her eyes and tried to work out the reason for the noise. The jarring sound came again but this time accompanied by a splintering of wood – a noise which would haunt Maggie for a long time.

She gasped with horror at the calamitous scene which met her eyes. A man, unsteady on his feet, swayed over Alex's yoal, his huge hand wielding a large stone, smashing it into the side of the boat. Again and again he struck and each time his devilish laugh, deep with delight, rang like a death knell.

Maggie was off her stool, her feet hardly touching the ground as she raced towards the aggressor.

'Tom Ratter! Stop! Stop!' she screamed, distraught at the sight of Alex's beloved yoal desecrated by this hulk of a man.

The slender hull was holed, the beautiful sweep of the wood to the pointed bow shattered into jagged pieces. Two more blows pierced the side below the waterline.

Maggie flung herself the last remaining yards and crashed into Tom, hoping to bowl him over and away from the boat. But seeing her, anticipating her fury, he stood firm and took Maggie's weight full force as if it was a mere wisp of wind.

His full-throated laughter boomed mockingly in her ears. He raised the stone high and flung it with all his force to shatter the wood in the bottom of the boat. Then he turned his attention to the woman who was fighting to drag him away from the object of his venom. His eyes blazed with the fire of drink and his breath reeked of whisky. He leered lecherously at Maggie and then with one powerful sweep of his arm flung her sideways. She cried out as she fell heavily on the ground and scraped her leg across a boulder.

She twisted round, pushed herself to her feet and, like some wild animal urged on by the need to protect her own, launched herself at the man who was now smashing an oar across the stern of the yoal.

'Stop it! Stop it!' she screamed in fury.

He dropped the oar and turned to meet her attack. As she hurled herself at him, her hands raised claw-like towards his face, his huge hands grabbed her shoulders and he took her full force without flinching.

Held in a vice-like grip, she saw dark evil in Tom's eyes.

'That'll teach Alex Fraser to get me thrown off the whaleships,' he boomed, his voice full of satisfaction at the destruction he had wrought.

'Thee was drunk and endangered the crew!' cried Maggie. 'Just as thee's drunk now.' Her eyes were filling with tears.

'Drunk maybe. But not too drunk to enjoy thee!'

The words echoed with horrifying meaning in Maggie's mind. 'No!' she screamed. She fought more desperately to free herself from him, but his grip was powerful.

Laughter welled from his chest, mocking her efforts. 'I like 'em when they struggle.' He gazed at her through eyes narrowed with anticipatory delight and sadism.

'No, Tom! No!' she screamed. Her eyes were wild with fear and desperation. She tried to raise her arms to fight off the horror of this man but could not escape his grip.

'I've allus fancied thee, Maggie Fraser. Now I'll have thee!'

Suddenly he changed his hold and his right hand grasped her head, forcing it upwards. Her free hand started to come up. 'Don't,' he hissed. 'I could break thy neck as easily as I smashed that yoal.' As if to emphasise his words he pressed her neck harder. She flinched and stopped her movement. She was helpless as his grip tightened and he forced her head backwards.

She felt his left hand come to the neck of her dress. His face was close, leering with the pleasure he was drawing from her helplessness. His fingers closed round the material and with a sharp wrench ripped her dress to the waist. Fired by the action he tore it from the shoulders so that, loosened, it fell to the ground. His hand closed on her bodice and in a moment that was ripped from her body too, leaving her breasts bare to his devouring glare. She tried to struggle but he forced her head backwards again. She gasped, trying to plead with him, but the words came only as a gurgle.

He fondled her breasts, taking delight from their firmness. His hand moved slowly down to the top of her drawers. It paused. He took in the frightened look in Maggie's eyes and then tore the clothing from her. In almost the same movement he flung her to the ground and before she could move was on her.

'Ma! Ma!'

Maggie's brain reeled. The children! The noise had woken them. They must not see this.

'Go back!' she cried. 'Don't look! Go back!'

But her words were lost and the twins realised only one thing – their mother needed help.

Tom half turned and met Alan's attack with a clenched fist which sent the boy spinning into oblivion. Fiona's feeble effort was dismissed with one swipe of the hand which sent her crashing to the ground. Her head hit a stone and she lay still.

'My bairns, my bairns!' cried Maggie.

All protestations, all calls for mercy were silenced as Tom Ratter raped Maggie Fraser.

*   *   *

145

Maggie lay still, physically exhausted by rough repeated thrusting and bruising blows; psychologically drained too, so that nothing in this world seemed to matter. Her own very existence mocked her. She felt stained, a defiled person who should no longer have life.

She moaned with the hurt and the shame. Silent tears streamed down her bruised cheeks but these tears of pity for herself did nothing to wipe away the awesome calamity which stalked her mind. She shuddered. She felt unclean, dirty. The horrific thought that people might look at her and know shocked her. She rolled over, drawing her torn dress to her in an effort to hide her bruised and defiled body from imagined prying eyes. She trembled when she recalled all the terrors she had suffered and was overwhelmed by a desire to cleanse herself, to try to wash away all contact with Tom Ratter. She threw the dress away, preferring to remain naked, then twisted on to her knees and squatted back on her heels.

She glanced round, trying to find some reassurance that this had been just a bad dream. But the two small silent forms nearby drove all such hopes into the realms of fantasy.

'Fiona! Alan!' The whole horrifying episode was brought back to her full force. She struggled to her feet and, fearing the worst, stumbled to her children. Relief swept over her when she saw her bairns were unconscious but alive, and that unconsciousness had been their saviour for they would not have seen their mother raped.

Maggie turned and walked towards the sea. Sand trickled through her toes but she was unaware of the sensation. Her mind was on the sea and its cleansing properties. All she could think of was washing away the grime and filth which she felt polluted her. The water was cold but she did not notice. She found relief as it rose around her with each slow step. It reached her ankles, swept her calves and then her thighs. It rose over her waist, across her stomach,

146

cooled her breasts and caressed her neck, salving the bruises inflicted by hard, callous fingers.

Maggie paused. She would go no deeper. She stood for a moment then suddenly ducked beneath the water. She came up, hair streaming. She ran her hands through it, turning it back over her shoulders. She repeated this three times before she drew nearer the shore. There she paused and washed herself vigorously with her hands, leaving no part of her body untouched. Only when she was satisfied that she had rid herself of every trace of her encounter did she walk slowly from the sea.

The air was cool. It tingled against her flesh, adding to the freshness she was already feeling.

Though the shock of what had happened still weighed upon her mind, Maggie was getting a grip on herself. Life had to go on. There were the children. She hurried across the sand. Alan was beginning to stir. Maggie ran to the croft and pulled on a dress before hurrying outside again.

Alan was sitting up, holding his jaw and trying to look around. Maggie fell to her knees beside him. 'Oh, Alan, my love.' She cradled him to her, a mother wanting to relieve her child of all pain and eradicate all unpleasantness from his mind.

'Oh, Ma,' he moaned drowsily. 'I feel funny.'

'Shhh, love. You'll be fine in a few minutes.' She eased him from her. 'Think you'll be all right while I see to Fiona?'

Alan nodded. He sat there still nursing his aching jaw while his mother went to his sister. The girl was still unconscious and a quick examination showed a nasty cut on the back of her head where it had hit a stone. Maggie lifted her in her arms and called to Alan. 'Can you walk home?'

'Yes, Ma.' There was a little more firmness in his voice. He got to his feet only to wobble as his legs threatened to buckle under him. He took a deep breath and made a determined effort to follow his mother, albeit with a stagger.

When he reached the house Maggie had already laid Fiona on the table. She poured some water into a bowl from a pitcher standing beside the stone sink and bathed the wound carefully with a piece of clean cloth. By the time she had prepared a salve and had bound the cut, Fiona had regained consciousness.

'Now to bed, both of you,' said Maggie when she was satisfied that they were over the worst of their ordeal.

They both did as they were told but before they closed the doors on their beds Alan asked, 'Why was that man attacking you?'

'He smashed your pa's boat and I tried to stop him,' Maggie explained.

'Why did he do that?' asked Fiona.

'He was drunk,' her mother answered. 'Now off to sleep.'

''Night, Ma,' they chorused.

'Good night, loves.'

Maggie returned outside and sat down wearily on the stool. She sat until the twilight had come and gone and only then, with what she regarded as the start of a new day, did she pluck up the courage to spear her torn and tattered clothes on a long stick and walk to the cliffs beyond the north side of the bay, to cast them to the waves far below.

Chapter Eight

'Land ahoy!'

The shout from the lookout high on the foremast sent excitement coursing through the crew of the *Hind*. None felt it more than the captain.

Shetland was in sight.

Their first land for over five months.

Firm ground instead of the deck of a heaving ship. Space to move. People other than the familiar faces of the crew, encountered day after day, week after week, month after month. Women to ease the tensions of long abstinence. Whisky and beer instead of the slop fresh water had become towards the end of the voyage. Good food instead of the tasteless concoction made from the remains of the flour now stale and weevil-ridden.

To Alex Fraser it was Maggie, the bairns and home.

To David Fernley it was Beth.

He was satisfied. It had been a successful voyage. There had been plenty of whales. The ship was full, something he had hoped for on his first voyage from London for Hartley Shipping. There had been no trouble with the crew. They had soon come to recognise his exceptional ability as a sailor and, on reaching the whaling grounds, his skill with the harpoon and the lance. They respected his authority, appreciating the fact that his firmness was coupled with fairness. Though there had been murmurings at his taking a Shetlander as mate, they soon agreed with the wisdom of the choice.

As soon as the ship was full, David had crammed on all sail to take advantage of a favourable wind. They had made a good run from the Arctic and now, with Shetland in sight, anticipation of home ran high. Eager to reach Lerwick and Beth, David took the *Hind* through the tricky waters of Yell Sound rather than using the longer route around the most northerly point of Muckle Flugga.

Rounding Lunna Holm, he ordered a southerly course and ran the ship through Lunning Sound. He held her close to Stava Ness and Moul of Eswick then angled her towards Kebister Ness, hoping that news of the sighting of a whaleship had penetrated to the croft overlooking Dales Voe.

With the Ness in sight David searched, eyes beating through the shimmering distance, hoping that Beth knew he was near and that she would keep her promise to be there on his return. The cliffs rose from a gently beating sea, bleak though bathed in warm sunshine, deserted and with no sign of life. Disappointment filled him but he continued to watch with a hope that the desolation would be washed away by the appearance of one special person whom he had held in his memory through the long, lonely Arctic days.

The *Hind* sailed on, buzzing with an excitement David felt no part of. He was disappointed. This was not the homecoming he had looked forward to. Kebister Ness was slipping by. He strode across the deck to the starboard rail to take one last look to the starboard quarter. Sad eyes fixed on the Ness. No one. Had she not thought of him? Forgotten him? Had he imagined the closeness he had felt certain was there even in the brief meeting in that tiny bay on the shore of Dales Voe? Oh Beth, where are you? His heart cried out for a sight of the sylph-like creature who had enraptured him.

The ship sailed on.

A movement. Had his eyes deceived him? Was the desire in his mind so strong that it played tricks with his imagination? He narrowed his eyes, wishfully drawing the Ness closer. Again a movement. Towards the highest point. Someone. A silhouette stood sharp on the skyline. An arm raised. A shawl waved. Beth! It must be. Joy surged in David's heart. She had come. She had kept faith. She had thought of him. He leaned out from the rail and waved in reply, hoping she would be able to see his answer. He watched for a few moments and then, as he saw the figure turn away, gave his attention to running the *Hind* into Bressay Sound and anchor, among the forest of masts opposite Lerwick.

With the *Hind* at anchor, David mustered the crew. 'We'll take on fresh supplies, sufficient for our run to London, and sail tomorrow morning. So if any of thee gan ashore, be back on board by ten tonight. I'll not come searching nor wait for anyone who's absent at sailing time. Understood?'

'Aye, aye, sir.'

'Good.' David dismissed them and turned to Alex. 'I'll pay thee off but I'd be obliged if thee would see to the supplies afore thee leaves. I'm ganning ashore.'

'Aye, aye sir,' replied Alex, and the two men started towards David's cabin.

David stopped. 'Roberts!' he bellowed.

'Aye, aye, sir!' Andy came running across the deck with the same eagerness he had shown throughout the voyage.

'I'm paying Mr Fraser off now. May as well pay thee as well, then thee can get me ashore.' Andy looked crestfallen. 'Something wrong?'

'Er . . . well, sir. I'd rather stay on board 'til thee sails,' spluttered Andy.

'Doesn't thee want to gan home?' asked David.

'I have no home. The *Hind* is all I have. I'd like to stay with her as long as I can.'

David looked thoughtful. He had taken to the youngster,

liked his enthusiasm and had seen him turn into a good and willing sailor during the voyage. 'Want to sail with me next year?' he asked.

Andy brightened. His back straightened and an eager gleam replaced the disappointment in his eyes. 'Yes, sir!'

'Right. Want to come to London now?'

Andy stared aghast at him. 'On the *Hind*, sir?'

'That's where she's sailing.'

'Yes, sir.' An air of hesitation suddenly replaced the enthusiasm. 'But what will I do in London, sir?'

David laughed. 'I think we'll find thee something to do. Now off with thee and organise a boat to take me ashore.'

'Aye, aye, sir.' Andy dashed off with a gleeful shout.

The two men chuckled at his renewed eagerness. 'What about thee, Alex? Want the mate's job next season?'

'If thee'll have me?'

'Couldn't find a better.'

David paid him off, including a generous allowance over and above his wages – his share of the proceeds of the voyage which David estimated from his knowledge of the market. Alex knew he would not lose out, for if the proceeds were higher than David's calculation he would receive the difference but if they were lower he would not be asked to make any return.

After a brief exchange of views on the voyage, the two men shook hands and proceeded on deck.

'Thee may be gone when I get back. If so, remember me to Maggie. And I'll see thee next year.'

'I'll look forward to that.'

'Over here, Cap'n,' Andy called from the starboard rail when he saw David and Alex appear on deck.

David smiled at the youngster. ''Bye, Alex.'

When he reached the rail Andy pointed to a boat which had drawn alongside the *Hind*. He had signalled it out from among the dozen or so which had come alongside, their occupants eager to sell their wares to men starved of luxuries during most of their Arctic voyage. 'Yon's Malcolm McCrea. He'll hire thee his boat.'

'Good. I may want it all day. He can stay aboard with thee until I'm finished with it.'

Once ashore David made his way quickly out of Lerwick. He climbed the hill beyond the town with long strides, urged on by the desire to see Beth, certain in the knowledge that she would be in the tiny bay where they had first met. Her bay. Now their bay. He paused at the top of the hill, breathed deeply on the pure air and let his eyes rove across the landscape. The land sloped away towards Dales Voe but their bay was hidden by a tantalising slight rise in the land. Away to his right he could see the Robinson croft but he avoided it and made straight for his destination.

When it came in sight as he topped the final rise he paused and drank in the view which had lingered in his mind throughout his voyage. Their bay. A slight indentation in the long shoreline of Dales Voe with the land at either end rising as if to make it snug, just for them, the shore washed by gentle waters from the larger expanse which filled Dales Voe. It seemed to have a secluded calm which could never be disturbed, a magic land which was all theirs, a place where time stood still and which they would share forever; a place to cherish for here their love was born, and here it would blossom into something deeper.

David saw her. She was sitting on the fine sand, her knees drawn up, her chin resting on them while she clasped her legs with her arms. She stared out across the water, lost in some faraway thoughts. He wanted to shout, to betray his presence, it was the natural instinctive thing to do, but the serene aura about her demanded not to be broken by anyone but herself.

He started down the slope, walking steadily, holding in check the desire to run and sweep her into his arms. He left the stunted grass for the soft, dry sand. His steps made no noise. He came up behind her and stopped. She did not look round. He did not speak. But their two spirits were in communion, locked in joy.

'David?' Her whisper broke the spell.

He dropped to his knees, his arms reaching out for her. She twisted round and in one swift movement was on her knees with her arms round his neck. His hands tightened round her waist.

'David, David!' she cried close to his ear, her voice filled with love and passion.

'Beth!' Five months' longing were expressed in that one word.

She kissed his ear, his neck, his cheek, and he responded until their lips met in unbridled passion. They sank slowly to the sand, side by side. She broke the kiss to look at him. His dark eyes were filled with tenderness. 'I love thee David Fernley.'

'And I thee, Beth Robinson.' He ran his broad fingers down her cheek and across her neck.

She shuddered under his touch. 'I missed thee, David. I came here every day wondering if it had all been a dream, fearing it might be, and yet knowing that somewhere on that vast ocean was the man I loved. It was as if I had drawn you to me to fulfil my destiny.' A wistful look had crossed her face.

'And I missed thee, love. My arms ached for thee. I wanted to feel thee, touch thee and love thee.'

His lips came to hers again and she accepted them willingly.

There was tenderness in their caresses and joy in their touch. With each passing moment they were drawn closer to their desires.

Beth moved away from him and rolled on to her back. She held his hand as he lay beside her, his eyes on the heavens. No word passed between them. It was a silence shared in the way only lovers can. They were in unison, each sensing the need of the other. Each waited for the other to make a move which would release the yearning which tortured them.

'Swim with me?' The words came softly from Beth.

She sprang gracefully to her feet and stood looking down at the man she loved. The wistful, wanton look in her eyes challenged him to take up the promises which were there.

She raised her hand to the top of her dress and pulled at the cord of wool which tightened the neck. She shrugged the dress from her shoulders and let it drop to her waist. A deft touch released it to fall at her feet.

David gasped. She was naked. His eyes devoured her smooth, milky skin, the small, firm breasts with hardened nipples, the taut stomach and slender waist. His gaze swept up her long, sleek legs, paused, and then moved over the rest of her body to meet the love in her eyes.

'Swim?' she whispered gently, and held out her hand in a tempting gesture before turning and running towards the water.

David propped himself on his elbows and enjoyed the graceful flight of her slender body. She met the water and moved on, deeper and deeper, until she pitched herself forward, sending spray around her. She made two firm strokes, turned and trod water.

Her plunge broke David's wishful thoughts and he rose quickly to his feet and stripped himself with equal haste, leaving only the jet cross on its chain around his neck before he ran swiftly to the sea.

She watched him come. He sent great waves of water rising around him as he raced deeper and deeper before flinging himself forward towards her. But she had already turned and was swimming further. Her tinkling, teasing laughter mocked his ears. He plunged after her. He reached her. She had let him. He grasped her arm. She turned towards him then plunged downwards. He went with her. They both surfaced, water streaming from their hair. They shook it away and stroked it from their faces, laughing. At last they were together in the caressing water which united their bodies and unified their love as if they were one.

David turned for the shore. He strode to the edge of the sea, turned to watch her and sank to his knees on the sand where the tiny waves lapped around him with sensuous touch.

She waited, allowing the sea to run across her body, heightening her pleasure. She swam slowly towards the beach. Her feet touched the sand and she stood, water up to her waist, before moving forward, parting the sea with her thrusting thighs. Water streamed from her as more and more of her body was revealed. She came from the sea like a goddess of the ocean seeking a lover.

David awaited her. Her every step set his mind alight with uncontrollable desire. She paused above him, her eyes taking him to herself, challenging, demanding and loving.

She sank slowly beside him. He reached for her and took her tenderly in his arms. He drew her close into a loving embrace as they sank to the sand.

Their kiss moved slowly towards overwhelming passion. Arms locked around each other, they rolled over and over in the shallow water. It ran across them, between them, around them, as it chose, to increase their sensuous pleasure.

'Take me, David, take me!' Beth gasped close to his ear. His kisses sought her breasts, her shoulders, her neck. She cried out again.

He took her in the peace of the sea in their bay.

They lay exhausted by the loving they had shared three times, in a fire which surged from their very souls and consumed them in a love which was like no other.

Now they lay contented, holding hands, wanting time to stand still.

'David, wilt thee always love me?' Beth broke the silence.

'Of course, my love.' The words were slow, deliberate, so that their meaning was clear.

''Til the end of time?'

'And beyond.' He rolled over and looked deep into her eyes. 'I love thee.' He slipped the jet cross from his neck and placed it round hers. 'To remember me by,' he whispered.

Her arms came up around his neck and she pulled him slowly to her loving kiss.

'Wilt thee be gone tomorrow?' she asked as their lips parted.

He nodded.

Tears came to her eyes. 'I don't want to lose thee.'

'That's tomorrow. We have this evening.'

'Aren't thee staying now?' Beth looked troubled.

'I've got to return to the *Hind*. Make certain everything is ready for tomorrow. I'm sure it will be, Alex was seeing to things. But I'd better check in case there's anything I need to see him about before we sail.'

'Thee'll be back this evening?'

'Of course.'

'Promise?'

'I promise.' He kissed her. 'Seven o'clock, here?'

'I'll be waiting.'

She watched him dress. He bent and kissed her. Without another word he strode away. She held him with her eyes until he was out of sight then rose slowly and slipped into her dress.

Having assured himself that the victualling of the *Hind* for her voyage to London was completed to his satisfaction, Alex Fraser took his leave of the ship.

He strode along the quay with a jaunty step, eager to be home to Maggie and the children. He was looking forward to the time he would spend with them until next season. Whaling put that extra money in his pocket which made the winters on Shetland more tolerable. It meant they were better off than most, could add a little comfort to their croft and survive the extra taxes the laird might levy. And he could supplement the meagre income from the croft by fishing. That was something else he was looking forward to – his boat and the time it gave him on the sea, free from the cares of land.

He swung out away from the town, lengthening his stride in time to the song he was humming. The sky was bright blue, hazed only a little as if a gossamer veil had been drawn across it. Small white clouds flowed across in gentle unison, cajoled by the soft breeze. Their shadows patterned the hills around the town and when Alex topped the rise from which he could see his croft, they were marking the sea and masking his boat. The croft stood in sunlight. He saw Maggie at the door, the children racing in chase. He paused and drank in the scene where he knew all was love and stability. It felt good to see all was well with his world. He raised his arm and waved.

Maggie responded then set off to run towards him. She called to the twins who broke off their chase and with excited shouts raced in his direction. With his face wreathed in a joyous smile, Alex ran, his strides lengthening with the slope of the hill. He dropped his bag. The children were upon him. He swept them into his arms and hugged them tight as they shouted their welcome. He released them, straightened, and held his arms wide to Maggie.

She flung herself into them. They closed around her and he hugged her tight. He sensed a tension in her. This was not the usual joyful Maggie he came home to. Her arms were around him, holding him as if she would never let him go. She clung to him as if she needed his comfort and protection, as if she sought safety and had found it in his arms.

'Oh, Alex, it's good to have thee home.' Though there was pleasure and joy in her voice, he detected strain also.

Something was not right. Still holding her, he eased her back. He wanted to look into her face but she seemed unwilling to let him. He exerted a little more pressure. 'Maggie, what is it?' he whispered gently. He saw that worry had clouded her eyes and driven away the first joyous rapture of welcome.

'Pa, Pa, hast thee seen thy boat?' the children yelled as they jumped up and down, still excited by their father's arrival.

'Hush!' cried Maggie.

'What about it?' asked Alex. He looked over his wife's shoulder, eyes spanning the distance to where the sun peeled away the shadow. His boat! His beloved boat. Smashed. His eyes widened in horror. He couldn't believe what he was seeing. Was this what was troubling Maggie? 'What happened?' he gasped. He looked back at his wife, seeking an explanation, but could pinpoint nothing in the mixed emotions in her eyes. Fright, sorrow, regret, apprehension, pleading, love, all mingled to cause him confusion.

'Man used a stone on it,' called Alan.

'Hush! I told thee to hush,' his mother scolded.

'Who?' demanded Alex. He gripped Maggie by the shoulders. 'Who?' His eyes had darkened into anger. He glanced at his son. 'Who?' he asked loudly.

The boy's hesitation was only momentary. He could not withstand the fierce expression which masked his father's face. 'The man who attacked Ma.'

'What!' Alex turned an astonished gaze back to Maggie.

'What happened?' The anger which had risen because of the damage to his boat subsided into loving concern for his wife.

She knew there would be no denying him until he got the whole truth out of her. Besides, hadn't he a right to know? Would telling him calm her fear that their relationship could never be the same? She needed to tell someone. That need had gnawed at her mind ever since the rape, but she had had no one. Now she had him. A fleeting prayer was made that he would understand, and that their love and passion for each other would not be marred.

'He flattened both of us,' put in Fiona, her eyes wide with the memory.

'He what?' gasped Alex.

'Away, you two,' said Maggie with a quiet authority that must be obeyed. 'Go mash some tea for thy father. Go on, now.'

The two children scurried away to the croft.

'Now, what happened?' asked Alex, taking her hands in his, recognising that she needed comfort and support.

'It was Tom Ratter,' she murmured as if the name brought back all sorts of horrors to her.

'Ratter?'

'Aye. He was drunk. Must have come out here looking for trouble. He had a stone and used it on the boat. I ran to stop him but it was no good.'

'He attacked thee?' probed Alex.

Maggie's lips tightened and she nodded.

'What did he do?' His mind was already fearing the worst.

'He knocked me to the ground. The children saw. They ran to help but he hit them both. Alan was flattened and Fiona hit her head on a stone which stunned her. Thank goodness they were unconscious and did not see what happened.' She bit her lips and looked away, tears filling her eyes.

He put a finger to her chin and slowly and gently turned her face to his. She looked up and saw tenderness in his eyes. 'Did he . . .?'

She nodded. 'Aye, he raped me.' She shuddered at the recollection of the experience.

'Oh, my love.' The words, full of feeling and compassion, were drawn out as he enfolded her in his arms and drew her to him.

She felt the power of his love and respect. She felt safe in his arms. She knew she had done the right thing in telling him for she felt purged of any feeling of having been defiled.

He held her, knowing she needed all the understanding and love he could give her. He was determined that this would make no difference to them and knew that their love would only be strengthened. At the same time anger was rising inside him, fury directed at Tom Ratter, a man who had committed a heinous crime, who had desecrated his wife and who must pay.

The enormity of it stormed his mind. Someone else had taken Maggie when she wished only to be his. It turned his stomach but for her sake he checked the feeling of revulsion. It must make no difference to them, but it would to Tom Ratter. The evil bully must not get away with it. He must be punished, and nothing was too harsh for him.

'The bastard!' The words escaped from between Alex's clenched teeth.

Maggie heard trouble in them. She pushed herself away from him and saw fury and revenge blazing in his eyes.

'No, Alex! No!' she cried, fear and alarm catching her voice.

'Love.' He gazed deeply into her troubled eyes. 'Tom Ratter must be taught a lesson. He can't get away with this. If we tried to get justice it would only be thy word against his, and thee knows what folk would say – a lonely whaleman's wife needing a man would encourage him.'

'Thee doesn't think that, does thee?' she cried out.

'Of course not, love, but that's what folk'd think. But I can't ignore this. I've got to deal with Ratter. He'll be boasting to his friends how he took the beautiful Maggie Fraser. Well, he's going to get a thrashing that he'll never forget!'

'Alex, no! Please leave it.'

'I can't, Maggie. I can't.'

She recognised his need. Just as she had needed to purge herself by telling him what had happened, so he had to expiate himself of that knowledge.

'Take my bag and go to the twins. I'll be back soon.' He turned and strode away up the hill in the direction of Lerwick.

She stood limp, tears in her eyes, and watched him go. She knew it would not be right to stop him.

Tom Ratter. Tom Ratter. The words beat into Alex's mind with every step nearer the town. Its grey buildings spilling down the hillside bore no charm today in spite of being bathed in sunshine. Instead they assumed an air of menace, harbingers of fate, hell holes which needed exorcising. Somewhere among them was the man who had raped his wife and Alex would not rest until he had sought him out and punished him.

He searched the ale houses, the whisky houses, all the haunts he knew Tom Ratter frequented, but to no avail. Frustration mounted until he learned that Ratter had been seen with his boat, that he had talked of going fishing. He hurried to the stone pier where he knew Ratter kept his boat. It was not there. He'd wait.

The gentle breeze subsided during the early evening, leaving an atmosphere of foreboding. Nothing moved. Ships in Bressay Sound and those tied up to buoys and quays seemed held in stagnant water. The few sailors and fishermen who had been about had gone, as if to clear the stage for the final act. Alex glanced around. Just as he wanted it. He could not have set the scenario better himself. No one about to witness his thrashing of Tom Ratter, or prevent it.

There was the sound of oars disturbing water. A boat. Alex moved to bring it into view while keeping himself out of sight. His eyes narrowed, seeking identification, but the man had his back to him. Two more strokes and he glanced over his shoulder to estimate his final manoeuvre to a flight of slimy, green steps. Tom Ratter! Alex's heart raced. Vengeance was close at hand.

Ratter shipped his oars and let the boat glide the last few feet. He reached over the side, his broad hands grasping at the stonework, halting his craft at the foot of the steps. He quickly tied up. Alex waited, expecting him to come to the quay, but Ratter turned his attention to his catch. He grasped a knife from the bottom of the boat and started to gut his fish.

Alex moved quietly to the steps, careful to make little sound. He was halfway down them before Ratter was aware that someone was approaching. He glanced up, knife poised in its movement. He froze when he saw Alex. His eyes widened with shock and filled with terror as the figure, silhouetted against the sky, seemed to tower over him, the harbinger of retribution.

'You bastard!' hissed Alex.

His words and the meaning behind them thundered into Ratter's brain. He knew instantly why Fraser was here, and knew it was no use denying it. He tensed himself, poised, wary and watchful, knowing an attack would be sprung at any moment. He swallowed hard, crouched, adjusted his balance and waited.

Alex stared at the man who had raped his wife. Hatred and anger churned in his mind and were urged on by an undeniable lust for revenge. At the same time he was alert

163

and cool, assessing the situation. Ratter had a knife and Alex knew he would not hesitate to use it. He began to move slowly down the steps, each movement closely watched by the man in the boat.

With two steps to go Alex hesitated slightly, trying to break Ratter's concentration, then he leaped into the boat alongside him.

It rocked precariously but both men balanced themselves. Ratter, quick to try to seize the initiative, slashed the knife viciously towards Alex's stomach but he side-stepped and the blade merely cut his jersey. At the same time he grabbed Ratter's knife-hand by the wrist and jerked it down, sending the man tumbling to the bottom of the boat. Alex smashed his hand hard across the stern. Ratter cried out with the agony and his hand automatically opened, allowing the knife to tumble harmlessly into the water.

Alex sensed the advantage he held and was not going to let it go. He slammed his fist hard into Ratter's face, drawing blood from a split lip. Ratter struggled to retaliate but Alex was not letting up. He grabbed him by the hair and smashed his head against the stern thwart. Again and again and again, Alex repeated his action in a fury in which he saw Ratter smashing his boat and then forcing his odious body on Maggie. His mind pounded, all reason gone in the pursuit of a punishment to fit the crime.

He heard a crack. It seemed to lance through his mind. He realised Ratter's head hung limp in his hands. Panting from exertion, he knelt down and stared into the wide unseeing eyes. He recoiled in horror as he realised that in his uncontrollable fury he had broken the man's neck.

Murder!

What had he done!

He had never meant to go this far!

He stared at the dead man a moment longer then buried

his head in his hands, his mind numbed by the crime he had committed.

How long he remained like that he never knew for he was unaware of anything until the swish of oars penetrated his mind. He uncovered his face to see a boat rowed by one man heading for the steps. He glanced round in fright, seeking some way out of the situation, but already he sensed it was too late. Desperation seized him. He must not be found with the body. Over the side with it. He bent down and tried to lift Ratter but something held him down. Alex tugged but to no avail. He looked round and saw that Ratter's right foot had caught under a thwart. He released his hold on the body and tried to free the foot. With success, he straightened – only to realise he was too late. The boatman had shipped his oars to let the boat glide in towards the steps and was already turning round to steady his final approach. Alex stiffened. There was nothing he could do but watch. The man grasped a rope tied to the bow, scrambled to his feet and turned, ready to jump on to the steps.

'Captain Fernley!' The words came automatically to Alex's lips.

David made his leap on to the steps and steadied the boat with the rope. 'Alex! What . . .?' He went silent for a moment when he saw the body, then asked, 'What's happened?'

'I killed him, Captain Fernley.'

'Thee what?' David stared incredulously at Alex. He couldn't be hearing right. Alex was no murderer.

'I killed him,' Alex repeated.

His delivery of those three stark words hit David with such cold finality that he knew they were true.

'Why? What happened? I thought thee'd be at home with Maggie.'

'Aye, I was. The ship was ready so I went off home,

only to realise something was wrong. Eventually Maggie told me this bastard Ratter had raped her.'

'What!'

'I came after him. Heard he was out fishing so I waited. I didn't mean to kill him, just to teach him a lesson, but I went mad with fury and didn't realise what I was doing.'

'They'll not take that into account if thee's caught,' pointed out David.

'I know, Cap'n. What can I do?'

The plea tore at David's heart. Alex Fraser was a good man. He was no criminal, no murderer. He'd been driven to this and blind fury had taken over. It could have happened to any man who had learned his wife had been raped. Vengeance always burned deep where a loved one was concerned. David's mind went ice cool. His friend needed help and it must be the best possible.

'I came back to the ship after being ashore earlier in the day and was just going ashore again. I see the ship's all ready and the crew are back on board. Thee get Maggie and the twins and whatever thee can take with thee and we'll sail for London. Get thee away from here. It's the only way. Stay in Shetland and thee's a doomed man. I'll dump Ratter overboard further out in the harbour, but when he's found someone will remember thee was looking for him. Thee must get away from Shetland. In London I can get thee a vessel for America.'

'America!'

'Why not? Thee'll be safe there. And thee can go into whaling. Hartley's Shipping have connections through their South Seas trade. I'll see thee's all right.'

'Thank thee, Cap'n Fernley. I have little choice. America it is!'

'Right, away with thee. Be back as soon as thee can. Use this boat. I'll take Ratter and then continue out to the *Hind*.'

Alex was on the steps. He started up them and then

paused, halted by David's words. 'And the fewer people who see thee the better.'

David quickly propelled the boat with Ratter in it along the quayside until, still in its shadow, he tipped the body overboard. Then he rowed quickly to the *Hind* where he made all preparations to sail as soon as Alex and his family arrived. All the time he regretted having to leave Shetland without seeing Beth again and without being able to give her an explanation for his leaving. That would have to wait for seven months.

Chapter Nine

Beth sat on the sand of their bay, her mind full of the moments she had shared with David. The mere thought of him sent joy skipping in her heart and shivers of ecstasy down her spine. She hugged herself. He would be coming soon. She watched the sea break gently and lap against the beach.

She sighed, a deep sound of contented happiness. This had been a wonderful day. The best in her whole life. Amidst the poverty and harshness of Shetland, she had never dreamed that there could be a day like this. Even the weather had smiled upon them. And now it was just as obliging for David's return. The breeze of the afternoon had dropped and the hush which embraced the land fitted her mood. The light which hung in the north held an ethereal quality and beckoned as if her future was bound up with the Arctic and the man who sailed its seas.

She fingered the jet cross which that man had given her. A token of his love. She would never take it from her neck. She looked down at it. It was plain, except at its four extremities. Each of these was exquisitely carved as a crown of thorns. On the cross itself was a delicate etching of Christ, his arms outspread, not in the horror of crucifixion but appearing as a gesture of love. There must be no other like it. The craftsman, whoever he was in faraway Whitby, could capture that deep expression and meaning in a figure on the cross only once. She ran her fingers over it, a gesture which seemed to bring David nearer.

She wanted this day to go on forever. Nothing must mar

it. That was one reason why she had not gone home since seeing David. The air of destitution around the croft, its reminder of oppression and degradation was alien to this day. Now, in the love she had found, she saw an escape to a new and different life. She had walked the cliffs and the shore lost in her thoughts, ecstatic in the joy she would experience when she saw David again.

She glanced around the sky. Instinctively she knew that the time for their meeting was near. Her heart beat a little faster with anticipation. She turned away from the sea to face the hill over which she knew David would come. This time she would watch him as he strode towards her. She would feel his love for her even across the space which separated them until she was finally in his arms and lost in the overpowering love which would bind them together forever.

She waited.

Time passed.

She frowned anxiously. Where was he?

A nagging disappointment began to gnaw insidiously at her heart. He had assured her he would come. What had happened? All manner of thoughts began to tumble in her mind. He had only been delayed. He would be coming. Be patient. He'd gone back to the ship. Maybe everything wasn't ready for tomorrow's sailing. She began to feel uneasy and restless.

Time moved on.

No one broke the line of the hill. She stared at it, willing him to come, wanting him, needing him here. The longing began to mock her. After twenty minutes she sensed he was not coming but only slowly accepted the fact.

Filled with disappointment she rose to her feet, sniffed the tears back and wiped them from her face. She walked slowly up the hill with only the wildest hope that she would see him hurrying to meet her. She reached the top. No one.

She searched the ships in Bressay Sound. The *Hind* was still there.

Why hadn't he sent a message? Her mind yearned for some word. Maybe he had. Alex would be leaving the ship so David could easily have given him one. She brightened.

She ran to the Fraser croft, her heart soaring on the hope that she might soon have news of David, but as she approached it apprehension gripped her. It seemed too quiet. The twins would normally be running riot outside but now everything was still. There was no sign of life and the croft held that atmosphere which settles on a building when there is no human presence.

Her steps slowed as she neared the door and she glanced anxiously about her. She knocked and, receiving no answer, tentatively pushed it. It swung slowly open.

'Alex?' she called in a voice which apologised for breaking the silence but was loud enough to bring a reply.

There was none.

'Alex?' she called again.

No answer. Not a movement. There was no one at home. They must have gone to visit some friends. Dejected, she turned away.

Reaching the hill above her bay, she walked along its ridge until she could get a better view of the ships at anchor off Lerwick.

One moved slowly towards the open sea. She recognised its set as that she had watched earlier from Kebister Ness. Her heart sank. A leaden feeling oppressed her. She watched, willing back the *Hind*, feeling helpless in the knowledge that there was nothing she could do.

'Oh, no!' A long-drawn-out moan, mingling disbelief with the feeling of being spurned and used, trembled through her body. She felt numb, but through the numbness anger began to swell slowly until it pounded in her brain: anger at David for not coming, for merely using her, and anger at herself for permitting it to happen and allowing herself to fall in love. And yet would she have prevented it had she been able? Even now she felt a loving ache in her heart and the anger was overwhelmed.

She stood dejected, her arms limp by her sides, swamped by the feeling that she would not see David again, that he had not kept his promise and did not love her as he had professed.

She shivered, chilled to the very depths of her being. The feeling of rejection consumed her. Tears filled her eyes and ran slowly down her cheeks until they could be held back no longer. They flowed in a torrent as sobs racked her body.

'Oh David, David, why did thee say thee loved me? Thee wouldn't be sailing now if thee did.' She swallowed hard. 'David!' Her heart-rending cry cleaved the heavens and she sank slowly to her knees. She watched the *Hind* taking her love away until she could see it no longer. 'David, I'll always love thee,' she sobbed as her fingers touched his jet cross.

'Where's tha been, lass? We've been wanting thee all day.'

Beth ignored the admonishment in her mother's voice for she detected sorrow and worry too. 'What's this?' she asked, indicating the two bundles and bag on the rickety table.

'We've got t' leave.' There was more bitterness in her father than she had heard before.

'Leave?' Beth glanced wide-eyed at her parents.

'Aye,' explained Will, pushing himself from his chair. 'The laird's men were here. He wants our land. We've t' get oot.'

Beth was speechless. She glanced at her mother for verification.

'We canna do a thing, Beth,' Bab said sadly. The enormity of the situation and what it meant choked the words in her throat.

'We aren't the only ones,' Will went on. 'He's repossessing all his crofts. Turning people oot so's he can turn the land over t'sheep.'

'But what are we to do?' cried Beth.

Will pointed to a leaflet on the table. 'We canna make all that oot but thee will wi' thy schooling, bit though it was. The laird's men summed it up for us.'

Beth picked it up. The heavy letters at the top hit her like a musket shot between the eyes.

PASSENGERS
for
NOVA SCOTIA

The words swam before her gaze. Nova Scotia? This couldn't be true. She started to read on.

A substantial coppered fast sailing ship, the *Good Intent*, owners Turner and Sleighthome, will receive passengers at Scalloway on 2nd September, and sail on 3rd September for Nova Scotia.

Beth looked up at her father. 'Nova Scotia? We're going?' An incredulous note tinged her voice.

'Got nae choice, lassie. The laird wants us oot and is prepared to do that for us.' He held out a piece of paper.

Beth took it and read it quickly. 'He's paid for our passage?' She could not believe what was happening.

'Aye. We're cast off the croft so it's that or nae roof for us in Shetland.'

Beth turned her attention back to the notice and read on.

The *Good Intent* is 200 tons burden, a fine ship, with every comfort for the passengers.

'The laird's men teld us the owners, Turner and ...' Beth's father faltered, trying to remember the other name.

'Sleighthome,' she prompted, her eyes still on the sheet of paper.

'Aye, Sleighthome,' he continued. 'They teld us they have land on which we can settle. We'll have a small farm and there'll be food for a year so we can get settled.' His voice had risen at the exciting prospects.

'Aye, Father, it says so here.' Beth tapped the notice. 'It also says their agent, George Hibbard, will accompany us.'

'It's too good a chance t' miss,' her mother put in.

'But this is home,' said Beth, glancing round the hovel. She knew it was a weak protest.

'Aye, lassie it is. But all that's here is poverty and nae hope.'

Beth knew her mother was right and in the light of what she had just read, Nova Scotia seemed to offer a new life. She turned to her father. 'I thought thee'd never leave Shetland.'

'Aye, so did I. It's home, it always will be.' He choked on the words, hesitated a moment then added firmly, 'But it has nothing for us. I canna do anything for thee or thy ma here. Maybe I can with this opportunity.'

Beth saw a little pride sparkle in a man who had known nothing but the harsh, soul-destroying Shetland life, with no chance to break out from it, no opportunity to better himself even a little. But now there might be just a chance. Her eyes skimmed the words again. It seemed too good to be true but she did not voice her doubts.

She could do nothing but go. Her parents needed her. They were old before their years and the rigours of life in the croft, with virtually no return for backbreaking work, had taken their toll. Beth only hoped that the voyage would give them strength to meet the challenge of a new world. She must help them all she could. Besides, if they went alone, what was there for her in Shetland? Probably even a harsher life than she had already had. Maybe she would end up in the whisky houses and brothels of Lerwick for she would never see the inside of the elegant houses of merchants and shipowners which existed but a few streets away. She might have done so if David had meant what he said about loving her, but he was like so many others she had heard about. Sweet talk and promises at first, and it didn't matter afterwards if you broke your word. He had been like all the rest. He'd had no good reason to sail that evening when all was arranged for a morning sailing. And if he had meant what he had said, he would have done all he could to get a message to her. If he had given one to Alex she felt sure her cousin would have made certain she received it before he went off visiting. No, there was no message. David's love was like a Shetland mist – here one minute and melted away the next. Oh, he would be back next year but he would probably not even bother to seek her out. Dare she wait on the off chance he might?

Her heart was in a turmoil. Could she let this opportunity of a new life go? She glanced at her parents and knew if she chose to stay she would be condemning them to a doomed life on Shetland, for she knew they would not go without her. She saw in their eyes a vision of hope and in their posture the belief that life had not deserted them. She could not be the cause of the utter dejection which would overwhelm them if she refused to go.

A vision of the stern of the *Hind* growing smaller and smaller swam before her eyes. David did not love her. If he did she would be in his arms now.

She sighed. 'Reet, we'd better get started for Scalloway.'

Word that the *Hind* had entered the Thames spread quickly to the offices of Hartley Shipping. Billy was the first to receive the news and burst into Lydia's room without knocking.

'He's back, Miss Lydia, he's back!' Excitedly, he slid to a stop in front of her desk.

She looked up sharply at the sudden intrusion, ready to admonish him for his lack of the poise she had been at such pains to teach him, but the news he brought swamped all such thoughts. David was back!

'The *Hind*'s back, Miss,' Billy added, brushing the unruly hair from his forehead.

'Yes, Billy, yes.' Lydia was on her feet. 'Get Tomkins and my carriage.'

'Yes, Miss.' He whirled round and raced from the office, along the corridor and out into the street. His feet hardly touched the ground on the way to the nearby coaching house where the Hartley carriage was kept whilst Lydia was at work. He found Tomkins polishing the carriage and imparted the mistress's order with the urgency he thought it deserved.

'Right, lad, give me a hand with the horse.'

As soon as the animal was between the shafts, Billy raced away.

'He's coming, Miss, he's coming!' he yelled when he saw Lydia standing on the steps of the office.

Heads turned as he weaved his way among the people on the street, some in amusement at the youngster's enthusiasm, others frowning at the disturbance.

Panting from his haste, he pulled to a halt in front of Lydia.

'Quieten down, Billy. There's no need for such a display,' Lydia said sharply.

'Sorry, Miss,' he muttered, downcast by her rebuke.

'Now, inside with you.' She stepped to one side and he shuffled past, closing the door behind him.

*　　*　　*

175

When the coach pulled on to the quay the *Hind* was not yet in sight but families of the crew, rejoicing that she was back safely, were already gathering in eager anticipation of her arrival. Lydia felt no less excited, for the *Hind* was bringing David. She had missed him throughout the summer months. The house had seemed empty without him, though he had never tried to force his company on her and had remained courteous, thoughtful and sociable throughout his stay. She had missed his voice, soft with a Yorkshire lilt, his laughter which softened his features with humour and pleasure, but most of all his dark eyes, sometimes brooding, sometimes searching, but ever with a joy of life which was only absent when they were touched with sadness. It was a sadness which she would dearly have loved to probe, not out of curiosity but from a desire to help the man with whom she knew she was falling in love. But she'd held her counsel. Those were David's private feelings.

Now, sitting in her carriage on the quay, awaiting his return, she felt her heart racing with excitement, eager to see him again. She stiffened, chastising herself for behaving like a love-sick girl, but then relaxed and let her feelings take over. Why shouldn't she if that was how she felt? Why shouldn't she be like these other people on the quay? Why should she keep her feelings on a tight rein? This was a happy time. David was home, safe from the rigours of the Arctic. Eagerly she anticipated his arrival, hoping that in the long days he had thought of her and that those thoughts had brought his feelings for her closer to those she felt for him. How she hoped absence had drawn them closer together.

'There's bone, bone at the masthead!' A sighting had been made and the news rippled through the crowd. It reached Lydia through the open window of her coach and sent a new wave of joy coursing in her veins for she knew what pleasure and pride it would give David that his first voyage from London had been a success.

She watched with fascination as the *Hind* was manoeuvred to the quay. Her eyes searched for and found David, and longing ached inside her. His tall, broad figure had a commanding presence on the deck of a ship. He looked every inch what he was: the officer in charge, who knew exactly what he was doing and expected his orders to be obeyed immediately.

He raised his hand and she knew he had seen the coach. She leaned towards the open window and waved back. Then she started. There was a woman on deck. Surprise and shock jolted Lydia. Who was she? Why was she there? Was she from Whitby? David's . . .

Two children ran across the deck to her side. A man joined them.

Relief flooded over her though her curiosity was still aroused.

Ropes were thrown from the *Hind*. Willing hands grabbed them and wound them round the bollards fixed to the quay. As soon as the mooring lines were fast the gangway was run out. Eager as the crew were to get ashore to their families and friends, they stood aside to allow their captain to be first. Knowing their longing, he was down the gangway almost as soon as it touched the quay.

When she saw him hurrying straight for the coach, she stepped out to meet him.

'Lydia!' David's greeting was accompanied by a broad smile. He held out his arms.

Her heart soared. She moved forward and hugged him as his arms came round her and held her tight. 'Oh, David, it's good to see you! Welcome home.' Her pulse raced at his touch, at the feel of his body — close, firm, strong, protective — but there was something missing. That final thrill of ecstatic joy on reunion with someone for whom you feel an overwhelming love was not there. But she would not despair for David held her in his arms and the barrier which still seemed to be there could be broken.

He released her and stepped back. 'It's good to be here and to see thee. Thanks for being here. I would have missed thee if thee hadn't come.'

'Nothing would have kept me away.'

The sincerity and affection in her voice tugged at David's mind. He had sensed her feelings towards him had gone beyond friendliness. As he looked at her he realised he had a great admiration for her and that that admiration had grown whilst he was away. He had looked forward to being with her again, a beautiful woman, gentle and kind, thoughtful and serious, yet able to act with a gaiety which made her popular with friends.

He had not realised until now how much he must have been looking forward to being with her again and it set up confusion in his mind for there was also Beth, the Shetland girl who like a whirlwind had captured his heart and loved him with a wildness born in the far reaches of the north.

He looked beyond Lydia to the coach and saw it was empty. 'Where's Dominic?' he asked, concern pushing all thoughts of Beth from his mind. Shetland was so far away.

'He's not too well,' explained Lydia. 'Oh, nothing serious,' she went on quickly to save David's worried frown. 'But, as much as he was looking forward to being here when you returned, he really wasn't fit to leave the house.'

'Oh, I'm sorry. We'll soon have him chirpy again. I've lots of stories to tell him.'

'I'm sure you have,' laughed Lydia. 'And I know how much he'll enjoy them. Poor Papa, no one but females around him. He'll enjoy men's talk.'

'I've someone for thee to meet,' he said, starting to turn towards the ship.

Lydia stopped him with a gentle touch on his arm. He looked back at her and their eyes met. 'I'm pleased you're back, and I'm looking forward to the winter as I never have before.' The words were out before she realised how presumptuous they were. Maybe David wasn't going to stay in London throughout the winter. He could have other plans and she had no hold over him. But they were said and there was no taking them back. David would have to make of them what he would.

There was a brief hesitation and for one moment Lydia thought she had offended him. She saw his eyes soften. 'And I too look forward to it,' he said quietly. He remembered last winter and how he had enjoyed the Hartley hospitality and company, especially Lydia's. There was nothing to take him away from it this winter – only memories and his son. 'I must go to Whitby,' he added, 'to see how things are with the firm, but more than that I want to see little Kit. I'll go soon and be back so that I won't get trapped by the winter snows.'

Lydia's heart rejoiced. Maybe this winter would see the barrier in David's affections broken down.

'Good.' She smiled. 'Now whom do you want me to meet? I see a lady on deck – and her family?'

'Aye, the Frasers.' David waved. Alex and Maggie picked up their bags and ushered the twins down the gangway. 'They had a croft outside of Lerwick.'

'Had?' interrupted Lydia.

'Aye. Thee needn't know the whole story. Better for a while if thee don't. They're a good family. Alex has sailed with me before. A good mate.'

'Ah, so he's the one Jeremy Kemp told me about when he got back,' she mused, then added quickly, anticipating David's question, 'He's recovered and will be fit for next year.'

'Good. Now, the Frasers want thy help.'

Lydia raised a quizzical eyebrow.

Before David could explain the Shetlanders reached them.

'This is Miss Hartley.' David started the introductions.

'Alex Fraser, Maggie Fraser and the twins, Fiona and Alan.'

'Pleased to know thee, Ma'am.' Alex touched his forehead with his first finger. Maggie slipped the threadbare shawl from her head on to her shoulders and bobbed a little curtsey. She was embarrassed, conscious that her worn and marked clothes contrasted with the smart green taffeta dress and matching shoulder wrap worn by Lydia.

'Welcome.' Her smile was warm and, sensing Maggie's feelings, she held out her hand in a friendly gesture. Surprised, Alex and Maggie hesitated a moment before returning the handshake. 'And you two.' Lydia's eyes sparkled as she bent down to Fiona and Alan who stood shyly beside their parents, overawed that a lady with a coach and coachman should shake hands with them. Taken by their wide, bright eyes, with a touch of shyness which she reckoned could soon be made to disappear, she added as she straightened, 'You've two lovely children, Maggie.'

Maggie smiled her appreciation of the compliment. She had taken to this lady and felt there was a genuine sincerity about her, in marked contrast to the haughty gentry in Shetland who had treated the likes of the Frasers as little more than dirt. Besides she had taken notice of the children and Maggie liked that. 'Thank thee, Ma'am. We think they are but they can be little devils at times.'

'Wouldn't be children if they weren't.' Lydia turned to David. 'You say your friends want my help?'

'Aye,' he replied. 'They need a passage to America as soon as possible.'

Lydia hid her surprise and made no request for an explanation. It was good enough for her that David wanted to help these people of whom he obviously held a high opinion. And Lydia too liked what she saw. There was pride and determination in Maggie's grey eyes as well as a love for her husband and children. She had felt Alex's hand to be that of a man used to and not afraid of hard work, and saw in his weather-beaten, craggy face someone who was not afraid of distant horizons and challenges.

'We have a whaler leaving for the Pacific in three days' time. I can arrange for her to call at New Bedford, if that will help?' offered Lydia.

'Ma'am, that would be just reet,' replied Alex, a tremor in his voice. 'But New Bedford ... won't that be taking tha ship oot of her way?' he added with a touch of concern.

'I suppose it will,' replied Lydia, 'but don't you worry about that. Captain Blundell can take on fresh supplies there and maybe pick up the latest information about where the American whalers are going.' She saw excited glances exchanged between Alex and his wife. 'The *Diana*, two ships down the quay, that's the one you'll sail on. I think Captain Blundell will be on board now, so let's go and get everything fixed up.' She started to move but Maggie stopped her with a light touch on the arm.

'Miss Hartley, we're so grateful.' There were tears in her eyes. She bit her lip to hold them back.

'We'll always be in thy debt,' Alex added his thanks. 'New Bedford! It'll be easy fa me t' get work.'

'You'll go back to whaling then?' asked Lydia with a slight inclination of her head.

'Aye, Ma'am. It's all I know, apart fra a bit o' crofting, an' I'm thinking there'll be nae crofting oot there,' he replied with a wry smile.

'Don't expect there is,' agreed Lydia. 'Well, if you're bent on whaling, I'll write you an introduction to Joseph Spence who sails whalers out of New Bedford. We've had some dealings with him. I'm sure he'll get you a berth.'

'Ma'am, this is more than I expected or even hoped for.' Alex's voice caught in his throat.

Maggie could no longer hold back her tears of joy but, when Lydia tapped her arm reassuringly, smiled gratefully as she wept.

'Spence,' added Alex thoughtfully. 'A Shetland name. I wonder if . . .?'

'I know nothing of his past,' Lydia interrupted. 'I'll give you a letter before you sail. Now let's go and see Captain Blundell.'

Lydia, with David beside her, led the way along the quay to the *Diana*. Alex and Maggie, hardly able to contain their excitement, commented on their good fortune to each other in guarded tones.

'Good day, Miss Hartley.' The greeting came from the big, broad-shouldered man at the top of the gangway. His presence seemed to loom large and his dark, full, neatly trimmed beard added to the air of authority which emanated from his stature. He was smartly dressed in a waist-length jacket cut away to tails at the back and calf-length breeches tucked into black, shining boots. Dark hair, greying at the temples, showed at the sides of a peaked cloth cap.

'Good day to you, Captain Blundell,' replied Lydia. 'May we come aboard?'

'Of course, Ma'am. You're always welcome.'

Lydia led the way up the gangway. Some of the twins' shyness had been replaced by excitement at going aboard another ship.

'Pleased to have you aboard, Ma'am,' said Captain Blundell, touching the peak of his cap as Lydia stepped on deck. 'May I enquire after your father?'

'He's not too well today otherwise he would have been here with me,' she replied. 'But it's nothing serious.'

Captain Blundell nodded. 'Give him my regards.'

'Thanks, I will. Now, Captain, you know David Fernley?'

'Aye, I do. Our paths crossed a few times last winter.'

He looked at David. 'I see you had success in the Arctic.'

'Aye, we did. Hope thee has the same in the Pacific.'

'Captain, this is Alex Fraser, his wife Maggie and the twins, Fiona and Alan. Captain Fernley brought them from Shetland.'

Captain Blundell nodded his greeting while his eye swiftly appraised the family as they returned his acknowledgement.

The twins stood in awe of his beard and his size. Alex summed him up as a man who ruled his ship firmly, with a no-nonsense approach, and woe betide anyone who stepped out of line, but in the pale blue eyes he saw a gentleness which spoke of a fair-minded man.

'They require a passage to America and I'd be obliged if you would take them to New Bedford,' explained Lydia.

'Certainly, Ma'am.' Captain Blundell knew better than to query. He would sail anywhere for the Hartleys and it made little difference to him that his voyage would be lengthened by his call at New Bedford.

'Alex was mate with me on a number of occasions when I was sailing out of Whitby and I had him this last voyage after Jeremy Kemp broke his arm in Shetland. He's a first-class sailor,' explained David.

'Anything I can do to help, I'll only be too glad.'

'I'll keep you for emergencies,' replied Captain Blundell. 'I'm fully crewed, so you look after your family.' He glanced at Maggie. Here was a fine figure of a woman, one who could turn any man's head, but he sensed an unswerving devotion to her husband and children and therefore anticipated no trouble with his crew. 'We sail on the evening tide three days from now. I'll show you where I'll quarter you and then you can come on board any time that day.' He turned and started across the deck.

He led them to a companionway near the stern leading to a short L-shaped passage. Turning the corner, he opened a door on the right and stepped into a cabin.

'I hope you and your family will be comfortable in here, Ma'am,' he said to Maggie.

'But, Cap'n, this is thy cabin,' Alex burst in before his wife could answer.

'Aye,' boomed Captain Blundell with a twinkle in his eye. 'You're welcome to it for the crossing. As you know, we aren't equipped for passengers but I can still see a lady has the best possible comfort we can manage.'

'Sir, I canna see thee turned oot,' protested Maggie.

'Nonsense,' he replied. 'I'll be all right, so think no more about it. It'll be a bit cramped for all of you but I think you'll manage.'

'Then thank thee, sir, I'm most grateful for thy kindness.' Maggie had never expected to find such thoughtfulness yet, within a few minutes of stepping ashore, they had found support from Miss Hartley and from Captain Blundell, with their passage to America assured.

Lydia added to her generosity by finding temporary accommodation for the Frasers and for Andy Roberts, the young Shetland sailor, in the same rooming house as one of her clerks. David quietly indicated that he would meet the cost, but Lydia turned down his offer with a smile.

'It's nothing. I'm only too glad to help.'

'Then thee should have an explanation.'

'Not if you don't want to. But if you do, do so in the coach on the way home.'

Home. That magical word. It gave David a warm feeling. It told him he belonged. And as he sat in the coach telling Lydia the Frasers' story, he could not help but wonder where his destiny was leading him.

Chapter Ten

Activity around the *Diana* intensified as sailing time drew closer. Men stood by the bollards to cast off when the order came. On deck, sailors were ready to haul the ropes aboard once they were released. The mate shouted instructions, making sure the crew were all prepared to get the ship safely underway.

The quayside buzzed with talk and rang with shouts from the throng of families and well-wishers who had come to bid their loved ones and friends a safe voyage. Final kisses and extra hugs were to be memories for over two years. Eyes were damp and tears mingled with whispered goodbyes.

'We'd better be getting aboard, Ma'am.' Captain Blundell, who had come ashore to have one final word with his employer, addressed his remark to Maggie.

She nodded and turned to Lydia. 'I canna thank thee enough for all thee's done for us.' Her voice was trembling. 'To arrange the voyage was enough, but new clothes and baggage were more than we could expect.'

'Please, think nothing of it.' Lydia held out her arms. 'It's good to have found new friends. And we did have fun together choosing the clothes, didn't we?'

They hugged each other tightly.

'I'll never forget thee, Lydia.' They kissed each other on the cheek in one final embrace and then Lydia knelt to take the twins in her arms. 'I've enjoyed meeting you. Be good, and look after your mother and father.'

Alan and Fiona pressed themselves close to her and gave her a kiss. They were silent in their sorrow to be leaving for Lydia had shown them breathtaking sights in London, but sailing on the *Diana* was an exciting prospect.

Lydia straightened and held out her hand to Alex. 'Goodbye, Alex. I'm sure that note to Joseph Spence will smooth your path in New Bedford.'

'Goodbye,' replied Alex quietly. 'Thank thee for everything. We owe our new life to thee and David.' He turned to his captain and the two friends exchanged a handshake which expressed a world of feelings – thanks for times shared in the Arctic, good wishes for the future, admiration of each other's ability, and regret that they would not sail together again. 'Thank thee, Cap'n. It's not much for what thee's done, but it comes fra the bottom of my heart. And may God be wi' thee where the whales spout.'

'And with thee, Alex,' returned David, giving him a friendly pat on the shoulder.

Captain Blundell was already halfway up the gangway. The Frasers, with good wishes ringing in their ears, hurried after him, Maggie ushering the children in front of her.

Once on deck they stood together at the rail.

The gangway was hauled on board. To Maggie it was the final break with the old life. She had regrets at leaving and apprehension at the unknown life which faced her. But she had her man and her children. They were all she wanted and with them she was prepared to face anything. Alex had confronted the unknown before – a whaleman always did when he sailed to the Arctic – so to him the sound of the gangway being stowed on deck spelt safety, escape from the law or someone's revenge – not that he thought either was likely to find him in England for who was there to really care about Ratter's death? Nevertheless the wide Atlantic would provide a safe retreat.

'Let go fore!' The shout rang crisply cross the deck. Two men on the quay heaved the rope from the bollard.

'Let go aft!'

The *Diana*, released of its securing ropes, eased from the

quayside and was manoeuvred towards the open river.

'Set the courses!' Sailors jumped to obey.

'Hoist y're main tops'l!'

David watched with mixed feelings. Any departing ship stirred his sailor's wish to be on board and that feeling was even stronger when watching a whaleship setting out on a voyage. But he had also been looking forward to seeing his son and spending Christmas with Lydia and her father.

The wind caught the sails. The *Diana* responded and seemed to move with a new sense of purpose as she took to the main course of the river.

The Frasers raised their hands in gestures of farewell and Lydia and David responded. They waved until the quay was lost to sight.

'Thy pa and I are going t' get settled in our cabin, thee two may stay on deck, but nae getting in the way and nae climbing on the rail,' Maggie instructed the twins.

She viewed the cabin and blessed Captain Blundell for allowing them to use his quarters; here was comfort and luxury compared to some ships she had heard about. A bed occupied one wall with a small table fixed securely to the floor beside it. Against the opposite wall was a table which served as the captain's desk. A drawing, the head and shoulders of a young woman and two children, hung above the table.

'Captain Blundell's family?' she queried, crossing the cabin to look at it more closely.

'Expect so,' replied Alex. He moved behind her and slid his arms round her waist, turning her to face him. 'Maggie, my love. Here's to our new life.'

She arched away from him and looked deep into his eyes. 'And it's a life in which I know thee's going t' do well. I feel it in my bones. Fortune has started to shine on us.'

'Aye, lass, thee's right. David's help, Lydia's kindness . . . how lucky we were.'

'And now we have Captain Blundell's cabin.'

'Aye, and decent food, unlike some emigrant ships I've heard of. And that letter of introduction can give us a good start.'

'In a captain's cabin! I reckon that's an omen. Thee'll soon have one of thy own.'

Alex laughed. 'Aye, maybe, Maggie Fraser, maybe.' He swung her off her feet and swung her round.

Maggie threw back her head and laughed joyously with him.

Two days out from Scalloway the *Good Intent* met the first heavy sea. She pitched and rolled at the will of the waves while keeping to her course. Nausea rose in Beth. She had fought it after her bout of seasickness on their first day out from Shetland, but now it tortured her body again. Sitting on the edge of the narrow wood which-served as a bed for herself, her mother and father, she leaned forward, trying to ease the vile sensation and hide her disgust at the conditions around her.

Three hundred emigrants were crammed into the hold of the small vessel. They had to share a space a little over sixty feet by eighteen and no more than eight feet high. The makeshift beds were no wider than two coffins placed side by side and had to be shared by three people. Beth was thankful that she had her mother and father for there were cases of strangers sharing with married couples. If anyone complained or protested they were given harsh treatment by the crew. The stench in the airless conditions was revolting, for the few buckets in the flimsy partitioned privies were inadequate for the numbers aboard. The vomit which swilled the deck still left its foul odour after the feeble attempts to remove it. Most emigrants felt too ill to bother.

Six weeks for the crossing they had been told. Beth shuddered and held her head. How could they endure this hell hole for six weeks? She wished she had stayed in Shetland, taken a chance on David's return, but without a roof over their heads there had seemed to be no alternative, especially as their fare had been paid. But they had not expected this.

They had been led to believe the accommodation would be adequate, and that even though they had to take their own food it need only be sufficient for two days as there would then be supplies available on board. This Beth was beginning to doubt for from the moment they had arrived at the ship they had been shown no compassion. Herded like sheep, they were hustled aboard by the crew when the order came for boarding. The tiny ship looked inadequate for such numbers and there were those who wanted to change their minds and stay, only to be forcibly persuaded otherwise by a hostile crew. Each emigrant aboard was money in their pockets and the captain was determined that no one should miss the voyage. Those who fell to the ground, their bodies racked by sobs, their wailing rising to the heavens, grasping at the ground of their beloved Shetland, were bodily lifted and taken aboard.

There had been no joyful goodbyes to those left behind, only sadness and tears, so that a depressing, melancholy atmosphere settled over the small town and harbour at Scalloway. The breeze carried the haunting notes of 'Cha till mi tuille', 'We Shall Not Return', played by a lone piper, across the quay and over the water, until the skirl of the bagpipes could be heard no more. With the last fading note Beth had wept openly.

Now she wept to herself and hoped that what they were enduring would lead to a better life.

A week later she doubted it. Most people had come to terms with the unending motion of the ship but not her father. He had continued to suffer from sickness and was plagued by bouts of uncontrollable shaking. His face was gaunt, his eyes, sunk in their sockets, bewildered and bemused by what had started as a voyage of hope but had turned into one of misery and suffering. When Beth approached one of the crew for help she was shocked by his unsympathetic reply and callousness towards her father. 'Maybe thee's the one that needs help.' He grinned meaningfully as he went on, 'Tha's a fine figure of a lass, with a body that could earn thee some favours.'

Her eyes flamed with anger and contempt. Her lips curled with revulsion. 'Thee'll get none o' mine!' She started to turn away but he grabbed her by the arm and swung her back to face him.

He thrust his stubbled face close to hers. 'Maybe at the end of six weeks thee'll think differently.'

'Six weeks and we'll be there,' she'd scoffed. She tried to draw back from the odious, tobacco-stained teeth and foul breath but he held her firm.

'There?' The man gave a short mocking laugh. 'We'll be little over halfway!'

Beth stared at him, wanting to disbelieve his words, but somehow there seemed to be a ring of truth to them. 'But we were told . . .'

'Aye, thee might have been *told*, but telling and reality are two different things,' he taunted her. 'I've done this voyage five times an' I tell thee, it takes eleven weeks.'

Beth's eyes widened as the horror of having to spend another five weeks in this stinking hold numbed her mind.

'But why tell us . . . ?' she began.

'Work that out for thyself, lassie.' He shoved her away with a harsh laugh. 'Maybe thee'll be ready to do me a favour then.' He walked away, leaving Beth's mind racing with the implications of what she had learned.

They had been given food for two days by the laird and by careful rationing they had stretched it to four when they became aware that any further supplies on board would have to be bought. Her mother, who had not been affected by the voyage as much as her father, had allocated what little money they had to provide a subsistence-diet for the six weeks' voyage. Now that money would run out with another five weeks to go. The thought of those final five weeks chilled Beth to the bone but she decided to say nothing of this to her parents.

'The blubber and whalebone from the *Hind* has brought a good price, David,' Lydia announced when he came into her office. 'That was a profitable voyage, thanks to your skill.' She smiled warmly.

'Not only mine. They were a good crew and I've signed them all on for next season,' said David as he sat down opposite her. 'I know Hartley Shipping is primarily concerned with whaling in the Pacific but I do think any ship thee sends to the Arctic could be profitably used in the timber trade from the Baltic, as we do with Whitby ships.'

'It's something to think about, but as you know we've never traded in timber.'

'Better than leaving the ship laid up all the winter, and I have connections in the Baltic ports I could turn to good use for thee.'

'Wanting to escape from us?' There was a teasing tone to her voice but her feelings ran deeper. She was enjoying having David at home, didn't want him to spend any of the winter away. There was no need.

'Not at all.' He smiled. 'It was just that I thought there could be something of advantage to Hartley Shipping. Oh, by the way, now that the *Hind* is all settled and laid up, I've booked a passage on the *Capella* to Whitby in three days' time.'

Lydia's heart sank. The knowledge that David had said he would go to Whitby for a few weeks did nothing to ease her sense of disappointment and loss.

They haunted her over the next three days and intensified when she took him in her coach to the *Capella*. If she could she would have held him back, but she realised he had to go to Whitby. How she wished he didn't. The urge to tell him she loved him was strong but she remained silent for she wanted to sense a reciprocal feeling instead of only the respect and consideration offered by a dear friend.

They reached the quay with only a few moments to spare. The coach had barely come to a stop when the cry of: 'All aboard that's coming aboard' rang across the quay. There was no time for lingering goodbyes.

'Good voyage, David, and good luck. Hope you find little Kit and your family well.' Lydia took his hand in hers. 'I'll miss you and will look forward to your return.'

'And I'll miss thee, Lydia.'

'But you'll soon forget in the excitement of meeting your family again.'

'Forget? I could never forget thee.' He bent forward and kissed her on the cheek. He was out of the coach and striding to the ship before any more could be said.

Lydia watched him with a longing heart. Was there more meaning behind those words than there appeared to be on the surface? Her heart wanted to think so. She raised her fingers and stroked the cheek he had kissed.

David reached the deck, found an empty space beside the rail, dropped his bag at his feet and waved. He saw Lydia reply instantaneously. Among the din of activity on the quay and on board to get the ship underway, and among the cries of those calling their goodbyes, he saw her mouth the words: 'Come back soon.'

A feverish excitement gripped David as he watched the familiar sight of the ruined abbey high on the cliffs come nearer and nearer. Home! This was home. Always would be. He scanned the cliffs and thought of the days when a red shawl waved for him. Now it was not there. Would it have been if Jenny had known he was coming? He felt sure it would. As the *Capella* passed between the piers and moved steadily up river, David drank in all the old familiar sounds of Whitby, in particular the sound of the gulls wheeling and swooping over the quays and around the ships. It was a sound like no other, a Whitby sound. The quays bustled with activity and David searched for the *Mary Jane, The Lonely Wind* and the *Ruth* but they were not there. They must still be on the Baltic run. He would soon know.

The *Capella* docked against the east bank of the river but David lost no time in crossing to the west bank and the building where newly painted letters above the door announced that these were the offices of Fernley and Thoresby. He paused and admired them. He was aware that eyes had been cast in his direction and he knew that word would soon be around that Captain David Fernley was in Whitby.

But word had not travelled before him for as he was about to enter the building Francis Chambers came out and pulled up sharp at the sight of him.

'Why, Captain Fernley, this is a surprise,' he cried.

David thought he caught a touch of apprehension in Francis's voice but it was gone so quickly that he could not be certain. The chief clerk seemed composed as he held out his hand in welcome.

'Here for long, Captain Fernley?' he asked casually.

'Must be back in London before the winter,' replied David as he shook hands. 'The ladies in?'

'They are. Hardly ever away these days.'

'Well, it's good to see them taking an interest, but I hope they don't pester thee.' He smiled at the thought of Jessica and Jenny taking to the shipping business.

'No, sir, but I think they do more good for the firm outside the office.'

'Socialising?'

'Aye, and hearing what's going on.'

'Good.' David was pleased with the report.

'Well, I must away, sir. Going to see about the sale of the timber.'

'Frank Watson?'

'Aye, but he seems to be interested in only two of the cargoes. Must see if I can persuade him to take the third.'

'And if not?'

'I have someone else who's interested.'

'Good. Now to surprise the ladies.'

David opened the door and stepped inside while Francis hurried away, thankful that there were no more questions.

When the office door opened without a warning knock both Jessica and Jenny looked up, prepared to admonish the caller whoever he was. But their affront was turned to joyous surprise when David stepped in.

'Davey!' Jessica sprang to her feet and flung her arms round her brother's neck. He dropped his bag and encircled her waist, hugging her tightly. 'Jess! It's good to see thee. And Jenny, thee too.' He held out his hand to her whilst still holding Jessica. She took it and he pulled her gently to him to kiss her on the cheek.

'It's good to see you, David. Whitby's not the same without you,' said Jenny as her eyes searched for any changes in him. But she could find none. Even though the harsh realities of his life in Whitby had marked his features, she could still see today the young man who had walked into her life seeking a berth on a whaleship.

'It certainly isn't,' agreed Jessica. 'When are thee coming back for good?' She slipped from his arms.

'Not sure,' he replied.

'Then how long are thee here for now?' she pressed.

'In Whitby? I don't know. I'm going to Cropton and will return to London in about eight weeks.'

'Thee won't be with young Kit for Christmas?' Jessica sounded a little shocked.

'I can't afford to be trapped by the winter's snow, and thee knows how long it can cut Whitby off – well into the

New Year. I've to be back in London and be ready to sail for the Arctic first week in March,' he explained.

'You're still going north?'

'Aye.'

'Not been tempted by those Londoners to go to the Pacific?' she asked.

'Not yet. That's a different proposition, away two to three years. Maybe one day I'll be tempted. Now, how are things here? I met Francis at the door. He told me the ships were full.'

'Yes,' replied Jenny. 'He got a good price for the blubber and whalebone. He's a great asset.'

'Good. I'm pleased to hear it,' said David. 'But I hope thee keeps an eye on things.'

'Oh, we do as far as we understand the running of the firm, but Francis does most of that. We sign final author-isations but he's good at explaining them.'

'What about Ruben? Does he . . .?'

'Well, thee knows Ruben,' put in Jessica. 'A sailor first and foremost, doesn't really like the business side.'

'Why stand here talking?' suggested Jenny. 'There's nothing to keep us. Mr Swan and Danny are here and Francis will be back soon. So let's go to my house. I baked some scones last night.' She glanced at David with a smile. 'Do you fancy tea, scones and home-made jam?'

'My mouth's watering already,' he grinned. 'And no doubt there'll be some of thy special fruit cake to follow?'

'No doubt,' laughed Jenny.

As Francis hurried through Whitby's narrow streets he decided on a change of plan. He had not been too worried that Frank Watson had initially said he would take the timber from only two ships. He had another possible purchaser for the other but it would have meant a shady deal with which he had intended to swell the money in

R. C. Shipping. Now, with David in Whitby, he would have to be more cautious. It would look better if he could persuade Frank Watson to take the timber of the third ship.

Confronting Frank, he came straight to the point. 'You've always taken all the timber we shipped from the Baltic but this time you've indicated you might only be interested in two.'

'Aye. Thee was driving a hard bargain.' Frank leaned back in his chair watching Francis closely. He was a man whom Frank had never really taken to but the Thoresbys seemed satisfied with him and who was he to question their judgement? But he knew he himself would never have left so much decision-making to an employee.

'Maybe I was, but I was thinking of my employers. It behoves me to get the best deal I can for them.'

'True,' agreed Frank. 'So what brings you here now?'

'It will save a lot of bother if all the timber can be dealt with in one sale. Saves us from having to store it until the other deal is finalised,' explained Francis.

'Thee mean thee haven't got a customer for the third cargo,' commented Frank.

'Not at all,' replied Francis testily. 'But it takes time to set up a deal with a new customer and I'd rather settle the whole thing quickly.' His tone eased a fraction. 'You've been a good customer of the Fernleys and now of the joint firm so it makes sense if I can persuade you to take the remainder of the consignment. How about if I let you have the third cargo at half the cost of one of the others?'

Frank rubbed his chin thoughtfully. Francis was offering him a good deal but he did not want to appear too hasty. 'When are the ships due?'

'Not certain, but I think they should reach Whitby in about four days' time.'

Frank nodded, pursing his lips. 'Mmm, that could fit in

196

with an enquiry I received yesterday. All right, I'll take all three.'

Frank stood up and they shook hands to seal the bargain.

When he reached the office again, Francis found that David had left with Jessica and Jenny and Mr Swan informed him that they'd said they would not be back. He dealt with a couple of enquiries and then instructed Mr Swan to lock up when he and Danny had finished their day's work.

Francis hurried through the milling crowds, going about their business, to the White Horse where he quickly had his horse saddled. He rode out of Whitby taking the circuitous route to Rigg Hall.

'Home early.' Ruth greeted him with a kiss but, noting a slight irritation in him, added, 'Something wrong?'

'Your husband's turned up.'

'What?' she gasped. 'For good?'

'Said he had to be back in London before the winter,' Francis replied.

Ruth nodded thoughtfully. 'That means he'll want to be there by early November, so he could be here up to eight weeks.' She paced the room. 'He'll no doubt go to Cropton. He'll have to spend some time there so he's not going to be around Whitby very long.'

'But it could be long enough to get nosey,' pointed out Francis.

Ruth swung round. 'Any reason why he should?' she demanded.

'No.'

'Well then, what bothers you? Is there anything to connect you with R. C. Shipping?'

'Nothing.'

'So there's no worry?'

Francis shook his head irritably, annoyed with himself

for showing a touch of nervousness. 'You're right. I expect I'm upset at having to change the timber deal.'

'You've what?' asked Ruth gruffly.

'I bumped into Fernley as I was leaving the office. So when I knew he was around I thought I'd better be safe and let Frank Watson have all the timber.'

Ruth's lips tightened. She was annoyed that David should influence her life even without knowing it. 'The proceeds from the third cargo were going to be ours. Now they won't be.'

'But we'll get our share. R. C. Shipping can put in a few more invoices,' said Francis. 'Better to be safe. Things are going along nicely, and I'm working on the sale of the ships.'

'Good,' said Ruth. 'As much as I want to get away, we must not jeopardise our scheme by rushing it.' Her eyes narrowed and her voice took on a hard tone. 'I want that firm utterly ruined.'

'It will be,' Francis reassured her as he slipped his arms around her waist. 'But now there are other things to think about.'

She accepted his kiss willingly, wanting it to drive the haunting thoughts of David from her mind.

Chapter Eleven

The *Good Intent* sailed on, weathering the Atlantic waves as best she could with her ageing timbers grating and groaning under the constant impact of the ocean. Her rigging's continuous creaking sent its melancholy sound below decks, a constant reminder to the emigrants of their precarious position in a tiny, leaking ship in the middle of a vast expanse of water which was beginning to seem limitless. The promise of a new life in Nova Scotia had become but a vision which grew dimmer with each passing hour.

Even though most emigrants had come to terms with the constant sway of the ship, the vile conditions in which they were now living and which they could not better, no matter how they tried, served only to foster a feeling of depression and despair.

Beth had been shocked to realise that the captain and crew did not care about their steerage passengers and regarded them more or less as cattle to be transported at a price, and that they were prepared to exploit them further by charging exorbitant prices for even the basic necessities.

Many who could not afford the high cost faced starvation and resorted to stealing. Thieving was rife, even by those who at home would have abhorred such dishonesty. Their sufferings brought out subterfuge and cunning so that no one dared leave their meagre rations and possessions unprotected, yet still there were those who tried to outsmart others. Friend turned against friend and even brother against brother in the desperate attempt to gain enough food to stay alive. Fights were frequent and punishment by an emigrant court rough and harsh.

The hold was one heaving mass of humanity, dressing and undressing, washing as best they could or ignoring it completely, arguing, quarrelling, pushing their way to the privies which frequently slopped over with the sway of the ship, and hustling to get their scraps of food cooked at one of the four fire grates installed at one end of the hold.

With little air and only unavailing attempts at cleanliness, the pestilential atmosphere which the emigrants were forced to endure became oppressive, lowering morale and resistance to illness further.

Beth's father continued to be unable to take much food and most of what he did came back. He grew weaker and suffered agonies with his uncontrollable shaking. Her mother spent most of her days lying beside him, gently wiping his gaunt face and mopping his brow. Her heart ached for the tall strong man she had once known, the youngster who, in spite of the harsh Shetland life, had promised her a better one when he had proposed to her. The better one had led only to this God-forsaken hold.

Beth watched with a sad and heavy heart. She wanted to do something to help, to relieve her father of his suffering. If only she could get a little more food, something more appetising. She was sure the crew would be better victualled and was certain the sailor who had hinted what he could do for her, and who eyed her lasciviously whenever he came into the hold, would be able to help if only she would bestow her favours on him. She shuddered at the thought of giving herself to such a loathsome creature and turned the inclination from her mind. But every time she looked at her father it came back.

Two days passed in this tormented state until she could stand it no longer. She could not let her father go on suffering in this way and, though she was filled with loathing at what she would have to do, steeled herself to go through with it. Her body was taut as a bow string as she awaited the sailor's daily visit to the hold.

The hatch opened, letting a flood of daylight stream downwards and a blast of fresh air sweep through the hold only to be quickly overpowered by the nauseating stench within.

Beth stiffened. She watched the burly figure clamber down into the hold. Apprehension filled her. She could not do it! She glanced at her father. She must, for his sake. She closed her eyes and ran her hand across her forehead as if it would banish the nightmare and she would wake up once more in the Shetland croft. But the swaying motion of the ship told her this was reality. She opened her eyes. The man drew near, carrying out his cursory inspections which meant nothing, only enabling the captain to say they had been done should anyone in authority question him. Beth moved away from her berth. She did not want her mother to overhear what she had to say.

She met his devouring look, only this time she did not glance away as she had every day since his first approach. She saw his surprise turn to expectation.

'Changed thy mind?' he grunted in a low voice.

'My father . . .' started Beth.

'Aye, what about him?' asked the sailor gruffly.

'He's desperately ill. He needs . . .'

'Let's look at 'm.' The man pushed past her and peered into the confined space which served as the family's bed.

He stepped back quickly, his face a mask of alarm. He turned, muttering, 'I'll fetch the captain,' as he brushed past Beth.

She stared after him in surprise.

'What is it?' her mother asked.

'Don't know, Ma,' she replied, relieved that for the time being her plans had been curtailed.

A few minutes later the sailor reappeared with the captain and another sailor. Silence gradually spread through the hold. Everyone seemed frozen as they watched the authorities, wondering what had caused them to visit the hold. With his hand to his nose, the captain crossed the deck quickly to peer at Will. He gave him only a quick look. His lips curled in disgust at the sight of Will's emaciated body, and the shivering which seemed to set his bloodshot eyes rolling in his vacant wide-eyed stare. He turned and nodded to the sailor who had brought him.

'Your name?' He directed his question at Beth's mother.

'Mrs Robinson,' she replied timidly, bewildered that the captain should visit them.

'Your husband?'

'Aye. Will.'

'He's very ill. We'll have to take him to better quarters.'

Bab swung from the berth, saying, 'I'll come with him.'

'You can't, Mrs Robinson,' growled the captain in a tone which would brook no argument. He was the master of the ship and as such his word was law.

'Then let me come,' suggested Beth in a brief moment of defiance. Fear was clutching at her heart. There was something terribly wrong; if there hadn't been the captain would not have ventured among this stinking mass of humanity. 'He's my father,' she added by way of an excuse.

'No one!' boomed the captain. 'Get on with it.' He shot a sharp look at the two members of his crew.

They reached across the bed space. One clutched Will's feet, the other his shoulders, and yanked him clear. His scream of agony as their grip dug into his frail, emaciated body pierced the far corners of the hold. The sailors' faces grimaced at the stench of clothes saturated in urine and vomit, as they hastened to follow the captain from the hold and get rid of their unsavoury burden.

Every movement brought fresh cries from Will and Bab collapsed, weeping, as she saw her husband being carried away without thought for the pain he was suffering.

The agony in his screams jerked Beth out of her confusion. She must go with her father. He needed her. He couldn't be allowed to have no one of his own beside him, to nurse him. She ran across the hold, pushing her way through the throng which was gathering at the bottom of the gangway leading from the hold. She reached it just as the two sailors finally hauled her father on to the deck. She started up the gangway, her face bathed in sweat, her lank hair straggling to her shoulders.

The hatch slammed down. The bolt was shot.

'Pa! Pa!' Beth screamed as she flung herself up the last few steps to cling close to the slats in the hatch. She tried to peer out, twisting to catch a glimpse of the movement on deck.

She saw the two sailors lift her father up with such ease he must have weighed very little. They moved out of sight. She pressed her face closer to the slats. She saw them carry her father across the deck. Then the horror of what they were about to do struck her. 'No!' Her shrill scream pierced the hold, striking a chill into everyone. 'No!' Her fingers clawed at the slats. 'No!' Her eyes widened at the harrowing sight.

The two sailors had reached the rail. Without hesitation they swung Will over the side and watched as he hit the waves, his scream torn away by the wind.

'You were right, Soames. Typhus.' The captain turned away without another thought for what he had ordered to be done.

Beth caught the one word as she sank back on the gangway, numb with the horror she had just witnessed. It automatically came to her lips. 'Typhus!' Her voice was low as if she was just speaking to herself, but it carried to the bottom of the gangway.

In a matter of moments it spread through the hold like the sweep of the wind through corn. It rose in crescendo as queries were raised by the ignorant, for the very word had a fatal ring about it. Alarm, fright and fear filled the air.

The hatch was raised, bringing the cries to a halt. All eyes turned to see who ventured into the hold. The steps came slow, deliberate, carrying with them an ominous ring. Four sailors, each carrying a short length of knotted rope, appeared. They stopped at the foot of the gangway, feet apart, testing the rope between their hands, conveying their intentions to anyone who interfered with what was to come. The captain reappeared and stopped on the fourth rung of the gangway, giving him extra height so that his voice would carry to the far corners of the hold.

'Most of you will be ignorant about typhus, but that's what Will Robinson has.'

Has. The word struck at Beth. She wanted to scream, 'Had! My pa had it. He no longer has because you threw him overboard.' But her mother's gasp of horror tinged with disbelief stopped her. She could not crucify her mother with what she had seen. Instead she put a comforting arm around her.

The captain was still speaking. 'It's caused by filth and that's what I find in my hold,' his voice boomed. 'I'll have none of it! You must get it cleaned up.' He glanced around, his eyes settling on four men in turn. 'You, you, you and you, are in charge of seeing the privies are emptied regularly. Don't let any of my men find them full or overflowing or it'll be the worse for you.' He moved into the hold and stopped in front of a group of women. 'You three are responsible for seeing that there are regular cleaning parties.'

'How clean can we get a stinking hold like this?' demanded one woman defiantly.

The captain's eyes narrowed as he looked her up and down. 'You'll do whatever you can.' He looked past her. 'Now, we're coming round to see if there are any more cases and if there are we'll take them to be better looked after.' He started round the hold, his sailors with him. He stopped at the third bed he came to. A middle-aged woman, her face drawn to the bone, her clothes saturated, lay helpless. The captain glanced at the haggard face of the man who stood beside her. 'She'll have to go.'

The man, thinking his wife would get better treatment, made no protest. He stood meekly by and watched two sailors carry her from the hold.

A few moments later they were back. Beth caught the nod they gave the captain and knew the woman had been cast overboard. He moved on with his examination. Two more emigrants were said to have the disease and were lifted from their beds. Relatives and friends watched, cocooned in the hope that their loved one would receive better treatment. Beth's mind screamed at her to tell them the truth, to disclose the fate that awaited the victims, but she forced herself to hold back. What good would be served if she revealed what she had seen? The captain would stand no nonsense. The crew could easily quell any insurrection and would carry out their grim task no matter how strong the protests. And she would be silenced.

The captain came to a bunk where a woman lay with her back to him, curled as if to hide something. He touched her on the shoulder. 'What have you got there?' he demanded.

She cringed as if trying to pretend she was not there. The captain gripped her shoulder and jerked her back. She screamed in fear and protest as she clung to the tiny bundle she had been trying to hide.

'Thought so,' hissed the captain. His glance at one of the sailors was an order.

The man grabbed at the bundle but the woman swung away. Her victory was only momentary, it could be no other in the confined space. A second sailor grabbed her by the shoulders and held her while the first prised the bundle from her arms. All the time she fought with what strength she had. Her sunken eyes were wild with the fury of a mother being forcibly parted from her young.

'Dead,' the sailor announced.

'Over the side,' ordered the captain.

'No!' The woman's scream pierced every cranny of the hold, its heart-torn agony bringing anguish to every mind. The grip on her shoulders had relaxed. She twisted free and flung herself after the man taking her child from her. She fell, hands grasping at his legs but finding no grip. Gasping for breath, she struggled to her feet. Her dishevelled hair straggled to her shoulders; her dress, torn and dirty, hung like a sack. She felt a hand clamp on her shoulder and turned with tears streaming down her face. 'My son! Let me take my son for a decent burial?' The pleading cry was wrung from her between sobs.

'Can't. Too long to go,' boomed the captain, and pushed her roughly aside.

She staggered but kept her balance. All her pent-up fury turned to hate as she flung herself at him, her long thin fingers clawing at his face. But they made no contact. As he parried the blows, a sailor grabbed her by the arms in a vice-like grip. She was helpless as the captain hit her. The blow was clean and sure. The woman slumped unconscious in the sailor's arms. He bundled her on to the sodden clothes in her bunk and rejoined the rest of the crew, ready to dispose of any more typhus victims.

Six more were diagnosed and carried from the hold. Beth, her head in her hands, sat silent by her mother. This was to be their life for five more weeks.

The *Diana* rode the Atlantic waves easily. Maggie and the twins soon found their sealegs, though Alan teased his sister when she was sick longer than he was. They began to enjoy the voyage and the fresh air with the tang of the sea borne on its spray as the whaler dipped its bow into the waves. The creaking ropes and the snap of the sails filled with the wind seemed to be the music of a new life. Maggie, wrapped up well, loved to feel the wind in her hair as she watched her children play chase under the watchful eyes of a kindly captain and tolerant crew. She was ever grateful for the comfort of the captain's cabin and they lacked nothing in food for, with a goodly supply on board and the knowledge that it could be replenished in New Bedford, Captain Blundell saw no sense in rationing.

'Good morning, Ma'am.' He gave Maggie his usual friendly smile when she came on deck. 'I trust you had a good night.'

She inclined her head in acknowledgement of his greeting and returned his smile. 'Indeed I did, thank you.'

'You've taken to the sea like a good sailor,' he observed.

'I've often wondered how the sea could entice you men in the way it does. Now I know.'

'Aye. She's a beckoning mistress, and there are those who can't refuse her.' He gave a contented sigh as if he gained great pleasure from being caught in her magical web. 'Tomorrow you'll leave her.'

'Thee means we'll be at New Bedford?'

'Aye, we will, mid-morning.'

'Land ahoy!' The cry which rang out from the main mast head sent excitement coursing through the ship.

'Whither away?' Captain Blundell's deep voice cut through the wind.

'Starboard bow!'

'Where, Ma, where?' the twins asked excitedly.

'I canna see it yet,' said Alex.

'Why? Why?' they demanded. 'The lookout can.'

'He's higher so can see things sooner,' their father explained.

Impatiently they waited. Maggie slipped her arm through his, snuggling a little closer to him, finding reassurance in his nearness and drawing from it the strength to face a new land and a new life.

'There!' Alex focused their minds on the future.

'Where?' gasped Fiona.

'There.' He pointed. 'See that smudge on the horizon.'

'Can't,' grumbled Fiona.

''Tain't there,' exclaimed Alan.

'Where?' asked Maggie doubtfully.

Alex chuckled. 'Landlubbers! Thee needs sea-eyes like me. Thee'll see it ere long.'

Impatience turned to excitement as the smudge became visible, emerging from the ocean as low-lying land.

The *Diana* was running north, with the coast curving away to the east and west forming a huge bay.

'Buzzards Bay, Ma'am,' a sailor informed Maggie pleasantly as he came to the rail.

She looked askance at him.

He smiled. 'It's right, Ma'am. So named 'cos hundreds of bustards roost along the shores.' He squatted beside the twins. 'See yon islands?' He pointed to the specks of land strung across the bay. The twins nodded. 'They're called the Elizabeth Islands, named after an Englishwoman, though who she was I know not. I prefer the Indian names: Naushon, Nonamesset, Onkatonka and Wepecket; Nashawena, Pesquinese, Cuttyhunk and Penequese.' The names tripped off his tongue with a swing. He laughed with amusement at the look on the twins' faces and repeated them with equal enjoyment. 'Picked them up on my first visit here and they've stuck with me ever since.'

'Indians! Are there really Indians here?' asked Alan, wide-eyed with astonishment.

The man nodded with a smile. 'Aye, you'll see some. They come into town trading. White men bought the land from them for some cloth, some skins, an iron kettle and a few other odds and ends.'

'Sounds to be the biggest bargain of all time,' said Alex as the man straightened.

'Aye, I guess it was.'

'Are they fierce?' asked Alan, peering up at the sailor. 'Will they frighten Fiona?'

'Quiet,' Maggie admonished her son, frowning at his teasing Fiona.

'No,' chuckled the sailor. 'They're peaceful now. The Indians around here have always been friendly except for one period about a hundred and twenty years ago when there was a fierce though short-lived uprising.' He nodded ahead. 'Soon be entering the Acushnet River.' He moved away towards the bow to be ready to throw out the ropes when they docked.

The Frasers took in the scene with a keen interest. The land was low and rounded, meeting the horizon without so much as a cliff or a crag to mar the smooth contours. Along the river bank it had been cleared to build the settlement, and further to provide rich farmland. Beyond the open ground were trees, trees and more trees spreading the landscape with a kaleidoscope of browns, yellows, golds, greens and reds. Colour ran riot with the profusion of fall tints enriched by the September glow.

'It's gorgeous,' murmured Maggie.

'Aye, it is, lass. Is such a fine sight an omen for the future?' wondered Alex, already thankful that they had been forced to leave Shetland. This looked a land of promise after the drab desolation of rundown crofts.

He turned his attention to the town. Not big, but plenty of room for expansion. The streets, laid out in a grid-like pattern, were wide. The warehouses along the river bank, opposite the wharves and quays, were close together, but beyond, the dwellings and shops and public buildings were well-spaced.

'Try-works.' Alex spotted the places set aside from the town for boiling the whale's blubber for oil. His eyes roved across the wharves ahead of them. He sensed a thrill surge through him at the sight of the activity. Whaling gear was being taken aboard two sloops. Two three-masted square-riggers rested at anchor as they were being cleaned and repainted, their huge sails hanging out to dry. Fishermen prepared their boats while others repaired their nets. Young men bustled about their business; older ones took their time summing up the activities with critical eyes and wishing for the days when they would have shown the modern whippersnappers a thing or two.

The news that an English whaler was coming in had attracted attention and there were several groups of people dotted around the quays watching the *Diana* being manoeuvred to a vacant berth. Sails were furled, ropes slung out, and soon the whaler was tied up.

When the Frasers brought their few belongings from the captain's cabin, they found Captain Blundell standing at the head of the gangplank.

'Well, the end of your voyage.' He smiled benevolently. 'I trust you have not suffered too much discomfort.'

'None at all, thanks to you, Captain Blundell,' replied Alex.

'You must have been a bit cramped, a family sharing a cabin meant for me.'

'We were most comfortable, and canna thank thee enough,' said Maggie, her eyes damp with gratitude. 'It was most kind of thee to let us have your cabin.'

'It was my pleasure.' Captain Blundell gave a slight bow. 'And it was an honour to have a lady aboard.' He took Maggie's proffered hand. 'May your life here be good.'

'Thank thee. If ever thee comes to New Bedford again, come to see us.'

'I will that, Ma'am.' The captain smiled at the twins standing quietly by their mother's side. 'Goodbye, you two. Be good to your mother and father.'

''Bye, sir,' they said meekly.

Captain Blundell chuckled, knowing full well the mischief the twins could get up to. 'Goodbye, Alex, and may all the luck you deserve go with you.' He held out his hand which Alex took in a warm and grateful grip.

'Thank thee for everything. You've been most kind and we'll never forget thee.'

The captain glanced ashore. 'I believe you have a note from Miss Lydia for Joseph Spence? That's him, talking to three ladies. Medium-built man, see him? Fawn trousers, frock coat, with the cane walking stick?'

Alex's eyes flicked across the people on the quay and settled on the man indicated by Captain Blundell. 'Got him. Thanks. I'll catch him now.'

Making their last goodbyes to the captain and his crew, and with well wishes ringing in their ears, the Frasers hurried down the gangplank. Curious glances were cast in their direction as they wove their way between the knots of people to the man indicated by Captain Blundell. It was unusual to see passengers dropped by a whaleship and an English one at that.

Nearing the group, Alex paused and spoke quietly to Maggie. 'Wait here a moment with the children.' He set down the bag he was carrying and, as Maggie ushered the twins to her, fished the envelope from his pocket and tentatively approached the group.

Not wanting to interrupt what appeared to be a pleasant conversation until an opportune moment arose, he hesitated a few feet from them. He judged Joseph Spence to be in his late forties, a man with a straight upright bearing, with a certain personal pride and dignity without being overbearing. He had a kindly face, gentle and understanding, and beneath the light brown brows his eyes were alight with life and interest in everything around him. At this moment they were paying particular attention to his companions but Alex knew that he was conscious of all the activity of the quay.

A moment later he glanced sideways and his eyes met Alex's. They looked away. Then, aware that the stranger was still looking at him, darted back.

'Good day.' His voice was soft with a Shetland lilt that was music to Alex's ears. 'You wanted me?'

'Aye, sir. I'm sorry to interrupt but I've a note for thee.'

Joseph's eyes lit up. 'A Shetlander? Can't mistake that accent.'

Alex smiled. 'Takes one to know one.'

'Then, well met.' Joseph extended his hand and the two men exchanged a warm handshake. He turned to the three ladies. 'Excuse me.' His voice filled with apology. 'A fellow countryman. I must have a word.'

The ladies made their pleasant goodbyes and moved away, exchanging gossip as they went.

'Now,' said Joseph, turning his attention back to Alex, 'the letter? You've just come ashore from the whaler. Is that your family?'

'Aye.'

'Bring them over.'

Alex turned and signalled to Maggie.

'I'm Alex Fraser. This is my wife Maggie and our twins Alan and Fiona.'

'I'm pleased to know you, Ma'am. And you two.' He doffed his hat to Maggie and beamed at the twins.

'And thee, sir.' Maggie bobbed him a little curtsey.

'Now what's all this?' said Joseph, taking the letter from Alex.

'Miss Lydia Hartley sends her greetings and said I should contact thee when we reached New Bedford,' explained Alex.

'Lydia! Ah, you ken Lydia? Fine woman. Good business head on her shoulders.'

'We only knew her a few days,' returned Alex.

'She was so kind to us,' put in Maggie.

'That's Lydia. How's her father?'

'Reasonably well, but I understand he's failed a bit these last six months,' said Maggie.

'Leaves Miss Lydia to look after the business,' said Alex.

Joseph had slit the envelope open and extracted a sheet of paper as he was talking. 'Excuse me,' he said politely and proceeded to read the letter. He looked up. 'Lydia says you've been a mate on English whaleships and asks if I can see you settled in New Bedford with a job. She speaks highly of you, even though you say you've only known her a few days. Someone who has a good opinion of you must have talked to her.'

'Captain Fernley.'

'David Fernley?'

'Aye. Know him?'

'My last voyage before coming to America was with him. Sailed a couple of times with Seth Thoresby. Grand man. Couldn't learn with anyone better. What news of him?'

'Lost in the Arctic. Boat towed by a whale through the fog. He was never seen again.'

Joseph shook his head sadly. He looked back at the letter. 'Well, let's see what we can do. After all, I expect Lydia's sent that whaler out of its way to drop you here. It'll be on its way to the South Atlantic or more probably the Pacific.'

Throughout the conversation Joseph had been making his own assessment of Alex. He liked what he saw. Alex's craggy face was open and friendly and there was determination about the set of his jaw, a readiness to accept any challenge. In his little asides to his family, as they were talking, Joseph read a deep devotion to his wife and children. There must have been a very special reason why Lydia had diverted one of her whaleships from its course to bring Alex and his family to New Bedford, but he would not pry. He preferred to make his own judgement and at this moment he liked what he saw.

'Right, the best thing will be for you to come home with me. Then in the next few days we'll get you fixed up with a house – I have some property and we can come to some arrangement.'

Alex and Maggie exchanged glances of disbelief. This couldn't be happening to them. Their luck must run out.

'Sir, I'm just overwhelmed,' cried Maggie. 'I never expected to find such kindness.' Tears welled in her eyes. She bit her lip, holding them back.

'Think nothing of it. One Shetlander helping another.' Joseph glanced at Alex. 'See yon two square-riggers? They're mine. The *Lunna* and the *Fetlar*.'

'Ah, a touch of Shetland in those names,' smiled Alex.

'Aye. I was born on Fetlar but we moved to Mainland, to Lunna,' Joseph explained. 'They've been in the Arctic. I have another, the *St Magnus*, on its way to the Pacific. First time I've sent a vessel there, but with the *Rebecca*, belonging to Jeremiah Whelden, returning from a two-year voyage to the Pacific and reporting plenty of whales, I thought I'd send the *St Magnus*.'

'Three ships. Thee must be the leading shipowner in New Bedford?' observed Alex.

'No.' Joseph shook his head. 'Jeremiah Whelden is. Very shrewd businessman and seems to be able to raise the capital whenever he wants it. Has connections in Boston. However, back to the *Lunna* and the *Fetlar*. They'll be sailing to the Arctic next season. I'll be needing a mate on the *Lunna*. Like the job, Alex?'

'What! Thee'll not be asking me again.' He could hardly contain himself at this good fortune.

'Right, I'll sign you on right away, then you can oversee the repairs to her. She had some trouble in the ice.' Joseph felt pleased with himself. He had brought joy, security and comfort to strangers in a strange land, but if he was any judge of character he figured the Frasers would soon settle and reckoned that in Alex he had a whaler of sound judgement and expertise. Lydia would not have recommended him otherwise.

Chapter Twelve

'Land ahoy! Land ahoy!'

The call rang out crisp and clear from the main mast-head where the captain of the *Good Intent*, knowing that they should soon sight land, had placed a lookout.

The cry brought relief to the crew, anxious to be rid of its cargo of diseased human beings. To George Hibbard, agent for the owners of the *Good Intent*, paid to see the emigrants to their new home, it brought relief that the voyage was nearly over but apprehension at the hostility he might have to face. But if he laid his plans right with the captain, he need fear no one.

The sighting sent excitement coursing through the hold. Land! The promise of a new life. The nightmare conditions would soon be at an end. They would have land, houses, food, fresh air and time to recuperate. Typhus had run rife. Over a hundred people had died. Every family had lost someone. Husbands had lost wives, wives had lost husbands, mothers and fathers had lost sons and daughters, children had lost parents and single men had passed away in loneliness.

The captain had let word filter through that none of those he had taken from the hold had survived. Beth broke the news gently to her mother and held back from her the fact that Will had still been alive when he was thrown overboard. Bab took the death of her husband stoically. She showed no emotion. It was as if she'd already known she would not see him again. From that moment Beth saw all the pride and self-esteem with which her mother had faced the harsh Shetland life slip from her. She showed no concern for her appearance and when the cry came from the masthead, showed only a mild interest.

Since the second week of the typhus epidemic, before it had really taken hold, the captain had allowed the emigrants to come on deck fifty at a time for half an hour. They had revelled in the clean fresh air and only reluctantly returned to the nauseating hold. Yet the epidemic seemed to have drawn them together in a common need for comfort. Thieving and squabbling stopped, efforts were made to improve their conditions, but it was difficult in such a cramped space which continually bore the marks of sickness and death.

Eager to see the new land, the emigrants in the hold who were strong enough to do so swarmed up the gangway to join the fifty already on deck.

The captain's immediate reaction was to drive them back but, realising he would have a near riot on his hands, he relented. He would allow them ten minutes.

'Come on, Ma,' Beth urged her mother.

'Nae, lass, I canna be bothered. Thee gan.' Bab's voice was weak, showing no enthusiasm. Seeing Beth hesitate, she added, 'Away w' thee.'

Beth pulled her tattered shawl around her shoulders and with a 'Shan't be long', joined the throng pushing up the gangway.

The sharp, cold air bit tightly at the lungs but Beth breathed deeply, relishing the sensation. It was good to be in the open. The hold was a sickening prison to a soul who had loved the freedom and spaces of Shetland.

The ship ran before a fresh breeze and swayed gently with the regular motion of the sea. Beth had thought she had conquered the nausea it brought but two weeks ago it had returned and affected her every morning when she woke up.

Now sickness was far from her thoughts as she strained to see land. The day was fine, the air clear, and the steep headlands of Cape Breton Island beckoned. Murmurs of excitement swept through the emigrants while in their hearts they regretted that their loved ones were not here to share their joy at reaching a new home.

Ten minutes and the captain ordered the emigrants back to the hold to take their turn in coming on deck at the appointed times.

The *Good Intent* ran with the island coast in sight, passing the headlands of a huge bay which separated Cape Breton Island from Nova Scotia. Beth was on deck drinking in the sights of her new homeland. The low-lying coast climbed gently to tree-covered hills, ablaze with autumn colours. The tranquil beauty seemed to spread to the water for the ship was now running on a sea as smooth as polished glass, its greys and blues mixed with the warm glow of the setting sun. She was overwhelmed by the beauty and longed to stay on deck when the fifty emigrants were ushered back to the hold.

A short while later they sensed the ship slowing until finally they heard the anchor drop. No one came to them. They waited and saw, through the hatch which had been left open, the light fade from the sky. As it darkened a myriad of stars pricked the heavens. They had one more night to spend in this unsavoury hold but no one cared. They had put up with it for nearly eleven weeks, could tolerate it for another night when the morning would bring a new life of comfort and plenty.

Someone began to sing softly, a lament for Shetland, yet it seemed to be casting off the old life to herald in a new one. The lilt spread through the hold as other voices joined in and one song merged with the next.

George Hibbard paused on his way to the captain's cabin. He stood by the rail and listened. The sound drifted on the still night air, rose and fell. Then one voice, female and crystal clear, rose gently above all the others as they settled to a low accompanying hum. Hibbard gazed across the water, shimmering in the moonlight, to the dark silhouette of the landscape. For a brief moment the beauty touched his heart but he shook off the sentimental pit he might fall into and continued on his way.

His knock on the captain's door was greeted by a gruff: 'Come in.'

The captain nodded when he saw Hibbard. 'Sit down.' He indicated a chair beside the small table at which he was sitting. He pushed a bottle of whisky and a glass towards Hibbard. 'Thought you'd be coming.'

Hibbard acknowledged the captain's gesture and poured himself some whisky. He raised his glass. 'Here's to tomorrow.'

The captain grunted, drained his glass and poured himself another measure. 'We'll move 'em out an hour after first light.'

Hibbard nodded. 'I'll see the spades and shovels ashore first so it looks as if we're organised for them. Then we'll get 'em all ashore and I'll come back to the ship saying I've forgotten the plans of their settlement. You be ready to sail once I'm on board.'

'Right.' The captain took another drink. The sound of the singing drifted through the ship. He gave a half laugh of derision. 'Poor gullible devils.'

Beth was awake early the next morning. She swung out of the so-called bed gently so as not to waken her mother. The feeling of nausea swept over her. She sat still on the edge of the board. Her lips tightened in annoyance. The ship rocked only gently. She had experienced worse than this in mid-Atlantic and felt nothing. Maybe it was just the combination of movement and excitement. She'd be better for some air. She tiptoed quietly to the gangway and stepped carefully upwards, thankful that the hatch had not been lowered during the night.

She slid to the rail and crouched behind a heap of ropes.

Light was moving in the eastern sky and as it spread she saw they were anchored in a cove shrouded in mist. As the sun came slowly above the horizon to lighten the landscape the mist eddied and rose with an ethereal, beckoning swirl to reveal a low, rocky shoreline dotted with about thirty wooden houses. The mist, gentled and teased by the sun, gave way and unveiled meadows behind the houses, rising gently to the tree-covered slopes of low hills. Along the shoreline the trees came almost to the water's edge presenting a thick and impenetrable aspect. A little way beyond the ship the cove widened into three small bays each fed by a small river.

'Beautiful,' whispered Beth to herself as she contrasted it with the harsh beauty of the Shetland landscape. She could be happy here once they got settled in the house they had been promised. She wondered if it was any of those she could see. She scanned them again and was surprised to see people begin to emerge from them and come to the shore to stand staring at the ship. She had expected the houses to be empty, ready for the emigrants to occupy. Maybe these were the agency's workers who had built the dwellings for the new arrivals.

Movement further along the deck drew her attention and she crouched lower behind her cover and watched spades, shovels, axes, saws, barrels of nails being loaded into two boats while a third was filled with casks which she judged would be the promised food supplies.

When the three boats were ready the order was given to pull away. Beth watched as they drew away from the ship expecting them to head for the houses but, to her surprise, they were steered towards the inlet farthest from the settlement. The goods were unloaded on the rocky shore and the boats directed back to the ship. Beth's heart sank. There were no homes ready for them, they were going to have to build their own. The task was enormous; there were a hundred and fifty people to house and winter was not far away. Maybe she was wrong, maybe there was somewhere ready for them. The agent would know, he would have everything in hand. In spite of easing her worries she still had a nagging feeling that all was not well. But right now she had better get back to the hold before she was discovered. She chose her opportunity carefully, when the attention of those sailors on deck was directed to their companions pulling alongside.

'Get 'em up!' The order was instantly obeyed by two sailors who came to the top of the gangway leading to the hold.

Not wishing to expose themselves to the stench of the abyss they yelled down, 'Up here, and don't rush. You're all going ashore. We'll take forty at a time.'

A surge of joy that at last they were going to their promised land lifted the gloom and depression which had been held by the wooden sides of the hold for the last eleven weeks. As eager as everyone was to feel their feet on solid land, to breathe untainted air, the emigrants began their evacuation in an orderly manner. The weak, the frail and the dying were helped by those who had been fortunate enough to keep some measure of strength and had escaped the dreaded typhus.

Supervised by George Hibbard, keeping a tally in case questions were asked later, and cajoled by the sailors, the emigrants scrambled down the rope ladders to the waiting boats. Eager to get a glimpse of their new homes, their eyes automatically turned to the wooden houses dotting the shore, but bewilderment and a strange feeling of foreboding filled them as they were rowed in the opposite direction. After the initial surprise most took solace in the fact that they were going ashore and that the agent no doubt had everything in hand.

Beth and her mother were in the second forty to be ordered into the boats. Though Bab was frail and weak from malnourishment and the shock of losing Will, she mustered the strength to scramble down to the waiting boat. Once ashore Beth helped her to a flat rock and both women sank down with relief that the constant motion of the ship was left behind. Maybe now, thought Beth, the sickness will stop.

They watched the rest of the emigrants being brought from the ship. Relatives or friends helped those too weak or too sick to help themselves. Around them people waited like lost sheep wondering where to go, what was to happen and what to do. They lacked someone to direct them and waited patiently for George Hibbard. The agent would answer all their queries and direct them to their houses and acres of farmland. But where? The sea was on one side and inland there was nothing but dense forest.

Hibbard came in the last boat. Once it was cleared he stood in the bow as emigrants shuffled nearer to catch the words they longed to hear.

'Well, here you are. A new land, a new life for all of you. I'm sure your courage in crossing those dreaded seas will be rewarded.' His words came clear but told them nothing.

'Where are the houses we were promised?' someone shouted.

'Ah, something has gone wrong. Those people you saw at the settlement were supposed to have them ready but they haven't done so. You'll have to build them yourselves – there's plenty of timber.'

A murmur of dismay ran through the crowd. Their hopes sank. Houses for nearly one hundred and fifty people – possibly ninety dwellings would be needed. The ground would have to be cleared, the timber cut and shaped, yet many of the able-bodied men were weak from the crossing. They needed time to recuperate in order to carry out the task before the winter set in.

'We were told there would be farmland,' yelled another.

'Aye.' Agreement rumbled through the crowd.

'And so there will be when you clear the forest,' answered Hibbard. He sensed the surge of anger in the people who faced him. 'But wait, you need to have your allocation of land made to you. I have the maps here.' He made a pretence of searching the bottom of the boat then he straightened. 'Seems I've left them aboard the *Good Intent*. I'll have to go back for them.' With that he turned and gestured to the sailors. Immediately they shoved off and started to row towards the ship.

For a few moments the emigrants stood in silence watching the boat move further from the shore. To some it still held hope, the promise of an allocation of land; to others it presaged a feeling of doom. There were no houses, no land to farm. Was there really a section of land for each family or had they been duped by promises which no one had ever had any intention of fulfilling? They started to give vent to their feelings and soon their words were rising in an angry swell. Their shouts across the water slowly died to a muted silence as the boat rowed on.

They watched as it drew alongside the vessel. They saw Hibbard go on board and stared in disbelief and horror as the boat was hauled to its davits. Sails were unfurled, caught the breeze, and the *Good Intent* moved slowly out of the cove. She gained speed as she met the waters of the strait and was lost to sight, hidden by the land beyond the cove.

Emptiness. All connection with the outside world gone. Helpless. Many sat down and wept, while others, dejected, sat and stared vacantly as depression swept over them. No one seemed to know what to do.

A movement on the water caught someone's attention. 'Canoe!' The word jerked many out of their stupor to see a vessel, propelled by three men, skimming across the steely waters of the cove.

Some of the emigrants moved closer as the canoe drew nearer. They waited in eager anticipation for they gained a glimmer of hope from the sight of men they judged to be from the settlement they had seen.

One final plunge of the paddles and the canoe slid to a halt on the small beach. The man in the front scrambled out and held the canoe steady while the one who had occupied the centre stepped out. The third man, who remained seated, laid his paddle in the bottom of the canoe, picked up a musket and set it across his knees. His actions were deliberate, meant to be seen.

All were dressed in well-made buckskins, two wore beaver hats, but the man who stepped ashore was bare-headed. He was tall and held himself upright, carrying an air of authority, the presence of a leader. He was well-built and, though his jacket hung loosely on him, there was still the impression of muscular strength. His rugged, chiselled features were weather-browned, which added to his attraction. He was a man to be noticed and one to take notice of. His eyes swept the newcomers.

'Who's your leader?' His voice boomed with an accent strange to the Shetlanders.

No one answered. No one stepped forward.

'Leaderless.' There was a touch of contempt in his voice. His eyes moved across the men nearest to him and rested on one. 'You speak for them. What's your name?'

The young man hesitated and then as some of his companions pushed him stumbled a couple of yards forward. He straightened and met the man's penetrating gaze. 'Er.' He hesitated then took a grip on himself. 'Tom Stubbs.'

'Right, Tom. I'm Ed Lucas.' The man ran his fingers through his thick black hair which came to the nape of his neck. 'Now where's thee from?'

'Shetland.'

'Shetland?'

'Aye. Islands off the north of Scotland.'

'And where is thee going?'

223

Bewildered, Tom stammered: 'Er . . . er . . . nowhere.'

'Nowhere? What brought thee here to Pictou?'

'We were promised passage, farmland, and houses which thee was supposed to build.'

'Us?' Ed's eyes widened in surprise.

'Aye, that's what the agent told us.'

'Oh, yes. And now he's gone with the ship, leaving thee with nothing but a few tools and promises he never had any intention of keeping.'

Mutterings and murmurings swept through the emigrants within earshot and they passed the word on until all knew they had been duped.

'Heard of it before,' Ed went on. 'You're left here to fend for yourselves with the few tools and the meagre food he's left you.'

'But what are we to do?' asked Tom. 'Can't thee help us? We've sick and dying folk back here.' He gestured and glanced behind him. When he turned to face Lucas again he knew he had made a mistake for the friendliness on Ed's face had become a mask of wariness and suspicion with a touch of hostility.

'Dying? Of what?' he demanded. 'Typhus? That's what generally comes with the ships.'

It was no use denying it. Tom knew that it only needed a cursory glance to reveal the worst. He nodded and then made his appeal. 'If we don't get help, if we don't get some decent food after what we suffered on board that ship, we'll perish. Few will survive.'

For a moment there was sympathy in Ed's eyes but harshness, tempered only slightly, was in his voice. He knew he could not give way. He must be firm. He owed that to the people of his settlement, the people who looked upon him as their leader, having appointed him before they left Philadelphia for a new life in Nova Scotia six years previously. 'There is very little we can do. We don't want you in our settlement, not with the typhus, not even near it.'

'Hast thee no compassion for the dying?' The yell from somewhere in the crowd brought hostile murmurings.

'Of course I have,' Ed shouted, an angry tone to his reply. 'But I've a greater duty to my own kind, the living who braved a new land and won. And it is they who get my loyalty first. You should have made sure what you were getting into before you set sail.'

Tom could sense the growing antagonism behind him. He knew it would take little to set the emigrants surging forward in an attempt to overwhelm these men. They had suffered on the voyage, they had lost loved ones, and now they found themselves stranded in a strange land instead of moving into houses with land to farm as they had been promised way back in Shetland. But he knew they would not stand a chance. These men were armed. Hadn't the man in the boat swung his musket into a more threatening position? Hadn't Lucas his hand on the hilt of his hunting knife, ready to draw it at the first sign of an attack? These three men could wreak havoc among the undernourished emigrants before they were overwhelmed. And even if the emigrants could win, they would suffer a bloody and fatal revenge at the hands of the other settlers.

'All right.' Tom raised his voice so that all could hear. They had shoved him into leadership so they must back his action and to do that they must hear what he had to say. 'Tell us what to do. Thee's had experience of this country. We'll listen. And we promise to make no move towards your settlement. We mean thee no harm.'

Lucas hesitated a moment. His alert eyes swept over the crowd. He sensed some of the hostility dampened by Tom's words. He liked the look of this young man whom he judged might from this moment take over some form of leadership. He looked to have survived the voyage better than most of the others and Ed judged that to be because he was supremely fit when the voyage started. He was tall, wiry, but there was a deep strength within him. His light brown hair was unruly but it added a certain charm to his long thin features in which deep-set brown eyes burned with a spirited fire.

'Right. Your first problem is tonight. You need some sort of shelter. The nights come in cold. Organise yourselves into groups and make what shelter you can from the branches of trees and whatever else you can find. Light fires for cooking and warmth. See what tools and food you have been left. Decide if there are any essentials you need to help you and when I come back you can tell me and I'll see what can be done.'

'Should we make a start on clearing the ground for houses?' Tom asked.

'Not yet, you'll have plenty on to see to your needs for tonight. Make a start and I'll be back before long.' He turned and climbed into the canoe.

The three back-paddled, taking it into deeper water. They deftly turned it and sped swiftly away from the shore. Tom watched them for a few moments, admiring their skill, and was curious as to why they were not heading for the settlement.

Then he swung round quickly. 'All right,' he yelled. 'Thee pushed me forward. I take it thee wants me to go on acting as leader?'

'Aye.' Agreement came readily from all quarters. No one else wanted the responsibility.

'Thee did well, lad.'

'Good idea to get his advice.'

'We needed his help.'

Tom was pleased with the praise which came his way. 'All right, I'll do it. But once anybody steps out of line or disagrees with my actions that's it. Thee can all fend for thyselves.' He paused and glanced round. 'Jim Rogers, Kirk Grant, John McCabe – I want thee three as my seconds in command.' The three men pushed forward to stand beside him. They were three whom Tom had noticed on the voyage were ever ready to help others and, because they were well organised within their own groups of family and friends, had survived the voyage better than most. 'I think the first thing thee three can do is to organise everyone into groups and oversee their preparations for shelter for the night. Martin Hamilton, will thee break open the barrels containing the food? Beth Robinson, get three helpers to sort out and allocate supplies.'

Beth waved her acknowledgement of the order and turned to her mother whom she had helped into a comfortable position propped with her back against a tree. They had waited patiently through all that had gone on. The utter despair they experienced when they saw the ship sail had been lifted, if only a little. Beth recognised that her mother was suffering from malnutrition for she had given up her portion of food to try to strengthen her husband and when he was taken from them her worry took away her appetite. Beth had watched her get weaker and weaker, not knowing how to cope. Now she feared her mother would not survive many nights in the open.

Beth quickly got three helpers and hurried after Martin Hamilton who picked up an axe from the tools which had been brought ashore and which were being allocated by Jim Rogers as soon as the working groups were organised.

Martin swung his axe at the first barrel and as soon as the top was split he moved on to the next. The four women wrenched at the shattered wood only to stagger back from the barrel with faces screwed up at the revolting smell which rose from the contents. They left it and went to the next where Martin was already shaking his head. The stench of putrefying flesh was overwhelming. It was the same with every barrel he split; meat and bread had rotted beyond all redemption. He called for helpers and the nauseating barrels were removed to be buried well away from the emigrants.

Activity went on apace. The fact that they now had a

leader who was organising them seemed to have put some life back into them. But even in the midst of activity there was death as four more succumbed to the typhus. The dead had to be buried. There was no time for ceremony. Graves were dug quickly, the bodies lowered into the ground and earth flung on top. There was time for no more. The living had to be cared for.

The crack of a musket shot brought a sudden silence to the scene. Everyone stopped, looking askance at his neighbour. Another crash shattered the stillness. Enemies? Marauders? Apprehension filled the emigrants. Were they all to be slaughtered? Shot down with no means of defending themselves? The silence seemed to hold an air of foreboding. The forest held an unseen menace. This was alien land.

Tom perceived the anxiety among everyone but there was no point in just waiting. Those shots were a long way off. Whoever fired them might not come their way. Better for all to be active and occupy their minds. 'Come on, we have work to do. We must be ready for night.'

His shout broke everyone's dismay and they quickly resumed their tasks. Tom resolved to ask Ed Lucas if he had any muskets to sell, but a more pressing need right at this moment was food. They could probably find some berries but they needed more sustenance than that.

It was a problem which was still worrying him an hour later when his attention was drawn to a canoe heading towards them from the direction taken by Ed Lucas and his companions.

As Tom watched he was joined by Jim Rogers.

'Said he'd be back, and he's as good as his word,' commented Jim.

'Aye. Wonder if he'll be able to tell us anything about those shots?' said Tom.

He received his answer before the canoe reached the shore for he saw two dead deer slung across the canoe.

As it ran aground the three men were quickly out of it and hauling the carcasses ashore.

'They might help you,' said Ed.

'Thanks,' replied Tom. 'We're grateful. The food we were left is all rotten. We've had to bury it.'

'Not surprised,' commented Ed. 'I'm going back to the settlement. I'll see what bread I can collect and send it over.'

Word about the fresh meat had spread quickly among the emigrants, most of whom left their work in the excitement of the prospect of some real food. As they flocked around the deer, calling out their thanks, Ed and his two companions, not wanting any close contact with the newcomers, got back into the canoe and shoved it away from the shore. They held it steady while Ed called out: 'Tom, we can't do much more. You'll have to fend for yourselves from now on. There are too many of you to stay here. There are other suitable places along the coast. You can reach most of them on foot if you follow the shoreline carefully. We'll let you have three canoes – you'll soon get used to handling them. Use them as you will. Transport your goods or move families to locations further away. But we can do no more.'

'That's kind of thee,' called Tom. 'We'll always be in thy debt.'

Ed waved his hand dismissively. 'Best of luck.'

The canoe sped away.

Two hours later four canoes, each propelled by one man, carried bread to the grateful emigrants. Twenty loaves were brought ashore together with four fishing lines.

One of the men eyed Tom as he was about to step into the canoe which was to take the four of them back to the settlement. 'Don't take Ed's kindness to mean you're welcome in our settlement. You're not.' He made his meaning clear by emphasising the last two words. 'We want none of your typhus.' With that he was into the canoe which was turned and driven away by strong strokes.

Tom watched it ripple over the still water. It seemed as if all contact with the outside world had been severed. They were alone in a strange land in which he knew they would feel the hostility of nature unless they could tame it, and that would be no easy task with their limited resources.

By nightfall all had some sort of crude shelter even though most of them were merely woven from branches. All had had some food, a piece of meat and a slice of bread, thanks to careful allocation by Beth and her three helpers.

Dawn broke silently over the forest night and spread its light across the water but as emigrants rose, shivering after the chill of the night, the promise of a fine day was not fulfilled. Dark clouds rolled up, thickened and sent down a steady stream of rain. Families huddled together, trying to find some warmth in personal contact; others, seeking better shelter, penetrated the forest.

Beth had woken to find her mother shivering with the cold, and however hard she pressed her body close to Bab's could not stop the shaking. Her voice was feeble, her eyes lifeless, and whenever Beth could make out the croak which rattled from her mother's throat she knew she was calling for Will. The rain sent a new chill through her and, though Beth did her best to shield her with more branches, she could not prevent the steady downpour reaching the emaciated body.

Beth knew she was fighting a losing battle but she tried for two hours. When the shaking stopped she knew she had lost. Silent tears streaming down her cheeks, she stared at the silent form. She had never felt more lonely in her life.

It was then that she experienced the stirring in her body and realised that the sickness which had returned to her each morning on board ship had nothing to do with seasickness.

Chapter Thirteen

The *Hind* slipped into the centre of the Thames, caught the breeze and headed for the estuary. David looked back. He could still make out the lone figure standing on the end of the quay. Not knowing whether she could see him among the activity on the deck, he raised his hand in farewell. He saw an answering wave and felt a deep pleasure in the knowledge that he and Lydia had a special affinity even across such a distance.

It had been a good winter. He had waited a week longer than he intended at Cropton, enjoying the company of his family. He knew that young Kit was well cared for by his mother and father and that Betsy doted on the child, almost regarding him as her own. His prolonged stay meant that he spent little time in Whitby, but he was not concerned. Whitby had too many harsh memories among the good ones for him, and knowing the business was flourishing under the capable hands of Francis Chambers, he had no cause to linger.

His return to London had been greeted warmly by Lydia, who had planned to make his winter stay memorable. They had spent evenings with friends, visited the theatre, attended concerts or spent the time quietly with her father or by themselves. They walked on the heath or by the river and David grew to look forward to the time when there was no one else to share it with. He guessed that Lydia held a deep affection for him. Nothing was too much trouble to her and she made Christmas a special time to remember. But he found himself confused by his own feelings. He liked Lydia a lot, but because memories of Beth still haunted him, dared not show the feelings he thought she wanted to see. He did not want to hurt her and so he held a barrier between them, a barrier which puzzled Lydia for she sensed at times that David was falling in love with her.

But now, as she watched the *Hind* sail, without David having expressed his feelings, she wondered if she had been blinded by her own hopes. Had she fooled herself by imagining what she wanted to happen?

She brushed a tear from her eye and waved again. She saw the answer and watched the *Hind* pass beyond her sight. She prayed for a safe voyage and that on his return David would reveal his love for her.

The *Hind* ran before the wind. David crammed on sail to take advantage of it. The exhilaration of being at sea again swept through him. The space, the beckoning horizon, the air sharp in the lungs, the bow hissing through the white-flecked waves, the snap of the sails, the creak of the ropes – David drank them all in as if tasting the most exquisite wine.

The further north he went the more his mind focused on Beth. His vision of the carefree Shetland girl began to dominate thoughts which had dwelt on Lydia as he left the Thames. Her eyes, wild and bold, challenged him; her lips, breaking into a disarming smile, tempted and stirred a restlessness in him.

He urged the *Hind* on. The abbey, high on the cliffs at Whitby, held his attention. He saw a lone figure, then it was gone. A figment of the imagination? Wishful thinking of the days when a red shawl would have waved for him? Jenny? But he had lost her, even in death, to Adam. Memories flooded back. Jenny, Adam, Ruth. Once the four of them had been close. Why had he lost the happiness

233

he once had? He shuddered, banished the memories, ignored the call and pressed on northwards.

Ruth stood on the cliffs and watched the ship run before the wind. A whaler, probably from London. The Whitby ships had already sailed and she hoped for a successful voyage, with the *Mary Jane*, *The Lonely Wind* and the *Ruth* returning full so that Francis could milk off some of the profits and bring the day nearer when she could leave Whitby and be herself again. She longed to escape the confines of Rigg House. It was becoming a prison and more and more she sought release by venturing on the cliffs in spite of the risk of being seen. But she was careful, keeping a wary eye open and avoiding being within recognisable distance should anyone else appear on the cliffs. And all the time she planned the day she would leave.

As Jeremy Kemp, back as mate after his accident, brought the *Hind* into Bressay Sound, David strolled to the rail beside Andy.

'Well, Andy, like what thee sees?' he asked.

'Aye, Cap'n, I do. It's heaven after that overcrowded, smoke-filled, good-for-nothing city that I saw,' he replied, screwing up his nose at the thought of the filth and squalor he had seen in London. Though his life had been hard on Shetland, there he had had open spaces, the sea and clean air.

'Then I'd better leave thee here,' suggested David with a teasing twinkle in his eye.

Andy straightened and swung round with a shocked look on his face. 'Cap'n, thee would nae do that, would thee?' he gasped.

David kept a serious face. 'Well, does thee think thee deserves to go to the Arctic again?'

'Course I do, course I do,' rapped Andy forcefully.

Seeing the look on David's face he hastened to add, 'I'll do anything thee says, Cap'n, anything. But please take me with thee.'

David held his serious expression for a moment then broke into a broad smile as he laughed loudly. 'Of course I'll take thee. Thee's become an important member of the crew.'

Andy stared at him. 'Then thee wasn't serious about leaving me here?'

Still laughing, David shook his head. 'If thee's not keen to gan ashore then thee can act as ship's keeper while the crew have some leave.'

'Right, Cap'n.'

Once ashore David hurried away from the harbour and out beyond Lerwick. As he topped the hill overlooking Beth's bay he paused. His eyes swept the shore and beyond. No one. The land lay still; only sheep moved as they champed the grass, and the odd gull wheeled and glided on the breeze. It was a place without humans. Disappointment swelled in David's heart until he called himself a fool for expecting Beth to be there. Why should she? She had other things to do besides be there in her bay. But this had been the place he had shared with her and he had expected it to be just as he had left it, with Beth as part of the scene.

Maybe she was at home. He turned in the direction of the croft. When he swung off the hill and rounded its curve he pulled up short. The croft lay in ruins. It was as if someone was seeking to destroy it. He was stunned. He could not believe what he was seeing. Then the impact of the destruction hit him. Where was Beth? Where were her father and mother?

He started down the hill to the croft, half expecting to find an answer but really knowing it would be futile. What could a heap of stones tell him?

He walked into the ruin. Beth . . . this was her home. This was her bay. Her spirit was here. He wanted to reach out and grasp it, to bring her back, to hold her. But the stones lay silent, dumb witnesses to lives which had been lived within their walls. Where was she? Where had she gone? He must find out.

His heart sad, his mind full of questions, he started up the hill in the direction of Lerwick. Halfway up he stopped for one more look across the bay. It shimmered in the sunlight, the water gently lapping the sand as it had done the day when he and Beth had experienced their overwhelming passion. He glanced back at the ruined croft. A tension came over his body. Two men, sledgehammers across their shoulders, were heading for the croft. Their step was purposeful, as if they were on a predetermined errand. The final destruction of what had been a home? David hurried back down the hill.

Before he reached the remains of the croft the first strike thudded against the stone. It was as if the blows were aimed at Beth, driving her away from him. He quickened his step. The crash of metal against stone pounded in his mind and anger tightened his chest.

'Stop! Stop!' he yelled.

The two men glanced up and, seeing him, straightened, letting the hammer heads rest on the ground. They eyed him with a mixture of curiosity, belligerence and amusement.

'What the hell does thee think thee's doing?' panted David as he stopped in front of them.

'What's it t' thee?' demanded the taller of the two.

'This is someone's home,' he snapped, his eyes flashing angrily.

The two men exchanged amused glances. 'Hame?' The tall man laughed derisively while the other chuckled deep in his throat. 'Do it look like a hame?'

'It was.' David's voice was sharp. Their mockery wounded him. 'Where are the folk who lived here?'

'What's it t' thee, Sassenach?'

'I knew them.'

The men's eyes darted at each other in a shared thought. A salacious grin touched their lips as they looked back at David.

'After the lass, was thee?' sniggered the short stocky man. 'Aye, she'd be a nice one to . . .'

The insinuation behind his words was not lost on David. He moved so swiftly that the man did not have a chance to defend himself. David's broad fist struck with an accuracy which sent his opponent reeling into oblivion. He swung round. The tall man, taken aback by the speed of the attack, was only just recovering from his surprise but had started to swing his sledgehammer in reflex action. Alert to the danger, David hesitated a second and in that passage of time judged the swing of the lethal weapon. At that precise moment, when the man could not alter his swing, David dived at his legs. He took them round the knees and his momentum, together with that of the sledgehammer, threw the man off balance. He crashed to the ground and lost his grip on the hammer.

David released his hold, twisted round and was on top of him before he had time to recover. His knees held the man's arms to the ground and his hands closed around his throat. His grip tightened. The man gasped for breath and stared up into a face dark with fury; a face which showed a determination to do murder if he did not get what he wanted.

'Where are they?' snarled David. He jerked at the man's throat as if to shake an answer from it. 'Where?'

'Gone,' the man spluttered, wanting rid of this Englishman who had suddenly become a mad thing.

'Where?'

'Nova Scotia.'

'What?' David couldn't believe what he was hearing. Beth gone from Shetland? It couldn't be true. 'Thee's a liar.'

'Nae. Why should I lie?' The man's eyes were wide with terror as he felt the pressure increase on his throat. 'They left for Nova Scotia.'

'Why? Why?' David almost screamed the words as the enormity of the announcement struck to his heart. Beth gone. Never to see her again.

'A better life. Lots have left Shetland.' The words choked in the man's throat.

David eased his grip. The terrifying tension which had held him began to lift. He straightened, still glaring at the man who gulped hard to temper the fire in his throat as he rubbed at the bruised flesh.

David stood up, towering above the man who still cowered on the ground. 'Thee telling me the truth?'

'Aye. Aye.' The man was quick to reply with a nod of his head. He wanted no more truck with this maniac.

David hesitated a moment then turned sharply and strode away, his mind numb with the news that Beth had left Shetland. If she had thought anything at all about him she would have waited. He could see no reason for her not to. A better life? Couldn't she have seen that that was what he could have offered her? He could have taken her, aye and her parents, away from the cruel life of Shetland. There was no need to go thousands of miles away. If she had given him but one thought she would have known he would have taken care of her. But she hadn't. She had gone. There had been no love for him. Their time together had been but a convenient interlude to her. Her words, her declaration of love, had been a sham.

Unseeing, hardly knowing where he was going, David climbed the hill. He did not stop. He did not look back. The bay meant nothing to him now.

He went straight back to the *Hind*, wishing that he hadn't given the crew leave. Surprised to see the captain back so soon, Andy noted the anger and disillusion which showed on his face. He held back his welcome and watched David stride to his quarters without a word. Something had upset the captain and Andy knew it was wisest to avoid any contact.

David stayed in his cabin for the rest of the day and only appeared the following morning to get the ship under way. His commands were terse, little things annoyed him and the whole crew felt the lash of his tongue. They guessed something had gone wrong during their stay in Lerwick. They wondered, murmured among themselves, and hoped the captain would soon get over his mood.

It did not pass until Shetland had sunk below the horizon. The sight of the land brought a deep resentment to him and seeing the headland where Beth should have been standing tore at his heart, but at the same time strengthened a resolve he had made during the night, to shake the past from him and look only to the future. What had happened had happened. It could not be brought back. There was a life ahead of him.

The *Hind* dipped into the waves. The wind sang in the rigging. Ropes creaked, canvas strained, and the sea hissed along the woden walls of the ship. David braced himself to the motion. He breathed deep of the clear air. This was the life. This was his world. Soon he would see that mysterious, ethereal glow in the sky, and would feel the silence on which the sounds of the ship did not intrude but only emphasised. The call of the north would be answered and David would know he was home.

The crew were pleased at his mellowing mood and the atmosphere became more relaxed.

Three days out from Lerwick David ordered the boats to be prepared. The crew was divided into crews and assigned to a particular boat which they got ready for the whaling. The boat itself was examined for any faults. The oars were checked and all the whaling gear examined and stored ready for use. The harpoons and lances were double-checked for on them depended final success after a sighting. When the boats were ready they were slung into position for instant use once the cry of 'Tha she blows, tha she blows!' rang from the masthead.

David decided to head for Davis Strait. Reports from whalers who had been there last season were good and although it meant a longer voyage into seas he had not sailed before, he expected it could pay off with a full ship sooner than staying to the east side of Greenland where the whales had been less plentiful last year.

Throughout April and May the whaling was good. The crew of the *Hind* were delighted with David's judgement and called the Whitby man a born whaler, but they were not so sure as the days moved into June.

At that time, as the sun sought to bring daylight through an overcast sky above Nova Scotia, a baby cried.

'Beth, thee's got a grand baby girl!' came the excited announcement from Sara Rogers.

Though Beth's smile was wan there was pleasure in it too.

She would ever be grateful to Sara and her husband Jim for they had taken her under their care after her mother died and she was alone. Sara had noted the signs of pregnancy during the last days of the voyage and judged that the girl could not survive the hard Nova Scotia winter alone. That and the typhus, still amongst the emigrants, had taken their toll.

With little to keep them where they had landed, the emigrants had split up to follow their own inclinations. Some headed into the forest, others used the canoes to find a new existence, but the Rogers, John, Sara and their three children, together with another family, had walked the coast until they found a secluded bay around which they could establish their homes. It had been hard, building shelters, shaping implements to complement the axe and spade they had been allowed to bring with them. But they had survived, and with the spring a new life seemed to come upon them. They built a raft and traded with friendly Indians further along the coast, obtaining seeds to cultivate. With the threat of typhus now gone from their small community, they had contacted Ed Lucas again to purchase a musket and some shot.

Beth did all she could to help but as the months moved on she was relieved of many of her duties. Sara was determined that the girl should have a healthy baby.

Now she held the child up for Beth to see and as her eyes rested on the little one all the love in her heart went out to her daughter. She held out her arms and Sara laid the baby gently in them. Beth cradled the delicate creature with loving care. She looked adoringly at the placid face, and the tiny fingers clenched fist-like.

'Thee's a little darling, a little love,' she said, her voice scarcely above a whisper. 'My dear, dear Ailsa.'

Tears came to Beth's eyes. Her mind touched on David for a brief moment. If only thee had stayed. If only thee had loved me, we could have shared this joy together. But thee didn't and now thee'll never know thee has a daughter. Thee'll never know my beautiful Ailsa.

As June moved towards its close David grew restless. The whales had vanished. It was as if they had deserted Davis Strait, as if they knew the hunters were about. As he sailed the *Hind* through July and August, the few sightings which were made all came to nothing. The crew grew restless. The skill and luck seemed to have deserted the captain in whom they had had implicit faith. The reputation with which he had come to them from Whitby had been proved correct on the first voyage but now on his second from London things had gone wrong.

When he ordered the ship on to a northerly course there were murmurings among the crew for they knew it would take them north of Disco into unknown waters where the risks could be greater, especially as it was getting late in the season.

Two days later David was standing on the deck beside Jeremy Kemp. Changes of lookout on the main mast had brought no sightings. They had remained silent all day.

'They're out there somewhere, Jeremy. I smell them on the wind.'

Jeremy glanced doubtfully at his captain. He saw the expression of the hunter sensing his prey burn fiercely in the captain's eyes. He knew David was no longer standing beside him on the deck of the *Hind* but was far out in an open boat, riding the waves with harpoon poised to dart at the dark diving bulk which represented a fortune to them.

'They're there and I'm going to find them.' His eyes narrowed as if piercing the distance, hunting. The willing acceptance and enjoyment of the challenge, filled with a determination to succeed, burned in his face.

'Hadn't we better not venture too far north, Cap'n?' Jeremy, as mate, felt he had to inject a note of caution.

'Ice! Ice!' The cry rang clear on the sharp air. It seemed to back up the mate's words.

David cursed to himself. He couldn't turn back. He knew there were whales out there. Besides, there was the ever beckoning call of the north. How could he explain to Jeremy that it had intensified in the last twenty-four hours? It had cast its mystery around him even more strongly and lured him with promises of greater beauty. It was a call which could not be denied. He could not free himself of the beckoning enchantment. He could not turn round. And there were greater rewards to be taken in the whaling. He knew it.

He swung on to the bulwark and climbed the ratlines, paused when he saw the ice. He studied it for a few minutes and then returned to the deck. He saw the helmsman glance queryingly at him.

'Hold your course,' he ordered.

'Aye, aye, sir.'

He knew his decision would not be popular with the crew. One thing whalemen feared was ice.

'I'm going aloft, Jeremy. Hold her steady.'

'Aye, aye, sir.'

David, in spite of the bulk of his clothing and hands thickened by woollen gloves, climbed nimbly to the cross-trees at the head of the main-top-mast. With a smile of thanks and a friendly pat on the shoulder, he relieved the lookout of his duty.

The man needed no second bidding. He was thankful to be away from the bone-biting cold and the screaming wail of the wind.

David huddled into himself and tried to find a little more cover from his only protection, a piece of canvas tied to the head of the main-top-mast and the heel of the top-gallant-mast, extending only from the cap to the crosstrees. He narrowed his eyes against the wind and stared towards the ice.

The crowded collection of drift ice was well broken and, provided the conditions remained constant, the *Hind* would negotiate this barrier without too much trouble.

Throughout the next two hours he brought all his skill, born of experience with the Thoresbys, to watching the relative position of every floe and anticipating their movements. Every piece of information and command came loud and clear to Jeremy who instructed the helmsman. The *Hind* answered his touch readily and her strengthened bow pushed through the drift ice without serious damage.

David, weary with concentration and numb with cold, was beginning to think he had embarked on a foolhardy venture. Maybe there was no open water between this drift ice and the solid mass which stretched to the Pole and beyond. But he could not see that solid mass and felt the presence of whales. The *Hind* sailed on, nudging her way through the ice.

David's head jerked. He started, opening his eyes wide. He took a firmer grip on his feelings. He must not doze. It could prove fatal. He had better return to the deck and send someone else aloft. One more look. His eyes narrowed, searching the distance. They crossed a point, paused and returned. He trembled with excitement.

'Water! Open water!'

The excitement his shout had brought to the crew overflowed into shouts of jubilation and relief.

He remained at the main masthead, guiding the ship through the last few miles of ice. When she burst from it a great cheer went up from the crew.

David relaxed wearily and eased his chilled limbs on to the ratlines. He paused and glanced once more across the open water. The tension of excitement surged back into his body. Spout after spout rose in the far distance. White puff after white puff sprayed from the sea.

Whales! He had been right! He tried to count the spouts but they rose in such numbers that it was impossible. He had never seen so many. Whales were there for the taking. Before long the *Hind* would be a full ship homeward bound for London.

'There she blows! There she blows!'

'Whither away?' Jeremy's call came automatically. The crew were intoxicated with the news.

'Dead ahead,' shouted David and immediately scrambled to the deck. He sent a man aloft to keep a check on the whales and ordered the boats to be got ready.

Every man knew his duty and was quickly at his boat station, eager to get their quarry and be heading for home. When he judged the time right, David ordered all boats away. The hunt was on and every man strove at his appointed task to obtain a full ship in the shortest possible time, for there dwelt in the back of their minds that the ice which they had successfully negotiated could close and trap them.

Whales were hunted, harpooned, lanced and killed, towed back to the ship, flensed alongside, cut up on board and the blubber stowed in barrels below decks.

In early August the wind changed. It moved almost imperceptibly round to the northeast as if trying to sneak up on the whalemen without the alteration being noticed but it betrayed itself by the ice which it pushed before it.

'Ice!'

The yell which came from the lookout startled the crew of the *Hind*. Instead of the hoped-for shout which would take them in pursuit of the two whales they needed for a full ship this chilling cry brought fear clutching at their hearts.

'Whither away?'

'Larboard bow!'

Jeremy climbed the ratlines to check the situation.

'Fairly solid pack being driven south,' he reported to David.

'Any immediate danger?' he queried.

'No, but we'd better run for it. If that ice we came through is still to the south of us . . .' Jeremy's doubts were cast aside by the cry from the masthead.

'Tha she blows! Tha she blows!'

'Whither away?' David's voice was charged with excitement.

'Starboard beam!'

David and Jeremy ran to the rail and stared across the undulating sea.

'There!' cried Jeremy, pointing at four spouts which rose on the cold air but half a mile away.

'Away all boats,' yelled David.

The *Hind* burst into activity as men raced to do his bidding.

'The ice?' Jeremy threw his question curtly.

'Catch quick, flense fast, and we'll be away, a full ship.' David did not wait for the mate's comment. He raced for his boat which the crew was already lowering.

Though caution tugged at Jeremy, he could do nothing but follow the captain and, as he ran to his boat, he was caught up in the whirl of excitement. He was not one to shy away from danger but intuition told him to be gone from these remote regions before it was too late.

The boats were away. The men, buoyed up by hopes of filling the ship, pulled hard for the whales.

Two hours later they were back with two dead whales. Men scrambled on board, the bodies were manoeuvred alongside, flensers wielded their flensing knives and spades, ropes and tackle moaned and protested at the strain of the blubber. The whole activity was one of perpetual motion, with each man knowing what he should do and what was expected of him. All the while the lookout kept reporting on the position and movement of the ice.

As the first carcass was cast adrift and the flensers moved to the second whale, the dull slap of loose canvas rapped harshly on David's ears. He frowned, glanced upwards and cursed the feel of the freshening wind. It could drive the ice into a death-gripping vice.

'C'm on, c'm on,' he yelled, urging his flensers to greater speed. 'Get thy backs into it.' But they needed no urging. They had felt the wind strengthen and knew they had a race on their hands.

Razor-like blades flashed and cut with the dexterity born of experience. Blood spilled to join the unending heave of the sea. Pulleys squeaked, ropes groaned as blanket-pieces were hauled on to the deck to be cut up as quickly as possible in the need to beat the threatening ice.

'Ice!' The alarm in the lookout's voice sent every man's heart beating faster.

'Whither away?' David's shout carried through the rigging and slapping canvas.

'Larboard bow, larboard beam, starboard bow, starboard beam, moving fast.'

Cold fingers clutched at more than one heart aboard the *Hind*.

'All aboard! All aboard!' David's command cut through the cold air, bringing men scrambling from the whale and forcing straining muscles to heave the attendant boats aboard. When he saw that all was clear he ordered the half-flensed whale to be cast off.

Jeremy already had men racing aloft to unfurl sails to make every possible use of the wind, seeking its aid to escape from the ice which it was driving towards them.

The ship came on to a southerly heading with everyone on board hoping that the ice they had encountered on their way north was no longer there.

With every nerve taut, anxious for his crew and his ship, David was continually on the move. On the deck, up the rigging, surveying, estimating and ordering. The manoeuvring, as man tried to outwit the forces of nature which were determined to capture and destroy, went on all day. Nature never wearied but fatigue overtook men in whom anxiety gnawed.

'Ice, dead ahead!' The dreaded information froze men's minds.

'Hell!' Jeremy cursed.

'It will be if we don't find any lanes,' commented David grimly.

But there were none, not even a crack from which they could gather hope for escape. When the lookout reported that the ice to the east and west was joined to that in the south hearts sank. Though they still sailed in open water the ice behind was moving relentlessly south, diminishing their area of clear sea.

David paced the deck restlessly, his rugged face scored with lines. The fate of the ship and its crew rested on his judgements. He went aloft and studied the ice ahead. A decision made, he returned quickly to deck.

'Jeremy, I'm going to take the *Hind* into the pack ice!' he announced.

The mate was taken aback. 'But, Cap'n, the ship could break up.'

'Aye, she could, but from the look of the ice, I don't think she will. If we stay in open water the ice coming from the north could crush us when it meets the ice ahead of us, but drive her into the ice, get her well locked, and we might survive the pressure. Then we'll drift south with the ice with the chance that we might escape when it breaks up in warmer seas.'

Jeremy looked thoughtful, nodding slowly as he considered the captain's reasoning. Maybe he was right, maybe running into the ice gave them the best chance. He gave his agreement.

'Right then, muster all hands,' instructed David.

'Aye, aye, sir.'

In a matter of moments all the crew had gathered on deck and David told them quickly what he intended to do. The silence which greeted his word was oppressive. He felt hope draining from his men and realised the best thing was to keep them occupied.

'Harrison!'

'Aye, aye, sir.' The sailor, short, stocky, tough, pushed his way to the front.

'Take Fletcher, Thompson, Skelton and Freeman below decks. Get shoring timber, matting and tools into the bow. Be ready to plug any holes which may appear when we strike the ice.'

'Aye, aye, sir,' Harrison answered crisply. He sought out the other men and they hurried away to carry out their orders.

'The rest of thee get aloft and when the order comes, furl those sails faster than thee's furled 'em afore.'

The crew scurried away. Orders came precise and sharp as David manoeuvred the ship so that he could get the best possible run at the ice. The *Hind* plunged on using the strength of the wind.

David's eyes were everywhere, assessing distance and movement. He must get this right. There would be no second chance. He needed speed to penetrate the ice but the big spread of sail had to be furled before the impact, or the opposing forces at that moment could snap the masts like rotten wood.

His eyes narrowed, watching the ice come nearer. Nearer. His muscles twitched with the anxiety of making the right judgement and his hands were damp with sweat in spite of the cold.

'Hold her steady, helmsman!' He gave the order more as a relief from the tension which gripped him.

The *Hind* raced on.

David concentrated on the rapidly diminishing space between the ship and the ice.

Now!

'Furl the mainsail!' His shout rang loud and clear.

Men, precariously balanced on the footropes on the yards, worked with all speed. They must get the sails in before they struck the ice.

'Furl the fore course!'

The *Hind* slowed but still moved quickly with only the topsails using the wind.

Relieved that they had finished their job before the ship struck ice, men swarmed down the rigging, anxious to be away from the nightmare height on a heaving ship whose progress was about to be sharply impaired.

The *Hind* struck. She shuddered, then plunged on, breaking the ice with a loud crack. In spite of bracing themselves, many lost their hold, stumbled and staggered and fell.

Below decks Harrison and his men were ready for action, their eyes searching everywhere for a tell-tale trickle of water.

Ice crashed and scraped along the hull like a giant's scratching fingers. The *Hind* had driven a hundred yards into the ice. She was held firm in an upright position and already the frozen sea was closing in behind her. It would form a protective barrier when the crushing ice from the north reached them.

'She's held well.' David was jubilant and his delight rose even further when Harrison reported all well below decks. 'Let's hope the drift south is quick and we can be out before the weather turns sour.'

That hope was dashed when, thirty-six hours later, he estimated that they had drifted less than thirty miles and the wind was easing. The ice from the north closed in and the *Hind* was caught fast in a frozen desert. The wind ceased to blow, leaving an eerie silence in the oppressive wilderness which weighed heavily on men's minds.

David climbed to the crosstrees but his survey brought no comfort. There was no sign of a break in the ice; it was solid to the horizon.

His heart was heavy when he returned to the deck for the crew had gathered round the foot of the mast, their faces reflecting their eagerness and hopes for good news. He shook his head slowly as he faced them but already they had judged the worst from the grim set of his mouth and the dull light in his eyes. Lines of despondency etched the faces of weary men whose hopes had finally died. They faced a winter in the Arctic, something which no whaler had done before and survived.

Chapter Fourteen

Francis Chambers was on the quay ready to check the consignment of wine he had ordered from London for resale in Whitby when the *Capella* docked. He turned up the collar of his long coat to block the bitter wind which drove from the northeast though the day itself was bright. He would be glad when he had checked the cargo and could leave the unloading to the men he had hired.

But all thoughts of the cold and cargo were driven from his mind by the news which Captain Midgley imparted. The London whaler, the *Hind*, Captain David Fernley master, was missing.

Francis left one of the men in charge and lost no time in reaching Rigg House.

His arrival, unusual for him at this time in the morning, surprised Ruth. 'What brings you back so soon? Something wrong?' She was puzzled by his agitated excitement.

'Ruth, David's missing!' he burst out.

'What!'

'Captain Midgley's just brought the news from London.'

The momentary shock which had chilled Ruth vanished as the implication of his news dawned on her. With the rapid turning of her thoughts she knew that any feeling for David that she had occasionally suspected still lingered had gone, for uppermost in her mind was the fact that he was no longer a threat to their plans. There was now no chance of his scrutinising the figures, and with Ruben taking no interest in the business side of the company, it would be easy for Francis to hoodwink Jessica and Jenny.

'This is good news,' she cried. 'Let's push our plans forward and sell the ships when they've sailed for the Arctic next year.'

For a moment Francis was surprised by her immediate reaction. He had expected some sort of regret, but there was none. His own eyes were bright with greed. 'No. With David out of the way we can afford to wait until the following year. That will give us chance to milk the takings from another whaling voyage and two winter voyages for timber.'

'But, Francis, I want to be out of here! You've no idea what it's like to be cooped up in this house,' she protested.

'But you're comfortable here, you want for nothing, you . . .'

'Oh yes I do,' she broke in roughly as she began pacing across the room with a step which mirrored her irritation. 'I want freedom. This place is getting like a prison. I need to be able to move about.'

'Ruth.' Francis stepped in front of her, grasped her hands and pulled her firmly down beside him as he sat on the sofa. 'Please be patient. You'll get all the freedom you want. But don't you see that we now have a better opportunity to be really well placed when we leave this country? You'll want for nothing.'

Ruth understood the reasoning behind Francis's words but she was anxious to have this whole thing finished with, tired of being a recluse, and yet if Francis saw this as a greater opportunity to ruin the firm completely wasn't that what she'd always wanted?

Francis saw hesitation in her eyes and seized the opportunity. 'Don't you see? With the extra money we'll be in a far better position to enter the whaling trade when we go to America, and your revenge will be complete. Jenny and Jessica will be penniless.'

She could see Jenny, the girl who had ruined her life,

destitute and on the streets. Nothing could suit Ruth better. The hatred which burned deep within her blinded her to everything but that revenge. It was within her grasp and it would be complete and utter. Jenny in poverty while she sailed to America and a new life of luxury and good living. That extra money could, as Francis said, make a lot of difference.

'All right,' she agreed. 'We'll make it the season after next. Once the *Mary Jane*, *The Lonely Wind* and the *Ruth* sail to the Arctic in 1797, you sell them and we leave.'

By the time Francis returned to Whitby the news that David was missing in the Arctic had reached the office. Jessica was in tears, numb with horror that she would never again see the brother she loved so dearly. She had encouraged him in his dreams and ambitions to become a whaler in Whitby not only because she wished him every success but also because she had seen in him the means of her own escape from a farm life in Cropton. Though she had been happy at home in the love of her family, she had a restless spirit which needed to escape to another world. Now the brother who had helped her would never tread the streets of Whitby again. And she mourned for Kit, the son who would never know his father.

Jenny, shattered to the very core, tried to comfort Jessica, even though she herself wanted to let tears take all the hurt from her. The man she had so nearly devoted her life to, for whom she had always held a special regard and a place in her heart, would no longer sweep into her life like a fresh Arctic breeze.

Francis offered his commiserations and suggested that he see to everything for the rest of the day, longer if they preferred, while they went home.

'Jenny, is it worth carrying on?' asked Jessica as they crossed the bridge to the east side.

She noted the tone of hopelessness in her friend's voice

and knew she must be strong for them both. 'Of course it is,' she replied sharply. 'The firm is partly yours and mine and as such belongs to our families. It's our duty to them and to ourselves to carry on.'

'But it meant so much to Davey. It won't be the same without him being involved.' The words came hard in her misery.

'But it's because David loved it so much, worked so hard for it, that we should keep it going. It's what he would want us to do. We must do it for him.'

Jenny's forceful words cleared the doubt in Jessica's mind. 'I'm sorry, Jenny. Thee's right. David's memory is precious and should be preserved in the firm he worked so hard to create. All our children will have something to remember him by.' She paused a moment and then added with a tentative nod of hope, 'Thee doesn't think there's a chance that he might . . .'

'Don't, Jessica,' Jenny interrupted. 'Oh, I suppose there's always a chance but it's so late now. All the whaling ships would be back and any that aren't have either been lost or are caught in the ice – and no one has ever returned from a situation like that.' The words choked in her throat and she sought Jessica's hand for comfort.

The two friends walked on hand in hand in silence, each lost in her own thoughts, mourning the loss of a dear one far away in the Arctic.

Lydia's devastation grew deeper as the days passed until she had to admit to herself that David and the *Hind* must be presumed missing and there was little likelihood of her seeing him again. The man she loved had been taken from her before she had openly expressed that love. Oh, how she regretted shying away from doing so, regretted waiting for his past to release its grip. Maybe if she had told him how she felt she could have broken that hold. Now it was all too late. David would never return, would never walk into her life again. All the plans she had for this winter were now but shattered dreams.

Dominic tried to comfort her, wishing he could take away the hurt his daughter was suffering. For her part Lydia knew how keenly her father was feeling the loss and realised he hid his feelings for her sake.

This was a winter of desolation for her as each night she cried herself to sleep, recalling that the whaling captains she had questioned all shook their heads with grave doubt when she asked about the possible chances of surviving an Arctic winter.

The *Hind* was held fast. As far as the eye could see there was ice. Wearily David picked up his pen and wrote in the log:

September 10. There seems no likelihood of escaping the ice. There have been no favourable winds to break it up. The men are in despair and there is nothing I can do for them. I am helpless and blame myself for being obsessed with gaining a full ship.

September 30. Despair fills the ship. We face a lingering death from cold and starvation.

October 10. Food supplies are running low. Very strict rationing in force but there is the threat of scurvy.

October 25. Martin Webster died today. The cold is intense and there are storm clouds on the horizon.

October 30. The gales have been severe. The lashing wind seemed to drive into every nook and cranny. Ice piled up but the *Hind* is a stout ship.

November 24. Three deaths this week. Crew in the depths of despondency. They have grown weary of the tasks which I set them to keep them occupied.

December 2. We have dismantled the upper masts and yards for firewood for warmth and to melt ice for drinking.

December 10. The men are weak. Two have died during the night. The pressure of the ice comes with shrieks and groans as it grinds mass against mass. This is very eerie during the night and drove Seth Hardy to madness. He leapt overboard and was never seen again.

December 25, Christmas Day. Our thoughts are with our families and the sad time they must be having not knowing our fate. Killed two fulmar petrels. They go with the few potatoes we have left to make some soup – our Christmas dinner.

David wearied of the bleak record where there was nothing good to report; even the coming of the New Year promised no better future. The *Hind* had drifted a considerable distance south with the ice but the pack showed no signs of breaking up.

January 15. The thing I dreaded has struck. Scurvy! Three men are complaining of pain and tenderness in the gums which are swollen and bleed easily. Our lime juice is all but gone.

January 30. The cold is killing. Scurvy is killing. Lack of food is killing.

February 4. Four deaths from the scurvy.

As his sombre entries went on David also had his own thoughts to contend with. The feeling that he had let his crew down had to be fought with all his will or he would have gone out of his mind under the pressure of remorse. His thoughts turned to Beth and how she had left without a word, leaving no sign, no message. As the memory faded, together with the disappointment, so thoughts of Lydia loomed more and more in his mind and he began to see her as a loving, desirable woman. Had he been a fool to think that Beth had ever been more than a momentary passion? Wasn't Lydia the one who should have occupied his thoughts, his dreams of the future? Hadn't she a love of ships, of the whaling trade, just as he had? As he thought back to the time he had spent in London he cursed himself for resisting the feelings he sensed she had for him. And, though he knew the chances were very much against them, swore that if he did come out of this situation alive, he would make amends for the time he had lost.

The winter had been dreary but with a change in the weather in the last week in February, thoughts in Whitby turned to the sailing of the whaleships.

Francis saw to the preparations and Jessica and Jenny were content to let his experience take the lead. The readiness of the vessels themselves was overseen by their captains and all were ready to sail by the first week in March.

As he watched from the quay Francis smiled at his own thoughts. In a year's time he would be hastening to complete the sale of the ships and he and Ruth would turn their backs on Whitby for a new life in America.

On the cliffs, cautious that there was no one else nearby, Ruth watched the ships leave the harbour and take to the sea. Her thoughts too turned to a year ahead. Her instructions to Francis should go smoothly with no David to upset them, then she could shake off the confines of Rigg House. She would have a new name and life in a new land.

'Miss Lydia! Miss Lydia!' Billy's piercing cry resounded down the corridor as he burst through the door on his return to the offices of Hartley Shipping.

Astonished and alarmed by the sudden cries, Lydia was on her feet when he flung open the door to her office. Behind him, across the corridor, the three clerks jerked open their door to see what all the fuss was about. They normally tolerated Billy's exuberance but there was something different in the tone of his voice today.

'Miss Lydia,' he panted, 'the *Hind*'s been sighted!'

The clerks gasped at the news before Lydia seemed to take it in.

She stared disbelievingly at Billy for a moment. What cruel trick was this boy playing? 'Nonsense!' she rapped, 'the *Hind*'s been gone over a year. She's lost with all hands.'

'No, Miss, no,' he yelled. 'She's been seen entering the Thames.'

'But . . .' Lydia was bewildered. Dare she believe this news?

'It's right, Miss, it's right. I heard it from more than one.'

Her thoughts ran wildly. The *Hind* in the Thames? No, she daren't believe it. David back? This couldn't be true, yet it must be. If the *Hind* was back, he must be. Dare she hope that he had survived? As she tried to cope with this astounding news she was aware of Billy yelling again.

'It is true, Miss, believe me!'

His shrill voice pierced the fog of bewilderment. She started.

'Get Tomkins and the coach, quick!'

Billy needed no second bidding. Like a flash he was out of the office and running down the street as fast as his legs could carry him.

Lydia swept the shawl from the chair where she had laid it, twirled it round her shoulders, picked up her hat and placed it neatly on her head. As she hurried from her room the clerks scurried back to their desks, their tongues not letting up on the good news that Billy had brought.

As she rode to the dock, Lydia tried to compose herself. Her heart raced excitedly and she chided herself for feeling like a schoolgirl hurrying to meet her first love. But why shouldn't she? David was home. The love she had thought had died was here again. Then a more sombre thought worked its way into her mind. Men must have died in the long hard winter when food would be almost non-existent. David might have been one of them. She tried to shut out the possibility. She closed her eyes and prayed.

Reaching the quay she found the word of the sighting had brought people flocking to the water's side. Wives anxious for news of their husbands, mothers of sons, relatives of their loved ones, and those with no connections who were yet curious to see a ship given up for lost.

Then she was there, a ship back from the dead. The excitement turned away to silence and all eyes watched the return of a vessel flying a tattered flag at half-mast.

The silence took on a heavy air, crushing those on the quay with the realisation that the *Hind* was bringing her dead back home.

Lydia stared at her. This was not the *Hind* she remembered, only the shattered hulk of the fine, proud ship which had left London full of hope for a successful voyage. Her top masts had gone; only a remnant of torn canvas carried her towards the haven which her crew had longed for and had never expected to see again. Her sides were splintered, crushed and cracked by ice, spars were missing, rigging hung loose, all but two of her boats were gone. Yet even though she listed to port, there was something defiant about her. There was an aura of a battle won, yet in that victory, regret and sorrow that some of her crew had not survived.

Boats had gone alongside. Men scrambled aboard and hurried to take over from the living corpses at the wheel who would never have been able to berth the *Hind* without further damage.

She came nearer and nearer, watched in respectful silence. No one raised a voice in welcome but it was there in their silent respect. They were shocked by the sight on her deck. Fifteen canvas-covered bundles lay neatly side by side. Five figures sprawled propped against the rail, the only indication that they were living human beings the odd movement of a limb or turn of the head.

Lydia searched the deck with wild eyes. David? Where was he? Was he alive or was he one of those canvas-covered corpses?

The men who had gone aboard were in full command. The *Hind* scraped the quay, creaking her way to a final rest. Ropes were flung and eager hands grasped them to secure the ship to the berth. The plank was run out. Weakened men raised weary smiles for their well-wishers, still leaning against the rail. A narrow opening appeared in the crowd as whispered word went out that Miss Hartley was here.

Her face grave, body taut, she moved half in hope, half in fear. Her eyes searched as she crossed the plank. When she stepped on the desk a figure moved unsteadily towards her.

Lydia stopped, her anguished eyes searching for identification, seeking something which would bring relief to her tortured mind. The gaunt figure shuffled towards her. She could see he was making an effort to walk more briskly, to hold himself erect and achieve some dignity.

David? Could it be David? Her heart pounded. This man was so thin; his tattered clothes hung loosely on him. Hollowed cheeks sagged below his eyes and were lost in the matted growth of beard. His hair was thick, uncared for, and straggled to his shoulders. Lydia felt nausea rise within her. One of those covered figures must have struggled back to life?

She wanted to turn and run but was held transfixed. Oblivious to people buffeting against her as they rushed on board to seek an answer to their hopes, she watched the thin man's arms reach out. She did not hear the cries of joy or the wails of lament which greeted the *Hind* in her homecoming. Her gaze was held by the eyes of the ragged man coming nearer and nearer. In them she saw a spark of life. There was joy and thanksgiving at being home again, and a defiant triumph at cheating death, mingled with the brightness of being able to see a future. The man pulled his body even straighter. He grew tall and seemed to fill out. His smile drove all doubts from her mind.

'David!'

His eyes brightened and in them, surely, was the revelation of a true love.

Lydia's heart sang. There was no need for David to say a word. She knew he loved her just as she loved him. She stepped into his arms. She could feel the bones in the body which she held but there was love also as he responded to her embrace. In their embrace was the promise of a shared future. They needed no words to proclaim that they were destined to be man and wife.

Chapter Fifteen

For four anxious weeks Lydia nursed David. There were times early on when she thought she was going to lose him, but she saw sparks of defiance and determination flash occasionally in his eyes and did all she could to encourage them.

Lydia spent as much time as she could with him, arranging for daily reports on Hartley Shipping to be conveyed to her home by Silas Farnham, her chief clerk. Whenever it was imperative that she go to the office, she always arranged for someone to be in attendance on David. Her father, though unable to do much physically, was a great support for he recognised the deep love his daughter had for the Whitby man.

Anxious though she was to know what had happened in the Arctic and how David had come to realise his love for her, she did not press the matter for she knew the experiences must have been harrowing. In his oft-repeated nightmares she heard David blaming himself for what had happened. She knew she must be patient. He would tell her all in his own good time, when he judged it right.

That time came during the fourth week. When Lydia came into the room with a bowl of steaming soup and David asked what was to follow, her heart leapt with joy for this was the first time he had done so. His spirit was back, there was a new light in his eyes, the corner had been turned, he would soon be well again. She sat with him throughout the entire meal, pleased that he was relishing his food again. Only the occasional word was spoken, for she did not want to spoil his enjoyment. When he had finished he sank back on the pillows.

'That was delicious,' he said with a contented sigh.

'That's the first time you've really enjoyed anything,' said Lydia. 'I'm so glad.' She took the tray and placed it on the table. She turned back to the bed and started to straighten the clothes.

He watched her for a few moments then said, 'I'm sorry for what I did to the *Hind* and its crew.'

She looked at him and saw the self-reproach in his eyes. 'David, you've nothing to blame yourself for,' she said gently. 'You were unfortunate to get caught in the ice.'

'My fault. I was obsessed with getting a full ship. Somehow I knew there were whales further north and I let them entice me when I realised it could be dangerous.' He bit his lip and his voice faltered as he went on, 'I killed those men.'

Lydia dropped to her knees beside the bed. She took his hand in hers, a gesture of concern for him and reassurance that he was wrong. 'No, David, no. You are not to blame. It was force of circumstance. You did what any captain would have done if he felt that whales were in the offing.'

'But would they?' he put in. 'Would they have risked their ship and the lives of their crew?'

'All captains do that when they sail, and whaling captains especially so,' she pressed, trying to soothe away the pain he was feeling.

'But I made the decision to go on.'

'Yes, and at that time it seemed right. That's what every captain does. It was just bad luck that the ice closed in when it did. You had no say over that.'

'Maybe, but if we hadn't gone . . .'

'You could say that every time you lost a boat when chasing a whale, and that can happen in clear water. These things are a hazard of the trade you follow. David, you must not dwell on them. The *Hind* is being repaired at this very moment.'

'But we can't bring back the men who died.'

'Sadly, no,' Lydia agreed. 'But they were whalemen. They knew there were risks and they were prepared to take them.'

'But I . . .'

'You did not,' she cut in sharply, anticipating the words he was going to say. 'From what I have heard, you have a lot to commend yourself for. More men would have died if it hadn't been for your leadership, for the way you kept their spirits up and your rigorous supervision of food and water. You could do nothing about the scurvy and the cold which I'm told took most of the men. You did well to survive an Arctic winter and it was thanks to you that so many came back.'

'How is Andy?' he asked.

Lydia felt some relief at that question.

'He's coming along well. Billy's been looking after him, he asked for the responsibility. Seems he took to Andy when he was here before. Silas has kept his eye on them, and his wife has been very good in looking to their food. And Dick and Stanley have been on hand as well.'

David nodded. 'That's good. I'm grateful to them all. Andy's a good lad, will make a good sailor one day. And the rest?'

'From what I hear, they'll all recover.'

'Good. And the dead . . . ?' His voice trailed away and he shook his head sadly.

'I have made a small provision for all those who lost someone,' said Lydia quietly, as if reluctant to speak of her generosity. 'They were men who contributed to Hartley Shipping's prosperity. I thought it only right that their families should have something to ease the hardship they would otherwise have to face.'

David squeezed her hand. 'Thee's so thoughtful. Very few shipowners would have done that.' He reached out and gently raised her chin so that she was looking at him.

'Thee says I kept the men going when we were trapped in the ice. Well, does thee know what kept me going?' She shook her head, her eyes fixed on his. 'Thee. The thought of thee to come back to. If I hadn't known that thee was here, I don't think I would have fought to stay alive.'

'David!' she whispered, and moved closer to him. He put his arm around her shoulders and she leaned her head against him.

'Through all the horrors, thee was there. Thy face was a vision I kept before me. Thee urged me on. Thee told me to fight the death-seeking cold, and thee kept my spirits up when the winds howled and the snow swirled and all about us was desolation and night.' He shuddered at the memory.

'Don't, David. Don't torture yourself,' she cried.

'It's all right, love. I want to talk about it.'

She listened, knowing that he was purging himself of the memories. She knew that though they would never completely disappear, they would cease to haunt him as they had done. He would be free to live his life again.

'And through all that it was thee who helped me. Out there, in that wasteland. I came to know thee better. What barriers I had put up between us, and don't ask me what they were, were torn down, gone forever. Lydia, I knew out there that I loved thee deeply.' There was love in his eyes as he looked at her. 'Lydia, I would like thee to marry me.'

'Oh, David. Yes! Yes! I love you so much. I have done since you first came to London. I've longed for you to feel the same.'

'And I do,' he whispered. He drew her gently to him and their lips met in a long kiss which revealed the depth of their love.

They talked excitedly of their feelings until, ten minutes later, David said, 'Lydia, ask thy father to come and see me, and don't tell him the news.'

She laughed lightly, swept up the tray and hurried from the room. A few minutes later she was back with her father.

'My boy,' Dominic beamed when saw David sitting up in bed, 'you look so much better. I'm so pleased.' He came across to the bedside while Lydia stood a couple of paces behind him.

'I feel it,' smiled David.

'Then we'll soon have you downstairs where you and I can have a good talk about the sea as we used to.' He smiled broadly and gave David a knowing wink.

'Sir, I'd like to talk to thee now. Well, for a few moments.' David's face took on a grave expression.

Dominic, taken a little by surprise by David's sudden seriousness, lost his own smile and looked askance at him.

'Sir,' went on David, 'I'd like to have thy permission to marry Lydia.'

Dominic did not speak. He looked sombre. Behind him, Lydia looked nervous. What was he thinking? 'Well,' he started pensively, 'I'm . . .' Suddenly his mood changed and his face lit up with a huge smile. 'I'm delighted. You have my blessing.' He turned to see Lydia radiant with excitement.

She flung herself at him and hugged him tight. 'Oh, Papa, you've made me so happy!'

Dominic laughed as he held his daughter. 'No, lass, it's David who's made you happy.'

Lydia laughed with him as tears of joy rolled down her cheeks. Still holding her, Dominic turned to David and held out a hand to him.

'Congratulations, my boy.' He glanced at his daughter. 'Your mother would have been pleased with your choice. If you're as happy as we were you'll be all right.' His eyes were damp. 'Be good to one another.' He swallowed hard then added, 'I'm delighted that Hartley Shipping is in good hands.'

Francis Chambers wondered how Ruth would take the news when he reached Rigg House. He had learned of David's survival when the weekly ship came in from the capital. He had watched the joy which had swept through Jessica and Jenny but had not hastened to impart the news to Ruth. Time enough for that when he returned from work.

'What!' She gasped at the news and leaped from her chair. 'Impossible. Nobody could survive an Arctic winter.' Agitated, she paced to and fro with short steps. She swung round to face him. 'Tell me it's not true!' she cried, her eyes ablaze with fury.

'It is and there's nothing we can do about it,' he said, quietly but firmly. He saw the fury rise in Ruth and knew a tirade was coming.

'Damn! We should have sold the ships this year as I wanted. Now they've sailed we'll have to wait.'

'You agreed to my plan,' he pointed out.

She tossed her head. 'More fool me. If we'd sold this year we could have been away. Now there's every chance that David will come to Whitby and start nosing around.'

'That's a chance we'll have to take. We've managed it before.'

'But David was only on short visits. He won't be sailing this season so he's likely to come home and be here longer.'

'Then we'll just have to be more careful and hope he leaves for London in time to be ready to sail next year.' Francis tried to take a calm attitude.

But fury burned in Ruth. Her plans could not be allowed to fail now.

Lydia and David married in June. After one night in London they sailed for Whitby.

David revelled in the smell of the sea and the feel of a ship beneath his feet. It was good to be on board again even though he was only a passenger. All the scars of his experience seemed to have gone. His thoughts went to the men who at this moment were hunting the whale in the Arctic, his beloved Arctic. In one way he wished he was with them, but he was happy here beside his wife, taking her to Whitby and then across the moors to meet his family. He just knew they would love her. They couldn't but help it. Her vivid deep blue eyes could charm anyone and he was sure her warm friendliness would break down any doubts that might be felt by his family when he arrived unexpectedly with a wife.

As he stood beside her on the deck with the wind catching the wisps of flaxen hair which had stolen from the confines of her bonnet, his heart was stirred by her beauty and he counted himself fortunate to have her for his wife.

For her part Lydia was enjoying every moment of sharing this voyage with David. She was looking forward to visiting Whitby, to meeting his sister and friends, and then seeing the Yorkshire moors for the first time and making friends with his mother and father and the rest of the family, not least his baby son. She was happy and looked forward to their life together with confidence. So much lay ahead for them. There was a thriving business to run, and though she knew David needed to sail the seas she also knew he would take a great interest in the business side of Hartley Shipping.

She slipped her arm through his and stepped closer to him.

Twenty-four hours later they were back on deck with the Yorkshire coast in sight as they began their run in to Whitby. The ruined abbey high on the precipitous cliffs caught Lydia's attention immediately. Her insatiable appetite for information brought questions pouring from her lips as David explained how there had been an earlier abbey on the site, ruled over by the holy St Hilda who had befriended Caedmon, the father of English poetry. He held her with the story of how that monastery had been destroyed by the Danes in 867, that it wasn't until 1078 that a new one was built and that it had stood until partially destroyed by Henry VIII.

Lydia expressed alarm at seeing the narrow entrance to the river between two stone piers.

David laughed. 'I suppose it looks small after the Thames and the long sail up the river, and I grant thee it's no mean skill to take a ship through that gap, but Captain Midgley's an expert. Done it many times.'

Lydia watched, fascinated by the expertise of the captain and his crew. One moment, with the sea running fast, it looked certain they would crash into one of the piers; the next they were safely through and entering the calm river water.

Orders flew thick and fast as the *Capella* was manoeuvred up the river beyond the drawbridge to the quay on the east bank, but Lydia was oblivious. All her attention was held on David's home port. Houses climbed the cliffs on either side, seeming to stand higgledy-piggledy on top of each other. Smoke curled from the warren of chimneypots and was whisked away on the breeze. Along the river ships of all sizes were berthed at quays, unloading goods from all parts of the known world or taking on board the merchandise on which Whitby's export trade thrived. Sailors and dockers bent on their work scarcely gave the new arrival a cursory glance, but there were those – housewives going about their morning shopping, urchins at play, sailors without a ship, merchants heading for a meeting, artisans pausing on their way to a job – who gave it more attention or cursed its arrival because they were held up at the bridge, drawn up to allow the ships to pass up river.

And all around the sounds of Whitby gave a welcome to Lydia. Orders and cajoling, shouts of greeting, the straining of tackle, the creak of ropes and rattle of chains, the rumble of carts, a piercing whistle, the lilt of a song – all swept her into Whitby's life. But above all she would remember the plaintive cry of the seagulls as they flew with a lazy beat of their wings or caught the current of air to glide majestically without a care in the world.

'Oh, David, I'm so happy to be here,' she cried with an edge of excitement to her voice.

'And I'm happy to have thee with me.' He smiled lovingly at her and added joyfully, 'Jessica's going to get a big surprise when I walk in with thee.' And not only Jessica, he thought to himself.

As soon as they were ashore David found two lads eager to carry their bags for sixpence. He threaded his way among the bustle of the quayside, guiding Lydia with care as she took in the activities of this important working Yorkshire port. She had seen such bustle on a larger scale along the Thames but here, confined by the cliffs on either side of the river, it seemed so much more vigorous. Almost everyone seemed to be involved, and if the number of greetings David was receiving was anything to go by, everyone knew him.

'Welcome back, Cap'n.'

'Pleased to see thee.'

'G'day, Cap'n. Take care.'

They crossed the bridge and a few moments later entered the premises of Fernley and Thoresby after David had told the two boys to wait and take good care of the bags. His knock was answered by a female voice. 'Come in.' He grinned at his wife and mouthed the word 'Jessica'.

Apprehension fluttered through Lydia now she was on the verge of meeting David's sister. As he opened the door she quickly smoothed her coat and adjusted her bonnet.

'David!' the cry burst from Jessica's lips. She was on her

feet, round her desk and flinging herself into his arms almost before he realised it. 'Oh, Davey, it's so good to have thee safe. We thought . . .' Her voice faltered and she stepped back. 'Let me look at thee.' Through her tears of joy, she looked him up and down. 'Thee's lost weight but we'll soon remedy that.' Then she was aware of Lydia, standing just inside the doorway.

David caught her glance. He stepped to one side. 'Jess, I'd like you to meet my wife, Lydia.'

Jessica's eyes widened. 'Wife?' She cast a glance at her brother, seeking confirmation that she had heard correctly.

He chuckled. 'Yes, Jess, my wife. We were married two days ago.' He turned to Lydia. 'My love, this is Jessica, my sister, and she's not usually as stunned as this.'

Jessica looked straight at Lydia, and liked what she saw. Someone about David's age, with warm, friendly eyes which at this moment had a touch of misgiving about them. She knew his wife had faced this meeting with some doubt, wondering how David's sister would react, badly wanting to be welcome. Yet there was pride in her bearing, too, just as David had described her on his previous visits. But he had never mentioned romance or marriage so having Lydia announced as 'my wife' had really caught her off her guard. Jessica quickly pulled herself together. She smiled and held out her arms. 'Welcome to the family, Lydia.'

Lydia saw sincerity in the greeting. Her doubts and fears fell away. She smiled and stepped forward into Jessica's arms.

'Thee'll be good for David, thank thee for marrying him.'

Joy flooded over Lydia. From what David had told her this was his favourite sister. They were close and to get Jessica's approval meant a lot.

For the next twenty minutes conversation flowed and in that time it was decided that David and Lydia would stay with Jessica for four days and then they would go to Cropton for ten days, return to Whitby and take the *Capella* back to London two days after that.

The arrangements had just been made when the door opened and Jenny came in.

She gasped when she saw David. 'Davey!'

He was on his feet. 'Jenny. It's good to see thee.'

'And you. What a relief when we heard you were safe.'

'Sorry I gave all of thee a bad time.'

They kissed and hugged each other. Lydia sensed that Jenny had captured a little bit of David's heart at some time and realised that there was a special relationship between them. She felt a little pang of jealousy but no animosity for she had an immediate feeling of empathy for Jenny.

'Jenny, I'd like thee to meet Lydia, my wife.'

Caught by the unexpected, Jenny looked startled but almost immediately took command of herself. A smile of genuine pleasure crossed her face. 'Oh, David, I'm so glad. Lydia, I'm pleased to meet you.' She stepped forward, took Lydia's hand and kissed her on the cheek. 'David spoke of you on his previous visits but we had no idea that you and he . . .'

'Two days ago,' said Lydia, 'and I'm so happy.' She took David's hand in hers.

Jenny knew that Lydia saw in David all that she had seen and more. She was obviously radiant and could not disguise her feelings for him. 'I'm so pleased for you both. Take your happiness while you can. You never know what tomorrow will bring.'

David realised that even in sharing their happiness Jenny was feeling the loss of Adam.

Lydia was made to feel very much at home during the next ten minutes until Jessica suggested that it was time to leave.

They had just risen from their chairs when there was a

knock on the door and Jessica's call of 'Come in' brought Francis into the room. He stopped in his tracks when he saw there were visitors. 'Oh, I'm sorry, I didn't know . . . why, Captain Fernley!' He quickly controlled his surprise and added, 'It's good to see you looking so well after your dreadful ordeal.'

'Thanks, Francis. We were lucky to escape, and my recovery is all due to my wife.' He turned to Lydia and missed the fleeting look of surprise which crossed Francis's face. 'Lydia, this is Francis Chambers who is the brains behind this firm, though I must add that Jessica and Jenny are doing very well also in learning the running of the business.'

Francis bowed and gave Lydia a charming smile. 'I'm so pleased to meet you, Ma'am. And may I congratulate both of you and wish you every happiness in the future.' He turned to Jessica. 'These are just some letters I thought you might like to see and sign.'

'Anything important?' she asked.

'No, just everyday affairs but I thought you might like to see them. They can wait, you're too busy now.'

'If they are everyday items you have the power to sign them. I can read them later.'

'Thank you, Ma'am, I'll do that.' He stepped back towards the door, then paused and asked casually, 'Will you be with us long, Captain Fernley?'

'Four days before we go to Cropton and a couple of days on the way back,' replied David. 'No time to worry you. Jessica and Jenny tell me the business is doing well and that's good enough for me. Besides, who wants to work on his honeymoon?'

Francis inclined his head in agreement. 'Have a pleasant stay.'

Francis made no haste to bring the news to Ruth. It would do when he returned to Rigg House at the usual time.

From his self-satisfied smile and the twinkle in his eyes as he greeted her, Ruth knew he had something to tell her.

'Well, come on, what is it?' she demanded, after she had returned his kiss.

'What's what?' he said teasingly.

'What you have to tell me.'

'Have I something to tell you?'

'You wouldn't be looking so smug if you hadn't. Come on, out with it,' she commanded, a note of irritation to her voice.

Francis met her gaze for a moment then said, 'David's in Whitby.' He saw the brightness in her eyes change to smouldering annoyance.

'Damn him! Here to blight us,' she snapped, then added a word of caution. 'You'll have to be careful, Francis.'

'Maybe there's no need to worry,' he replied, his smirk revealing that he knew something she didn't. He paused then went on in answer to her unspoken question, 'He won't have time – he's here on his honeymoon.'

'His what?' gasped Ruth, eyes widening at the news.

'Honeymoon.'

'Well well, so David's found himself a wife. Who is she?'

'She was only introduced to me as his wife. But I've heard Jessica and Jenny talking about a Lydia Hartley after David's previous visits. If it is she then she's the daughter of the owner of the firm for whom David sails, and an only child.'

'Mmm.' Ruth tapped her chin thoughtfully. 'That means that David could become a partner in that firm, as she will inherit. So the harder we hit Fernley and Thoresby the better. It's just as well we aren't selling the three ships until next year.' She paused then chuckled. 'But maybe I could do him more harm by revealing he's a bigamist.' She flounced away, enjoying the thought. The laughter on her face only served to drive home the barb her words had plunged into her lover's mind.

Francis's face clouded with anger. He stepped forward and grabbed her roughly by her arms. He towered over her, eyes burning with an unmistakable threat. 'Don't!' he hissed. 'Don't ruin everything I've done. I want my share and I'm going to have it, so get any such fool notion out of your head.' There was menace behind the tightening grip on her arms.

She stared up into his eyes and saw how love could quickly turn to hatred and loyalty to mistrust. For one brief moment she gazed back with defiance and was tempted to carry out her idea. Then she relaxed with a laugh. 'You really thought I meant it?' Her eyes teased, leaving him wondering whether she meant it or not.

He released his hold on her with an impatient gesture.

'It was an exciting idea, but that's all it was. It would spoil the revenge I want on Jenny.' Her eyes narrowed, smouldering with the thought of fulfilling her desire. 'On her and David. Nothing, not even proving he is a bigamist, will deter me from that.'

'As long as we understand each other,' rapped Francis.

'Of course we do. And we'll do it together.' She came closer and raised her face to him. She needed his help, not his antagonism. Her eyes sparkled with enticing charm and Francis was lost.

He crushed her to him and his lips met hers with a passion which resealed their bargain.

Chapter Sixteen

'Oh, David, I've had such a happy time.' Lydia hugged herself with pleasure as she watched Whitby recede with the *Capella* on course for London. The mid-morning sun penetrated the curling smoke to set the red roofs of Whitby ablaze with colour. 'Your family are all so kind.'

David smiled, recalling how his parents' shocked expressions when he'd introduced Lydia as his wife had changed quickly to warm welcome. His mother and Lydia had got on so well and he knew his father admired her even though she was a 'London lass'.

'Betsy was wary at first.' Lydia's comment broke into his thoughts.

'Wary?'

'Oh, yes. Maybe you weren't aware of it, taken up as you were with young Kit. I believe she was frightened she was going to lose him.'

'Yes,' David mused. 'I hadn't thought of that.'

'Don't forget she's been a mother to him. She adores him and it would be a big wrench if we took him. She would be wondering if we were going to and what sort of a mother I would be to him.'

'Did she say anything?'

'Not directly. The wariness disappeared when she had made her assessment of me and I hinted that we wanted to get settled before we even thought of Kit's future.' She cast a querying glance at her husband. 'Would you want to bring him to London?'

David looked thoughtful. 'I'm not sure. He's known

nothing but the country. Maybe he has farming in him. We'll just have to see.'

'Well, you know I'd love to have him if that's what you want, but be careful about breaking Betsy's heart.'

'Thanks, love, I will.' David blessed the day he had taken this kind and considerate woman to be his wife.

Three months later, in the middle of September, Lydia joyously told David she was expecting a child.

Alex Fraser cast a glance at the billowing sails as the *Arctic Fox* ran before a favourable northwest wind. She was a full ship on a southeasterly course out of Davis Strait for her home port of New Bedford.

He counted himself lucky to have been given command of her after one voyage as mate on the *Fetlar*. His ability and knowledge of whaling in the Arctic had been recognised by her captain and after that voyage he had been strongly recommended to take command of Joseph Spence's new vessel, a full rigged merchantman which he converted to a barque with fore-and-aft sails on her mizzenmast. She had all the good points required by a whaler. She was strong, built of durable oak. She was unusually tub-shaped for a merchantman but that fitted her well for a whaler for her capacious hold was ideal for stowing the accumulation of blubber gained on a whaling voyage. She was not fast but that did not matter in a whaler, in which steadiness and dependability were greater attributes.

All was well and the crew were happy to be heading home at the beginning of August, the weather looking to be set fair.

Alex had already charted his course, keeping in mind that taken on his first voyage out of New Bedford. He would avoid the long run round Newfoundland through the broad Atlantic by taking the shorter and more sheltered route through the Strait of Belle Isle, into the Gulf of St Lawrence and thence via Cabot Strait into the Atlantic for the run down the coast to New Bedford.

With Cape Charles and Belle Isle in sight and with the wind still blowing from the northwest, Alex altered course to take them into the strait, with the wind coming on to the beam. Progress was good and continued so in the wider waters of the Gulf of St Lawrenec. East of Anticosti Island he ordered the sails to be freed off and set the *Arctic Fox* on a dead run for Cabot Strait.

All went well for twelve hours, then the wind began to veer north and slowly to drop. Alex grew anxious. If the wind played no more tricks they would make the run through Cabot Strait, albeit more slowly. Pacing the deck, he kept an eye on the weather. He felt a certain nervousness had come over the crew. It was heightened all the more because they had had such a good run from the whaling grounds and home was only about ten days' sailing.

Twelve hours later all semblance of a wind had gone. The sails hung limp and the *Arctic Fox* lay becalmed, so tantalisingly close to completing her run through the strait. For two days she was set in a sea which hardly moved. The stillness and silence became oppressive, carrying an air of foreboding. Anxiety stalked the minds of the crew, and though no one voiced their thoughts they prayed that when the wind returned it would be favourable. All they could do was watch and wait.

The glass-like surface of the sea rippled. There was a faint slap of sailcloth. An elusive breeze touched stubbled chins and was gone. Alex started. Men jumped to their feet. Wind! The word was in everyone's mind. Wind to take them home.

Though still light, it made its presence felt again. But Alex was not happy. It was coming from the south. His orders flew fast and men ran to obey as they endeavoured to get the vessel underway for the Atlantic. But within a few minutes they knew it would be useless for the wind was increasing fast and worse still was backing rapidly to the southeast, blowing from a quarter which would prevent their getting out of the strait.

Alex seized on the situation quickly for the sea was beginning to run high and the weather was showing every sign of an approaching storm.

'Aloft. Aloft. Furl all topgallants!'

Men raced to the rigging and climbed swiftly.

Alex had studied his charts while becalmed and knew that with the wind blowing hard from the southeast they would never make the Atlantic. He would be better seeking the shelter of Cape Breton Island and the northern coastline of Nova Scotia until the storm blew itself out. He lost no time in tacking and heading off southwest.

'Stow all mizzen sails!'

Six hours later, with the sky darkening and the wind strengthening, his cries rang out again.

'Stow foresail and mainsail!'

No sooner had this been done than the storm hit them. Rain lashed the ship. The sea, its whitecaps torn into shreds by the piercing wind, pounded her from stem to stern. A gale howled in the rigging and the topsails and inner jib, on which Alex kept the *Arctic Fox* running, cracked with the sharpness of a musket shot as the wind sort to tear them from the ship.

Alex held her to her course and, with Cape Breton Island to the east offering some barrier against the storm's ferocity, prepared to outrun it. He did not sleep that night but remained alert, anxious for his ship on this his first voyage as captain. He desperately wanted to return safe and undamaged, with his cargo intact. His anxiety grew towards dawn when, with no let up in the maelstrom which battered them relentlessly, he realised that the coast of Nova Scotia would soon present a barrier upon which the *Arctic Fox* could be beaten to destruction.

Two hours later, with Alex weighing up the chances of running between Prince Edward Island and the mainland, he detected a slight change in the wind. His hopes rose. The clouds were breaking, the rain thinning and it had lost some of its driving torment. The rain ceased, the clouds were slowing and the *Arctic Fox* was able to take charge of her own fate.

Alex decided to drop anchor in a suitable cove and allow his crew to recuperate. Anxious as he was to reach New Bedford he needed an alert crew, not one exhausted after the beating they had taken. Besides there was no longer any need to run before the wind; he could find shelter and wait for it to change to a quarter which would enable him to sail northeast and then successfully negotiate Cabot Strait.

Surveying the coast, comparing it with his charts, he dropped anchor off the tiny settlement of Pictou with the expectation of finding fresh supplies.

As soon as the *Arctic Fox* was at anchor he ordered a boat to be lowered and in a few minutes he was being rowed ashore by four members of his crew. The sight of a ship drawing into their cover and dropping anchor had already brought people from their houses. Those busy in the fields behind the settlement dropped their hoes and came for a closer look at the vessel, curious as to its purpose. When they saw the boat strike the water and turn towards the shore, they moved to the water's edge, looking to Ed Lucas for a lead.

The boat ground into the shallows. Two men leaped out and held it steady as Alex rose to his feet and came ashore.

'Good day, everyone,' he greeted them pleasantly, trying to ease the curiosity tinged with suspicion which he felt emanating from the gathering. He noted axes held loosely by several of the men and that some had brought muskets from their houses. It was to be expected. Who could blame these people? A strange ship could mean danger. They had a right to regard him with suspicion.

He singled out a tall, upright man who had stepped a little in front of the others. He carried an air of authority. Though Alex addressed his remarks to him, he used a loud enough voice so that all could hear.

'I'm Alex Fraser, captain of the *Arctic Fox*. We were heading home for New Bedford from a whaling expedition when the storm drove us off course. We are all right, we just need to rest and wait for a favourable wind. We will not trouble you except to buy fresh supplies if you have them available.' He expressed himself with an amiable tone and friendly gaze.

Ed stepped forward and held out his hand. As he took it Alex could feel the tension leave the crowd. 'G'day to thee, Cap'n. Pleased thee survived that storm. It was a hard blow.' He glanced skywards with a shrewd eye. 'Within twenty-four hours the wind will be right for thee. Time for thee to recoup and take on fresh supplies. We'll let thee have what we can.'

With bargains struck, fresh bread, venison, eggs, potatoes and vegetables were taken on board and the crew revelled in the change from their meagre supplies which were always low at the end of a five months' whaling voyage.

When he awoke next morning, Alex found that Ed's judgement of the weather was correct. During the night the wind had dropped and was now blowing lightly from a westerly direction. He allowed his men to sleep on but by mid-morning, with the wind freshening, all hands were busy preparing to get the ship underway.

'Cap'n, canoe approaching.' The call from the mate brought Alex to the rail. Two men paddled the craft with strong, skilled strokes, bringing Ed Lucas to the *Arctic Fox*.

'Permission to come aboard?' he called as the canoe was brought alongside.

'Granted,' Alex called. He watched the well-built man climb the rope ladder and swing over the rail, then held out his hand. 'Welcome aboard, Ed.'

He shook hands. 'Thee'll be leaving soon?'

'Aye,' smiled Alex. 'Thee was right about the weather, so we'll be underway before long. Thanks for the food and your generosity. My crew are grateful.'

'Only pleased to be of help,' returned Ed. 'There's one more thing, a request I'd like to make.'

'Name it. We'll help if we can.'

'Could thee take a passenger to New Bedford? Well, two really, a woman and her baby?'

Alex tried to hide his surprise behind a question. 'Has she folk in New Bedford?'

'No.'

'Then what am I to do with her?' asked Alex quickly before Ed could go on. He was sensing difficulties when he reached port.

'That could be a problem,' agreed Ed, 'but I think it's one which could be resolved somehow. She's capable, resourceful, but has had a very hard time. I feel she needs to be where there are more people, not in this wilderness which has dealt her terrible blows.'

Alex looked thoughtful but said nothing. Not sure of his reaction, Ed went on, 'Let me tell thee more about her. It's a hard story. She and her parents were driven off their holding and shipped aboard an emigrant ship whose passengers had been told there would be houses and farms at Pictou for them. Conditions on board were horrifying. They were herded like cattle, disease killed many of them, her father included. Here there was nothing for them. They were dumped across the cove there.' He indicated the place with a gesture. 'Very little food and only a few spades and axes. We could do little for them, there were too many.

282

Winter was coming on and the cold killed many of them. They had broken up into groups, hoping to find somewhere to build their homes along the coast or deeper in the forest. Her mother died shortly after they landed. Realising she was pregnant two families befriended her and took her with them when they went to settle along the coast.'

Alex was already moved by the story for he had heard of the vile conditions aboard many of the emigrant ships and realised how lucky he and his family had been to come to America on board a whaleship with a kindly captain. He made no comment for he sensed there was worse to come.

Ed drew a deep breath and continued, 'All went well for them until one day some Indians appeared. They were reasonably friendly but some member of one of the families insulted them and they were driven off.' Ed looked exasperated at the recollection. 'This was only the second time they had met Indians, they were ignorant as to how to deal with them. The result was the Indians returned and massacred them.'

'And the woman? How did she survive?' asked Alex.

'She had taken the child and gone into the woods. She was on her way back when she heard screams. She hid near the edge of the wood and witnessed the slaughter. She was terrified. Hid there after the Indians made off. How long for I don't know. But then she made the thirty miles to here on foot along the coast in terror, fearing the Indians might return. She was completely spent when she reached us. We thought she would die but she had the will to survive, maybe because of the child. She's scarred by her experience, is afraid to go out, that's why I think she would be better taken away from here.'

'The father of the child?' asked Alex.

'I don't know. She has never mentioned him. Evaded the question when we asked her. I suspect she conceived before she left Scotland.'

Alex was moved by the story and without hesitation offered to take her to New Bedford. 'Is she in agreement?' he asked.

'It hasn't been mentioned to her. I didn't want to do that unless thee were willing. Come ashore with me and we'll see how she takes it.'

The two men climbed quickly into the canoe and once at the settlement Ed led the way to his house. His wife was at the door to meet them.

'Sally, my wife. Captain Fraser.' Greetings were exchanged and then Ed asked, 'Where is she?'

'In the kitchen.'

Ed led the way through a large room furnished with chairs and a table stoutly made from forest timbers. A door led into another room which ran half the length of the whole building. A large open fireplace occupied the left hand wall. Outside through the long window Alex could see the fields and beyond them the forest. A table occupied the centre of the room at which a woman was kneading dough, her head bent to her task. She glanced up as Ed entered the room followed by Sally and Alex.

Her hands ceased to move. She stared in disbelief at the visitor.

Alex stopped in his stride, frozen into immobility by shock. His mind was numb, unable to cope with the unexpected.

'Beth, what is it?' asked Ed, seeing the look on her face where silent tears were already beginning to flow. He swung round to Alex and was astonished to see he had gone ashen white. 'Thee looks as though thee's seen a ghost.' His statement came almost as a question, demanding an answer.

'Alex, is . . . is it really thee?' He was looking at the cousin he had last seen thousands of miles away in Shetland. But she was different. So thin, and with lines of suffering marking her face which had a gaunt appearance. Her eyes, which he remembered had always shone brightly with a love of life, were dull. But in spite of the changes there was no mistaking her.

He was round the table and hugging her with all the love and compassion he could muster, ignoring the doughy hands which held him tight as they sought reassurance that he was real and this was not another nightmare come to haunt her.

He let her sobs of joy and relief play themselves out while he offered a brief explanation to Ed and Sally.

'Then there'll be no need to worry about what she will do in New Bedford?' said Ed when Alex had finished.

'None,' he replied.

Beth eased herself from his arms. 'New Bedford?' she queried with a sniff.

'Aye,' replid Alex. 'We emigrated and now I'm captain of a whaler bound for there. Ed came to ask if I would take a woman and her baby there. He didn't mention your name, hence my shock. He's told me everything and thinks it would be best for thee to leave here, if thee wants to?'

'Oh, yes, yes! Please.' Beth turned to Sally and Ed. 'Oh, please don't think me ungrateful after all thee's done for me.' Her eyes were damp as she looked lovingly at her two friends.

'We know thee's not,' said Sally with a smile as she hugged her.

Excitedly Beth packed her few belongings and went for the child who had been sleeping peacefully in a corner of the kitchen.

'Ailsa, come and meet thy cousin Alex,' she said with a smile. She held the child proudly for him to see.

Ailsa's dark eyes shone brightly as she gurgled and smiled at him. He was startled by their depth. He had seen eyes as dark as that in only one other person: David Fernley. His gaze fell on a jet cross round Beth's neck. It was special. It was unique. And the last time he had seen it, it had been round David Fernley's neck.

Chapter Seventeen

It was mid-morning when the *Arctic Fox* crossed Buzzards Bay towards New Bedford. The voyage from Pictou had been good. The weather had held and the ship took the rolling Atlantic with ease. The crew enjoyed the final few days' worth of fresh food taken on at Pictou and were in good heart, anticipating the warm welcome their full hold would receive.

Alex had given his cabin over to Beth and Ailsa and she revelled in the comparative luxury after the harsh wilderness. The sharp sea air soon brought colour back to her cheeks and Alex was pleased to see that a new light was returning to her eyes and that she had thrown off the mantle of depression which the horrors she had witnessed had cast over her.

All hands were on deck, and Beth, holding Ailsa, stood close to the rail near Alex as they came up the Acushnet River and headed for the ship's berth. She was thrilled to see the town, neatly laid out beyond the immediate vicinity of wharves and warehouses. She had never seen anywhere so spacious and attractive and felt an air of friendliness, as if the place itself was making her welcome, saying: 'Make your home here.' She had never felt as happy since those last moments she had spent with David. David . . . He had not been true to her. She shuddered at the memory and cast him from her mind. It was no good looking back. The past was gone, her future lay here.

She was dying to ask Alex questions, to have him point things out to her, but he was busy concentrating on bringing the ship safely to rest beside the quay.

Ropes were thrown out, grabbed and attached to capstans. The gap between the ship and the quay closed amidst cheers and shouts of welcome from the people who had flocked to see the return of a whaler with bone at its masthead. A full ship meant money to Joseph Spence and to New Bedford.

Beth was stirred by all the activity. The quay buzzed with chatter through which shouts and calls penetrated as orders for the safe docking of the ship were given. Her eyes took in everything of what to her was a magical scene. Here were people going about their ordinary lives, safe from the hostility of the wilderness. She felt certain she could be happy here; she would feel safe and the harshness of her past life could be banished forever. A group of ladies, elegantly dressed in colourful, patterned gingham frocks with matching bonnets, focused her attention. She had never seen anyone looking so smart. Some had parasols opened to stop the sun spoiling their complexions. All chattered gaily to a man smartly dressed in knee-length breeches and pale stockings. His shoes were black with bright silver buckles and he wore a high hat and carried a walking cane. Beth noted that as working men in their coarse breeches and short sleeveless coats passed him they touched their three-cornered hats. He always acknowledged them with a nod of his head and a word.

With the ship finally at rest, the gangway was run out and Alex came to Beth.

'Well, how does thee like it?' he asked. He had noticed the awed expression on her face as her eyes darted about, drinking everything in.

'Wonderful, Alex, just wonderful!' she replied excitedly. 'Oh, my goodness, black men.' She had noticed some working on the next wharf. Her eyes were wide with disbelief. She glanced at Alex, seeking reassurance.

He laughed. 'Of course, the first thee's seen. They're harmless and friendly. And by the way, thee may see some

Indians in town from time to time.' Her excitement vanished and a scared look came to her eyes. 'Now, there's no need to be afraid,' he went on quickly to set her mind at rest. 'They're peaceful. Come into town to trade.' He turned to the scene on the quay to divert her mind from her sufferings in Nova Scotia. 'See yon?' He indicated the man with the top hat.

'I've been wondering who he was,' said Beth. 'And those ladies with him – I've never seen such dresses.'

Alex smiled. 'Thee shall meet him.'

Beth swung round in astonishment. 'I will?' she spluttered.

'Thee'll have to. He's Joseph Spence, owner of this ship and of others. He'll want to know what I'm doing with a woman on board.' Beth swallowed hard at the thought of meeting someone as rich and influential as Joseph Spence. 'You'll like him,' went on Alex. 'He's one of us.'

'Us?' Her brow puckered.

'A Shetlander. Emigrated here and made a fortune. Come on.' He led Beth to the gangway and escorted her to the quay. Joseph Spence was coming to meet them.

'Welcome home, Alex.' They shook hands. 'You've had a good voyage?' Without waiting for a reply he turned to Beth, bowed slightly and doffed his hat. His eyes were full of curiosity.

'Sir, I'd like thee to meet a cousin of mine, Beth Robinson. She's from Shetland but I found her in Nova Scotia.'

'Pleased to meet you, Ma'am. And that's a fine bairn you have.'

'Thank thee, sir.' Beth bobbed a little curtsey.

Alex quickly explained the circumstances which had brought Beth to New Bedford.

When he had finished, Joseph, who had listened with interest, said, 'You get off home with Beth. I'll see to things here.'

'Thanks,' said Alex. 'I'd like to get her to Maggie. I'll fetch our bags.'

'Where are they? In your cabin?'

'Aye.'

'Then off with you. I'll get them brought on.' He turned to Beth. 'I hope you settle down and like our town.' Before she could reply he was striding up the gangway and slipping out of his coat as he did so.

'He's not afraid of work,' Alex explained as they made their way along the quay. 'He remembers that's how he made his fortune. He'll do my job of supervising the arrival in port.'

Beth admired the fine buildings as they made their way along Union Street to the corner of Fourth Street. Here Alex stopped in front of a two-storeyed house with a central chimney. Five steps led to a panelled front door with a brass knocker.

Beth stared at him in disbelief. 'This yours?'

'No. This is where we live. It belongs to Mr Spence who rents it to us for a very modest sum.' He smiled. 'A far cry from the Shetland crofts?'

'Aye, it is that, Alex. Who'd ever have thought it? Thee's done well.'

'Aye, and now thee can share it. Come on, let's see Maggie.'

When she opened the door to his knock, Maggie flung her arms round him in welcome and the twins came running to add theirs. For a moment Maggie did not realise that her husband had someone with him. Then she stared in amazement over his shoulder and her eyes widened. 'Beth!' she gasped. 'How? What?' she spluttered.

'It is, Maggie,' said Alex as he eased her from his arms.

Maggie's welcome was profuse. Beth's tears of joy at her reception were allowed to flow. She settled in quickly and took delight in what to her was luxury – carpets, comfortable chairs, spacious rooms, a soft bed with sheets and blankets and feather pillows. Alex told Maggie the story of finding Beth and of how she came to be in Pictou. He left out the horrifying tale of the Indian massacre to spare Beth the memory and only told Maggie of it in the privacy of their bedroom.

'And what of the child?' she asked. 'Who is the father, and where is he?'

'Beth has never told me and I have never asked. It is up to her to tell us. But did thee notice those eyes?'

For a moment Maggie looked askance at him but, with her mind recalling Ailsa when she had taken her into her arms, her gaze turned to one of astonishment. 'Thee don't mean Captain Fernley?'

'Aye, lass, I do,' he replied. 'I've never seen eyes as dark as that in anyone else. Besides, that jet cross thee admired – the last time I saw it it was round David Fernley's neck.'

The silence between them was charged with conjecture. Maggie broke it to ask, 'Do we say anything?'

Alex looked thoughtful as he crossed to the window and looked out across the moonlit town. Then he turned and said, 'There's nothing to be gained. If Beth wants us to know Ailsa is David's, she'll tell us. Maybe she doesn't want him to know. If she doesn't there's no point in her returning to England, and she's given no indication that she wants to do so. After all she's been through her life is here with us, if thee agrees?'

'Of course I agree, love. Beth's more than welcome. We'll say nothing. What about us? Have thee told her how we came to be here?'

'I told her we emigrated.'

'Then let's leave it at that. There's no need for anyone to know the real story. That's our secret.'

At the turn of the year Lydia broached the subject of the whaling season with David. 'You'll have to be preparing the *Hind*.'

'That's been taken care of,' he replied. 'I've appointed Jeremy Kemp as captain. I'm not sailing.'

'But you must! You missed last season because of your late return. You go, love. I know you want to.'

'There's no denying I would like to, but I'm not going. Thee's expecting and I'm staying with thee.'

'That's sweet of you, and I'll be only too pleased to have you here, but I'd understand if you went. Andy will be disappointed.'

'He'll be all right. He knows Jeremy, gets on well with him. It'll do him good. He's got to sail with other people. Now no more about it. I'm not sailing.'

In March he watched the *Hind* depart with mixed feelings.

On the Yorkshire coast *The Lonely Wind*, the *Mary Jane* and the *Ruth* left Whitby and headed north.

As soon as he saw the ships pass between the piers at the mouth of the river, Francis Chambers hurried to the offices of Chapman and Hern, merchants and shipowners. This was the day he had been waiting for, the day when he would be rich and would leave Whitby for good with the woman he idolised.

For the past two months he had negotiated with James Chapman for the sale of the three ships. Both men had sworn secrecy over the deal for there could be repercussions from other shipowners if it became known that Fernley and Thoresby were selling and Chapman and Hern were buying. It had been agreed, on Francis's suggestion, that the deal would be finalised the moment the ships sailed for the Arctic.

Now he hurried to complete the transaction. He had the necessary papers in his pocket and smiled to himself as he recalled how easily he had slipped the authorisation to sell among the day-to-day papers for Jessica to sign. She trusted him implicitly and very rarely read what she signed, a weakness which Francis had never bothered to correct when he was instructing her and Jenny in the business. He had told them only as much as he wanted them to know.

As sailing day drew near arrangements to leave Whitby had been made by Ruth. The day couldn't come quickly enough for her to escape to the freedom of the outside world.

When they had broken the news to Emily Judson that they were leaving it had come as something of a surprise, even though she'd known that one day Ruth would want to throw off the restrictions of Rigg House. She had become devoted to Ruth, recalling the happiness she had brought Jonathan, the former master of Rigg House, who she believed had died tragically in a fall from the cliffs when out riding. Faced with a life of loneliness, known now as the recluse of Rigg House, Emily had welcomed a suggestion that she should accompany Ruth and Francis to America. She had successfully negotiated the sale of the house and was all prepared to leave. They, on their part, were pleased to have the only person who shared the secret of Ruth's existence with them.

Francis knew that when he arrived at Rigg House the two ladies would have the coach ready to leave immediately for Liverpool.

With a light step he entered the offices of Chapman and Hern and was shown immediately to James's room.

'The ships have sailed,' he announced, 'and here is the authorisation for the sale.' With a satisfied flourish he drew a sheet of paper from his pocket and placed it in front of James, who was sitting behind his desk.

He picked it up, cast a quick eye over the wording, lingered on the signature for a moment and replaced the paper on the desk with a grunt of satisfaction. He had long been an admirer of the three ships but had never entertained the possibility of acquiring them until two months ago when he was discreetly approached by Francis. He was surprised but, when the opportunity presented itself, sought no reason for the sale.

He opened a drawer in his desk and withdrew a note. He glanced at it and handed it over. 'The necessary Bill of Exchange.'

'Thanks,' said Francis. He glanced at the note, taking in the figures which sent a wave of satisfaction through him. He leaned forward and the two men shook hands. 'I hope they return full,' he added. 'Now I'll bid you good day.'

He left and hurried to the offices of Simpson and Holt in Grape Lane where he withdrew most of the money from the Fernley and Thoresby account, presenting his authorisation to do so.

The banker stared at the closed door for a few moments when Francis left. He was puzzled as to why so much cash was required, but that had nothing to do with him. He had the note authorising him to pay the money to Francis Chambers. He shrugged his shoulders and filed it away.

Francis hurried to the stables at the White Horse and was soon leaving Whitby for Rigg House. As he reached the heights above the town he paused for a brief moment and looked back across the red roofs to the river and beyond to the sea. His life here was finished. Whitby had given him the opportunity to better himself, he had seized the chance and it had come with the woman he had once only been able to worship from afar. Now she was his and a new life awaited them in America.

He turned his mount and kicked it into a gallop for Rigg House.

He was admitted by Emily and hurried straight to the withdrawing room. Ruth jumped to her feet when he entered.

'We've done it,' he laughed. 'Cash to get us to America.' He tapped his pocket. 'And this!' He waved the Bill of Exchange.

'Ruined! Ruined!' cried Ruth, savouring the poverty

facing Jenny and Jessica. 'I wish I could see their faces when they find out.' She flung her arms round Francis's neck. 'You've done well. How can I ever repay you?'

He gazed at her with smouldering eyes. 'There's one way. Marry me.'

'What, and make myself a bigamist?' She started to turn away. 'Leave things between us as they are,' she added coyly. 'We satisfy each other.'

He grabbed her by the arm and turned her back to him. 'I want you for my own,' he hissed. 'Don't play with me, Ruth.'

For one moment she looked at him defiantly then, realising this was no time for confrontation, eased the tension with: 'I won't, after what you've done for me.' She stood on her toes, reached up and kissed him.

He held on to her when she would have broken away. 'Here's to a new life,' he added, and kissed her passionately again.

Their few remaining belongings were quickly put into the coach. As Francis was helping her into the seat, she stopped and turned to face him and Emily. 'Don't forget, I'm Ruth Hardy from now on. We daren't risk the name of Fernley being recognised. And we come from Hull. That's where we learned the whaling trade.'

Once Ruth and Emily were settled and he had tied his horse on a lead behind the coach, Francis climbed on to the carriage box, picked up the reins and sent the two coach horses forward. The vehicle rumbled through the gates and headed for the moorland road from Whitby to Pickering.

Ruth gave Whitby only a cursory glance. It seemed a lifetime since she had come here as a teenage girl. Her ambitions, strengthened when she discovered her aristocratic background, were wrecked on jealousy and hatred of the girl she was sure had taken David's heart. Now she had had her revenge and Whitby meant nothing more to her.

They reached Liverpool without mishap, cautious in their contacts on the way even though they knew Francis had permission to be absent from his work and would not be missed for two weeks.

Francis sold the coach and horses and booked passage on the American ship *Clementine* bound for Boston. An individually owned ship experimenting in the passenger trade between Liverpool and Boston, it carried timber from America and returned with passengers. Their cabins were comfortable and spacious, the best which money could buy, and the passengers were free from the usual mass of emigrants, for American ships were not yet concerned with that trade.

Emily Judson did not take kindly to her first voyage and spent most of the time in her cabin. After two days Ruth found her sealegs and, along with Francis, found walking the deck as the ship sliced through the Atlantic swell exhilarating. She enjoyed relaxing in the well-appointed saloon and dining at the captain's table where the stimulating conversation was accompanied by a variety of well-cooked food – mutton and pork served in various ways and always accompanied by an excellent claret. She was keen to hear about America, and particularly of life in Boston and New Bedford. She already knew of the latter as a whaling port, albeit on a small scale, but from what she gleaned realised that it was now being seen as a place which could develop into an important port. She was determined to be part of its exciting future. There she would turn their gains into a fortune. Nothing and no one would stop her.

Sailing into Boston, Ruth felt elated. She drank in every aspect of the town. This was the beginning of her new life. Soon she would be putting her foot ashore in America and the past would be forgotten.

When the captain came to say goodbye to them at the gangway, he said, 'You'll be wanting a hotel for the night, bound as you are for New Bedford. The stagecoach leaves early morning, you'll arrive in New Bedford early evening.' He glanced down at the quay swarming with people, some greeting passengers, others going about their business, others just idle sightseers. 'Boy, boy!' he shouted. Two black boys, about fourteen years old, detached themselves from a group and ran to the bottom of the gangway where they stopped and looked up expectantly. 'Come aboard,' the captain called.

The two boys ran up the gangway. They were dressed in torn shirts and short trousers, with nothing on their feet. 'Massa,' they said brightly, their eyes shining in anticipation of something worthwhile, for the arrival of a passenger ship could mean money for them.

'Take this luggage, and guide these ladies and this gentleman to the Excelsior Hotel.'

'Yes, Massa.' They started into their task.

'Sir,' said Francis, turning to the captain, 'can they direct us via a bank? We must acquaint ourselves with American money.'

'Of course,' he replied, then directed his order to the two boys. 'Go via the National Bank.'

'Yes, Massa.'

At the bank Emily remained outside, determined that nothing should happen to their luggage. Ruth and Francis quickly made the acquaintance of the manager, changed some of their English money and received a recommendation and introduction to a private banker in New Bedford for as yet there was no incorporated bank in the town. They obtained rooms at the Excelsior and were woken the following morning in time to catch the stagecoach for New Bedford.

The roads were rough, in some parts little more than tracks, but in the skilled hands of their driver the coach made up time on the better sections. There were no other passengers going all the way to New Bedford but at some of the several stops along the way they picked up people travelling shorter distances. Buffeted and shaken, Ruth sometimes longed for the steady motion of the vessel which had carried them across the Atlantic.

Their final stop was at Acushnet at the tavern of Jabez Sherman which they had been told by a passenger was the most cheerful and inviting inn between New Bedford and Boston. They found his words true for in the friendly hands of Jabez and his wife the tavern's atmosphere was warm, the food good and the wine excellent. A genial welcome was given to travellers and the Shermans were more than interested to learn that they had visitors from England coming to take up a new life in New Bedford.

'You'll be needing a place to stay in Bedford while you look for a place of your own,' said Jabez as they were leaving, 'so might I recommend you go to my sister's on Water Street? Esme Taber, and her husband's John. You'll be very comfortable there.'

'If your tavern and hospitality is anything to go by, I'm sure we will,' said Ruth with a gracious smile.

'Tell her I sent you,' Jabez added as he helped Ruth into the coach.

The news of the coach's arrival brought a number of people flocking around to greet relations among the other five passengers, or pick up the latest news from Boston or a message from one of the stopping places. Luggage was handled quickly and the coachman collared two youngsters from among the crowds who were milling round the coach. 'Jimmy, Mark, help these good folk with their luggage and take them to Mrs Taber's on Water Street.'

They led the way to a solid-looking, clapboard house with a large brick central chimney. The windows were neatly curtained, the outside of the house well maintained, and it looked as though it had recently been painted. Their knock on the door was answered by a woman who could have been no one else but Jabez Sherman's sister. She was well made like him, her round face looking newly scrubbed. Her straight hair was drawn back and tied in a neat bun at the nape of her neck. Her blue eyes sparkled with interest at the strangers she found at her door.

'Good day, Ma'am,' said Ruth. 'We seek accommodation. We've just arrived on the Boston stage. Your brother at Acushnet told us to call on you.'

Esme smiled broadly, showing even white teeth. 'Anyone my brother sends is welcome. Come on in with thee.' She stepped to one side, holding the door open.

Ruth entered, followed by Emily and Francis. The two boys brought the luggage in.

'Put them down there, Jimmy.' Esme pointed to a spot close to the bottom of the stairs.

Francis tipped the two boys, who expressed their gratitude. Jimmy added, 'If you need any help, Ma'am, we'd be pleased if you'd call on us.' He addressed his remarks to Ruth. 'We live two doors away.' He indicated the direction.

'Thanks, Jimmy. We may need a guide until we get to know our way around.'

'Now, Ma'am, what accommodation would thee be wanting, and for how long?' asked Esme, who believed in getting down to business right away. The niceties could come later.

'Three rooms, please.'

'New out from England, I'll be bound?' Esme hinted. 'Aiming to settle here?'

'The answer is yes to both questions,' replied Ruth. 'We'd like rooms until we can find a house to buy.'

'Very well,' said Esme. 'I'll show thee what I have.' She led the way upstairs and the newcomers found the rooms neat, tidy, and adequately furnished.

'We'll take them,' said a satisfied Ruth when Esme quoted her terms.

'That includes all meals,' she added, 'and I guess thee'd like something now?'

'I would think only something light,' said Ruth, who received a nod of approval from Emily and Francis. 'Your brother fed us well.'

When they came down for their meal John Taber had arrived. He introduced himself. 'Esme tells me thee'll be looking for a house?'

'Yes,' Ruth affirmed.

'Shouldn't be too difficult. There's land being sold on Walnut Street. Good sites. Thee get one of those and I can organise the house to be built for thee. I'm a carpenter, cooper and wood carver, and work with the builders.'

Ruth was delighted. Their luck was in, and she realised this even more so after she had plied John with questions and indicated their reason for coming to New Bedford.

'If thee has knowledge of the whaling trade, thee's come to the right place to settle,' he said. 'Mark my words, New Bedford will expand on the whaling trade and there'll be fortunes made. There are signs of it already. A ship, thee says? Well, thee could go to Joseph Spence, Sam Arnold, Ben Hudson – all of them are beginning to get a grip on the whaling trade here.' He paused, looked thoughtful for a moment then added, 'But maybe thee'd be best going to see Jeremiah Whelden. He and his son, Lewis, are having two new ships built specifically for the Southern Atlantic and the Pacific. There's talk of them pulling out of the Arctic trade. They might just be prepared to sell one of those ships rather than convert it.'

That night, when Ruth discreetly visited Francis in his room, she made plans as she lay in his arms. 'Tomorrow morning a site for a house. Tomorrow afternoon a whale-ship. Oh, Francis, we'll build a whaling empire on the back of that ruined firm in Whitby!'

Chapter Eighteen

Immediately he had seen the *Capella* safely to her berth in the London Docks, Captain Midgley left the ship in the capable hands of her mate and hurried through the busy street to the offices of Hartley Shipping.

His urgent knock was answered by Billy who quickly ushered him inside at his request to see Captain David Fernley.

'Simeon.' David rose from his seat behind the desk. For two weeks Lydia had been feeling unwell and David had insisted that she remain at home while he saw to any urgent matters in the office. Silas Farnham, their chief clerk, was quite capable of seeing to everyday matters so Lydia complied with David's wishes. He shook hands with the man from Whitby. 'Good to see thee. What brings thee to Hartley Shipping? News from Whitby?'

'This,' replied Simeon. He held out an envelope which he had withdrawn from his pocket as they were speaking. 'Your sister said it was urgent and that I was to give it to thee personally so that she knew thee had received it.'

A puzzled look crossed David's face as he took the letter from the envelope. The matter must be serious for Jessica to be so cautious.

Dearest David,

I am sorry to report that we are in serious trouble. Francis Chambers has disappeared, taking with him the greater part of the Fernley and Thoresby account. But worse – the three ships are no longer ours! I went to make arrangements for the sale of the oil when they returned only to be told that that had already been done by Mr James Chapman. I couldn't understand it so went to see him. He said the ships were his and showed me an authorisation to sell signed by me. Oh, David, I never signed such a document!

He said Francis Chambers had taken the Bill of Exchange. When I checked it seems that this happened the day he told me he was to be absent from the office for two weeks. He has not been seen since.

We don't know what to do. We face ruin. Please help.

Your affectionate and troubled sister,

Jessica

David frowned. This was a catastrophe. The three ships gone, owned by someone else? It was something he just could not imagine. Those ships were steeped in Fernley and Thoresby history. They were his beloved ships. Each one meant something special to him. He must go at once. But there was Lydia . . .

'Bad news?' Simeon asked.

'Almost the worst,' he replied. 'The ships have been sold without Jessica's or Jenny's knowledge. Francis Chambers seems to be at the bottom of it. He's disappeared.' He did not give Simeon time to comment but asked, 'When does thee sail?'

'Morning tide.'

'Right. I'll be with thee, almost certain, but if I'm not when thee's due to weigh anchor, gan without me.'

Simeon nodded. 'And if there's anything I can do, please ask.'

'Thanks.' David raised his voice. 'Billy!'

The youth darted into the office. 'Yes, sir?'

'Show Captain Midgley out and then get Tomkins with the coach.'

'Yes, sir.'

'And quick! It's urgent.'

As Billy hurried from the office with the captain of the *Capella*, David picked up several papers from his desk and crossed the passage to see Silas Farnham. 'I have to go to Whitby. I don't know how long I'll be away. Thee must take charge here. If there are any important decisions, then refer them to Mr Dominic.'

'Very good, sir.' Silas had been with Hartley Shipping so long that he knew the running of the firm as well as anyone. David knew he was leaving the business in capable hands. He instructed him about the papers he had brought from his office, bade him and the other clerks goodbye and left.

The coach was approaching when he went outside and he told Tomkins to lose no time in driving to Russell Square.

He hurried into the withdrawing room where Lydia was sitting in a comfortable chair, with her feet resting on a stool. She was near the window from where she could look across the square and had been surprised to see David arrive.

'You're home soon, love,' she commented as he came to her. He bent and kissed her, but she was troubled by the expression on his face. 'Something wrong?'

'This,' he replied, handing her the letter he had received from Whitby.

She read it quickly, then looked up at him. 'Of course you must go.'

'But thee's not well,' cried David, torn between two loyalties. 'I shouldn't leave thee.'

'Nonsense,' replied Lydia sharply. 'I'll be all right. It's just a minor upset. I'll take care. I've got Father and Mrs Dove as well as Millie and cook. I'll be well looked after. He should go, Pa, shouldn't he?' She held out the letter and David passed it to Dominic, who had stopped reading when David arrived and had been puzzled by the exchange.

302

He read the note. 'Most certainly you should go. You cannot allow your firm to be ruined. You must see what is wrong. Lydia will be all right with us.'

'Are thee sure?'

Both father and daughter approved most emphatically and within a few minutes David's objections were broken down.

Grey clouds tumbled in the glowering sky, parting only occasionally to allow shafts of sunlight to flirt with the crowded red roofs of Whitby's east side. The mood of the day matched that of Jessica and Jenny as they walked to the quay where they hoped David would arrive on the *Capella*.

Their depression lifted when they saw David standing beside the rail. Smiles and shouts of greeting were exchanged as the ship sailed the last few feet to her berth. As soon as the gangway was run out David was on the quay, hugging his sister and then holding out his arm to Jenny.

'It's so good to see thee, Davey.' There were tears in Jessica's eyes and her voice caught in her throat. 'I was so sorry to send thee that letter.'

'We're glad you're here. We didn't know what to do.' There was concern in Jenny's voice.

'Tell me all about it when we get home. I presume I'm staying with thee, Jess?'

'Of course.'

They picked their way quickly through the throng of people on the quay and were soon at Jessica's. Once they had settled with tea and some of David's favourite fruit cake, she told him all she knew.

'I've no idea how the ships came to be sold nor how the money was taken from the account, but Francis must have been at the bottom of it. We had given him permission to be absent for two weeks after the ships had sailed. When he didn't return we thought he must be ill or have been delayed. We didn't bother for a couple of days, and then we thought we had better make some enquiries. We visited his lodgings only to learn that he had given them up the day he started his leave.'

'His landlady had not heard of him since that day?'

'No. We feared he must have decided to leave his job but thought it strange for we trusted him and he seemed to like working for us. We gave him a lot of responsibility as thee knows and he seemed to enjoy that.'

'Maybe we gave him too much,' put in Jenny. 'We carried on but received another shock when we went to draw some money from the bank. We were told that most of it had been withdrawn by Francis on the day he quit his lodgings. Mr Simpson told us he thought it was strange but he had a note of authorisation signed by Jessica.'

'I don't remember signing such a note,' she said.

'What about the ships?'

'I just don't know,' she replied, her voice low with guilt and worry. 'The day I wrote you the letter I had been to make arrangements about having the blubber boiled but was told that James Chapman had made arrangements for the cargoes of our three ships.'

'We just couldn't understand it,' said Jenny, taking up the story as Jessica faltered. 'We went to see Chapman, only to be presented with a note authorising the sale of the ships to him. And that was signed by Jessica.'

'I remember no such note,' she cried in dismay, on the verge of tears.

'Take it easy, love,' soothed David. There had been some trickery and though he knew Jessica must bear some of the responsibility if those signatures were genuine, he did not want to lay the blame. 'Do thee think Francis could have forged your signature?'

Jessica looked thoughtful for a moment then seized on the chance to exonerate herself. 'I suppose so. How else could they have got on those letters?'

'Could he have slipped them in with other things to sign?'

Jessica hesitated. 'Well, it's possible.'

'Don't thee read everything he brings thee to sign?'

'Well, not when I know it's just everyday things. Francis will wait while I sign and explain anything he thinks needs explaining,' she related nervously.

'Then he could have slipped those two letters among some others?' pressed David gently.

'Oh, my God, what have I done?' Jessica hid her face in her hands. Tears began to flow.

David came to sit beside her. 'Don't, love. Crying won't help.'

She looked up with tear-filled eyes. 'But I've ruined the firm through my carelessness. I've sold the ships thee loved so much. Oh, David, thee'll never forgive me.' She flung her arms round his neck.

He held her tight, trying to take the hurt from her. 'Don't blame thyself. If Francis was determined to sell those ships, he'd have found some way to do so. He's been crafty, no doubt diverting thy attention when thee came to those particular notes. And if thee had noticed I'm sure he'd have had some glib explanation. Now, there'll be nothing we can do about the money he took from the bank, but maybe there's something we can do about the ships. I'll go and see Chapman.'

When David reached the offices of Chapman and Hern his request to see James was met immediately.

'David Fernley. I'm surprised to see thee,' said James without rising from his seat behind a large oak desk which was set at an angle to the window, giving him a view across the harbour. He eyed David as he crossed the room to the visitor's chair. James Chapman had always held a contemptuous jealousy for the farm boy who had come to Whitby and made good in the whaling trade. David

Fernley had done it the hard way, serving in all the capacities on the whaleships until he became a captain. He had the respect of the Whitby folk for his hard work and diligence, and the fact that he had risen from the lowest of the low. Whereas James himself had never gained that respect. He had come into his father's firm and had never had to soil his hands on a whaleship. Everything had been laid on for him. That jealousy had been appeased when Chambers had come to him with the proposition of selling him Fernley and Thoresby's three ships, provided the Bill of Exchange be made out to him personally and that no one but their two selves should know this. James had been tempted and succumbed to Francis's glib tongue. With those three ships added to his own fleet he would become the biggest whaling concern in Whitby and Fernley would be ruined. 'I thought you were living in London now?'

'So I am, but I still have my interest in the firm here so when I received a letter from my sister asking for my help because our three ships had been sold to thee without her knowledge, I lost no time in getting here.'

'Then you've wasted your time. Those ships are legally mine whether your sister knew about it or not.' He threw up his hands, adding emphasis to his words as he said, 'But she must have done, she signed the authorisation.'

'But she says she never saw it.'

'Then your sister must have a poor memory.' He reached into a drawer, took out a piece of paper and placed it on the desk in front of David in such a position that he could keep his hand on it while David scrutinised it. 'There is her signature authorising the sale.'

David recognised Jessica's signature. His heart ran cold. This legally binding document deprived him of his beloved ships and there was little he could do about it. He read the words and saw there the answer to something which had been puzzling him but which he had not voiced to Jessica and Jenny. He had not been able to understand how Francis had absconded with the proceeds from the sale of the ships when the Bill of Exchange would be made out to Fernley and Thoresby. But there in black and white, as part of the authorisation, were words allowing the Bill of Exchange to be made out in the name of Francis Chambers. He was numb, hardly able to take it in. The firm was ruined.

'Satisfied?' There was mockery in Chapman's voice which irritated David.

He straightened and gave James a withering look. 'No. What about that?' He pointed to the words he had just read.

Chapman glanced at them and then back to David. He shrugged his shoulders. 'What about them?'

David glared angrily. 'They speak of collusion to me.'

James bristled. 'What are you getting at? Everything's straightforward.'

'Thee never gets such wording authorising payment of such a large amount to an employee. Thee should have queried it unless thee'd agreed it first with Chambers.' David was on his feet, leaning forward, hands planted firmly on the desk. 'Just how far were thee and Chambers in this together?'

James sprang to his feet. His temper was rising. 'What are you insinuating?'

'That thee and Chambers set out to ruin my firm. One of thee suggested it to the other and then . . .'

'That document's legal,' snapped James. 'And there's nothing you can do about it. The ships are mine, and mine they'll remain.'

David knew he was caught and the fact lent him added determination. He knew their raised voices would be heard in the clerk's office so kept his loud as he said, 'One day I'll have them back.'

'Like hell you will!' James sneered. 'It'll cost you double

to get them.' He was certain he had put them out of David's reach. After all, Fernley and Thoresby had no future and now David was a mere whaling captain sailing out of London.

David moved swiftly to the door and jerked it open. As he'd suspected the door into the clerk's office across the corridor was open. He knew that an argument involving their master was too good to miss. He was into their office in two quick steps. He grabbed the nearest man and propelled him into James's room. The man was so startled that when David fired his order at him, he obeyed automatically.

'What did Mr Chapman just say?' The fierce anger in his voice and the thunderous look he gave him frightened the clerk.

'It'll cost thee double to get the ships,' he spluttered.

'Right,' cried David. 'Thee's a witness.' He grabbed a quill pen, dipped it in the ink and wrote quickly on a sheet of paper: 'I promise to sell the *Mary Jane*, *The Lonely Wind* and the *Ruth* to David Fernley when he can pay .... for them.' He thrust the paper and pen at James, who had been so startled by the speed of events that he had barely sized up the situation. 'Sign,' rapped David.

James hesitated. David rounded the desk and grabbed hold of his neck. 'Sign, or else I'll break thy blasted neck!' He gave James a sharp jerk.

'All right, all right,' he protested. 'I'll sign.' David released his hold and James picked up the quill. 'It'll make no difference. You'll never be able to afford them.' His voice held a triumphant note. He wrote his name with a flourish.

'Fill in the amount. And don't falsify it. I'll check thy ledger.'

When James had completed the form, David glanced at the amount. 'Twenty-one thousand pounds! If that's double, thee got them cheap.' He handed the quill to the clerk. 'Witness,' he snapped.

The man trembled as he wrote but his signature was legible.

'Date it.' The man did so. 'Now go.' The clerk scurried from the office like a frightened rabbit.

David took the piece of paper, folded it carefully and slipped it into his pocket. He looked up to see James leaning back in his chair with a supercilious look on his face.

'Useless, Fernley. You'll never be able to afford those ships.'

David's eyes narrowed as he looked down at James. 'One day, Chapman, one day.' His voice was scarcely above a whisper but it was penetrating, leaving no doubt in Chapman's mind that he would be back one day to settle a debt, formidable task or not.

David turned and strode from the room.

Chapter Nineteen

Once the *Capella* had docked, anxious for news of his wife, David lost no time in reaching the house in Russell Square.

He had spent three fretful days in Whitby waiting for the ship's next sailing. He had done what he could to ease the troubled firm, trying to raise capital for a new vessel but failing. His thoughts turned to the possibility of getting Lydia and her father to approve the loan of a vessel for a share in the proceeds. If so, they could start with a winter voyage to the Baltic for timber, once the *Hind* had returned from the Arctic.

As he stepped from the carriage which had brought him from the dock, his glance took in the front façade of the house. The curtains were drawn across every window. For a brief moment he stared, not realising the significance. Then it hit him like the cold blast of the icy Arctic wind.

'Oh my God! Dominic!' He did not realise he had uttered the words for his mind was racing with concern for Lydia. The blow of losing her father could be devastating at a time like this. He raced to the front door, let himself in, flung his cloak on to a chair as he crossed the hall. He burst into the withdrawing room.

With the curtains drawn it was dim. Only a single oil lamp sent out its yellow light, casting grotesque shapes across the walls. 'Lydia . . .' His voice broke on a sharp intake of breath. Lydia's chair, the stool for her feet – no one occupied them. The only figure was sitting in Dominic's chair. A choking sensation was rising in his throat as he stepped towards his father-in-law. His mind was whirling. Those curtains couldn't be for Lydia. She couldn't be . . . ? No, she must be resting upstairs. But why the drawn curtains? He stopped beside the chair.

Dominic looked up slowly and David saw an old man from whom life appeared to have drained. His eyes bore unfathomable sadness. His hand reached up for David's, an effort which seemed almost beyond him. David dropped to one knee beside the chair.

'David, my boy.' Dominic's words came in a croaked whisper then faded away, choked by overwhelming despair.

'What happened?' He could scarcely frame the question.

'Lydia took a turn for the worse. The baby came early. Complications.' He shook his head. 'Oh, I don't know, but the doctor couldn't save her.'

'I should have been here!' David's face twisted in agony. He was riddled with guilt. 'I shouldn't have gone to Whitby.'

The anguished cry stirred Dominic into realising he wasn't the only one who was suffering. David had come back, full of life and eager to see Lydia – only to find that his beloved was dead.

'You can't blame yourself, David. If you had been here you couldn't have saved her.'

'I could have been with her, maybe given her strength, maybe helped her to live.'

Dominic shook his head slowly. 'She wouldn't have. The doctor assured me nothing could have been done for her.' He laid a comforting hand on David's shoulder. 'But you have a son.'

Startled, he looked up in surprise. He had assumed that because his wife had died, the child had died too. 'The baby lived?'

Dominic nodded. 'A fine healthy child. Lydia would have been proud of him.'

'Where are they?'

'Upstairs.'

David pushed himself to his feet and hurried from the room. His thoughts were whirling as he took the stairs two at a time. At the cry of a babe from the room to his left, he paused a moment on the landing then moved slowly to the room he and Lydia had shared. He hesitated, drew a deep breath and pushed it open. He stepped into the room and closed the door quietly. There was peace here which did not want to be disturbed.

The drawn curtains had taken almost all the light from the room. He moved slowly to the bed, his eyes on the still figure upon it. He paused and looked down at her, silent, untroubled, untouched by the world. 'Lydia, my love, why?' His whispered words choked on the enormity of the question to which there was no answer. This was the end, here time ceased, but he could not let her go in the dimness of this room. He went to the curtains and drew them back so that light touched the bed. He walked back to take his last look at his wife. Her flaxen hair had been combed and drawn up to her crown where it had been neatly pinned in place, just as it had been when he first saw her. Her skin was smooth, almost translucent, unlined. The years had fallen away and she had assumed the looks of the beautiful girl she must have been before he knew her. Love swelled in his heart and his mind cried to heaven with loss and grief. He bent down slowly and kissed her. The cry of a baby filtered down the passage.

'Thank thee for my son,' he whispered. 'There'll always be part of thee with me.' He turned slowly to the door, paused and looked back as he opened it. 'Goodbye, my love.'

Two days later Lydia was laid to rest. It was a big funeral. Such a likeable person had attracted many friends and she and Hartley Shipping were well known in the city's shipping and merchant circles. Dominic had insisted on going. In fact, he had shown remarkable strength. It was as if the death of his daughter had laid more responsibility on him which he was determined to accept and fulfil by throwing off the shackles of age.

With sympathisers all gone, Dominic took David to his study. He poured two glasses of brandy and handed one to David with the words, 'Thee needs this after this harrowing experience.' He sat down behind his desk and looked hard at David. 'My boy, this has been a sad and terrible experience for us both, but though we mourn her she will not be far from us. We have our lives to live and a child to look after. Lydia loved life. She would not want us to mourn. She loved Hartley Shipping. She would want us to see that it thrived and gained strength, for you have a son who will own it one day.'

Seeing David was about to speak, he held up his hand to halt his words. 'Before you say anything, David, hear me out. You may have thought I was not fully with you these last few days. There were times when I wasn't – the shock of losing Lydia was too great. But I was also doing a lot of thinking. What would she want me to do? Now I want you to hear my conclusions.' He paused and sipped his brandy. David, respecting the old man's wishes, said nothing.

'Well, one day the firm would have been Lydia's. Now it will be yours. I will transfer her portion to you. It would not come to you automatically as her husband for in her will it states that her shares must revert to me if anything should happen to her. It was arranged that way just in case she married anyone who turned out to be unscrupulous. I will alter my will so that when I join her the firm will be yours in its entirety, with a proviso that it passes from you to your son. Lydia's son. I make this proviso because you already have a son and, who knows, one day you may marry again.'

David started to protest that that could never happen. The love he had for Lydia would never allow it. But

Dominic stopped him. 'She would not hold it against you if you did find someone else. I know, and she knows, that even if you did, you would never forget her. Now, how does my proposition sound to you?'

'What can I say? Thee's too generous.' David was overcome with emotion. Dominic could have been bitter. His only child taken from him in the prime of her life. In that bitterness he could have blamed David, could have turned his wrath on the child. But he did none of these things. Here he was showing the face of understanding and true generosity of spirit.

'It's what Lydia would have wanted, and I do too. Now that's settled, what are you going to call the boy?'

'Daniel,' replied David. 'Lydia said that if we had a son she would like him to be called Daniel Dominic.'

'Admirable.' A little smile of pleasure appeared and Dominic took a sip of brandy as if to hide it. 'I have something else to say. Because you are taking Lydia's place with the firm, does not mean that you have to stay ashore. I know you love the sea and like nothing better than to be on the deck of a ship with the wind in your hair and the taste of salt on your lips. You'll always be a sailor who keeps his eye on the business side of things whenever he's at home. I think it would be a good thing for you to get away to sea as soon as possible. Help you to forget.'

'But I can't. If thee's being so generous in letting me have Lydia's share of the business, the least I can do is to remain ashore and put my mind to it.'

'Nonsense,' interrupted Dominic. 'This is what I propose. We promote Silas from chief clerk to manager. He's been with us long enough to accept more responsibility. He understands our policies and operations. Dick Castle and Stanley Harris can share the work Silas does now. I will be here and Silas can confer regularly with me. With that arrangement you are free to make voyages and can come back with all manner of tales to tell me.' The bright light of enthusiasm shone in his eyes and David knew he was seeing himself as a young man on the deck of a ship with the sails taut in a stiff wind, the spray curling from the bow and the weather set fair. He wanted to sense it all again, through David. He would not be disappointed.

'But what about Daniel?' he asked, seeing the babe as an obstacle to Dominic's plans.

'No trouble. We'll get a nurse for him. I'll be here, and you know Mrs Dove and Milly will fuss over him. Oh, Daniel will be all right, never fear.'

'Very well.' David was pleased to accept his father-in-law's suggestion. He knew it would do him good to get away, especially back to the life he loved.

'Good,' said Dominic. 'Take a whaler to the Pacific.'

'What!' David gasped. 'But that means two years. I can't be away that long.'

'Why not? Daniel's only a babe, he'll not miss you. Now if he was two that might be a different matter . . . Besides, the South Seas will do you good, so different to the Arctic, and we don't want you trapped in the ice again.'

'Thee seems to have it all worked out,' smiled David.

'All for the best, I hope.'

'There is just one request I would make of thee?'

'Name it.'

'My trip to Whitby . . .'

'Oh, I'm sorry, in all the upset I never asked you about that. And as you did not mention it, I assumed everything was satisfactory.'

David shook his head slowly. 'I'm afraid it wasn't. I did not tell thee about it, it wasn't the right time, only now . . .'

'We've time.'

David told him how Francis had defrauded the firm, bringing it to the edge of ruin. Dominic came to the same conclusion as he – that Chapman had been in collusion with Chambers.

'I'm afraid I cannot raise that amount to buy those ships

315

back,' said Dominic with a regretful shake of his head. 'I only wish I could.'

'I'm not asking that,' said David. 'What I am asking is the loan of a ship to keep the firm afloat. Say the *Hind* when it returns from the Arctic? Let it do a winter voyage for timber sailing out of Whitby, and then to the Arctic whaling again next year. We'll split the profits.'

Dominic tapped his glass thoughtfully, took a sip and licked his lips. David was tense, waiting for the old man's reply. 'We'll go one better than that. We'll add to that the voyage you are doing – we'll split the profits on that one too.' His voice was firm, brooking no arguments.

David relaxed. 'Thank thee, sir. I'm even more in thy debt.'

'Nonsense.' He waved away the obligation with a shake of his hand. 'I'm afraid it won't raise enough money to buy those ships but it'll be a start. I can see how much they mean to you. I only wish I could help more.'

'Thee's done enough. Thy generosity will keep the firm afloat until the day I see those ships sailing under the Fernley and Thoresby flag again.'

Six weeks later, with everything organised to his satisfaction for the care and welfare of his son, David took a ship, renamed the *Lydia*, down the Thames bound for Cape Horn and the Pacific.

Within a fortnight of their arrival in New Bedford, Ruth and Francis saw a start on building their house on Walnut Street and had an appointment with Jeremiah Whelden and his son Lewis.

Ruth had attracted the eyes of the men and the curiosity of the ladies. Here was a mature woman who liked to hold centre stage; in fact, her very presence, the way she held herself, seemed to be aimed at one thing: drawing the attention of the menfolk. But at the same time she knew how to charm their ladies, who, though wary and ready to hold her at arm's length from their husbands and sweethearts, secretly admired her poise and charm. Their curiosity extended to her background. Who was she? Why was she in New Bedford? Was she a widow? Who was the handsome Francis Chambers? A lover who had come between man and wife? Had they fled to escape her husband's wrath? And who was their travelling companion? Relative, servant or merely friend?

Rumour had it that they planned a fine house on Walnut Street and that they were interested in the whaling trade. If so, then they were not short of money.

Such curiosity could not go unanswered and Ruth soon found herself invited to take tea with the wives of the most influential men in New Bedford.

She gave them only as much information as she wanted them to have on each occasion so that further invitations would follow, as they did until individuals trying to outdo each other extended their invitations to intimate dinner parties. Patience and subtle manoeuvring brought their reward when Ruth secured an invitation for her and Francis to the home of Jeremiah and Miriam Whelden.

Meanwhile Francis, precluded from the ladies' tea parties, studied the activities of the whaling port, and came to know some of its captains and sailors by visiting the wharves and taverns. Curious about the Englishman, they were impressed by his knowlege of whaling, albeit confined to the Arctic trade, though he had never sailed on a whaler. They were eager too to talk of England and her attitude to their newly independent country, and only too willing to talk of their town and its trade.

He realised that they were proud of it, eager to see it expand, and that they foresaw this as being on the back of the whaling trade. He learned that this had been set back by the American Revolution which had brought an abrupt end to its prosperity and forced ships to be idle. In 1778 the British had marched into New Bedford, burning buildings, wharves and ships, completely devastating the business and waterfront area. Recovery came only slowly and seven years passed before a whaler sailed from the port again. But now there was every sign that New Bedford was thriving. Blacksmith's shops, cooperages, ropewalks, the candle manufactory and other industries connected with the whaling industry were rebuilt. The shipyards and wharves bustled with activity once again, and in 1791 the *Rebecca* sailed to the Pacific, the first American whaler to round Cape Horn, after British whalers from London had found an abundance of whales there two years earlier.

New Bedford seemed determined to oust Nantucket from its position as the leading whaling port in America, a position the latter had enjoyed since whales were first hunted along the New England coast. Francis saw that they could be part of this new boom and there would be money to be made. He therefore welcomed the news when Ruth told him that they were invited to the Wheldens'.

'It's the Pacific trade we must look to,' he enthused as he briefed her while they were dressing for their evening out. 'There are still whalers going to the Arctic, and some are whaling in the Atlantic. They are short voyages and the blubber is brought back to be tried out down by the river. But I've seen tryworks being erected on the decks of new whaleships so that the blubber can be turned to oil to overcome the longer voyage and hotter weather experienced in the Pacific. That is what we have to aim for.'

Ruth was swept along by his enthusiasm and they were both in buoyant mood when they arrived at the Whelden house. It was situated on the corner of Union and Second Street and was of large proportions, Ruth thought probably the biggest in New Bedford. It certainly had an air of affluence, situated on a slight hill beside a row of poplar trees. They were admitted into a large square hall by two dark-skinned maids dressed in neat plain brown dresses with spotless white bib pinafores and white mobcaps. One took Ruth's cloak and bonnet while the other attended to Francis's hat, cane and gloves. They were then escorted to a room on the right where one maid opened the double doors and the other stepped inside to announce clearly, 'Mrs Ruth Hardy and Mr Francis Chambers.'

As Ruth glided into the room, Miriam Whelden rose from a winged chair and came to meet her. She was of medium height, carrying an air of confidence coupled with a touch of sophistication. She wore a perfectly fitting dress of black silk watered faille, trimmed with beading and inset with lace.

Ruth breathed a sigh of relief that she had not chosen her own black dress for this evening. Instead she was wearing a white silk gown embroidered with flowers in yellow, red and blue, with a white Alençon lace fichu. She carried a brown silk reticule embroidered in colours to match. By choosing white, usually a colour reserved for young girls, she had attracted everyone's attention.

'Ah, Ruth, so nice to have you.' Miriam took her hand in friendly greeting.

'It's a privilege. Our thanks to you for inviting us.' Ruth stepped graciously to one side, half turning as she did so. 'May I introduce Francis Chambers?'

He bowed politely. 'Ma'am, the pleasure is mine.'

'Come, meet everyone.' Miriam turned to the other people in the room. 'Mrs Laetitia Spence and her husband Joseph, one of the leading whalemen in New Bedford.' Greetings were exchanged, Laetitia offering a polite smile while her eyes assessed Ruth's appearance.

Joseph bowed and as he looked up, said, 'I've been curious since Laetitia said she had met you at one of the tea parties and that she thought you must be from the North of England. I'll put it closer than that. I'd say you were from Yorkshire.'

Though her heart missed a beat, Ruth held her composure. 'You are right. We're from Hull. You know it?'

'No. I'm from Shetland. Sailed with two Whitby captains once, Seth Thoresby and David Fernley. David's first voyage as captain, my last as I decided to emigrate. I wonder if you ever met them?'

Ruth felt tension suffuse her body but held the emotions which threatened to overwhelm her in check. David's name was the last she had expected to hear so far from England. Thank goodness she had changed her name to Hardy! 'Naturally, being in the whaling trade I've heard of two such experienced whalemen but I've never met them.'

Both Ruth and Francis were thankful that Miriam moved them on to meet her husband, Jeremiah, a tall well-built man with a commanding presence. In his early sixties, he had an ample girth which he made no attempt to hide. He had made good, was affluent, and his dress and manner showed it. He was proud of his achievements but they had not turned him into a snob and he had the welfare and progress of New Bedford very much at heart. That was one reason he had encouraged his wife to arrange this dinner party. Newcomers to New Bedford, especially those who appeared to have money and were looking for an opening in the whaling trade, interested him. He had heard stories of the new arrivals from England but wanted to see for himself.

Miriam introduced her daughter Felicity, a dark-haired young woman of twenty-six whose open-fronted dress was of pale muslin with skirt ties passing round her slim figure to meet in a bow just below her breasts. Like her mother, she had a friendly, open face and gave Ruth and Francis a warm greeting, apologising for the absence of her husband, away on a whaling voyage.

Next Miriam took the two guests to the young man standing at one side of the fireplace. Ruth was curious to meet him for she had felt his eyes on her ever since she had entered the room.

'My son, Lewis.'

He bowed gracefully as he took Ruth's hand. She felt an odd sensation at his touch and knew he had meant to cause it. Now that she was close to him she wondered if he really was as young as she had first judged. Maybe not, maybe he was more her own age, but he certainly bore time well and knew how to create the impression of looking younger. He was elegantly dressed, his clothes fitting perfectly. They were of the best materials and their grey colour seemed to be purposely chosen to catch a female's attention. He held himself erect, Ruth would have said that he had a military bearing; if he was no longer in the army he must have served at some time. He was handsome and he knew it yet he did not exude an air of arrogance. His eyes were intriguing and Ruth felt that in spite of everyone else's presence in the room those eyes were only for her. They swept over her, appraising and assessing, and already sending out a signal that he hoped something might come of this meeting.

Throughout the evening she was always aware of him though he did not push himself. He did not attempt to monopolise her but mingled with everyone else.

By the time the evening ended Ruth had learned a lot about New Bedford and saw that with men like Jeremiah and Joseph, and sons like Lewis to carry on their business, New Bedford could boom on the whaling trade.

Although Jeremiah's parting words as they were leaving, 'As you want to set up in whaling both of you come to see me at my office tomorrow. I might be able to help,' were more than encouraging, she wondered if her future lay in someone else's hands.

Chapter Twenty

'Well, my dear, after your visit yesterday I've thought out a deal which might interest you.' Jeremiah leaned forward on his desk and fixed Ruth with a firm but friendly gaze. 'I'm taking two of my ships off the Arctic trade and I'm increasing my fleet by two more which are at present nearing completion in Freeman's shipyard. I could sell you one of the Arctic ships and, if you so desire, offer you a share in one of the new ones.'

Ruth inclined her head graciously and as she did so glanced quickly at Lewis, who sat beside and a little behind his father. He had never taken his eyes off her since she and Francis had arrived. She was not sure how to take this attention but of one thing she was certain – it was not going to distract her from the business in hand.

'That is very generous of you,' she said.

'A business proposition, Ma'am,' Jeremiah smiled. 'Also I have New Bedford at heart. It's a growing town. People with business in mind and money to support their efforts need encouraging to stay here. I detect in you and Francis just such persons. You are keen to invest to make money, and if you do New Bedford will benefit.' Jeremiah warmed to his subject. 'There's waterfront and warehouses out there just waiting to be occupied and used by those who have a vision of New Bedford as the leading whaling port in the country. With your knowledge of the trade you can fit in very well and take advantage of the opportunities.'

While he had been speaking Ruth had been making up her mind about his offer, but before she could present her opinion Francis, not wanting to appear the junior partner, spoke up. 'We would certainly like to purchase one of the ships and would like your advice about fitting it out for a voyage to the Pacific. As regards a share in one of the other vessels, I think we'll forgo that for the time being.' He glanced at Ruth. 'Don't you?'

She smiled at him without warmth. She did not like being pushed to one side. Lewis observed her reaction, veiled though it was, and was pleased. He liked his women strong-willed. It made the play for them and the final conquest all the more satisfying.

'I entirely agree,' she replied. 'Please don't think us ungrateful for not taking a share in the second ship but we would like to remain completely independent.'

Jeremiah nodded his agreement. 'Then you shall have the *Aurora*.'

'A good ship,' interjected Lewis. He glanced at his father. 'They'll need a crew. I suggest Captain Morgan Black stays with the *Aurora*. I think he'll be willing.' As his father nodded, he looked back at Ruth. 'He's tough, he's rough, but he'll get the job done. He's always returned with a full ship. His last voyage was to the Arctic but he's had experience of taking whales in the Atlantic and he's been round the Horn.'

'Will he recruit the crew?' Francis asked.

'Yes. They'll be mixed, some Americans, some Portuguese who've come back from the Azores to stay in the whaling trade, maybe the odd Indian or two. But they'll be good, Black will see to that.'

'Very well.' Francis looked at Ruth again. 'I think our first voyage should be a short one into the Atlantic. If we do that we'll get some return fairly quickly and then the second voyage can be to the Pacific.'

'That's a good idea,' Jeremiah approved.

The terms were agreed and Jeremiah told them he would have the necessary document ready for signature in three days.

They were about to leave when Lewis spoke. 'I gathered last night that Francis will be managing the everyday running of the business so will want an office? I suggest, Father, that we lease them the small warehouse with offices above that you recently purchased, overlooking the docks at the end of Middle Street.'

'An excellent idea, my boy.'

Lewis cast Ruth a look of satisfaction and she knew that he had purposely opened a door to collusion if she would step through it.

As they walked home Francis was ecstatic with the progress they had made. 'This is better than we thought. We visualised a struggle to become established but this has been easy. A ship which will sail in two weeks, bringing back profit within six months. And then greater profits from the Pacific.'

But Ruth was only half hearing him and answered automatically for her thoughts were on Lewis, a man who was offering an exciting liaison. She recalled how his eyes had swept over her the previous evening and how she had sensed he knew the effect he was having on her. He had taken that further this morning and she found herself wondering what it would be like to be taken by this man. Her thoughts ran on. Was it fortuitous that their paths had crossed? He was rich. His father had the leading whaling company in New Bedford and as the only son it would be his one day. Win him and she would have all the power she had ever wanted. Power which she had once had in Whitby but had lost. Maybe her destiny lay here in New Bedford. But there was Francis . . .

They had no ties. There was nothing to hold them together, or so she tried to delude herself. He was still infatuated with her and would not give up easily. However, things might be arranged and given a push if necessary.

Two weeks later, they watched the *Aurora* sail. Captain

Black had gathered his crew. They were such a mixed and rough-looking bunch that Ruth thought he must have searched the lowest taverns in the town. But he seemed to know them and reassured her that they were good whalers and would bring back a full ship. As for the man himself, she felt a little in awe of him at their first meeting. He was big, powerful, even his clothes did not hide the strength in his muscles. His hands were broad, fingers thick. His angular jaw was covered by a thick, short beard, its colour matching the deep black of his hair and eyes. It seemed as if his name had been chosen to identify his colouring. He had a black patch over his left eye which was lost, so stories said, in a fight in which a deadly whale lance was used. It seemed to amuse him that he should be working for a lady, an attitude which was eradicated when he realised she was a shrewd businesswoman, that she wouldn't be outsmarted, and that she would be generously appreciative if he kept the right side of her.

Lewis was among the gathering of people who came to wish the *Aurora* well on her first voyage under new owners.

As the ship caught the river breeze and headed for Buzzards Bay and the open sea, he said quietly in Ruth's ear, 'I think this is an occasion you and I should celebrate together.'

She looked coyly at him. 'Just what do you mean?'

'It would be spoilt if I told you.'

'Are you daring me to find out?'

'Take it as you will. I also think you have interests other than whaling. Maybe you'd like to share them with me?'

'Maybe.'

'There's a little inn about four miles out in the country. I know the landlord. He's discreet so you need have no fear. No one will know you have been there and shared a meal with me.'

'A meal?' Ruth pursed her lips thoughtfully.

Before Lewis could reply, Francis came hurrying over to them. 'Isaac Waitman wants to discuss some business with me. Will you be all right?'

'Think no more of it, Francis, I'll see Ruth reaches home safely.'

He hurried away to join Isaac, who was strolling slowly towards the office in which Francis had spent a great deal of time during the last two weeks, putting the new business on a firm footing.

Lewis smiled as he looked at Ruth and said, 'It couldn't have worked out more perfectly.'

Lewis drove the gig the four miles with an expertise which Ruth admired. She was fascinated by his long fingers which handled the reins delicately but kept command. She wondered what it would be like to feel those fingers touching her.

As they pulled up outside the inn she noticed the sign above the door announcing it to be the Harpooner. A black boy ran from the corner of the stoutly built wooden building and steadied the horse while Lewis climbed down and helped Ruth to the ground. 'Thanks, Toby.' He flicked a coin in the air which Toby caught deftly. He led the horse and gig to the back of the inn.

'You're well known here.' Ruth's words were an observation rather than a question.

'Oh, yes.'

'Then I'm not the first woman you've brought here?'

Lewis turnd her to face him with a light touch on the arm. She looked up into dark eyes which probed as if reading her soul. 'You're not a person to meddle with, nor to try and fool. I'll be blunt. You are right, you are not the first I've brought here, but you are the most intriguing. Let us go inside.' He escorted her into the inn.

'Good day, sir. Good day, Ma'am.' A stout, round-faced man, his straight hair tied back with a greasy ribbon, greeted them on their entrance. 'Nice to see you again, sir. Your usual room is ready and the meal will be ten minutes.'

'Thanks, Clay.'

The landlord crossed the floor to a room on the right. He opened the door and stepped to one side to allow Ruth and Lewis to enter.

She found herself in a compact room in which a fire burnt brightly in a grate. The day was not cold but the fire had a cheering, cosy effect. A two-seater cushioned settle stood to one side of the fire while a wing-chair stood at the other. An oak table set for two with high-backed dining chairs stood against one wall across the room from a neatly curtained window. A bowl of punch steamed on a small table set in front of the settle.

'Let me take your cloak.' Lewis slid it from Ruth's shoulders and laid it carefully on a chair beside the door, where he also placed his hat and cane. 'Do sit down. A cup of punch?'

'Seems as though you had all this planned,' said Ruth as she sat down. 'You anticipated my accepting?'

'I felt sure you would,' replied Lewis smoothly as he glanced up from pouring a cup of punch. 'After all, you are as intrigued by me as I am by you.'

She ignored the comment and instead said, 'But what if Francis . . . ?'

Lewis gave a little chuckle. 'I have a business interest with Isaac Waitman.'

'You put Waitman up to keeping Francis occupied?' said Ruth, amused by the audacity of the man.

'Let us say that I hinted at a business proposition which would tempt Francis and suggested to Waitman that it would be better put to him immediately.'

Ruth laughed. 'You were sure of yourself.'

'A man gets nowhere if he isn't.' Lewis raised his glass and Ruth acknowledged him.

'May I ask what the business proposition is?' she said. 'After all, I am involved, having put up most of the money to establish us here.'

'Now that interests me.' Lewis was watching her carefully for a reaction to his next question. 'Just what is your relationship with Francis?'

Ruth sipped her punch, looking over the rim of the glass to meet Lewis's penetrating gaze. In those seconds she considered her answer carefully. 'We are business partners. We were back in Hull, and decided that there was more money to be made here.'

'But there's more to it than that. You live in the same house.'

'Just let's say we satisfy each other's needs.'

'Nothing more than that? Nothing more permanent?'

Behind these questions Ruth saw an eager anticipatory light in his eyes and knew that Lewis's feelings were beginning to run deeper than physical attraction, even though they had known each other such a short time. Play this right and she could land the biggest catch in New Bedford.

'No,' she answered. 'But you haven't answered my question about the business proposition.'

'There's no need for you to bother your pretty little head about it. It will keep Francis occupied for about two weeks then nothing will come of it. And then there will be others to keep him occupied.'

'You plan ahead,' mused Ruth coyly. 'You expect me to come again?'

'I think you'll want to after today, after we've used those stairs.' He glanced in the direction of a door in one corner of the room and Ruth realised that it hid a staircase and that they were almost isolated from the rest of the inn.

'You flatter yourself.'

A smile appeared. 'We shall see.'

*   *   *

With the house in Walnut Street finished Emily Judson was able to take over the role of housekeeper more fully and was pleased when Ruth let her have a free hand to engage servants and run the home. This was the life she liked. Knowing this, Ruth played on it for she wanted to gain Emily's trust and discretion. Her liaisons with Lewis had become more frequent and she knew the day would come when he visited the house.

For the rest of New Bedford Ruth reciprocated with tea and dinner parties, and though there were some questions asked among themselves about the relationship between Ruth and Francis, the New Bedford ladies and their husbands accepted them into society.

Ruth found life good. She enjoyed the social occasions, using them to promote interest in the whaling firm she was creating and to advance its prospects. Already she was talking about another ship but, although Francis was enthusiastic, they decided to wait to see what profit came of the *Aurora*'s first voyage. Ruth's ambitions were fired the more contact she had with Lewis. She saw him as the key to riches and power, and was determined to have both. She had played the recluse in Rigg House long enough in order to attain her desire. Now she was determined to build on that, and nothing would stand in her way. Not even Francis.

Her meetings with Lewis became more frequent as they sought to assuage their mutual passion. But Ruth played for higher stakes in the knowledge that Lewis had fallen in love with her.

Two weeks before the *Aurora* was due back, Lewis asked her to marry him.

'Are you sure, Lewis? It's not just because we are good with each other?' Ruth put on a cautious air, even though she could see all her planning coming to fruition.

'It's because I love you,' he murmured as he held her close. 'I have since the first moment I saw you. I knew that one day you would be mine.'

'You're sure you want to spend the rest of your life with me?'

'There's nothing of which I am more certain. You're a fascinating woman, Ruth. A gentle lover, a passionate woman, hard-headed and shrewd in business, and there's an air of mystery about you I have not fathomed yet but which makes you all the more attractive. Say you love me. Say you'll marry me?'

'Oh, Lewis, yes, yes! Nothing would make me happier.'

Their lips met in a kiss which sealed their future.

'Just one thing, Lewis. Don't let's announce it yet. I have Francis to contend with. Let me get that over before we do.'

'Just as you wish. But make it soon. I want to announce my good fortune to everyone.'

Though they were discreet in their meetings, rumours began to circulate and two days before the *Aurora* was due Ruth returned home from an afternoon with Lewis to find Francis already awaiting her return.

As soon as she entered the room she knew there was trouble, but tried to pretend she had not detected the seething anger he was feeling.

'You're home early, love,' she said lightly. 'No trouble preparing for the *Aurora*'s return, I hope?'

Francis ignored the question. 'Where have you been? With him?' His voice matched the fire in his eyes.

'What do you mean? Who?' Ruth parried his demands coyly.

'Don't play the innocent with me,' he snapped. 'I've heard rumours for a week or two. I took no notice but they persisted, grew stronger, until today I could ignore them no longer.'

'What are you talking about?' she returned, a touch of irritation in her voice.

'Lewis Whelden! You've been seeing him. Why? What about me?'

Ruth gave a little half laugh. 'Oh, him. Yes, I have been seeing him.'

Francis grabbed her by the arms. 'You bitch!' Expecting her to try and slip away he tightened his grip. He was confused when she did not try to do so. He went on, 'I share you with no one so put a stop to it immediately.'

She looked up at him mildly. 'Oh, Francis,' she said softly, 'you've got it all wrong. I don't love Lewis. It's you I care for.' Her words caressed him. 'Only you. We've been through too much together to spoil things now.' She saw the anger subside and in its place came bewilderment.

'But why are you seeing him?'

'For us, Francis. For us.'

'Us?'

'Yes. Don't you realise that Lewis as an only son will take over his father's whaling business? It's the biggest in New Bedford. Keep in with them and we're made. Who knows where it could lead?' Ruth moved closer to him. He still showed doubts. She took hold of his hands. 'Play things right, get Lewis into our grip and we could finish up owning that firm.'

He smiled. This was the old Ruth, the schemer. 'You're a crafty bitch.'

'After what you did for me in Whitby, do you think I could desert you?'

'Then marry me.'

'I would still be a bigamist,' she protested.

'Who'd know out here? Besides, it would put an end to speculation about our relationship,' pressed Francis, his hands moving to her waist.

'Maybe you're right,' she mused. 'But let's wait until the *Aurora* sails for the Pacific. We'll get her fitted out as soon as she returns, give the crew some leave. She should be away in a fortnight.'

Francis drew her close and his lips met hers with a fire which seemed to him a pledge.

Ruth returned his kiss but her mind was elsewhere. No one, not even Francis, must stand in the way of her becoming mistress of the leading whaling firm in New Bedford. The town would become the premier whaling port of America and Whelden's the leading whaling firm. What she had once dreamed of in England would become reality in America.

Chapter Twenty-One

During the next fortnight Ruth played the two men off by reassuring Lewis that Francis was no obstacle to their marriage, whilst confirming her promise to Francis of marrying him after the *Aurora* had sailed.

Knowing that Lewis was out of town, and that Francis was preoccupied with working out the profits from the Atlantic voyage, she secretly visited Captain Morgan Black two days before the ship was due to sail.

The following evening as she and Francis were finishing their meal Ruth brought up the question of their profits.

'I thought they would have been higher. Are you sure you worked everything out correctly?'

Surprised, he looked at her across the rim of his glass of Madeira.

'Of course.'

'Didn't you expect to make more?' Ruth pressed, watching him warily.

'I didn't really know what we would make. After all, sperm whales yield differently to the right whales we were used to before.'

'That's just it.' Ruth seized on the point. 'The unfamiliar could lead to mistakes. We should check them.'

'We can, but I think you'll find my figures are right.'

'Let's go and see.' Ruth started to rise from her chair.

'What? Now?'

'Yes. Why not?'

'But it can wait until tomorrow.'

'No. The *Aurora* will be sailing and if there are any questions we need to ask Captain Black about the Atlantic voyage it will be too late. We'd better do them this evening. Come on.' She started for the door.

Francis sighed. In these effervescent moods he knew there was no holding her back. He drained his glass, stood up and followed her.

The light was fading fast when they approached their warehouse with the offices above. Close by, the *Aurora* lay peacefully at her berth.

'She's a fine ship,' commented Ruth, pausing ostensibly to admire her but in reality checking to see if a figure was leaning on the rail.

'She is,' agreed Francis as he slipped his hand in hers. 'And she'll bring us a fortune back from the Pacific.' He squeezed her hand and turned to unlock the door into the warehouse.

They went upstairs to the office where he lit an oil lamp and placed it in a central position on the desk. He lit a second lamp and placed it at one end of the desk. He arranged two chairs, unlocked a cupboard and brought two ledgers to the desk. Opening one of them, he started to explain the expenses incurred in the voyage. Ruth kept halting him for further explanations on the pretext that she didn't understand or had not fully grasped the meaning of what he was talking about.

Ten minutes had passed when they heard a knocking on the warehouse door.

'Who on earth can that be?' said Francis, looking up with a puzzled frown.

'There's only one way to find out,' replied Ruth.

'Shan't bother, they'll go away.' He looked back down at his figures.

The knocking persisted.

'You'll have to go,' said Ruth.

The rap came again but seemed more urgent.

With his lips tightening in exasperation, Francis picked

up one of the lamps and started for the door.

'Coming, coming,' he muttered to himself as he went downstairs and across the warehouse floor with the knocking growing louder at every step.

He reached the door, unlocked it and held his lamp high as he opened it. The draught sent the flame flickering and its dancing light made shadows weave across the face which stared at him out of the darkness. Francis started. One eye was covered by a black patch, the other shone out with a look of satisfaction.

'Captain Black.'

'Sorry to disturb ye, sir. I saw a light and wondered . . .'

'Oh, it's all right. It's just Mrs Hardy. We're going through some figures.'

'You won't be called upon to do that any more, sir.' Captain Black gave him a hearty shove in the chest and stepped into the warehouse as Francis staggered backwards.

The captain sent the door shut with a flick of his left hand while the other produced a belaying pin from behind his back. One step forward and he struck at the surprised and horrified Francis. The blow took him on the temple, driving him into unconsciousness. He collapsed to the floor, the oil lamp shattering. Oil spilled and flames licked, but before the rivulets of fire could get a hold Captain Black was stamping them out. As the last was doused Ruth appeared at the top of the wooden stair holding a lamp in her left hand.

Light danced across the walls as she came down slowly, her eyes on the form which lay sprawled at the foot of the stair, silent and still. She resolutely controlled her thoughts which were tending towards the past. Francis's silent devotion, culminating in risking his life to save her from the sea, his scheming to help her bring misery to Jenny and Jessica and ruin to David; the days and nights she had spent with him while both appeased their desires. Such thoughts were soon banished. Now there were greater prizes to be won.

She reached the bottom of the stairs, her eyes still on Francis. She looked up and saw Captain Black watching her carefully. The light sent his shadow climbing the wall behind him so that he seemed to dominate the scene. For one brief moment her heart missed a beat with fear but she drew herself up and met his gaze.

She held out an envelope. 'It's all there.'

He took it with his massive hairy hand and slipped it into his pocket. 'Thank you, Ma'am. You'll hear no more of this.'

'I don't want to. This is between us two. No one else. You've been well paid.'

Captain Black nodded. He bent down, grabbed the front of Francis's coat, hauled him up and slung him over his shoulder.

As she watched all thoughts of the past were gone. Ruth dwelt only on the future. She had drained herself of all feeling towards Francis. Her heart was cold as she saw his head and arms dangling like a rag doll as Captain Black, without another word, left the building.

She mounted the stairs quickly, put the ledgers away and locked Francis's coat, hat and cane with them. She would dispose of them later. She took one last look round the office and left the building.

Her steps were swift as she hurried home, hoping that by this time Emily would have followed her usual practice of retiring early. She let herself in quietly and went straight to her bedroom.

The next morning when she came down to breakfast she told Emily that Francis had left early for the Boston stage as some urgent business matter had arisen which demanded his attention in that city.

'It's a great pity, he'll miss the *Aurora* leaving for the

Pacific,' she concluded. 'You'll be coming to see her sail?'

'Ship's aren't much in my line,' replied Emily. 'I had enough of them when we crossed the Atlantic. When do you expect Mr Francis back?'

'Don't know,' replied Ruth. 'It depends how long the business takes.'

A flicker of consciousness returned to Francis. Confusion stalked a mind not yet fully aware of his situation. As his brain cleared slowly he began to recall the last thing he remembered – Captain Black at the warehouse door. What had happened? Where was he? It was pitch dark. He tried to clear his troubled mind to bring sense to his situation. He moved. His head throbbed. He raised a hand to it and felt a huge lump. It recalled Captain Black raising his hand and then a blow. But why?

Then recollections came flooding back. He had been at the office with Ruth. Panic gripped him. What had happened to her? What had Black done? What was this attack all about? He tried to struggle to his feet and became more aware of his surroundings. The faint swish of water. The creak of timbers. Wooden planks, shaped, spars, the hold of a ship. Captain Black . . . The *Aurora*?

He got to his feet, stumbled and put out an arm to steady himself. He felt casks. Casks for oil? It must be the *Aurora*. What time was it? She was due to sail on the morning tide. What was he doing here in the confines of the hold, unable to get out?

Alarm gathered to the point of hysteria until he calmed himself with the thought that there must be a ladder to reach the hatch which gave admittance to the hold. He started to grope his way around. He tripped, staggered, fell, bruised his shins, scraped his arms and cut his hands. How long he sought a way out he never knew for time mocked him in his urgent desire to know why he was here and what had happened to Ruth.

337

The futility of his efforts and the frustration of getting nowhere overwhelmed him like a heavy cloak. He sank to his knees, sobbing.

He started. Voices. Faint, distant. He looked up with renewed hope. He pushed himself to his feet. Footsteps overhead. He yelled. No reply. He shouted again. No answer. All his efforts to attract attention were either unheard or ignored. Voices again. This time louder as if they were shouting orders.

The ship creaked, shuddered. Movement. Francis tensed, his head tilted to catch tell-tale sounds. They came more frequently. The motion became more noticeable, the swish of water louder. The ship was leaving her berth. Panic overcame him. He had heard of men being shang-haied but had never associated it with the whaling trade. But why had Captain Black shanghaied him? He had a full crew.

Helpless in his situation, all he could do was wait until someone opened the hatch, but resignation to his fate did nothing to alleviate the horror which was filling him.

'She's a fine vessel,' commented Ruth to Lewis as they, along with relatives of the crew and well-wishers, watched the *Aurora* slip her ropes and move from her berth into the Acushnet River.

'She'll bring you back a good return on your capital,' commented Lewis.

Ruth made no observation for her mind had drifted to Francis, bidding him a silent farewell.

She started when Lewis went on with the remark, 'I'm surprised Francis isn't here to see her sail.'

'He left on the early stage to Boston. He had some business to see to.'

The *Aurora* picked up more speed as more sails were unfurled to take advantage of the freshening breeze.

*　　　*　　　*

338

The motion of the ship grew stronger and Francis reckoned they were in the river. No one came. He was still a prisoner. Then he was aware of a tremor running through her. He felt her pitch and heard the louder swish of water along her sides. They had reached the sea.

Minutes passed then he was roused from his depression by a noise overhead. He realised that the hatch was being unfastened. A moment later it was thrown back and light flooded into the hold, momentarily blinding him. He looked down, letting his eyes readjust from the darkness.

'Get up here!' a voice boomed.

Francis looked round, seeking the means to obey. Seeing the wooden rungs he scrambled to them and started to climb. Reaching the top he swung himself over·on to the deck, stumbled and fell as he tried to take in his surroundings. He pushed himself to his feet, steadying himself to the ship's motion.

A group of men, eyeing him with curiosity, stood in a semi-circle around the hatch. Beyond them, far beyond the ship, he saw land astern. Anger swelled inside him and with it came the strength of determination.

'Where's your captain?' he demanded forcefully.

No one answered but several men glanced in the direction of the stern. Francis followed their gaze and saw Captain Black standing beside a man at the wheel. He noticed that he was watching the scene at the hatch. Francis, his clothes torn and dirty, his face smeared and hair unkempt, straightened his shoulders. He had to put on a bold and determined front. After all, the man was in his employ.

He pushed his way through the crew and walked quickly to Captain Black, who eyed him all the way. He stood with feet astride, hands clasped behind his back, drawing his shoulders tight. He seemed to tower over everything with an aura of impregnability.

Francis was not to be put off, not even by the black

patch and the one eye which seemed to gleam with extra ferocity.

'Captain, bring this ship about and take me back to New Bedford.' Francis kept his voice strong.

The captain, amused by his attempt to be masterful, chuckled deep in his throat. 'Can't do that, Mr Chambers.'

'I'm ordering you to!' snapped Francis.

'Still can't.'

'Why not?'

'Orders.'

'Orders?'

'Aye. From higher authority than yours. Wouldn't pay me to take you back.'

Francis was puzzled. Higher authority? That could only mean one person. 'What happened to Mrs Hardy? She was with me the night you . . .'

'Mrs Hardy's perfectly safe,' cut in Captain Black. 'So you needn't worry about her while you're on this voyage.' He did not wait for a reply but shouted, 'Connors, take Mr Chambers below. Get him more suitable clothes.'

'Aye, aye, sir.' Connors, a short, stocky man, ran forward.

'Suitable clothes? What are you talking about? Take me back at once.' In spite of his show of defiance, Francis was already feeling his words meant nothing.

Captain Black's one eye seemed to glare more fiercely. 'If you want to get ashore you'll have to swim and I don't think you'd make it.' He nodded towards the receding shoreline. 'Now, you're on a two-year whaling voyage and you're going to work as hard as anyone else. You'll see New Bedford – if you survive. Take him below, Connors!'

With that Francis knew his position was hopeless. If he resisted he'd be thrown into the hold again. There was nothing he could do but submit. He turned and followed Connors, knowing that comments were passing amongst the crew.

Connors's words were few while showing Francis his bunk in the cramped quarters of the fo'c'sle and the clothes which had been placed there in preparation for his arrival. As he changed he realised it had all been planned and that only one person could be behind it – Ruth. She had persuaded him to return to the office the previous evening on the pretext of wanting to check some figures. They could have waited until today but no, she had to have them there and then. He had given way as she knew he would under her persuasive spell. Then Captain Black had arrived. He could not have known they would be there unless he had been told. And only Ruth could have done that by planning every move.

Francis's lips tightened into a grim line as his mind hit on the reason for her actions. Lewis Whelden! She had fooled him with her reason for that association. She hadn't both their interests in mind, only her own, and now she planned to marry into the richest family in New Bedford and use Lewis to become the most influential person in the whaling trade, satisfying her lust for power.

He realised he was not meant to return to New Bedford. Somewhere in the vast ocean, today, tomorrow, next week, a month's time, even a year maybe, Black would get rid of him. He was at the mercy of the captain's whim.

When he went on deck Francis confronted him again, drawing him to one side so that their conversation could not be overheard.

'Whatever Mrs Hardy paid you, I'll pay you double.' Francis put his proposition forcefully so that there was no doubting that he meant it.

The captain rubbed his stubbled chin thoughtfully. 'Tempting,' he muttered. 'Tempting. But that woman would see that I paid for it. My life would be worth nothing.' He shook his head. 'Can't be done.' He started to turn away.

Francis grabbed his arm and stopped him. 'Please,' he

cried. 'Anything you want.' His pleading tone was touched by fear. 'Put me ashore, anywhere.'

'And let you get back to New Bedford? Not likely. She'd dispose of us both if you turned up, and you would – for revenge.' Captain Black eyed him disdainfully. He had little respect for employers who gave the orders but knew nothing of the physical side of whaling, content to grow rich on the hard toil of their crews. He fixed Francis with his one eye. 'You're on this ship, you're part of the crew – and by God you'll do your share.' He glared at Francis, which left him in no doubt that he meant it, then turned away and went back to the man at the wheel.

Dejected, Francis stared at land which was now but a smudge on the horizon. Yesterday everything had seemed all right with his world; now he was condemned to hell, for no doubt Captain Black would make it rough for him and whatever he did would be emulated by the crew.

His whole world had been sacrificed to the ambitions of one woman, a woman he had idolised, for whom he had stolen and cheated. He had known how ruthless she could be but never once had he suspected that her ambitions would override the love he thought she had for him. Even in that he had been mistaken. She had used him for her own ends all the time and he had been blind to it, overcome by her charm and persuasive guile. He cursed the day he had first seen her. He could swear revenge, but would it ever be fulfilled? He was condemned to hell and final destruction on this whaleship.

A fortnight after the *Aurora* had sailed, Ruth presented a problem to Lewis when he called to take her for a meal at their quiet inn outside New Bedford. It was an enlargement of the concern she had purposely voiced to Emily that morning.

'I'm worried about Francis. You know he went to

Boston the day the *Aurora* sailed?' She glanced at Lewis, who was concentrating on handling the horse over a tricky section of road. He nodded. 'I would have expected him to be back by now.'

'You've not heard from him?'

'No.'

'Where was he going in Boston?'

'To the bank to see about getting more funds through from England. He thought it might take a few days but I didn't expect him to be this long.'

'Would you like me to get our agents in Boston to check?'

'Oh, would you, Lewis? I am concerned.'

A week later he informed her that the agents had made enquiries and that Francis had never been to the bank. Ruth displayed a worried expression on hearing the news and turned this into dismay when over the next month Lewis's agents failed to elicit any news of Francis. It seemed he had disappeared without trace.

With the passing of time, Ruth began to modify her concern until she appeared to accept that Francis was never going to return.

'One good thing has come out of it,' she confided to Lewis one day, 'there's no one to stand in our way and now we can meet openly.'

'And marry,' he added.

'Yes. But give me time to get over the shock of Francis walking out.'

'Of course, love,' he replied. 'We won't rush things. We can't.'

'What do you mean, can't?' Ruth was puzzled.

'You may have charmed the men in my family, but I can't say that for my mother. She is always suspicious of outsiders until they win her over. She won't approve until you've done that.'

343

'Must she approve?'

'My God, yes.' Lewis was taken aback by Ruth's question. 'Cross her and I would be cut off without a penny, without a business, with nothing. I don't want that and I'm sure you don't.'

'Then I'll win her heart,' replied Ruth coyly, determined that no one would come between her and her ambition.

Chapter Twenty-Two

The *Aurora* sailed aimlessly on the calm Pacific, going nowhere in particular but ever searching for whales.

Men sprawled on the deck, idle in the endless days of monotony. Two whittled at bones kept from the last kill, while four etched sperm whales' teeth, using penknife and nails, with crude pictures of whaling scenes or reminders of far-off home. Others slept while some played dominoes fashioned from bone, the dots burnt in with an iron heated in the tryworks fire.

Francis dozed under the intense sun which shone from a clear sky, the only respite coming from the shadows of the sails as they moved with the swaying of the slow-moving vessel. He had survived this hell only on his determination to do so, and the burning desire to wreak revenge on the woman who had used him and then betrayed him at the moment when all their plans and desires seemed to have been fulfilled.

But how was he to gain vengeance he did not know for he could see no escape from the fate he was sure was to be executed by Captain Black. The captain's treatment of him so far had been harsh. He did not even wait for Francis to find his sealegs.

The only time he had been at sea before had been for the crossing of the Atlantic and that had been made in comfort. On board the *Aurora* life was rough: he lived in confined quarters which smelled of unwashed bodies and dirty clothes and were awash with water when they experienced storms, especially rounding Cape Horn. The food had been barely palatable but he ate in order to survive. He had heard of captains who ran a tyrannical regime on board ship; now he was experiencing it. Black was harsh on the men, and since he was backed by an equally despotic mate, life aboard the *Aurora* was brutish.

The crew moved in fear of the captain and knew that any objections they voiced would bring reprisals. They viewed Francis with some curiosity at the start of the voyage. They wondered why he had been shanghaied but knew better than to ask questions. They did not expect him to survive the rough life for long but as the days progressed some of them came secretly to admire his endurance. But none became friendly. They did not want to incur the displeasure of the captain for it was obvious that he was intent on making life for Francis as near hell as possible, and any friendliness on their part would be dangerous.

Francis raised his eyes aloft. Soon the order would ring out sending him up the mast to swing with it in its slow circular motion high above the mesmerising movement of the sea in the search for whales. Francis hated it and Captain Black knew it so gave him more than his fair share at the topgallant crosstrees. But he was never to climb the rigging again for within five minutes came a shout which electrified the ship.

'There she blows! There she blows!' The cry sounded across the deck. For one moment the men froze in disbelief. They had waited nearly two weeks for this call so that when it came it momentarily stunned everyone.

'Blows! Blows!'

The ship erupted. Men ceased their lazing, stopped whittling and etching, scooped up their dominoes and scrambled to their feet.

'Whither away?' the captain yelled.

'Larboard bow!'

Men crowded the rail, the heat and monotony forgotten, for whales could mean a full ship and home.

Captain Black shielded his eye against the sun shimmering from the sea. There it was, the tell-tale spout. Excitement gripped him. Nothing pleased him more than the chase and the power over these monsters which he held in his hand at the moment of the kill. Another spout and another and more. There must be a large pod.

'Helmsman, bring her round three points larboard. Lookout, sing out when we're on them. Muster all boats, Mr Mate.'

'Aye, aye, sir.'

The *Aurora* came round slowly. The mate sent his commands resounding round the ship. Men raced to their appointed positions at each boat.

'Dead ahead!' yelled the lookout.

'Steady there, helmsman!' shouted Black as the ship eased in her turn. 'Hold her steady!'

The ship sailed slowly towards the spouting whales. There was no need for the lookout to indicate any more sightings, the spouts were plainly visible.

'Carpenter!' called Black.

'Aye, aye, sir.'

'All boats will go. Bring her to when the boats are away.'

'Aye, aye, sir,' replied the carpenter, knowing that as shipkeeper he was in charge of the vessel during the whale hunt.

The *Aurora* moved gently with the stealth of a predator. Captain Black eyed the distance to the whales critically. Nearer. Nearer.

'Away all boats!' His orders came with the speed of a gunshot.

Ropes whined through the well-greased blocks as the boats hit the water. Men eager to make a kill sent them away. There was no need for any more orders. The crew knew exactly what the captain wanted. They knew his method. Four boats to go for a strike, the fifth to stand by to lend assistance wherever needed.

As soon as the boats were clear the carpenter and the remaining crew brought the ship into wind.

The boats cut through the water. Muscles bulged as brown bare backs, steaming with sweat, bent to the heavy oars. Francis heaved in unison with the rest of his crew. Now he was used to the effort, knew how to control it so that he was not over-exhausted. His hands had become accustomed to the oars too and were no longer bruised and aching at the end of the chase.

Francis kept his eyes on the boatsteerer, watching for the signal which would tell the oarsmen that they were near the whales. He saw the man frown, his lips tighten in annoyance. He took a quick glance over his shoulder. The water ahead churned as tails turned up and the whales sounded. Something had disturbed them, something had warned them of the hunters. Now they had escaped the attack.

All the boats followed the lead of the captain, who had moved his boat ahead of the rest. He let his boat drift over the spot where he had last seen the whales. Standing in the bow, harpoon in hand, he searched the sea in the boat's immediate vicinity.

A dark mass streaked upwards and burst from the water a few yards away. The water churned, rocking the boat violently, but the captain kept his balance and at the same time arched his body like a huge bow. Then, with the coiled tension released, it sprang forward, sending the harpoon on a perfect trajectory. It struck with a dull thud, piercing the skin and grabbing hold on the blubber.

A loud whoosh as the whale drew air warned the captain that it was going to sound.

'Stern all!' The order flew with fierce urgency.

Muscles rippled aross broad backs as the crew attempted to drive the boat away from the whale. Sixty tons of flesh and muscle towered over them. The massive tail, streaming water, hung above the boat like some figure of retribution.

'Bend y'backs. Bend y'backs . . .'

The captain's urgent cry was cut off as the flukes shattered the boat. Cries were cut short in that moment of horror. Battered bodies were pitched into the sea along with the splintered remains of the tiny vessel.

Francis, resting on his oars, was transfixed by the maelstrom. The terror which assailed his mind was only relieved by the thought that Captain Black would no longer be able to carry out Ruth's orders. He was safe. He would find his revenge in New Bedford.

Already the nearest boat to the scene was among the wreckage, hauling bodies from the sea. By the time Francis's boat was near enough to lend a hand the task had been completed.

He saw the captain pulled from the blood-stained sea and stiffened in disbelief when he saw him sit up and shout orders to his tiny flotilla. He ordered the rescue boat to return to the ship with all speed. The others were to continue the hunt.

Dejected by the miraculous survival, Francis automatically bent his back as the harpooner called directions. His eyes were dull as he watched the captain's boat reach the *Aurora* and the crew were taken on board.

The four remaining boats scattered across the sea, searching for whales.

Five minutes passed before the harpooner who had remained standing in the bow called out: 'Whale!' It was circling about fifty yards from the *Aurora*.

The boatsteerer turned the boat in its direction.

'My God!' The gasp from the harpooner was tinged with horror. The boatsteerer, eyes wide in disbelief, signalled the men to stop rowing. These orders brought them twisting on their thwarts to seek the cause.

The enormous sperm whale, bigger than any they had ever seen, was heading straight for the ship. There was a thunderous crash and a tearing of splintering timbers as the huge blunt head pounded into the *Aurora*. She shuddered and faltered in her movement. Men were sent sprawling and tumbling across the deck, while others, holding grimly on to the rail, gaped with terror at the monster which blew close to the ship, sending stinking oily vapour across the deck.

The whale rolled and moved away, churning the sea into a boiling foam with its massive tail and champing teeth-filled jaws. It circled and came at the ship again. It struck with immense force, widening the gap in the side of the ship, allowing water to pour in. There was nothing the carpenter and his men, who had gone below after the first attack to try to repair the damage, could do. Water swirled around them, climbing higher with frightening rapidity as they struggled to reach the deck.

The ship rocked under a third crunching impact. The *Aurora* floundered like some great stricken bird. The sea took over quickly. The stern came up, seemed to pause for a moment and then slid to its watery grave.

Shock enveloped Francis's boat. No one spoke. They had just witnessed an unbelievable sight. Whales had been known to attack boats, in fact they had just experienced one such incident, but it was unheard-of for a whale to attack a ship the size of the *Aurora*. Yet they had seen it with their own eyes.

The *Aurora* was gone and Captain Black with her. Francis found some cause for joy in that, just as he had when he'd thought the captain lost from the boat. But then there had been the chance of reaching New Bedford on the *Aurora*. Now she was gone and four small boats were left on the wide ocean under a blazing sun.

Numbed by what they had witnessed and the thought that they were left in open boats, with no shade from the powerful sun, burning with a white fierceness from a cloudless sky, and no protection from a sea whose placid swell could turn into merciless fury, the men propelled their boats to the flotsam.

The harpooner in Francis's boat had assessed the situation quickly and realised that each of the other boats was striving to reach the floating debris first. The desire for survival had already made them rivals. He called to his men to bend their backs. The boat skimmed across the water as they put in an effort to grab all they could.

Boat clashed with boat. Men hauled casks of water and boxes of food from the ocean before those who had once been their companions could get them. Men fought with men in another boat and fell into the sea, ignored by their fellow sailors. It would mean fewer mouths to feed if they did not make it back into the boat of their own accord.

From being comrades in the same cause the catastrophic event had turned them into animals, bent on their own survival and willing to fight for it. There was no chance that these men were going to pool their food and water and those few who proposed it were shouted down. What each boat had got they wanted to keep for themselves.

When the proposition that they should stay together was made it was regarded with suspicion. Was it a ruse to give an opportunity to steal provisions? Each boat distrusted the other and with no agreement made they started to drift apart.

In Francis's boat the harpooner, who had been mate on the *Aurora*, took charge. He had the men row a short distance and then told them to ship oars.

'Let's see what we've got,' he ordered.

'Two casks of water here,' called the boatsteerer.

'One here,' called Francis.

'Good,' appraised the mate. 'I got a box of biscuits.'

'One here,' the bow oarsman called.

'Any more?'

Men looked around at their companions, hoping for an affirmative answer, but none came.

'Right,' called the mate. 'Better than nothing. We'll have to have strict rationing.'

'Any idea where we are?' someone asked.

'Yes,' replied the mate. 'I'd been working on the charts with Captain Black just before we sighted the whales. It's not a pretty picture. We're about mid-Pacific, just north of the Equator. That's just about the loneliest stretch of water in the world. The charts are not accurate for this area so I can't say for certain if there's any land hereabouts. I doubt it so we'll assume there isn't.' Men shifted uneasily and a low murmur ran through them. 'That means the nearest land, the Marquessas, is fourteen hundred miles away.'

'Bloody lot of savages there,' came one comment.

'Right,' agreed the mate. 'I don't feel like tangling with them. The next nearest known land is South America, three thousand miles away.'

The statement brought groans and complete hopelessness hung over the boat like the hand of doom.

'What about north?' Francis asked.

'The charts are bad for that area,' replied the mate. 'I reckon we ought to head for South America.'

'Three thousand miles!' Gasps expressed how ridiculous they thought the attempt.

Francis's mind had been working fast. If the mate thought that was their best chance then he was with him, but it needed an effort, both physical and mental, from them all if they were going to survive, thin though that chance was. And he had a burning desire to survive and wreak revenge on Ruth, who had brought him to this.

'I'm with the mate,' he shouted. 'Head for South America.'

'We'll never make it,' someone replied but Francis was not to be put off.

Before the mate would speak he went on: 'What else would you do? Sit here and wait? Finish up in a cannibal's pot? Head for the unknown? There's only one thing to do – try to make that three thousand miles. We can do it if we pull together, every man playing his part, no one attempting not to do his share. Work and think as one and we stand a chance. At least it's worth trying. Who knows? We might find uncharted land, might sight a ship. I for one am not going to give up without an effort.'

'Good for you, Chambers,' called the mate. 'You hear that? There's a man not used to the whaling life, not used to the sea, not like you – and yet he's willing to challenge it. Now what do the rest of you say?'

Shamed by the effort of the Englishman, the other four men agreed.

The harpooner scanned the ocean. No other boats were to be seen among the endless undulations. They had drifted away or had set course on what they expected would be their salvation.

He proceeded to lay down rules, work out rotas for rowing, for steering, for distributing food and drink, and allocated men to each watch.

The tiny sail, which was only used under certain circumstances to take a boat silently on to a whale, now served to supplement the oars.

For three days their progress was good in weather which held fine with a favourable breeze. The men gained a little heart but cursed the sun which burned and dried their bodies. Covetous glances were cast in the direction of the water casks but no one made a move for extra rations.

The fourth morning brought some relief with clouds covering the sun but it also brought a freshening wind with portents which were not pleasing to the crew. For two days they ran before the wind and were beginning to think their fears were unfounded when on the morning of the sixth day the clouds thickened and darkened. To the west vivid flashes of lightning streaked seawards; thunder rumbled, mingling with the rising howl of the strengthening wind. Dread clutched the hearts of the men in their frail boat.

With heavy hearts they watched the storm overtake

them. The sea heightened, buffeting the boat with increasing strength. The sail was dropped, the oars shipped and the boat allowed to run before the storm. Men crouched low against the gunwales, seeking some measure of protection as the first rain lashed them.

The troughs deepened. The waves swelled into mountains. The boat rode high, hung precariously, then plunged with ever-increasing speed to the depths, paused, then climbed again. Waves pounded down, broke around them in a swirl of foam, threatening to swamp them.

'Bail! Bail for your lives!' The mate's cry was torn from his rain-soaked lips. His eyes narrowed against the wild wind, water ran from his hair, lank from constant soaking. 'Bail! Bail!'

One man grabbed a tin, another the bailing bucket, and the rest anything which would serve as a bailer or else cupped their hands in an effort to overcome the water which threatened to send them to the depths of the Pacific. Frantic action driven by desperation counteracted the chill from the penetrating wind.

It seemed to the gasping crew that they were doing no good yet the boat remained afloat. The sky wrapped them in the darkness of hell, split only by flashes of fearful lightning. In breaking the darkness it revealed towering waves from the top of which the wind whisked a canopy of streaming water.

The storm raged on. Minds cried out with weariness. Bodies screamed at the torture of wind and cutting rain. They seemed caught in an eternity of despair.

After eight hours they sensed some of the fury easing yet their numb minds would not let them believe it was true. It was only after the intense black had lightened to grey, when the flashes of lightning were more remote, the thunder less loud and the waves not so fearsome in their height, that they began to realise they had won.

Gradually all violence eased. The sky brightened, the

clouds began to break and the sun, which only a few days ago they had cursed, was greeted with a welcome. The sea no longer threatened and the wind dropped to a steady blow.

Men flopped against the gunwales. They licked the rain from their lips and ran it with their hands from their sodden hair to their mouths, anxious to supplement their meagre water ration before the sun parched them once again.

For two more days they ran with the wind and waves. They regained some strength, reorganised themselves and prepared for their lonely vigil.

The sun woke them on the ninth day with a fierce intensity. It beat all day with a heat which burned. At first men fidgeted under the glare but, as the sun climbed and shone with energy-sapping ferocity, they remained listless, steeped in ungainly relaxation lest any movement helped to intensify the sun's power. Rowing was out of the question.

The wind dropped and they floated on a mirror-like sea. The scorching sun seared into their minds as well as their bodies. They were in a huge oven from which there was no escape. Parched, cracked lips began to mumble and tremble, heaping curses on the whale which had condemned them to this fiery death. They cried out for water, yelling obscenities at Francis, who had been made keeper of the casks. Disoriented minds began to accuse him of keeping it for himself.

He wanted water as much as any of them and it took all his effort to keep from sneaking a drink. Give way to that, give way to them, and there could be chaos. Each man would take the law into his own hands, and men driven to the boundaries of sanity could do terrible things in the urge to relieve a thirst which was burning them up.

The mate decided that they must row at night and sleep by day. For the next week this was their life, with each man getting physically weaker and closer to insanity every day.

On the eighteenth day after the whale had sunk their ship a faint breeze blew against the men sprawled in the bottom of the boat. As the mate stirred he heard an attempt at a call. He pushed himself into a sitting position and through narrowed eyes saw a figure raise a feeble arm.

'Mr Mate,' a voice croaked in its dryness, 'Tim won't wake up.' The words trailed away and the arm flopped down.

The mate made the effort and pushed himself to his feet to stagger along the boat. His arms hung limp by his sides. His shirt was in shreds and his trousers torn and filthy.

Reaching the man who had called, the mate stared down at him. His head hung limp on one side, his mouth was open and his eyes were wide. The stark reality jolted the mate's mind into clarity. He knelt down and placed a hand on the man's heart. Not a flutter. The mate turned to Tim. A moment's examination told him he was dead too.

The mate tapped the two nearest men with his foot. They both looked up wearily. 'Over the side with these two,' he ordered.

The men stared at him in disbelief.

'They're dead! Damnit, they're dead!' he yelled, wanting to dismiss their accusing stares.

The two startled men scrambled to their knees and with some effort rolled the dead men over the gunwales into a watery grave with hardly a sound.

The sun did not relent and the four remaining men lay at its mercy, only managing to move for their rations, which they demanded more frequently and which the mate didn't refuse for by now he saw nothing but death for them all. Refusal might only hasten the end as men on the edge of insanity would fight for what they imagined should be theirs.

Four more days were spent in this burning furnace. The water was gone, the biscuits finished. The end was near.

Francis wept. This was not the finish to his life he had planned and imagined. That should have come as a rich man in New Bedford with Ruth by his side. Instead she had condemned him to this torturous end far on the wastes of the Pacific with revenge but a figment of his imagination. Anger stirred him. He sat up, croaking vengeance at the heavens where Ruth's face swam, with a mocking smile.

His croak stopped in mid-sentence. He drove the narrow slits of his eyes to focus across the gently moving sea. His mind jarred. He sobbed, knowing the sea was mocking him. It couldn't be. They were alone on this vast ocean where nothing else moved. He started to shake with the misery of the delusion. But still his eyes insisted that they were right. The vision of a ship persisted. He shielded his eyes with bony fingers. It was still there.

'Sail!' The word croaked from his parched, split lips. He wanted to shout louder but the dryness wouldn't let him. 'Sail! Sail!' He turned his head, his long hair and unkempt beard shaking with the excitement he was trying to transmit to the others.

The mate heard this distant noise. He stirred.

'Mr Mate, sail!' Francis made an extra effort to make himself heard.

The three men scrambled to their knees, ignoring the pain of the hard wood on their protruding bones in their anxiety to verify Francis's words. Eyes were screwed up against the dazzling reflection from the sea.

'Where?' someone rasped.

'Over there.' Francis waved a bony arm.

The men searched through burning eyes.

'Damn you!'

'Blast your soul!'

'You bloody bastard!'

Curses hissed from burnt throats and eyes filled with

disgust condemned him. The men flopped back in the bottom of the boat.

'But ... but ...' Francis's voice trailed away. They hadn't believed him. Had he been mistaken? His mind was too weak to cope. He slid down to his resting place, his final one he was sure.

Chapter Twenty-Three

David Fernley lay on his bunk trying to find some respite from the heat. He had been on watch until half an hour ago and the blazing Pacific sun had drained his energy.

This fiery furnace was a far cry from the Arctic he knew and loved but he did not regret experiencing it. The voyage had been good. They had taken several whales in the South Atlantic, weathered the storms round Cape Horn, and sailed into the far reaches of the Pacific, taking whales fairly regularly. He reckoned they had come far enough. Tomorrow they would set course for home for he felt certain they could fill the ship on the return voyage.

His thoughts turned to Lydia as they often had. He had mourned for a short while for he knew she would not want him to fill his whole life with memories. Though they could never be eradicated and would always be there, he had his own life to live. Lydia would not want to be forgotten but she would not want the rest of his life to be filled with sadness. Dominic had been wise in suggesting he do this voyage for it had eased the pain to be with the sea he loved.

He dozed.

He started fitfully. A call? He shook himself awake. He was mistaken. It came again. The lookout. He swung off the bunk and hurried on to the deck.

'What is it, Mr Mate?' he called.

'Lookout's seen something, sir.'

'Whales?'

'No, sir.'

'Whither away?'

'Dead ahead, sir.'

The crew had stirred themselves from their languid occupations and were at the rails, peering ahead.

David swung on to the ratlines and climbed to get a better view.

'Lookout,' he yelled. 'What is it?'

'Lost it, sir. Looked like a boat.'

'Boat?'

'Aye, sir.'

David was puzzled. He had every faith in the sharp eyes of the man he had placed high on the mast, but a boat in this wilderness of the ocean? Impossible.

'There it is!' The cry came from the lookout. 'Keeps disappearing in the troughs.'

The sea was not running high but David knew that something the size of a boat, no more than twenty-eight feet long, could soon be lost in the troughs and might only be glimpsed as it came to the crests of the waves.

'Hold her steady, Mr Mate!'

'Aye, aye, sir.'

The *Lydia* sailed on.

The lookout reported more frequent sightings.

Then David saw it. A tiny object in the vastness of the ocean. But what was it doing here? Lost from a ship in a storm? A few minutes later he identified it as a whaleboat. Maybe it had been towed far from its parent vessel when a whale ran.

'There's someone in it,' called the lookout.

A buzz of bemused curiosity ran through the crew.

'Sign of life?' David shouted.

'None,' replied the lookout after a moment's scrutiny.

It was the answer David half-expected for no one could survive in an open boat in this heat for long.

'Stand by number one!' David's order brought instant action from the crew of number one boat.

'Bring to, Mr Mate!'

'Aye, aye, sir.'

The mate brought the *Lydia*'s head to the wind and the vessel came to a stop.

'Away number one. Take her in tow.'

The boat was launched with the skill born of experience. As soon as she touched the water the crew pushed her away from the *Lydia* and in a matter of moments were rowing strongly to the derelict vessel.

David watched intently. He saw the boatsteerer manoeuvre the two boats stern to bow, fasten a towline and head back for the *Lydia*. They were brought alongside and from the rail of the ship the crew saw four objects they could hardly recognise as human beings. Willing hands brought them gently on board and laid them in the shade.

Even some hardened men recoiled at the sight of the emaciated bodies. David's stomach churned. He felt bile rising in him but could not give way. He must keep a grip on himself. These men, little more than skeletons, with skin shrivelled and burnt dark brown, with matted shoulder-length hair, beards bushy and marked with salt spray, needed his help if there was still any life in them.

A croaking sound rattled in one man's throat. David started. There was life. It galvanised him into action. A speedy examination showed a flicker of life in all four men.

'Set course for home!'

'Aye, aye, sir.'

The mate's commands brought men into action and the *Lydia* picked up the wind again and headed southeast.

David supervised the treatment given to the four men. A little water to dampen parched and cracked lips and soothe burning skin. He knew they could not rush matters and that patience would be needed to bring these men back from the edge of death. A little broth, carefully made in the galley, was spoonfed to them. It was only after two days that three of the men showed some realisation that they had been saved. The excitement for one of them was almost too much and he had to be restrained. The fourth man continued in and out of delirium but showed some signs of recovery, though as yet he had not opened his eyes. He kept muttering something about the sun and David concluded he was frightened of the harsh brightness he had experienced in the boat.

After four days David learned, from the broken-voiced men, of the horrors they had faced. Hearing that they were from New Bedford, he promised to take them there. He also decided that they would feel better and look better with their hair cut and their beards trimmed. The task was done gently and the three men who were showing signs of gaining strength were grateful, though the fourth showed no improvement and seemed barely aware of what was going on. However David thought he should be treated the same as the others and hoped it might help him to rally, though it seemed he might still succumb to his ordeal.

As his hair was being cut David stood by and talked in a gentle voice to him, telling him it was all right to open his eyes, that he was no longer in the boat and that he was going home to New Bedford.

'Thee's in good hands. We'll look after thee. Thee's gannin' home. Thy family . . .' David stopped, brought up short by the revelation which had come with the clean-shaven face. It couldn't be! And yet . . . He doubted his own eyes, even his own mind. He must be suffering from delusions. Francis Chambers? No. How could he be here in the vastness of the Pacific. He had gone missing in Whitby. But here he was, pulled from the sea. He wasn't a seaman. If only he would open his eyes.

David leaned closer. 'Come on, open those eyes. It's safe to do so. Thee's on board a ship. Thee's in the shade. Nothing is going to hurt them.' The eyes remained shut.

David knew this skeletal man was hovering on the brink of death, but he wanted him alive. If this was Francis Chambers he needed some explanation of how he had brought the firm of Fernley and Thoresby to ruin. David kept the excitement out of his voice, spoke softly close to his ear, all the time watching the face intently, eager for some flicker of response.

'Francis, thee's safe. Thee's no longer in the boat. Francis Chambers, remember Whitby? Come on, Francis, open those eyes.'

A low groan came from Francis's throat.

David kept on speaking.

The man turned his head as if seeking the source of the voice.

'Open thy eyes, Francis,' David made his words a little more forceful.

The eyelids twitched.

David encouraged him.

They twitched again, fluttered, half opened and then closed again as if frightened of the light.

David cajoled.

There was a tremor. The eyes opened, shut again and then almost immediately opened. They blinked several times as they adjusted to the brightness they had sought to shut out.

They remained fixed on David but showed no recognition. Maybe his eyes had been scorched into blindness.

'Francis, can thee see me? It's David Fernley.'

A tremor ran through the man's body. He blinked again. Gave a little shake of his head as if to throw off a yoke which was holding him back. 'Captain Fernley?' The words were soft, hardly above a whisper. As if needing the reassurance of physical contact, his claw-like hand came up to touch David's.

'Yes, it's Captain Fernley and thee's Francis Chambers?'

Francis nodded his head. David saw the tension in his body ebb as if a burden had been taken from him by this meeting.

'Captain Fernley, I'm sorry for the part I played in your ruination.' The words came slowly with much effort.

'Don't talk now, Francis. Thy story can wait.' David patted him reassuringly on the shoulder. He started to stand up but Francis stopped him.

'It can't. I'm dying and I need to tell you the truth.'

'Thee's going to live. Don't use thy strength up now.'

'No, Captain Fernley. I need to tell you. My story can only have one ending. If I live, I will see that it ends properly. If I don't I know you will, after you hear what I have to say. I need to be certain that Ruth pays.'

'Ruth?' David was puzzled. 'Ruth who?'

'Your wife.'

'But she's dead.' Francis must still be delirious.

'No, she's very much alive.'

The words hit David like a thunderbolt. Was this true or just the figment of Francis's deluded mind?

But as he told his story David knew that he was as sane as anyone for he seemed to gather strength in the telling. He was determined that it should be told. With the final word he sighed with relief for now he could die in the knowledge that he had wreaked his revenge, though he was thousands of miles away.

The next day David said a few words over Francis's wasted body, wrapped it in sailcloth and slid it into the deep waters of the Pacific.

David watched New Bedford come nearer and nearer as the *Lydia* sailed up the Acushnet river. Beside the rail the three New Bedford men were ecstatic in the joy of seeing their home port again even though they knew their homecoming would bring sadness to those who had lost men to the strange whim of a whale.

Though pleased for them, he felt unable to share their excitement for in his mind was the thought of the grim task he had in facing Ruth, the wife he'd believed dead for several years.

News of an approaching English whaler had brought a crowd to the wharf and the sight of the New Bedford men acknowledging their calls sent excitement through the crowd.

As soon as the ship was tied up, the gangway was run out and the three men were ashore and into the loving arms of their relations.

Leaving the mate in charge, David went into town.

'Captain Fernley!'

The call stopped him. He spun round.

'Alex Fraser!'

Joy wreathed the faces of the two men as they clasped hands and hugged each other with friendly slaps on the back.

'Heard there was an English ship in but never thought thee'd be her captain. Heard thee picked up some shipwrecked whalemen.'

'Aye, lucky to be alive,' David confirmed. 'But how's thee and the family?'

'Fine,' grinned Alex. 'I'm back from the Arctic a fortnight ago. Yon's my ship.' He indicated a vessel tied up at a neighbouring wharf. 'Captain now.'

'Well done. Thee deserves it,' said David.

'It's all thanks to thee and the note Miss Lydia wrote to Mr Spence. By the way, how is she?' He was concerned when he saw the look of sadness cross David's face.

'We married. She died in childbirth. Dominic suggested I did a whaling voyage to the Pacific. It helped ease the pain and showed me I could cope with life for the sake of the son she bore.'

'I'm sorry.' Alex made his commiserations and then asked, 'How long is thee going to be in New Bedford?'

'I reckon maybe a week. Give the crew a break. Besides, I have some business to attend to.'

'Then, thee must stay with us. Maggie will be delighted to have thee.' Alex was trying to decide whether to tell David about Beth or leave it as a surprise when the decision was put aside by David's next request.

'Thee may be able to help me, Alex. I'm looking for my wife.'

'Wife?' A puzzled frown marked Alex's forehead. 'But I thought thee just said . . .'

'Aye, I did. This is Ruth.'

'I thought she'd died in the shipwreck off Whitby?'

'So did I until I picked up these men in the Pacific.' David went on to give Alex the essential details quickly.

He shook his head slowly when David had finished. 'Never heard of Ruth Fernley. This Francis Chambers arrived here with a Ruth Hardy and lived with her on Walnut Street.'

'Hardy! Of course. Francis must have forgotten to tell me she changed her name. Ruth Fernley was supposed to be dead so she took the name of her true father.' He looked at Alex with excitement in his eyes. 'Right, take me to Walnut Street.'

'Wait.' Alex laid a restraining hand on David's arm. 'Ruth Hardy is to marry the heir to the biggest whaling firm in New Bedford the day after tomorrow.'

'Is she? Trust her to aim for the top! All the more reason to stop her and save him from marrying a bigamist. Come on, show me the way.'

The sky was darkening as the two men walked quickly to Walnut Street. Oil lamps were being lit in houses along the way.

'Here we are.' Alex stopped outside an imposing house.

David surveyed it quickly. He was impressed. It stood out among the others he had passed on the way. 'She would have the best,' he muttered to himself, and glanced at Alex. 'I hope I shan't be long.'

'As long as thee likes. I'll wait.' Alex wandered a few yards along the roadway wondering how David would react to meeting Beth after finding Ruth still alive. He almost wished he had not invited him to stay.

David's knock was answered by Emily Judson, who held an oil lamp high so that she could see the caller.

'Yes?' She queried when David did not speak. She peered at the face highlighted by the lamp's glow, trying to identify the visitor. 'Oh, my God. Captain Fernley!' Her face drained with the shock of the unexpected.

'Is my wife at home?' David asked, and stepped forward. He was not going to brook a refusal of admission. Emily Judson moved to one side. She hastily closed the door behind him and turned to stare at him as if seeking confirmation that he was real. 'Mrs Fernley?' he asked again, his voice more assertive.

Emily's hand was shaking, causing the lamp to send shadows flickering across the walls. The woman she had served with adoration after the death of her beloved Jonathan, because she had brought him happiness, was now threatened. She sought a way to withstand the menace but there was none. Inadvertently she had glanced at the door to the right of the hall.

David noticed. 'In there?' he said. He did not wait for an answer but was across the hall in three strides, ignoring Emily's cry of 'No!' He flung the door open and strode into a room elegantly furnished and decorated. The light from two oil lamps revealed Ruth sitting in a chair beside the fire which burnt cheerily in the grate.

Startled by the sudden crash of the door, she spun round to see a powerful figure striding across the room.

He uttered one word. 'Ruth.'

She knew that voice. Only one man had ever spoken her

name with that intonation. The light from the lamps caught the contours of his face.

She stared, her mind in dismay. It couldn't be! This was some ghost come to haunt her before her wedding, to remind her of the past when she had trodden the ways of dishonesty, fraud, licentiousness and murder.

'Ruth.' That voice again. Then he was beside her, as real as she.

'David!' The word came in a whisper drawn from the very depths of disbelief.

'Yes, it is.'

'But . . .'

'Francis Chambers. Thee did not reckon on the whale which sank his ship before Captain Black had carried out thy orders. Thee did not reckon on my wife dying. Oh, yes, I married again thinking thee dead. That took me on a whaling voyage to the Pacific to ease the pain of my loss. I found Francis and three others barely alive. Those three survived. He didn't, but before he died he recognised me and told me the whole sordid truth.'

Ruth gasped. This was no apparition. His words struck home. David knew everything. He could ruin her. Even his presence spelt doom to her forthcoming marriage. She saw her position as the head of the biggest whaling firm in America, the power and the wealth, all jeopardised. She could not let it be so. She must do something about it. Her thoughts were racing, seeking some way out of her dilemma.

'Tha'rt evil, Ruth, only thinking of thyself, letting nothing stand in thy way. I hear thee was to marry the day after tomorrow. Thank goodness I've arrived in time to stop another poor fool from falling under thy spell!'

As the words drummed into her brain Ruth resolved to fight. She had riches at her fingertips, she was not about to relinquish them easily.

'You wouldn't David.'

'I would. Thee's still legally married to me.'

'Thee doesn't want me. We mean nothing to each other now.' Her words came like a whiplash. She paused, then softened her tone. 'You could just leave. Go back to England. No one here need even know about us. I'm Ruth Hardy. No one here knows you.'

'And leave this poor unfortunate man, whoever he is, to become a victim of thy greed and twisted ambition? No, Ruth. I can't stand by and see him ruined, a pawn in yet another of thy schemes.'

Ruth's lips tightened. Her eyes flashed with anger and hatred. 'You're only doing this for revenge,' she hissed. 'Revenge for what I did to thy precious firm, the firm which spelt our ruin.'

'Not the firm, Ruth, but thy jealousy. Now it's thy turn to pay. I'll not let thee spoil other lives.'

'You forget I did a lot for your precious firm. You owe me some consideration. I tried to save it when things went wrong, even to killing Jonathan to get his money, but he tricked me! Please, just go. Forget you've seen me. There's nothing to stop you doing that.' Ruth had put all her persuasive powers into her words but David knew her ways and resisted.

'No!' He strengthened his voice and in the force of this one word Ruth sensed her doom, but she would not give up.

'I'll give you back all the money I took from the sale of the three ships.'

'It won't do.'

'Anything you want. I'll have plenty after I am married.' Her tone was pleading.

'Nothing will buy me off. You are the one who is going to pay now. Call that wedding off. I sail in a week. Be ready to leave with me.' He swung on his heel and stormed from the room, throwing the half-open door wide.

Ruth flung obscenities after him and paced the room in

exasperation. As she turned she became aware of Emily standing in the doorway. She was silent. Her eyes were cold, accusing. Ruth stopped. She realised Emily had heard everything. She knew that Ruth had killed her precious Jonathan.

'Well?' Ruth demanded haughtily. 'Something you want?'

Emily stared a moment longer then let out one word. 'Bitch!' The venom lashed Ruth. 'Bitch!' Emily screamed again. Her eyes filled with hatred. Gone was all the respect and adoration she had held for Ruth. Once she would have done anything for her, covered up her misdeeds, helped her all she could, because of the love she'd thought Ruth had had for Jonathan. 'You killed him!'

'It was necessary,' snapped Ruth.

'Don't give me any of your glib talk. I've closed my eyes to a lot of things. I could have disclosed that you were still alive back in Whitby, but I didn't because of the way you appeared to have changed Jonathan's life. He was a different man when you were at Rigg House. But if I'd known what you did to him, I'd never have held my tongue.' Her eyes had grown wild with all the anger which had been building inside her. Ruth recoiled momentarily then, realising she must counter Emily's viciousness, tried to deflect her tirade.

'And haven't I been good to you? Where would you have been without me? Didn't I bring you out here, and now I'm on the verge of giving you an even better life.'

'Probably brought me here to keep an eye on me so that I wouldn't reveal you were still alive. You scheming hussy! And what about Francis? You used him until you saw better prospects, then cast him aside – no, murdered him!' Her eyes widened with the desire for vengeance. She had the power. 'Thee deserves to die, and die you will!' Her voice had risen to a piercing scream. At the same moment she hurled the oil lamp she was holding across the floor.

It shattered, leaving a stream of oil which the flame readily burst into a channel of fire. Almost before Ruth could move Emily swept one of the lamps off the nearby table. Oil streaked the curtain and in a moment flames licked greedily at the fabric.

Ruth screamed and made a dash for the door. Emily swung round, caught her by the waist and flung her to the floor. The carpet was alight. Flames tried to catch her dress. She pushed herself to her feet and made another run for the door. Her way was barred by Emily, who stood there like an avenging angel.

'Let me out! Let me out!' Ruth screamed as she fought to escape.

Emily grasped her wrists in a powerful grip. She gave a harsh laugh. 'Thee's afraid to die. I'm not! I've nothing to live for and you'll be better dead.'

Ruth fought until she could fight no more. She broke down in helpless sobs while Emily's laughter rang with insanity.

The wooden structure was soon alight. The room became an inferno and flames roared beyond to engulf the whole house.

Chapter Twenty-Four

David strode from the house. He had been dimly aware of Emily Judson in the hall but it had meant nothing to him. He looked round for Alex and saw him hurrying towards him.

'This way,' he said as he reached David.

They sat off in step without a word. Recognising a pent-up fury in him which he was trying hard to bring under control, Alex did not pry. He knew if David wanted to tell him anything, he would do so.

They had gone about two hundred yards when a flare of light brought them swinging round to see what had happened.

'A fire,' gasped Alex and started to run back along the street.

David caught him up and matched him stride for stride.

'My God, it's Ruth's!'

By the time they reached the house it was ablaze. Flames curled out of the windows and shot skywards. David raced for the door, ignoring the yells of people who were trying to organise a chain of buckets. They knew it was hopeless, the building was too well alight, but they had to make a gesture.

David jerked the front door open and was into the hall. The fire was everywhere. It beat at him, driving him back. Shielding his eyes he made another effort, paused inside the door and glanced in the direction of the room in which he had left Ruth. It was a raging inferno and David judged it to be the seat of the fire. If she was still in there she hadn't stood a chance.

'David!' The yell came from behind him. He started towards the room but felt a firm grip on his arm. He looked round. Alex's face was contorted with frightened concern. 'Get out,' he shouted above the roar of the flames. 'There's nothing we can do.'

'Got to try. In there.' He shook himself free and started for the door.

'Don't!' Alex's voice was lost in the sound of falling timber.

David reached the door. Smoke and flames billowed around him. He covered his nose and mouth with a handkerchief. In a momentary parting of the flames he saw two figures on the floor, one pinning the other down. The woman on top looked up for a brief moment. He saw it was Emily Judson, on her face a look of deranged triumph. Flames swirled and roared, driving him back, but he heard the insane laughter of one who had won even at the cost of her own life. He did not know what it meant, did not care, but he sensed vengeance had come upon Ruth.

He made one final effort to go forward but was driven back. At the same moment he felt arms fasten round him in an inescapable grip. They dragged him from the house, away from the flames and smoke. He breathed deeply, coughing, spluttering and gulping at the fresh air.

'There's nothing we can do.' Alex's words were final.

They stood and watched, utterly helpless and dejected. Before they turned away David passed the word that he had seen two people in the house, Mrs Hardy and Mrs Judson, and that he was sorry that he had not been able to effect a rescue.

It was a silent walk to Alex's home, each man lost in his own thoughts, Alex wondering about the coming meeting between David and Beth, and David amazed at the irony of fate. As next-of-kin he would recover the money Ruth had stolen. With that and the help of Hartley Shipping he would be able to hold James Chapman to his promise to resell him the three ships.

When David stepped inside the house he sensed a happy home, one of warmth and comfort. The building itself seemed to be welcoming and threw out a friendliness which David now realised had been missing when he'd entered the house on Walnut Street.

Maggie appeared from the kitchen. 'Hello, love, I . . .' The sentence faltered on her lips and she stopped in her stride. 'Captain Fernley!' She shot a sharp glance at her husband who was standing just behind David and knew by his slight shake of the head that he had not told their visitor about Beth. After the initial shock, her face broke into a warm smile. She came forward and took David's outstretched hand.

'It's good to see thee, Maggie.'

'But how come thee's here? And why the mess?' She indicated the dishevelled and smoke-stained state of the two men.

Alex led the way into the kitchen and explained briefly how David had come to be in New Bedford. Maggie was shocked to hear of Lydia's death and extended her sympathy.

The news of the fire stunned her. 'Poor Mrs Hardy, and her to marry in two days' time. It will be a terrible blow for Mr Whelden.'

Alex glanced at David. If he wanted to reveal Ruth's true identity it was up to him but he could see no reason to do so now she was dead.

'Oh, forgive me, Captain Fernley, you'll want to clean up.'

'Here's fine, Maggie,' he said as he crossed to the sink, beside which stood a pitcher of water. 'And forget the Captain Fernley, it's David.' He poured some water into a bowl and in a few minutes was feeling much fresher.

'I've asked David to stay while he's in port,' said Alex as he prepared to wash.

'Good,' replied Maggie. 'The spare bed is made up.'

'Thee's sure it's no trouble?' asked David.

'Of course not. After all thee did.'

When Alex was ready Maggie suggested they went into the other room while she prepared a meal. As they stepped into the hall David was aware of someone coming down the stairs. He glanced up. At almost the same moment the person coming down the stairs saw him. They both froze, their eyes locked in incredulity.

'Beth!' David seemed to flounder in bewilderment.

Her mind was telling her this was not true yet the evidence stood before her. Her thoughts were whisked back to a lonely beach in Shetland where she had waited in vain, and the sight of a whaleship sailing away, leaving her with a broken heart.

'David.' Her voice had an edge to it.

He was surprised. He had thought she would have been more welcoming than this. Besides, he saw she still wore the jet cross!

She came slowly down the stairs. His eyes never left her. She was more lovely than ever and the simple dress of black with a white flower motif made her look even more attractive. Her dark hair was drawn to the back of her neck, a little too severely David thought for he remembered it loose, flowing to her shoulders and blown by the Shetland wind. Her face bore the marks of trials but still held that frankness he had admired all too briefly. He recalled her carefree wildness, her love of life in spite of the harsh Shetland existence, and as she reached the bottom of the stairs he saw it still in her deep blue eyes.

She saw the David she remembered, a little older and with the marks of life etched deeper on his face, though if anything they made him more attractive. His dark, deep-set eyes still had the power to overwhelm her and she realised her heart was beating faster.

Alex had opened the door to the sitting room. Maggie fussed behind them. 'The meal will be ready in twenty minutes.'

'I'll help thee.' Beth made the offer to seek some way out of the confrontation with David.

'It's all right, I can manage. Alex will help me.' She cast at him a glance which left him in no doubt that he should return to the kitchen. 'Thee talk to David.'

Beth said nothing but stepped past them and went into the sitting room. Better to get this over now. David followed, a little confused by her coolness. Alex closed the door behind them.

'Beth, why did thee not wait for me?' David saw no point in holding back.

'Wait for thee?' she showed astonishment.

'Yes, thee knew I would be back.'

'How could I? Thee never said.'

'Thee knew the whaleships called at Lerwick every year and that I would be on one of them.'

'Oh, yes, I knew the ships would return, but how was I to know thee would? And if thee did, how was I to know thee would want to see me? We had arranged to meet. Thee left knowing I would be waiting for thee. Left without a word. How would thee expect me to take that as anything but a sign thee didn't really love me in spite of thy glib words?'

'I had to leave quickly. I couldn't contact thee.'

Beth tossed her head and snorted in disbelief.

'It's true,' went on David. 'I had to get Alex and his family to London quickly.'

'Just so they could sail to New Bedford?'

David realised she did not know the truth behind the Frasers leaving Shetland. They had obviously seen no reason to tell her and now he could not break a confidence.

376

'Believe me, it's true, I couldn't stay in Shetland any longer.' His voice rang with conviction. Beth saw his eyes pleading with her to accept his explanation without question. 'I thought thee'd be waiting when I came back and that thee and I would meet in our bay. I see thee still wears the jet cross, thee must have felt something for me. So what happened, Beth?'

'We were turned out of our croft and given a passage to Nova Scotia with the promise of a smallholding near Pictou. I didn't want to go, but I thought thee didn't love me when thee didn't turn up so I didn't resist the dreams of a better life which my mother and father held. Pa died on the voyage. It was hell on that ship.' She shuddered at the memory. 'Ma died just after we reached Nova Scotia. I was alone. The smallholdings weren't there. We had been tricked. The emigrants split up. Two families took pity on me and I went with them along the coast. I was away from the settlement when they were massacred by Indians. I found my way back to Pictou and was there when a storm drove Alex to find shelter. He brought me back here and he and Maggie have been kindness itself to me since. I have a lot to thank them for.'

David was distressed for in these brief words he could imagine the ordeals Beth had gone through. 'And I thought thee didn't love me when I returned to Shetland and was told thee had left. Oh, Beth, we've both been so mistaken. Can we ever forgive each other?'

Before Beth could answer Ailsa came running into the room. 'Mummy, Mummy, Aunt Maggie says the meal will be ready in five minutes.' She stopped, her voice trailing away, and looked sheepishly at the stranger.

David stared at her, then looked up at Beth. 'Thee's married?'

She did not reply. 'Ailsa, come here, love.' The child came to her and, with eyes fixed on David, snuggled up against her mother. Slowly Beth slipped the jet cross from her neck and placed it round Ailsa's.

David's brain spun as he watched and inferred the meaning of the gesture. He looked at Beth, an unspoken question in his eyes. She met his gaze and nodded, confirming the thoughts she knew were going round in his mind.

'Beth!' His whisper was charged with love. He recalled Dominic's words after Lydia's death. 'Beth, I've a lot to tell thee, but will thee marry me and come to England?'

A week later, when Beth and Ailsa came on board the *Lydia*, David sensed an air of acceptance about the ship, as if Lydia herself was welcoming both Beth and Ailsa into the bosom of her family.